Origins

Song of the King's Heart

Book One

Nicole Sallak Anderson

Literary Wanderlust | Denver, Colorado

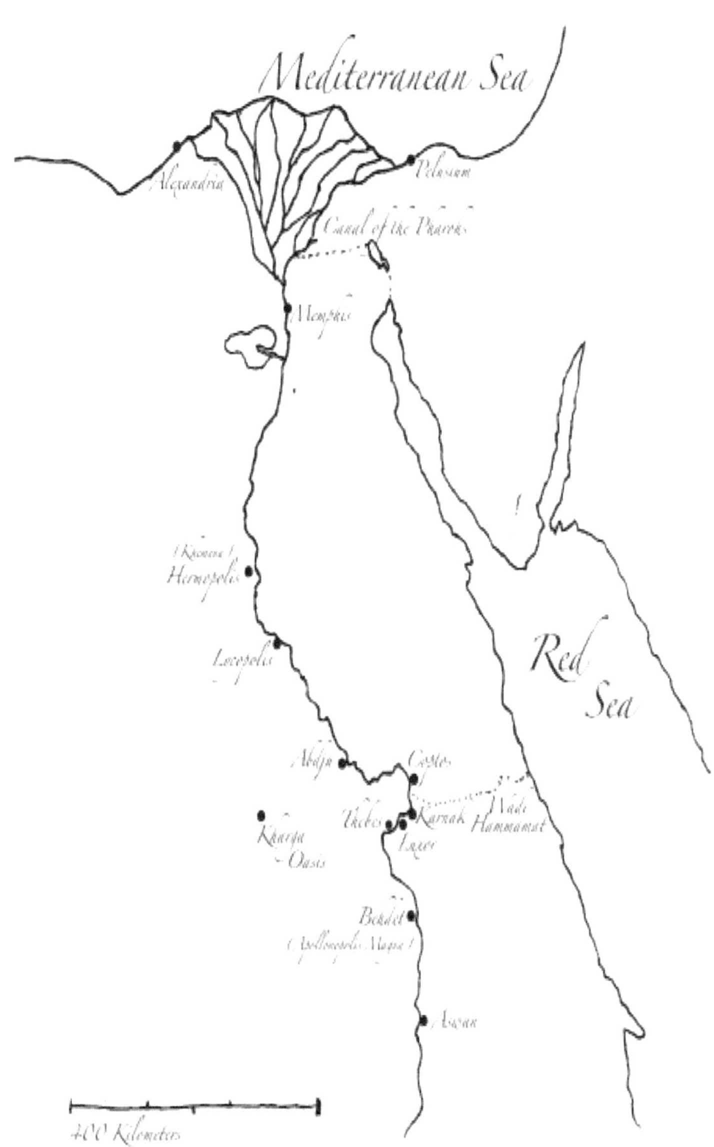

Mediterranean Sea
Alexandria
Pelusium
Canal of the Pharaohs
Memphis
(Khemenu)
Hermopolis
Lycopolis
Red
Sea
Abdju
Coptos
Thebes
Karnak
Wadi
Hammamat
Luxor
Kharga
Oasis
Behdet
(Apollonopolis Magna)
Aswan
400 Kilometers

List of Characters

Agathoclea: Ptolemy IV Philopater's mistress. Sister of Agathocles.

Agathocles: Favorite and advisor of Ptolemy IV Philopater.

Alexa: Daughter of Tyia. Priestess of Isis. Mother of Sethe and spiritual companion to Chanax.

Ankhmakis: Second son of King Hugronaphor and Queen Keket. Father of Helena with his spiritual companion, Natasa. Married to his half-sister, Weret. General of the rebellion. Known to the Greeks as Chaonnophris.

Ansel: One of Ankhmakis' guards. Greek heritage.

Antonius: Friend of Senmen during his training in Memphis. Greek heritage.

Arsinoe III: Queen of Egypt 220–204 BCE. Sister and wife of Ptolemy IV Philopater and mother of Ptolemy V Epiphanes.

Bastyre: Royal Midwife of Behdet. Teacher of medicine and herbalism.

Bithiah: Second daughter of King Hugronaphor and his second queen, Mafuane. Promised to Nefermaat but forced to marry her half-brother Chanax.

Corinna: Nursemaid of Nefermaat and Natasa. Mother of Eleni with her husband, Hecataeus.

Djed: Metakryon's assistant in Memphis.

Eleni: Natasa's younger half-sister. Daughter of Corinna and Vizier Hecataeus.

Ennaeus: Assistant of Vizier Hecataeus. Appointed by Ptolemy III Euergetes.

Epiphanes: Son of Ptolemy IV Philopater and Queen Arsinoe III. Fifth Ptolemy to take the throne.

Hecataeus: Greek Vizier of Behdet, originally assigned by Ptolemy III Euergetes to spy on the royals of Behdet. After the death of Euergetes, betrays Ptolemy IV Philopater and helps King Hugronaphor procure an army and launch the rebellion. Father of Natasa with the High Priestess Neferu-ankh-maat. Father of Eleni with his wife, Corinna.

Helena: Holy child of the temple. Daughter of Ankhmakis and Natasa.

Hugronaphor: King of Behdet, nobleman of Southern Egypt. Father of Silus, Ankhmakis, and Senmen with Keket. Father of Ruia, Bithiah, and Weret with Mafuane. Father of Nefermaat with his spiritual companion the High Priestess Neferu-ankh-maat. Launched the rebellion against the Ptolemaic Empire in

205 BCE. Known to the Greeks as Haronnophris. Pharaonic name is Horwenefer.

Ikui: Weapons trainer and master smithy for the rebellion.

Inman: Lead excavator in the temple of Seti I.

Isidor: High Priest of Set in Behdet. Mentor to Chanax. Spiritual companion of the High Priestess Neferu-ankh-maat.

Iu-Amon: High Priest of the Houses of Healing.

Kawit: Daughter of Tyia. Priestess of Isis. Spiritual companion to Silus.

Keket: Queen of Behdet. First queen of King Hugronaphor. Mother of Silus, Ankhmakis and Senmen.

Kyros: Greek military officer hired by Vizier Hecataeus to train and build the rebel army.

Mafuane: Priestess of Isis. Second queen of King Hugronaphor. Mother of Ruia, Bithiah, and Weret. Died giving birth to Weret.

Metakryon: High Priest of Memphis and the Lower Kingdom of Egypt. Head of the Cult of Set and training in Memphis.

Min: Son of the priest Zethus and a royal nursemaid. Twin brother of Pontius. Ankhmakis' captain of the guard.

Molyruse: Daughter of a southern nobleman. Classmate of Natasa and Alexa's.

Natasa: Daughter of the High Priestess Neferu-ankh-maat and Vizier Hecataeus. Heir to the Temple of Isis. Mother of Helena and spiritual companion of Ankhmakis.

Neferu-ankh-maat: High Priestess of Isis in Behdet. Spiritual companion to King Hugronaphor and High Priest Isidor. Mother of Nefermaat with King Hugronaphor. Mother of Natasa with Vizier Hecataeus.

Nefermaat: Son of the High Priestess Neferu-ankh-maat and King Hugronaphor. Royal Guard. Originally promised Bithiah's hand in marriage, but betrayed by his father when she's married off to his half-brother, Chanax, instead.

Pabasa: Teacher in Memphis. Scribe of High Priest Metakryon.

Pontius: Son of the priest Zethus and a royal nursemaid. Twin brother of Min. Guards the Princes of Behdet.

Philopater: Fourth king of the Ptolemaic Empire. Reigned from 221–204 BCE. Pharaoh when the Great Revolt of 205 BCE was launched. Father of Epiphanes with his wife, Queen Arsinoe III.

Qeny: Friend of Senmen during his training in Memphis. Native Egyptian.

Ruia: Eldest daughter of King Hugronaphor and his second queen, Mafuane. Mother of Senui with her husband and half-brother, Silus.

Sebastos: Horse trainer and master falconer of Behdet.

Senmen/Chanax: Third son of King Hugronaphor and Queen Keket. Becomes Chanax when initiated into the Cult of Set. Priest of Set and father of Sethe with his spiritual companion, Alexa. Married to his half-sister Bithiah.

Senui: Eldest son of Silus and Ruia.

Setep: High Priest of Thebes and the Upper Kingdom of Egypt.

Sethe: Holy child of the temple. Son of Priest Chanax and Priestess Alexa.

Silus: Eldest son of King Hugronaphor and Queen Keket. Father of Senui with his wife and half-sister, Ruia. His spiritual companion is Kawit.

Sosibuis: Favorite and advisor of Ptolemy IV Philopater.

Stamatia: Oracle of Memphis.

Tatianna: Acolyte in the temple. Fellow student of Natasa and Alexa.

Tsui: King Hugronaphor's first general. Trained the rebel army.

Tyia: Priestess of Isis and assistant to the High Priestess Neferu-ankh-maat. Mother of Kawit and Alexa.

Weret: Youngest daughter of King Hugronaphor and his second queen, Mafuane. Married to her half-brother, Ankhmakis.

Zethus: Elder Priest of Horus. Father to Min and Pontius.

Published in the United States by Literary Wanderlust LLC, Denver, Colorado.
https//www.LiteraryWanderlust.com

ISBN print: 978-1-942856-40-5
ISBN eBook: 978-1-942856-44-3

Cover design: Pozo Mitsuma

Printed in the United States of America

Acknowledgments

A novel has a life of its own. When you begin, you need a cheerleader, someone to bounce ideas off of, someone to encourage you even when the well seems dry, someone who loves you as much as you love your characters. For The Song of the King's Heart trilogy, that person was Regan Caruthers. She read every chapter as I wrote them, asked questions, and encouraged me at every step. It's not an exaggeration to say that without her, this story never would have been told.

The second phase in the life of a novel is taking the mess you call the first draft and turning it into something presentable to pitch to the agents and publishers you hope to impress. I wrote The Song of the King's Heart as a single novel, simply letting the story flow without paying attention to the nagging voice in my head that kept saying, "Excuse me, but no one will look at a novel that's more than 100K words.

Stop now!" When I was done with the first draft, the novel was over 300K words. That's when I jumped on Upwork and found editor/author Stephanie Diaz. She spent months helping me break the story into three books, polishing each one and create a submissions packet for the trilogy.

She was also very encouraging during the next phase, the agent search. I won't go into the details, nor the number of form-letter rejections I received during that year of hell, but it was Stephanie who encouraged me to pitch Ankhmakis one last time, in a Twitter #pitmad of all things, and that 140-character pitch is what led me to Literary Wanderlust, and a publishing contract for all three books. If you're ever in need of an editor to make sense of your literary mess, you can find her on Twitter @stephanieediaz.

Which leads to this last phase, publishing. Thanks to Kylee Howells at Literary Wanderlust for actually reading the first book, Origins, and taking it on as a project. I love the work we've done together and look forward to sharing it with the world. I can't wait to edit the next two with you. Thanks also to Susan Brooks, our publisher, for making my dream—holding this story in my hands, as a book I can sniff—come true.

The writer's life isn't possible without love. Thanks to my husband, Walt, who shares me with my characters, my sons, Jackson and Michael, who know writing is what keeps their mother kind, Jillian Briscoe Chelson, who always cheered me up when I was down, and Maureen Kilkeary Noonburg, my only friend who understands the strange spell one is under when a story demands to be written.

Dear Reader

Several years ago, while researching rebellions in general, I stumbled upon a Wikipedia entry about the Great Egyptian Revolt of 200 BCE. A mere five sentences about a native Egyptian, most likely of Nubian origin, named Hugronaphor and his son, Ankhmakis, who in 205 BCE, launched a rebellion against the Ptolemaic Empire in Upper Egypt, claiming 80% of the territory and holding this kingdom until 186 BCE, the year Ankhmakis was betrayed by his priests, captured by the Greek General Conanus, and publicly put to death. This short entry captivated me. I had to know more, and as I dug deeper, I fell in love with ancient Egypt, Ankhmakis, and the mystery of the Rebel King. I knew I had to write his tale, and so the hunt for historical material began.

In general, I used primary source materials, such as Herodotus's *Histories* and actual ancient Egyptian poetry taken from scrolls that have survived as well as temple walls. I also studied books by archaeologists, books about ancient warfare, Alexander the Great and the history of the Macedonians in the region, and college level ancient Egyptian history textbooks to build Ankhmakis and Natasa's world. Aspects of their daily lives, such as embalming, temple building, farming, seasons, what they ate, climate, animals, basic customs, etc. Their belief in the Ba, Ka, and Khat (body) are also well documented. Two topics though were a bit trickier: sex magic and Ankhmakis himself.

Let's start with Ankhmakis. He's mentioned only in passing in histories of the Ptolemaic Empire. His rebellion, as well as others in the Delta, are often mentioned as a reason that Philopater's reign is considered the beginning of the end of this particular Macedonian Empire. But that's about all. He only exists as a whisper in time. When I first wanted to know him, I searched everywhere and finally found a website from UC Berkeley by a professor who had done his best to piece together the Great Egyptian Revolt of 200 BCE. It appears Philopater's son, Ptolemy V Epiphanes, spent two years removing every trace of the southern Egyptians who had ruled most of his kingdom for twenty years. The professor found the data in sources such as tax collector journals (the Macedonians were unable to collect taxes because of the rebellion), merchant logs (obtaining gold from Nubia was impossible due to the rebellion), as well as slave sales in the Alexandria slave yard (the wives and children of many natives involved in the rebellion were sold into slavery). However, Ankhmakis's own writings are gone. We're not even positive where his home was, except that it was south of Thebes. I tried my best to recreate the Rebel King's story by taking those dates the professor shared as actual data points, as well as reading up on both Ptolemy IV and V to include those historical figures who took part in it, as well as the timelines, mostly based on Theban records that document the various crownings from 205–186 BCE. The general who eventually arrests Ankhmakis is also a historical figure. The rest of the characters in The Song of the King's Heart trilogy are fiction.

In addition to these more exoteric sources, I also did general research into ancient Egyptian religion and that quickly led me down a rabbit hole of esoteric writings. There are obviously many mysteries with regards to the Egyptians, and I decided early on to write the story from the viewpoint of an initiate in their magical system. Two of the most intriguing mysteries for me were the sex magic of Isis, a.k.a. *Anit-Shadya*, and the Wands of Horus, featured in books two and three of the trilogy. In general, it was against the law for any priest to have sex in the temples. Yet there is a rumor that in three locations, the highest form of magic, sex magic, was practiced. None of the sex magic temples, except the one in Luxor, are named. Beyond random websites that sounded more fantastic with each click, I only found one decent book about Egyptian sex magic, and it is a channeling—not a proper source, I imagine. Yet it inspired my imagination, and I wanted to include the art and magic of ecstasy in the storyline. So, I began to research sex magic from the Wiccan standpoint, using the Great Rite as a starting place as well as Tantric sex, which uses the same breathing techniques as the Wiccan tradition.

What becomes clear, from the older Wiccan writings up to the sex magick of Alastair Crowley, and the many various cults of the late 1800s to mid-1900s that practiced alchemy, is that they all believe that their practices came from these secret temples in ancient Egypt. Yet none can prove this for there is no actual line of documentation to track it. The practitioners of modern sex magick claim this lack of historical proof is because the practice of Isis sex magic was so holy, only a few learned it, and none committed the knowledge to writing.

In the end, I used Wiccan books about the Great Rite combined with Tantra and what I learned about ancient Egyptian astral travel, the Ba and Ka relationship, and a pantheon of deities to imagine the practices and took the liberty of recreating sex magic in an Egyptian temple in Behdet. I also make the attempt by the end of the trilogy to suggest how the European pagans might have received this information, as well as how the sex magic of Isis eventually arrived at Luxor, the only temple documented to have practiced the art.

I have no proof that the man known as Ankhmakis practiced *Anit-Shadya,* but he managed to achieve something in his short lifetime that none of his ancestors had—take Thebes from the Ptolemys and hold it for sixteen years. Magic is written in the temple walls of ancient Egypt, and I'd like to think he had that on his side. Besides, in a world where sex is used to sell cars and beer, why not share a story where it's used to launch a rebellion, as well as travel the cosmos, instead?

Sincerely,
Nicole Sallak Anderson

For Our Lady of Love,
whose work is the work of life.

"In the beginning, the First Ones were sung into existence by the Mother, to be her hands upon the Earth. These first hands of the Earth were immortal and perfectly connected to the planet's light and energy. All were one, yet many.

They created the first civilizations at the dawn of time, forming cities in the North and South, East and West, in all quadrants of the Earth. They molded, shaped, and created with the Mother, begetting life on the Earth. For millennia, they birthed Spirit into matter with hearts of joy. Until the greatest among them no longer desired immortality and bonded with the forces of death to create a second humanity— these to be the hands of the Earth, living many different physical lives. Thus, the First Ones fractured, and in chaos and fear, a new human race was born. The new humanity feared death, and some among them turned to darkness for their power. Chaos gained control and tainted the Mysteries with blood.

In their defeat, the immortal First Ones retreated to the

mountaintops and islands of the world, isolating themselves from the anger of men. The humans called them Gods, for their magic was great and their lives were long. But the evil of humanity was too great for the Gods to bear, and they fled the world, becoming legends, abandoning the Mother to man's chaos, darkness, and bloodlust.

Time marched forward. Humanity conquered the world. At the turning of the tide, some remembered their past, their power, and their majesty. They wished to reconnect to the Gods, to open the veil and reclaim their inheritance. The Children of the Light returned to bathe the Earth in hope. For the light is within humanity, waiting to be found. The plan is in each one, waiting to be activated. Those who choose to open their eyes will see the path to everlasting life."

~ "The Dark Goddess," by Finnian, Scribe of the North

1

A Light in the Darkness

This is the lost story of Lord Ankhwenefer, known to the Greeks as Chaonnophris the Rebel—the last native Egyptian Pharaoh, though no monuments stand in his name. Ptolemy V Epiphanes spent years destroying all evidence of the Rebel King's rule, erasing his name from every gleaming surface, battering his alabaster temples to the ground, and burning his records under the blazing desert sun. The brilliance and heartache of his rebellion weave a tale that history has forgotten—until now.

The City of Memphis, Egypt 211 BCE

The High Priest of Memphis, Metakryon, lay prone in the torch lit room. The moonlight from the night god Khons's silver boat poured in through the open window, and the candle flames danced in the slight breeze. Metakryon took unhurried breaths, exhaling to such an extreme that, in his trance state, he appeared dead. His attendants stood still as statuary around the altar, protecting him during his journey. His Ba had left his body, and he traveled the cosmos, searching for the answer to the question that had plagued him his entire life—what was Egypt's path to freedom?

The darkness of space remained silent. Long ago he'd lost the ability to see. Every trance journey was in vain, for the universe had turned its back on him and his beloved country. With a heavy heart, he returned to his body and cleared his head, sending his thoughts down his spine, through each energy center, to his feet. He felt the cold stone slab beneath his thin, white robe and knew he'd returned to his body. His old bones cracked as he lifted himself from the altar and breathed Amon Ra's light into his abdomen, filling his body with the power of the gods, thanking the goddess for her protection while, in the exact same thought, cursing her for her silence.

As Metakryon stood, a young priest stumbled into the dim room, hurtling himself through the door as if chased by a coalition of cheetahs. The boy's dark, bald head shone in the torchlight, and his brown eyes glittered intensely.

"Djed, why are you crashing into my quarters so late at night?" Metakryon demanded. The young priest would never dare disturb him without gravest cause.

"Master, Stamatia speaks. She has seen something," Djed answered, wringing his hands, whether in fear or excitement, the high priest couldn't discern. "You must come with me."

"Have you informed Aster?" Metakryon asked, forcing his voice steady and hoping to hide his own nervousness. Metakryon was the true high priest of Memphis, born of the ancient Egyptian blood passed down by his holy father, but by Ptolemy's decree, he shared this role with Aster, the pharaoh's relative and informant. Nothing Egypt did in the temple could be hidden from Ptolemy IV Philopater. Or, that's what the pharaoh liked to think. In truth, the man knew nothing of the plans that stirred in the hearts of Egypt's powerful magicians.

"No, sir, she called only for you," Djed replied.

Metakryon nodded and let go of the breath he had been holding. The Oracle's revelations would be his and his alone. He looked to his attendants, "Fetch me my black robe and staff."

They jumped into action, no longer silent sentinels, and soon Metakryon was ready for the long walk to the Oracle's chambers. Stamatia was but a child, yet her tenure had granted a wealth of visions and knowledge to the priests. For his part, Metakryon harbored a jealous hate of the girl, as he longed for such accurate abilities. She was loyal to her post, spending her entire life underground in a trance, serving Egypt's highest good with her every breath.

The two men entered the Oracle's chambers in silence and reverence. She sat in the center of the room on a tall, stone dais, her legs folded and arms gently resting on her thighs. She too was bald, and she wore a golden cuff around her neck and a white linen tunic. Her feet were bare, and her arms were covered with multiple golden bands. Her eyes were shut yet moving rapidly under her eyelids. In the candlelight, Metakryon could make out her thick eyelashes and red lips against her pale, moon-shaped face. Despite her wild insanity, she was beautiful to behold, as glorious as the goddess herself.

"Stamatia," he said in a quiet tone. The Oracle didn't respond to demands or loud voices. "You sent for me?"

Her eyes flew open, whites fluttering as they rolled in her head, revealing the madness of her mind. In the temple, she was a fearless channel of the goddess, but outside, the men and women of the world would find her terrifying. Her visions made her unfit for a normal life—to be the Oracle of Memphis was to live underground, in service, away from regular people.

She turned to face her high priest and trembled. "I have seen it, my lord," she whispered.

Metakryon drew closer. Djed followed by his side. The two men kneeled on the solid wood rests at her feet and raised their hands to the ceiling.

"Dearest Isis, Our Lady and Protector, show us Osiris's message," Metakryon said.

Stamatia stood, raising her own hands, and threw back her head.

"Hear me now." She spoke with empyrean effect, and Metakryon shuddered as her voice eddied upon the crisp temple air. "Egypt's day of Resurrection is near. The men of the south shall rise to the throne, and the pretenders will be swept from our shores. The Golden Child shall be born to him whose banner claims Thebes, and through this miracle, Egypt will return to her glory."

Stamatia fell to the ground in a heap, panting and groaning like a woman in the throes of childbirth. Her attendants approached her, giving her drink and wrapping her in a leopard skin blanket.

"The time for war is at hand," Metakryon said as he struggled to stand on unstable legs. He wasn't sure if it was old age, or the anticipation Stamatia's prophecy had sowed within him, but his body refused to cooperate.

"I didn't hear her mention war," Djed replied as he held out his arms to help the older priest.

Metakryon grasped Djed's hands, his joints creaking as he stood. "Excuse me?"

"She spoke of a child, and the men of the south, but not war," the young priest explained.

Metakryon held up his hand to quiet the acolyte. "War is the only way to drive the Ptolemys out of these lands. I know what they do in Behdet. It appears the work of their temple has come to fruition, and they will bear us the warriors we need. This Golden Child will be the one to truly inhabit Ra and restore us to the glory of the kings of old."

Djed looked at his master and remained silent. It was against temple code to contradict the high priest of Memphis, and Metakryon appreciated the boy's faithful nature to his duties.

"We must send word to King Hugronaphor of Behdet and his High Priestess, Neferu-ankh-maat. They need to know this," Metakryon said with a huff as he shuffled toward the exit of the Oracle's chambers. His lungs felt heavy, and nothing the healers did would clear them. Perhaps he was beyond their abilities? He was old. Very, very old.

"What do we tell the High Priest Aster and the Greek priests?" Djed asked.

"Do not speak of it to them," Metakryon warned. "Ptolemy Philopater must not know. After three centuries with only wooden staves to protect ourselves, our esteemed pharaoh armed Hugronaphor and his native army to help win the war against Antonius in Syria. We need to keep those armaments if our plans are to succeed."

"Understood, Master," Djed replied as he bowed his head.

Metakryon wasn't sure the young man could be trusted.

"You must go to Apollonopolis Magna and inform the royals of Behdet yourself. King Hugronaphor runs an efficient military operation with the approval of the pharaoh, of course. Go pay the high priestess of Isis a visit, and you'll see how powerful the men of the south are," he ordered as they made their way out of Stamatia's chambers, leaving the poor child heaving and suffering upon the stone dais. She always had fits after an important prophecy. "You deliver the message to them, and I'll deal with Aster."

Djed nodded and left his master's side to make for his

quarters, but Metakryon grasped the younger man's arms. "There's something else."

"What, my lord?" the young priest asked.

"Tell King Hugronaphor that the time has come for him to send me one of his sons," the high priest said, recalling the deal that had been struck with the young king years ago.

Metakryon had convinced Ptolemy IV Philopater to let Hugronaphor keep his troops after the war with Antonius—for a small price. "Hugronaphor must fulfill his promise of tribute to the pharaoh."

Djed raised his hand and lifted two fingers. "Tell them the Golden Child is at hand, and that a prince must be sent to Memphis as tribute."

"Yes, tell King Hugronaphor these things, and he will understand."

Metakryon let the man's arm go, and the acolyte flew out of the room. Rather than return to his meditation, the high priest sat in his favorite chair by the fire and lit his pipe. As he stared at the flames, he fingered the ibis heads carved upon each arm and sank into pillows made from leopard and jackal pelts. There was no use sleeping after such an exciting event. The upper kingdom would rise, and Egypt would finally be free. Launching a civil war against the Empire would take years of planning and secrecy, but there was no stopping destiny. Of this, Metakryon was sure.

2

Coming of Age

Ankhmakis was born into a precarious situation. The middle son of a powerful native noble, and only twelve months younger than the eldest, yet vastly more talented, he was the best of the heirs to the throne of Behdet, and eventually Egypt. But first, he had to deal with his brothers. For while the natural order of inheritance belonged to the eldest son of the high queen and king, simple succession was rarely guaranteed.

Behdet, Egypt 211 BCE

Ankhmakis stood by himself in the antechamber. He could hear the crowds gathering in the Great Hall. Music and song filled the air. Nobles from Upper Egypt had traveled for days to grant their blessing on the newest heir to the throne of Behdet, the House of Hugronaphor, and the stewards of Pharaoh Ptolemy IV. Few native families still existed such as his, of this he'd been made quite aware in his years of study under Vizier Hecataeus and his father. To be a royal in Behdet was to be a member of the last line of native kings in Egypt. And today, he would be welcomed as a man into that line.

He straightened his white kilt and checked that his leather sandals were tied. Upon his head, he wore a prince's crown, a simple golden circlet with a lapis stone at the center of his forehead. At his hip, he gripped his sword. Now that his father had secured an army, the men of Kemit were once again warriors. He felt the leather-wrapped handle of the dangerous weapon and drew it from his scabbard, lifting it high above his head. The metal hummed a song in the still air as if singing a ballad of glory to his noble heart. In the silence of that moment, he could almost see himself commanding armies along the Nile, making their way into Alexandria.

"My lord?" a voice asked.

He lowered his sword and sheathed it quickly. Turning, he found his best friend and newest member of his guard, Min. The two had grown up together in the gardens, fields, and eventually the training ring. Now that they were coming of age, they were each assuming their roles. Being a son of the priest Zethus and a nursemaid, Min had no access to the throne. He'd been offered the life of a scribe but had turned it down, stating he preferred to be a Royal Guard and stand beside Ankhmakis as he grew in power. Min's twin brother, Pontius, had made the same choice and was now serving in the Queen's Guard. Knowing Min was going to be by his side as he navigated his now complicated and bureaucratic life provided the young prince great relief. No one knew him like Min.

"Yes, Min," Ankhmakis answered.

"They say it's time," Min replied. "I'm to hold the door for you as you make your entrance."

"What will you do?"

"Take my place among the Royal Guard, while you get the glory." He grinned.

"Ah yes, that's the way of this now, isn't it?" Ankhmakis said.

Min slapped him on the back. "Let's get this over with. Silus has arranged a wonderful afterparty that the fellows can't wait to attend."

"Afterparty?" It was the first Ankhmakis had heard of it.

"Yes, with your father's concubines," Min replied.

"The concubines?" He blushed and looked away, unable to hide his surprise.

Min laughed. "Of course. Now that you're a man, you have access to the women of pleasure."

"But," Ankhmakis began. Why hadn't he known this? His thoughts lingered on his First Rites with the high priestess. The candlelight. The heat of her. The Rising. All edges, all boundaries, melting in her embrace. "I assumed I was to be taught in the temple."

"Seriously?" Min laughed again. "You thought you'd have regular access to the high priestess?"

Ankhmakis could feel his cheeks burning with embarrassment.

"My lord," Min said with a crooked smile, hand on his hip and head tilted as if in jest, "you'll need to practice your lessons with someone, eh?"

"Yes, of course. I'm nervous right now, Min. Every noble in the south is here, waiting to see the latest heir to our throne."

"Right, business first, of course. But pleasure later, okay?"

"I want them to see me," Ankhmakis admitted.

"What do you mean?"

"I want them to see me, not as a child, but as their future king."

Min was silent, his mischievous smile fading into a grim, tight-lipped line. To speak of such things was dangerous.

"Tell me, when you look at me, do you see a king?" Ankhmakis asked. "Be honest."

Min swallowed but did not speak. His silence was unbearable.

"I serve the entire royal family," Min said after a moment of consideration.

"You mean you serve both Silus and me," Ankhmakis clarified.

"And eventually your younger brother, Senmen," Min admitted.

"But when you look at me, do you see a king? You haven't answered my question."

Min shifted in his place. He was stalling. A priest entered, releasing Min from the situation.

"Prince Ankhmakis, second son to Hugronaphor, your king awaits you."

Ankhmakis glared at Min, angry that his best friend couldn't step out of politics long enough to see the truth. Everyone was so careful around the palace. It frustrated Ankhmakis, for it felt disingenuous.

"They will see me as king," he whispered, his throat tightening with emotion.

Ankhmakis lowered his shoulders, lifted his chin, and walked to the door to enter the Great Hall. He gazed upon the sea of faces that had gathered, and the size of the crowd overwhelmed him. Fires burned in several braziers and around them lounged hundreds of people, who rose to attention when he entered the room. A line of priests and priestesses flanked a long, woven mat that led to a small dais where his father, King Hugronaphor, stood dignified in his full regal attire. At his hip, he too wore his sword with pride. Ankhmakis looked his father in the eye and received the acceptance he needed.

Hugronaphor was no fool; he knew who the competent son was.

The green-eyed temple girl Natasa stepped forward, dressed in gold with flowers woven into her dark hair. She stood beside the king and bowed to Ankhmakis. She raised her hands and sang, *The Song of the Men of the South*. He'd heard it sung the previous year at Silus's coming of age, but this time it sounded like a personal blessing bestowed upon him by the goddess herself. Ankhmakis looked at the girl and felt his stomach flutter, followed by a surge of power. He nodded to his father and began his walk across the room to receive his blessing.

As he walked, the girl continued to sing, each note giving him confidence and grace. She sang not for him, but to him, and of him. Ankhmakis, a man of the south. A prince. One who could be, would be, king. He strode by the guests, nodding to them and meeting their gaze. They nodded in return. He had command of the room, each soul beckoning him to become a man, to join his father as a warrior and savior of this land. When he approached his father, he looked Hugronaphor in the face again and lowered himself to one knee. The girl's song climaxed, and her final notes cascaded across his back and throughout the great room. As the last note faded, the hall remained silent. He wasn't sure if the silence was normal or not, but knew he had to remain kneeling until his father called his name. After what seemed like an eternity, Hugronaphor cleared his voice.

"Rise, my son."

Ankhmakis did as he was told and stood. His father held in his hands a beautiful golden collar, decorated in jewels and symbols of the royal family. Hugronaphor wore the collar of the king of Behdet, passed down at the coronation. He had given Silus his own personal prince's collar the year before. The one the king now held had been made new, a special design created for Ankhmakis. In the center of the collar was a large lapis lazuli stone, upon which the image of a black phoenix over a fire had been engraved. This was a new symbol for the family, one he had never seen before.

"In honor of your becoming a man, I give to you the collar of your days as a prince. The Phoenix is the promise of our house to the people—from the ashes, we will rise anew. From destruction, we birth hope. You, Ankhmakis, are hope made flesh, a warrior and keeper of our sacred mission, that Egypt may rise again and the glories of old may be renewed."

The crowd roared at the king's speech, and Ankhmakis felt the weight of the world rushing over him. Whatever had possessed him to want to be king? The pressure was enormous.

"My son," Hugronaphor continued, "do you vow to protect the people of Egypt, your kinsmen, your countrymen, and serve them with honor and strength?"

"My oath is given," Ankhmakis replied with more confidence than he felt.

"Will you serve your king and your house in faith, and uphold the law of the land?"

"Yes, I will."

"Let it be written that on the First Month of Perit, the eleventh day, in the tenth year of the rule of Ptolemy IV Philopater, I crown you, Ankhmakis—Prince of Behdet."

Hugronaphor placed the collar over Ankhmakis's head and slid it down onto his chest, where it shone with the brilliance of the sun upon his dark skin. The prince turned to the crowd as his father laced the collar behind his neck, their faces glowing in the firelight. They looked upon him with a mixture of awe and trepidation. All but the girl, Natasa—she looked right through him. It was unnerving.

"People of Behdet. Men and women of the south. Upper kingdom of Egypt. I present to you Ankhmakis, second son of the throne, and newest heir to the House of Hugronaphor."

The room buzzed around him as people clapped and patted him on the back. He was ushered to the king's corner and seated at his father's right-hand side, for this evening. Tomorrow, it would be Silus, the firstborn, who sat in the place of honor. But for tonight, Ankhmakis would bask in everyone's favor, including his father's.

Food and wine soon arrived, and the members of the king's retinue laughed and sang his praises. To his father's other side sat Keket, Ankhmakis's mother and the high queen of Behdet. Next to her sat Vizier Hecataeus, High Priest Isidor, and High Priestess Neferu-ankh-maat. Her mere presence made Ankhmakis ache with desire. He recalled the glorious moments in her arms the night before and longed for her once again. He leaned toward her, trying to catch her eye, but the older woman had none of it, instead focusing her attention on Isidor, whom everyone knew was her lover, partner, and companion. Together the pair ruled the temples of Isis and Set. Ankhmakis's ribs squeezed tight with envy at the sight of them.

"It's impolite to stare," Silus whispered into his ear, shoving him.

"What?" Ankhmakis demanded, focusing now on his brother.

Silus smiled and drew a long drink from his wine goblet. He snapped his fingers, and in an instant a servant refilled it. "Fill my brother's cup. He needs it more than I do."

"What are you talking about?"

"I know what you're thinking because I thought the same

things myself a year ago. First Rites with the high priestess are every bit as divine as we're told, aren't they?"

Ankhmakis felt his cheeks warm again. He hated knowing less than his brother.

"Don't think you'll be getting many lessons from her," Silus continued.

"But she said we'd meet again," Ankhmakis cried.

"Yes, you will. Six times, but you won't have sex," Silus said with a sigh. "Which is a shame."

"What will we study, if not sex?"

"Anit-Shadya of course, you idiot," Silus reprimanded with a seriousness that Ankhmakis hadn't expected from his elder brother. "She'll teach you a special way of breathing, fill your head with the true meaning of Isis and love, make you see channels of light around the body, and she'll demand you master the daily rituals that are expected when you take a spiritual companion."

"When will I receive a spiritual companion?"

"Goddess knows," Silus said, his face wistful like a child on the eve of his birthday. "I was told I'd get one when I'm ready."

"What does that mean?"

"When *they* feel like it, I'll be bonded to a priestess. I imagine I'll have some say. We have more freedom in this than in choice of wives."

Silus nodded to the place where the children of the court were sitting. Their half-sisters and future wives, Weret, Bithiah, and Ruia, sat at their places, proper and prim as was expected of the royal females. Senmen and the other boys of the court were also there, making a racket. Next to Senmen sat the two young temple girls, Alexa and Natasa.

"Yes, wives. How horrible," Ankhmakis admitted.

"In many ways, bonding with a spiritual companion is more serious than taking a wife," Silus said.

"How?"

"We can have as many wives as we want. As long as they're of the royal bloodline and we produce heirs, no one cares. But you only get one spiritual companion. One woman with whom to serve the goddess. One woman to open your path to Horus, and to explore the chamber of eternal life."

"You sound like a priest, Silus," Ankhmakis joked. This time it was his turn to shove his brother.

He took another drink of his wine and found he was getting woozy. It felt good. He snapped his fingers, and in less time than it took him to belch, an attendant refilled his glass.

"All I'm saying is under most circumstances this pairing is for life, unless one is crowned king," Silus continued.

"What happens then?"

"The king always pairs with the high priestess of Isis. So, each time there's a change of king or high priestess, the pairings change. Father's original spiritual companion was Tyia, Alexa's mother. And Neferu-ankh-maat's original companion was Isidor. But when the old king and the high priestess died, Father took Neferu-ankh-maat as his companion."

"When I become king, I'll be paired with Neferu-ankh-maat? But she'll be so old."

Silus took another drink from his cup and shoved a handful of stuffed pork into his mouth. He chewed each bite with care, taking his time, gaze set upon Ankhmakis. He washed it down with a gulp of wine and leaned in close to his younger brother's face.

"First, dear brother," he said in a low and steady voice, "Neferu-ankh-maat will be dead by the time Father passes. She's older than him."

"Then who?"

Silus glared at the children's table again. "Natasa, her daughter, of course."

"That little girl?" Ankhmakis exclaimed.

"She won't always be a little girl," Silus answered.

Ankhmakis considered Natasa as the high priestess and felt the room spin again. He grabbed some meat and cheese. Maybe he was hungry.

"And second," Silus continued, colder now and holding Ankhmakis by the shoulders, "you won't ever be king. *I'm* the eldest, remember?"

Ankhmakis brushed Silus's arms off and sat up straighter. He was several inches taller than his brother, and as he looked down upon him, he could sense Silus's disdain, but also his fear.

"Succession is never guaranteed," Ankhmakis taunted, the copious amounts of wine making him bolder by the minute.

Silus glared from under his painted eyebrows, and Ankhmakis could tell he was fuming. Ankhmakis was ready to stand and make a scene when Min appeared.

"Hey, brothers," Min said, eyeing the princes with concern, "are you two done here? Because the men are starting to lose patience back there."

Min glanced over his shoulder at the group of guards and soldiers, all of them Silus and Ankhmakis's fellow classmates in training. They were a young, reckless, and lustful group, eager to take the celebration into the arms of the women who lived to please them. Not priestesses, but whores, paid for by the king to keep the soldiers and men of the palace satisfied. The thought both excited and repulsed Ankhmakis. Yet, he was grateful for the distraction. Fighting with Silus never made him comfortable. He looked at his older brother and smiled, letting him see that, for now, he regretted his words.

"Silus, we're brothers and princes. Our father is going to live forever it seems. Let's not fight. Besides, we don't need priestesses or wives. Too much work, don't you agree? We shouldn't keep the ladies of the evening waiting."

Silus nodded, his jaw still clenched, but he smiled regardless. "I agree."

Min looked relieved as the two princes excused themselves from the meal. Hugronaphor laughed when he heard his sons's request.

"What, do you find us boring?" Hugronaphor jested.

"Father, it's time to make a real man of my brother," Silus said, hugging his brother close and winking at the high priestess, whose face remained nonplussed.

"Ah, yes. I was young once. I remember," Hugronaphor replied, also winking at Neferu-ankh-maat. "Go and enjoy my women."

Ankhmakis bowed to his father and left the room. It was too much for him, and the night was still young. Silus was right; he'd rather drink and spend his time in the arms of a woman than play the part of the prince. Life was too short and being a member of the House of Hugronaphor was too serious.

As he followed the group of young men out the door, Ankhmakis couldn't help himself and glanced over his shoulder, not to sneak a glimpse of the high priestess—instead his gaze fell upon the girl, Natasa, who was watching him with her bright, green eyes—such a beautiful contrast against her dark skin. Once again, a shiver ran up his spine, and he shook his head. He wrapped his arms around Min's shoulders and took his leave.

3

The Osirion

The Osirion in Abdju was an ancient mystery, long buried by the desert when Seti I was crowned in 1290 BCE. Egyptians were archaeologists studying their own history even in the ancient days. Each time a new temple was built, additional aspects of their past were revealed. When Seti's builders uncovered the long-fabled Osirion, they decided to build the new temple around it, and eventually, they opened the ancient doors and uncovered the lost secrets of eternal life. Legend held that the mysterious Resurrection Bath was the true power of the Ramisside period of prosperity and dominance.

Abdju, Egypt 211 BCE

Two days after the crowning of Prince Ankhmakis, Natasa, daughter of the high priestess, boarded one of the king's finest ships and headed down the Nile with the youngest prince, Senmen, toward the ancient city of Abdju. The waters of their sacred river rushed by the cedar-crafted vessel, and the adults worked purposefully around the decks while the two friends fished for dinner.

"Not bad, for a princeling," Natasa said with a laugh, shaking her head as beads of gold and precious jewels clacked together at the end of her long, kohl-black braids. She fidgeted with her fishing pole at the edge of the boat, legs crossed under her thin, white shift.

"What's that supposed to mean?" Senmen asked as he rose to stand and tugged a heavy fish from the river and onto the deck, wearing only a white loincloth himself—commoner's clothes despite his noble birth. He crinkled his brow at her comment, and she smiled. Natasa liked the way his cheeks blushed when she teased him.

"Everyone knows the royals don't fish. Servants do your work for you because you're helpless."

"Nonsense," Senmen answered as he turned, pole in one hand, holding his catch by the tail with the other. He glanced her way and continued to talk as he whacked the thrashing fish's head against the wooden deck of the boat. "I've been fishing with my brothers since I could walk. What do you think we do, sit around all day?"

"Your sisters do," she said.

"Ruia, Bithiah, and Weret *are* helpless," Senmen agreed. "I supposed it's the way of women." He freed the fish from the pole with ease and placed it in a bucket made of fired river mud. He nodded at her pole, still strung in the water, and shrugged. "You haven't caught a fish yet. I guess that's because you're a girl?"

Natasa jumped from her place and thrust herself at Senmen, but he twisted out of her grasp as fast as the flowing waters of the Nile. She ran after him, chasing him up and down the boat, their brown skin glistening with sweat under the warm gaze of Ra, the Sun God who rode his chariot across the daylight skies. The king's sailors stepped out of the children's way, reprimanding them for causing a ruckus.

Natasa had spent the first thirteen years of her life delighting in Senmen's company. Whether climbing the Royal Garden fig trees, which were old and sturdy, but not too tall, or hiding from their nursemaids in the secret places of his father's palace, the two were endlessly chasing each other, swimming in the canals, and disturbing the adults.

Their lives were heaven, but their heaven was about to end.

They were on their way to the ancient city of Abdju. This was to be Natasa's last adventure with her father before she began training under her mother, Neferu-ankh-maat, the high priestess of Behdet. Senmen was on his way to Memphis as a tribute from his father to the Ptolemaic Empire, to be vetted in the holy priesthood of Pharaoh Ptolemy IV Philopater himself. Natasa knew she shouldn't be chasing Senmen in this way, they were disturbing the work of the men, but these were their last days together before each of them were swept away by the adults in their lives.

They rounded the prow of the ship and found the High Priest Isidor standing with his hands clasped behind his back. The older man oversaw the temple of Set in Behdet and was also the king's main advisor as well as her mother's lover. Together the pair ruled the temples and the religious life of King Hugronaphor's people. Isidor's gaze was stern, and beads of sweat dripped down his cleanly shaven head. His red robes stretched tight around his waist. At his neck, he wore a golden necklace with a red stone.

"My Lord Isidor," Natasa said as she halted in place, and Senmen stumbled over his feet to stop, avoiding an embarrassing crash into his new master.

Isidor folded his hands across his chest. "Senmen, this

behavior will not do. You are no longer a child of the court, but a priest-in-training. To that end, you will stop acting like a wild animal and join me in my cabin for prayers."

"Sir," Senmen protested, "I haven't even begun training."

"Not officially, no," Isidor continued. "But I can see we must begin to cure you of your unruliness before we get to Memphis. Which means we begin. Now."

Isidor never liked it when the two of them played, and he grabbed Senmen by the shoulder to herd him away. Natasa felt her lip tremble as she fought back tears of anger.

"That's not fair," she cried out, knowing she would pay dearly for her outburst. "He doesn't even want to go to Memphis."

Isidor grasped Senmen's shoulder even tighter, and her friend flinched in pain.

"Natasa," Senmen said, his voice lower than normal, "don't say such things."

"But you don't," Natasa continued, daring to come two steps closer to the priest. "We know it should have been my brother, Nefermaat, a holy child of the temple, not Senmen, son of the high queen."

"That's enough from you," Isidor said, raising his hand to shush her. "It is not your business which son the king sends to Memphis as his tribute."

"But I heard you and Mother fighting," Natasa replied, unable to silence herself. "You asked for Nefermaat, and she denied you."

"Natasa, please," Senmen said, still struggling under Isidor's grip. "Let it go."

Her father Hecataeus arrived, stunning and sharp in his Greek-styled robe, affixed over his shoulder with a golden pin. His olive skin almost glowed in the sunlight next to Isidor's darker, native skin. On Hecataeus's head of golden-brown curls, he wore a tall blue and red hat that marked him as the Greek vizier to King Hugronaphor's court in the upper kingdom of Egypt. The hat was a sign of his authority over the native population, and it had always given Natasa pause. Was her father a spy for the pharaoh, or champion of her mother's people?

"What is this?" Hecataeus asked, giving Natasa a harsh glance, shushing her in an instant. She hated disappointing her father.

"Hecataeus, it appears your child thinks she has the right to give her opinion on a matter that is not her business," Isidor said.

"I'm not surprised." Hecataeus laughed as he ruffled Natasa's hair. His face softened, and Natasa's fear disappeared. "Natasa is bound to be nosey. She's Neffa's child, isn't she?"

Isidor's gaze narrowed at her father's use of her mother's nickname. It hinted at the intimacy they'd once shared. Natasa didn't know why her mother had chosen to have an affair with Hecataeus, but her father had confessed once, after a jug of wine, their brief union still troubled Isidor.

Hecataeus gave them a charming grin. "Best to wash up. We will approach the docks of Abdju in moments." He turned to walk toward the crew as they began raising the sails to slow down the boat.

Isidor released Senmen. "Fine. Go on, boy, make yourself presentable. You can leave your things in your room on the boat. Tomorrow we continue on to Memphis."

As the adults left, Natasa breathed a sigh of relief. Why did people their age have to make life so complicated? Moments later, they disembarked at the docks of Abdju. It felt good to be on solid ground again. After paying their fees to the Greek dockmasters, her father lifted the two children into a wagon stationed nearby.

"Now you behave," Hecataeus said to them. "If you're good, I'll take you to the excavation site this very afternoon."

"Wonderful, Papa," Natasa answered, looking at Senmen with a huge smile. She loved to be involved in her father's architectural digs in Abdju, a hobby he'd begun after he'd been assigned to King Hugronaphor's court, fifteen years prior. Hecataeus often said the historical wonders of Egypt made living away from Athens worth the sacrifice. Natasa sometimes feared he'd leave her to return to his homeland, but Hecataeus seemed content with his life in Egypt.

The sunny days on the boat had darkened Natasa and Senmen's skin, and now they looked like commoners rather than royal heirs. Senmen's hair had grown long enough to cover his face, and he used a thin, flaxen rope to tie it back.

"They're going to shave my head when I arrive in Memphis," he said as he tucked a dark strand behind his ear.

"No," she exclaimed. "That's horrible."

"They'll do it to you too," he warned her.

"Ugh," she said, playing with the beads at the bottom of her braids, "but hair is so nice. Why do we shave it off?"

"The gods must like it."

"I doubt that," she said. "I think the adults like it, so they can wear their stupid hats and wigs."

Senmen laughed and brushed up against her. He leaned closer, and his face became serious as the smile faded. For the first time in their lives, Natasa felt an awkward silence with him.

"Senmen?" she asked. "What is it?"

"Your mother gave Ankhmakis his first rites," he said.

Natasa felt a knot in her stomach. Her mother's role as the

high priestess of Isis involved many things, and one of those was to initiate the royal males in Anit-Shadya, the sex magic of Isis. It had never bothered Natasa until her mother had initiated Ankhmakis, the second son of King Hugronaphor. Natasa wasn't sure why it had disturbed her—when her mother had begun to teach the eldest prince, Silus, in the ways of love, Natasa hadn't cared one bit. But the image of Ankhmakis in her mother's arms made her heart beat like a hurried horse's hooves upon stone. As Senmen scooched even closer to her side, she worried he might hear the pounding in her chest.

"What of it? She's the high priestess of Isis. It's her job to initiate the royal men into the sexual arts. You included," she burst out, trying to hide her discomfort. "It's part of your purification, to prepare you to inhabit Ra himself if ever crowned pharaoh."

He blushed. "Will you do it as well?"

"Do what?" she asked.

"Practice Anit-Shadya."

"Without the ancient magic of Anit-Shadya, Egypt will fade into nothing," Natasa answered. "We must preserve it."

"You've decided," Senmen said. "You're going to train to become a royal spiritual companion, like your mother."

The way he looked at her made her cheeks feel hot. "It is what my mother expects of me," she whispered.

The strange silence engulfed them, and Natasa struggled to breathe. What was going on in his mind? Moreover, what was happening inside her?

Senmen leaned in toward her face. She could feel the warmth of his skin and smell his sweat. The next thing she knew, he kissed her on the lips, and then, quick as a slave master's whip, jumped off his seat and into the dusty road. She placed a finger on her lips as he ran around the wagon and out of sight. Confused, Natasa called out for him, but he didn't return. She launched herself out of the cart to chase him down.

"Natasa," her father called. "Get over here."

She turned and ran toward her father, who was riding his horse behind the wagon.

"Did you see Senmen?" she asked while jogging to keep up with the caravan.

"Girl, you get yourself in that wagon. I won't have children's nonsense right now."

"Yes, Papa," she said through gritted teeth, frustrated with both her father and Senmen. But she obeyed and climbed back into the wagon, paying attention to the landscape as they approached the town.

The Nile had recently retreated, leaving behind acres of dark, mineral-infused earth and heralding the beginning of Perit. This was one of Natasa's favorite seasons. The Inundation had ended and gone were the rains and threats of floods. As their caravan approached Abdju, the small city nestled in the valley emerged. Along the river stretched dark plots of farmland outlined with ancient walls built long ago to guide the river as it flooded into cultivated farm plots, making it easier to plant, grow, and harvest the crops. To the east rose the city, and beyond, Seti's temple complex. To the west, she could see the mountains and the gap between them that led to the desert wastelands.

Her heart soared as they entered the village. Abdju was a place she'd been many times before, filled with memories of treasure hunting with her father. Here she would be his assistant in research, not some child told to shush. She turned to look for Senmen but still couldn't find him. They stopped at their destination, a low bungalow built of red brick her father owned, and the men unpacked the supplies.

Natasa leaped from the wagon and skipped to Hecataeus. As she did so, a man ran up beside them, as excited as a pack of golden jackals descending upon an injured gazelle.

"Lord Hecataeus," cried the lead excavator, Inman, waving his hands. "We've found something."

Natasa ran forward with her father, and Senmen appeared right behind her. She stopped to tug him aside.

"Senmen, where have you been?"

"Why do you care, silly girl?" he replied, acting as if it were her fault he'd kissed her.

Frustrated with her friend's behavior, Natasa shook her head and turned away, instead walking beside her father to hear Inman's report. Senmen followed on her heels.

"What is it, Inman?" Hecataeus asked the worker.

"We've uncovered a new room, deep below the temple," Inman said in between gasps. He must have run from the temple to find Hecataeus. "One we've never seen before."

"Could it be the fabled Osirion?" Natasa asked, bouncing on the balls of her feet. She was beyond excitement herself.

"Wouldn't that be wonderful?" Hecataeus agreed.

"We discovered the room days ago and have made it safe to enter. Follow me," Inman instructed.

Inman guided them toward the temple of Seti, which had been an excavation site for as long as anyone could remember. Built over one thousand years prior by Seti I, the temple had been completed by his son, Ramesses II, but was abandoned when their dynasty ended. Over time, the palace, gardens, and temples had fallen into ruin. What now remained was an outpost for the Greek merchants moving goods up and down the Nile. Abdju reeked of the unfortunate poverty of a native class that served the Greek aristocracy in all ways, yet never reaped any of the economic benefits. As one traveled farther north on the Nile, it was evident the Egyptian people had become slaves, producing goods for the privilege to breathe.

The Egyptians believed Abdju was at the exact location where Osiris, after being killed by his brother Set, had returned to power. The Resurrection of Osiris was celebrated each year in Abdju, with priests and priestesses playing the roles of the different gods and goddesses. When Seti I built his temple in Abdju, he chose it as a way of aligning himself with the god Osiris. Legends told that somewhere within the complex, Seti had hidden his secret treasure, lost to those who ruled after his dynasty ended.

What was so fantastic that the pharaoh had decided to hide it from his own people? Natasa had spent months searching his temple, figuring Seti had buried his treasure where he was worshipped. Yet years later, she still hadn't found anything other than broken pottery, golden medallions, and cups—things any old king would have. If they'd found the Osirion, maybe she would uncover the mystery of the fabled Resurrection Bath—a treasure worthy of a king. It was rumored the bath had given Seti's dynasty their military power.

They entered the temple from the front and crossed its various courtyards and chambers until Inman led them to a long, narrow path that ran deep under the entire structure. The entrance to a tunnel loomed ahead. Inman turned to them.

"We found the well," he said. "But nothing else."

He grabbed a torch from the wall, and they entered the tunnel. Hieroglyphs surrounded them, depicting bewildering scenes.

"What do the walls say?" Senmen asked.

"We believe they depict initiation rites," Inman explained. "The things priests and kings had to do to enter the chamber in Seti's day before it fell into disuse."

Eventually, the tunnel emptied out into a large circular chamber, twenty feet in diameter. In the center of the room, there was a pool of water. The air was cool and crisp. The walls were bare, save one large form on the far end. As she entered the space, Natasa felt the hair on her body rise. Her pulse quickened. This place was important, she knew it.

"This room is like the one under the Great Pyramid in Giza," Natasa said, recalling what her mother had told her. "So old no one knows who made it."

Inman nodded as she walked deeper into the chamber. Her father gazed at the bare walls, searching for evidence of a secret door or passage, but Natasa only had eyes for the pool. It had been constructed of local stone from the mountain, and as she approached it, Natasa could see a set of steps leading down into its depths.

"Is it the Resurrection Bath?" she asked, her heart pounding in her ears.

"No," Inman said. "It is a sacred pool, yes, but it can't provide eternal life. The Resurrection Bath would be something that renewed the Ka, not the physical body itself. During our lives, the forces of death destroy the Ka over time, which in turn ages the body. Thus, the bath would have been something energetic in nature, something that could renew the magnetism of the Ka. Water can't do such a thing, and it doesn't make one immortal."

Inman continued walking toward the wall. "From what I can gather, the initiate would enter the pool to be cleansed, and exit to approach this form." He stopped in front of a familiar geometry—a large circle that held within itself thirteen smaller, interlaced circles, forming flowers where they connected.

"I've seen this before," Hecataeus said. "In the temples in Athens."

"Have you?" Inman frowned.

"Yes, on the floors in the temple on Delos. I've also seen it in other places in my travels along the Mediterranean Sea."

"Like?" the excavator probed.

"Gaul. And Jerusalem."

"We call it the Flower of Life," Inman said. "It's interesting that the same form is here, deep in this ancient room, as well as in the temples of Greece."

"What does it mean?" Hecataeus asked.

"Maybe it's a doorway?" Natasa offered.

"There aren't any seams," her father said as he ran his fingers around the form.

Natasa glanced around the cavern. Senmen stood by the pool, gazing into it. The torchlight cast an eerie shadow across his face, and for a moment, he looked possessed, like a ghoul from one of the tales her nursemaid had told her to scare her into staying in her bed at night. To her surprise, Natasa feared him. He turned to grin at her, nothing now but sweetness in his gaze, and she shook the cold visage from her imagination. Senmen was her best friend, not someone to be feared.

"This place is strange," Hecataeus sighed. "We finally managed to break into the Osirion's inner chambers, only to find this empty room. I can find no way out of here. It's a dead end."

Natasa studied the room, chin up and lips pressed, determined to discover the mystery the cavern held. Her father was right; there was only one entrance, the ancient pool, and the Flower of Life carved upon the wall. Yet she felt an energy course through her being.

"Papa, I don't know," she said. "I think there's more than meets the eye. It's a water bath, but that doesn't mean it isn't the treasure you've been searching for."

"No, little hawk," Hecataeus replied, "I think Inman's right. Something else would be needed to keep a man alive forever. If water could do the trick, we would never die."

Natasa stood next to the pool, bent down to put her hand in it, and jerked back in shock. "The water is warm, Papa." She licked her finger. "And salty."

The rest of them placed their hands in the warm, briny water.

"I agree with Natasa," Senmen said in a soft voice, his mouth open as he continued gazing at the pool. "This place is powerful."

Hecataeus shrugged. "We'll come back tomorrow to investigate further. Natasa, why don't you give Senmen a tour of the rest of the complex while I catch up on the recent surveys?"

Natasa didn't want to leave the room. Here was a puzzle in need of solving, and for some reason, she felt she was the only one who could do it. What a funny thing to think; she was a child. How could she hold the answer to such a mystery? But she knew within her very soul that somehow her life held the answer. If she could unravel the secret, she would discover the power of the old kings.

"Go on now," Hecataeus said, breaking her thoughts and handing her a torch. "Show your friend around. He's never been here before."

She nodded and did as she was told, spending the rest of the day sharing her favorite tunnels, stela inscriptions, statuary, and dusty hiding places with her dear friend. Later, as Ra began his nightly descent, Natasa and Senmen stood on the top of her small house. The ancient city at the base of the valley turned from gold to pink, the dying sun reflecting off the marbled tops of the temples and buildings. Abdju sat at the point where the alluvial Nile plain met the desert in the east and a limestone mountain in the west. In this crescent-shaped mountain, which cradled the ancient village in its protective embrace, there was a strange cleft splintering the mountain. The kings knew it as the Stairway to Heaven. Natasa held her breath as the sun descended into the crevasse, setting in a blaze of gold and vermillion. The sky lit up behind the mountain, and a cool breeze sighed across the plain, blowing Natasa's hair around her face.

"It is written," she said, her voice low and serene, "that the stairway in the mountain leads to the Halls of Amenti, the realm of Osiris, the lord of Abdju."

As Ra made his dramatic disappearance, a brisk desert chill formed around them. Senmen shivered. "I believe it," he agreed. "It feels like we're standing in the palm of god."

Senmen had a strange look in his eyes again, and despite the desert chill, Natasa's cheeks grew warm. This time when he kissed her, she knew what was coming and surrendered. If this was how he wished to spend their last moments together before he left for Memphis, she wasn't going to argue. She enjoyed feeling so loved and adored by him.

When they climbed down from the roof to enter her father's bungalow, they found Isidor and Hecataeus at the table in her father's study. Natasa made to shush Senmen, and he took his place beside her to spy on the adults. The pair settled under a window and tried their best to be as still as stone.

"Neferu-ankh-maat has her reservations about sending

Senmen to Memphis," they heard her father say.

"She has already shared her concerns," Isidor answered. "She and I are very close."

Silence. Then the shuffling sounds of men sitting on uncomfortable chairs.

"Yes, I'm aware the two of you spend a lot of time together," Hecataeus said. Natasa detected some sort of anger in his voice. She looked at Senmen, who shrugged.

"Then she must have told you I will do what I can to protect the boy while he's training with Metakryon," Isidor answered.

"Will you remain in Memphis the entire three years of his training?" Hecataeus asked.

"Of course not," Isidor replied. Silence again, and then the sounds of wine being poured into clay goblets. "You'd like me to stay away though, wouldn't you?"

"I have no idea what you mean," Hecataeus said.

"The last time I was in Memphis for years, you managed to steal my lover and make that half-breed of a child."

What did he mean, half-breed? How dare he? Natasa made to stand and yell at the older man, but Senmen grabbed her and placed his hand over her mouth, shaking his head.

"You're unbelievable," Hecataeus answered with a laugh. "Half-breed. Do you tell Neffa that when she's in your arms? Does she know what you think of her beloved daughter?"

Silence again.

"That's what I thought, Isidor," Hecataeus replied. "You keep much from her, don't you?"

A chair scraped the floor as someone rose from the table.

"I will take my leave now," Isidor said. "We leave for Memphis at sunrise."

"As you wish," Hecataeus replied, remaining in his seat.

They heard the patter of footsteps as Isidor walked toward the door.

"Isidor," Hecataeus called out. "Be careful. You can't keep anything from her, so I'd suggest you do a better job of guarding your secrets. She's bound to find out who spends time in your chambers when she's not around."

"I don't need advice from you, Greek," Isidor hissed.

His footsteps faded into the distance. Inside, Hecataeus must have poured himself another drink but remained at the table. The children crawled on their bellies like adders to the back of the house, careful and silent, until they knew the coast was clear.

"Why is your father worried?" Senmen asked. "Why should I need protection from the priests in Memphis?"

"I have no idea," Natasa admitted. "I've met Metakryon, he's older than Seti the First." Senmen laughed at her remark. "But harmless," she continued. "Perhaps there's something else going on? Besides, how dare he call me a half-breed?"

"He's an elitist," Senmen said. "Though you are half Greek, which does make you different."

"Yes, but the way he said it made it sound like a disease."

Senmen's eyes locked onto hers, and she felt her heart begin to beat faster. What was going on between them? How could they be spying on the adults one minute, and feel excited inside the next? She looked at his handsome face and brushed the hair from his forehead. She tucked the dark lock behind his ear, and the next thing she knew, he was kissing her again. The kiss was still hesitant, but wetter this time. Natasa didn't stop him. Instead, she allowed herself to feel his adoration. How strange she'd never noticed it before.

After a moment, he drew away and looked at the ground, moving his sandaled foot back and forth in the dusty street.

"Senmen?" she asked. "Why are you kissing me?"

"Don't you know?" he answered, looking up at her, lips parted and face flushed.

She shrugged. "No, I don't. But I like it. I thought you should know."

Senmen grabbed her, planting one long, last kiss upon her lips before walking away. "I'll see you tomorrow," he said, a slight bounce in his step.

✝

The following morning, as the Great Ra was rising from his slumber, Natasa found Senmen sneaking into her room. In his hand, he held an amulet. He kissed her on the cheek and placed it in her hand.

"Bloodstone," he whispered. "It will protect you from witches."

"But I am a witch." She giggled.

"Not to me," he answered. "To me, you're a goddess."

He kissed her on the mouth once again, this time with complete confidence in his newfound skill, and stood to leave.

"Kissing gets better each time you do it." She smiled and he laughed, which made her even happier. "I'll miss you, Senmen." She could see he had tears in his eyes and didn't even attempt to hide her own. "Please be careful. Mother wouldn't be worried unless something was wrong in Memphis."

"I'll miss you too," he said, moving to sneak out of the room before her father heard them. When he got to her window, he glanced over his shoulder one last time.

"Please don't forget me," he said, his voice cracking as he wiped his eyes.

Then he slipped from her window, and her sight.

4

The Brotherhood of Darkness

At the heart of Egyptian magic was the understanding of the threefold nature of the human being—each person has three bodies to care for and maintain—Khat, the physical body; Ka, the life force that surrounds the Khat; and Ba, the eternal spirit of the individual. Being a part of nature, the Khat eventually dies, releasing the Ba to travel the cosmos and return to a body again in time. Thus, the religion focused mostly on the Ka, and the practices needed to regenerate and renew it with power and everlasting life. These practices ensured a long physical incarnation, as well as a strong connection to the Ba. For within the Ba, all wisdom is already known. This understanding of the threefold nature of the human was taught only to those who were initiated into the mysteries, for in the wrong hands this knowledge would yield a force of darkness, destruction, and despair.

Memphis, Egypt 211 BCE

Senmen's instruction in the temple of Memphis was filled with the knowledge of the Khat, Ka, and Ba, and the various practices for maintaining the health of each.

Nutrition, herbalism, massage, movement, music, song, dance, breath work, meditations, imaginations, and countless other items of knowledge were set upon him and the other acolytes. They slept in dorms on woven mats upon the hard floor, wore scratchy gray robes, ate plain foods, and kept their heads shaved. The goal of the first phase was to teach the knowledge they needed to serve in the priesthood, while also laying the foundations for discipline deep within the boys's souls—for without discipline, they could never hope to pass into the other worlds and gain Divine wisdom.

Five months into his training, he was excelling at his studies. Boring at times, but better than he'd expected. Senmen, of course, missed the life of the court; in Memphis, he was nothing but an initiate, not a prince. In addition, even though the priests in Memphis were teaching the alchemies of Horus, they had an obvious Greek influence, something Senmen hadn't witnessed in Behdet. Gods from the Greek pantheon were often included, and Greek art infiltrated the temples. The most interesting aspect to Senmen was the realism in their paintings. Where the walls in Behdet were still engraved with figures that were quite like one another, in Memphis, faces took on personal appearances. There was one new fresco that had been painted in honor of the Greek God Dionysus, which looked like Ptolemy IV himself.

On the day Pharaoh Ptolemy IV Philopater arrived to meet with the priests in Memphis, Senmen and his other classmates were busy copying texts from the temple walls onto broken, discarded shards of pottery, things the temple artisans had deemed unworthy for the gods or the burial chambers of the kings and nobles. The learning of letters and hieroglyphs was important, for they believed the written word was filled with the energy of the gods themselves. If something was written on the walls of a tomb, like a spell or magical incantation, it would remain alive for as long as the tomb walls existed. Writing was sacred, a means of passing on power from one generation to the next. Thus, priests were taught how to write, and the best of them were often offered the job of scribe—one of the most sought-after occupations in the entire kingdom.

"Boys," their instructor, the scribe Pabasa, called out, "please finish your work. I have received a message declaring the pharaoh has demanded to see each of you for inspection."

Senmen looked up from his work and turned to Qeny, a boy from the Delta he'd bonded with early in the training.

"Inspect us? What does that mean?" Senmen asked.

Qeny shrugged. "I have no idea. My father never mentioned inspections by the pharaoh."

"It's his way of making sure his future priests are fit to fulfill their role," Antonius, a young man from a prominent Greek house, answered. He was not Senmen's favorite person.

"Why wouldn't we be?" Senmen demanded. "We're here at his command already."

"No," Antonius replied with a tone that suggested he knew best, reminding Senmen of his older sister, Bithiah, "we're here because he demanded tribute from our fathers to train in his priesthood. Our fathers chose us. Now our pharaoh decides if he approves of their offerings."

"His priesthood?" Senmen exclaimed. "This is a priesthood of Ra himself. Only the gods can own it."

"Isn't our Lord Philopater a god?" Antonius answered. "The priests of Memphis and Thebes crowned him Ra, didn't they? Thus, he is Ra on Earth, and we serve him with our hearts and minds. You need to understand your place here, Nubian."

Senmen rose from his place and looked down upon the

overconfident Greek. He wanted to crack his writing tablet over the boy's head.

Qeny grabbed him. "Senmen, it's time to go."

Senmen stomped across the room and dropped his work onto Pabasa's desk. The old priest squinted at it with discernment as he determined the value of Senmen's work.

"You have a talent for words, Lord Senmen," he said with approval. "Have you ever considered becoming a scribe?"

Senmen rolled up his sleeve and cracked his knuckles, still irritated by Antonius's comments. "No, I'm a prince. The only vocation I've considered is king."

Pabasa made a gesture of protection around himself and waved a finger in Senmen's face. "Watch yourself boy, you don't want to draw the pharaoh's attention."

He dismissed them, and Senmen followed the others to the sleeping quarters to put on his ceremony robe—a white tunic and leather sandals. He ran his hands over his bald head, wishing he had hair and grateful Natasa hadn't seen him in this state of priestly poverty. Would she find him handsome? When he was finished changing, he looked for Qeny, and the two took their places in line with the others. There were twenty-two boys in total, one from each nome of Upper Egypt, sent as tribute from their noblemen fathers. Senmen noted that most of them were Egyptian; it appeared the Greek nobles didn't have to pay tribute in the same way. To his side stood Antonius, wearing a smug grin in addition to his ceremony attire.

"Excited?" Senmen asked him.

"Of course," Antonius replied, puffing out his chest. "Meeting the pharaoh is an honor."

"Why are you here?" Senmen demanded.

"What do you mean, Nubian? For the same reason, you

are. Tribute from my father."

"Yes, but why? There are only two light-skinned tributes in the bunch of us. I can see why the pharaoh demands loyalty from my father, but why yours? I thought the Greek nobility was exempt from such acts of groveling."

Antonius's nostrils flared, but before the boy could reply, Metakryon appeared before them. Isidor wasn't with him. The high priest of Behdet had taken part in the training so far, as this had been his school as a young man. But for some reason, he was nowhere to be seen.

The acolytes bowed to Metakryon, who held up his old arms and nodded, his head bobbing up and down at the end of his long neck. He reminded Senmen of a black cormorant floating upon the surface of the Nile.

"Young men, you are going to meet your king, our lord, and pharaoh of this great land. Follow me and show respect," the ancient priest commanded.

"How old do you think Metakryon is?" Senmen whispered to Qeny, who shrugged and fought off a bout of nervous giggles. "Look at him, he walks like he's already dead."

Antonius punched Senmen in the side. "Quiet, Nubian."

Senmen shoved him back and stood straight to march into the hall.

Ptolemy IV Philopater sat on a throne at the front of the room, wearing the pharaoh's regalia over his Greek robes. His golden circlet crown lay crooked upon his brown curls, as he leaned to one side and watched the boys enter. If Metakryon reminded Senmen of a bird, then Philopater was a sweaty swine—round in the middle and smacking his lips as if the boys were food scraps. They followed Metakryon up to the dais, formed a straight line in front of the pharaoh, and bowed low to their ruler. Ptolemy IV snorted and told them to stand.

From this close distance, Senmen could see the pharaoh's eyes were bloodshot, his cheeks were red, and his robes were too tight. Senmen had overheard rumors in Behdet that Philopater was a disgrace to Egypt from Greeks and Egyptians alike, but had never seen proof of this until now. It was clear to Senmen that his pharaoh was a sloppy man, a man nothing like Hugronaphor, who wore his station with pride. Philopater was slumped, messy, slurring his words, and appeared out of his mind.

"My Lord Ptolemy IV Philopater, Ra and Dionysus, pharaoh of our lands, I present to you our recent recruits into the priesthood in Memphis," Metakryon said with a raspy, shaky voice.

"Yes, yes," Philopater said. He swallowed hard and parted his legs. Senmen looked away, not at all wanting to catch a glimpse of what was under the man's skirts. "I see. And I like what I see."

"I'm glad, my lord," Metakryon continued. "Now if I may, we will take your leave and let you continue with your business—"

"Not so fast, Metakryon," Ptolemy IV said, leaning forward in his throne. "You know our agreement."

Senmen heard the door behind them close, followed by the sounds of the guards bolting it shut. He felt a sense of danger fill the room. He searched the older priests' faces for an indication of what was happening, but none would look at him or the line of terrified boys. Instead, they gazed at their feet, or at Metakryon himself. The old priest nodded to the pharaoh, flinching. He hunched over on his staff, resigned.

"I'll take the Egyptians," Philopater continued, "and that one, what's your name, son?"

Senmen glanced over his shoulder at Antonius, who stood

at attention.

"Antonius, Sir. Son of Benor, house of Belos."

"Yes," Ptolemy IV cooed. "Lord Benor's son. I've been waiting for you."

"Sir," Metakryon said, wringing his hands. "I'm sorry, but you can't have every Egyptian. Remember what High Priest Isidor said—"

"Isidor." The pharaoh laughed. "Do you see him anywhere?"

Metakryon shook his head.

"Then he has no say right now," Ptolemy IV spat. He looked over the line of boys and called out, "Son of Haronnophris, step forward."

Senmen stood still, not wanting to be seen. What was going on? Qeny nudged him, and Senmen stumbled forward. He could feel the lust in the pharaoh's predatory gaze undressing him.

"Yes, you," the pharaoh purred, his eyes darting over Senmen's body. "I've also been waiting for you."

"Your Majesty—" Metakryon begged.

"Quiet, old fool!" Ptolemy IV yelled, rising from his throne in a fury. He swayed as he stood and gripped the arm of his golden throne to steady himself. "This is my temple. My court. My father might have bowed down to your every wish, but I will not. The priests bow down to *me*. Now, send them to my private chambers. My colleagues and I are looking forward to meeting them."

Senmen eyed the other men in the room and noted the various looks upon their faces—wide-eyed, lips drawn tight, faces grave, each one looking at the floor, or the ceiling— anywhere other than the boys. He wiped the sweat on his forehead, fear coursing through his veins. From deep within his mind, he recalled the worst rumor of all—that Ptolemy IV Philopater and his friends used young boys for their private recreation. He turned to his classmates, who now shook with terror. They too had heard the stories, and so had their fathers. Yet, each of them had still been offered up.

One Greek boy was wrenched from the group while the guards surrounded the rest of them, herding them through a door. Senmen felt his heart grow cold and his lungs stop drawing in air as a soldier shoved him into a dark room, filled with smoke, candles, and naked, wild-eyed men.

☥

Isidor hurried through the halls of the temple, knowing he was too late. Djed, Metakryon's assistant, had rushed out to try to summon him from the city the moment he'd heard the boys had been taken, for he'd known that Isidor had explicitly stated Senmen under no circumstances could be offered up to the pharaoh for his pleasure. Unfortunately for the boys, and for Djed, it took him hours before he found Isidor in a dirty alchemist's shop in the seediest part of Memphis, where Isidor had been visiting old friends and purchasing questionable magical objects.

"When did he take them?" Isidor asked as they ran toward Metakryon's chambers.

"Hours ago, my lord," Djed replied. "I'm sorry I took so long, I had no idea you'd be in that part of town."

"Don't speak of it," Isidor warned, holding the sack he was carrying closer to his chest. "How dare Metakryon go against my orders?"

"My lord," Djed continued, wringing his hands and panting hard to keep up with Isidor's furious pace. "The high priest did try to remove Senmen from of the lineup, but—"

"Never mind," Isidor snapped as they approached Metakryon's quarters. Five Royal Guards stood at attention. It appeared he would see the pharaoh after all.

"Out of my way," Isidor demanded.

"I'm sorry, but I must ask who calls," one of the guards said.

Isidor shoved the guard from his path and let himself through the door. He found Metakryon sitting at the pharaoh's feet, while Philopater the Filthy drank of his wine and laughed with his favorites, Sosibuis and Agathocles. The room stank of opium smoke.

"*Metakryon,*" Isidor yelled as he stepped toward the men.

Metakryon attempted to stand but swayed as if a young willow in the breeze. The old man rubbed his eyes and fell back to his supplicant position on the floor.

"Ah, Isidor," Philopater purred with satisfaction. "Do come in. We were discussing the old days when I was an acolyte in this wonderful, esteemed school."

Isidor handed his bundle to Djed, who took it without question and strode to the pharaoh's side, kicking Metakryon out of the way. He didn't bow or greet him. Instead, he stood above him, placed his hands upon the arms of the king's chair, and leaned in, his red robes falling into the pharaoh's face. Ptolemy swatted at the robes, trying to get out of Isidor's grip.

"Since when was the raping of young boys a part of this school's practice?" Isidor yelled.

Philopater looked up at Isidor with his pink, pudgy, pig-like face. He shoved Isidor back, raised his cup in a toast, and smiled.

"Since I became the pharaoh," he slurred. "It's my religion, therefore you must follow it."

Isidor turned on Metakryon, who tripped on his robes

as he struggled to stand. The sight of his master's fragility enraged Isidor.

"Is it true? Did he abuse Senmen?"

"Senmen," Philopater simpered. "Oh yes, I like him. He's a good boy."

Isidor made to strike the pharaoh, but held back, considering the consequences he'd suffer for such an action. Getting jailed at that moment was what Philopater wanted, but would be of no help to Senmen.

"I think I'll take him back to Alexandria with me," Philopater continued, "and make him my pet."

"You will not," Isidor snarled. "You will not lay a hand on him again, or trust me, Philopater, there will be war—a war that will destroy you and your line."

"Why speak of such treason?" Ptolemy IV demanded. "Haronnophris will do no such thing."

"If he hears you have made his son your sex slave, you can be sure he will destroy the entire nation if necessary to make you pay for your crimes."

Philopater blinked at the thought, his lips turning into a grin. Enraged by the man's arrogant smirk, Isidor grabbed the pharaoh's tunic and heaved him out of his chair.

"Touch him again, and you will pay," Isidor said, his grip growing tighter by the moment. "By Hugronaphor's sword you shall die, and by the power vested in me by our lord and god Set, you shall suffer in eternal agony. Remember, dear pharaoh, I'm not a priest of Memphis. I am the high priest of Set, lord of chaos, and I am his chosen one. Trust me when I say I will unleash his fury as I see fit."

He dropped the fat man back into his seat, the form of fear now surrounding him. Isidor's message had somehow been heard. He rounded on Metakryon, who trembled before a wooden table covered in jugs of wine, ale, and opium paraphernalia.

"We will discuss your failure later, Metakryon," Isidor hissed. "The priests may crown the pharaoh, and the pharaoh may rule this land, but no one can evade the wrath of Set."

Isidor turned and walked toward the door, grabbing his parcel from Djed's hands. Without being excused, he made his way back up the long hallway from Metakryon's chambers to the dorms where the boys slept. Gone were the jovial sounds of the boys's banter, replaced instead with soft moans and hushed tears. He entered the room and found them tucked up into balls, some crying, others rocking in silence. One boy was hitting his head on the wall, over and over, creating a morbid rhythm. Senmen was sitting on his mat, staring into space with open, deadened eyes.

"Come with me," he whispered to the boy.

Senmen turned and looked up at Isidor. His lips trembled yet he didn't utter a word.

"Come, now," Isidor said again, grabbing the boy by the shoulder and raising him to stand.

Senmen obeyed and followed Isidor to his quarters. He still didn't speak. When they arrived, Isidor sat Senmen down on his couch and shut the door behind them. He took a place beside the child and waited in silence for him to say something, but Senmen sat still, staring into the fire. In the torchlight, Isidor could see signs of struggle on the boy's arms and wrists. He felt nauseous as he thought of what that meant.

"Senmen," Isidor began, "I know what they did to you, and I want you to know that they did it without my permission."

Senmen turned on him, his whole body now shaking. "Where were you?" the boy screamed. "You were supposed to *protect* me."

"I had business in the city. I didn't know the pharaoh would be here—"

"You knew this was part of the training, didn't you? So did my father. Everyone knows," the boy continued yelling. He gripped the chair beneath him and ripped at it. "And you offered me up, a sweet gift for our perverted king, in exchange for your precious army."

"No, Senmen, that's not true. You have to believe me," Isidor cried.

His heart was breaking for this boy. He'd promised both Neferu-ankh-maat and Queen Keket that he'd protect him, but had failed. It was impossible to keep him safe in this horrible place. He himself had endured a torture of a different kind during the long years he'd spent under Metakryon's training. But he couldn't remain with Senmen for the entire three years. He had to go back to Behdet. He was needed there.

"Senmen, listen to me," Isidor continued, placing his hands on the boy's shoulders and settling him down. "I'm sorry this happened to you. I've spoken with the pharaoh, and while I can't promise you'll never have to experience his cruelty again, I can tell you he won't be near you in the immediate future."

Isidor rose from his place and walked to the table where he'd deposited his parcel. He opened it and took from it three objects—a wand made of onyx, a second, longer wand made of silver, and a skull carved from crystal. He placed the wands and the skull on the table and turned to Senmen.

"I can't protect you," he admitted. "I'm due home and will leave within a fortnight. I've already been here too long."

Senmen's eyes grew wide, and the wild, fearful look returned.

"There are ways you can protect yourself," Isidor

continued. "What happened was unfortunate, but it can be used to our advantage. What do you feel right now?"

Senmen glared but said nothing.

"Disgust?" Isidor suggested. "Disappointment? Fear?"

"Hate," Senmen hissed.

"Whom do you hate?" Isidor asked.

"You," Senmen answered. "My father. Metakryon."

"How do you feel about the pharaoh?" Isidor probed.

"I loathe him."

"Good, good," Isidor answered. "In the temple of Memphis, you will learn many things. But much will also be kept from you. This is to protect our magic and knowledge from the Greeks. If they knew our true power, they would use it against us. Thus, it has been guarded for generations."

Senmen continued to stare, his breaths shallow, fists clenched.

"Hate and loathing are powerful emotions," Isidor explained. "Normal men are told to ignore them, or perhaps inflict pain on a weaker opponent until they feel better. But emotions are energy, and they're charged with immense power that if directed in the right way, can not only protect you but create circumstances to your advantage."

Senmen remained silent, but his breathing slowed.

"I want you to feel your hate as it surrounds you and weaves its way through you," Isidor instructed. "Now close your eyes and imagine the hate around you, like a form. See it snake through your veins and your body, dancing around your arms and legs. Can you see it?"

Senmen nodded.

"What color is it?"

"Gray," the boy whispered in a low voice. "Dark gray."

"Good, you have seen hate, for its form is gray, and it

covers the world in smoke," Isidor continued. He walked to the boy and put the onyx wand in his hand. "This is a wand of the Dark Brotherhood. It's not well looked upon in Behdet to use these objects, but the time has come for me to instruct you in the dark arts sooner than I'd planned." Isidor sighed and placed a hand on the boy's bald head. "Now, Senmen, I want you to picture Ptolemy IV standing in front of you—"

"No!" Senmen gasped, opening his eyes and jumping from his seat.

"Sit," Isidor commanded. "Trust me." Senmen hesitated and did as he was told. "Do as I say. Close your eyes and picture the pharaoh." He paused, giving Senmen a moment. He could see how badly the child struggled. "I know it's hard but do it. Recall your hate, your loathing, and see him standing before you."

After a moment, Senmen sat up straighter.

"Good," Isidor whispered. "Now see the force of hate around you. When you can feel its charge, when its energy pours through your body, raise the wand and point it at Ptolemy IV. Send the power of your hate toward the evil, vile man, and cover him with it. See it choke him and strangle him."

Senmen nodded and raised his arm, pointing the wand out in front of him. Isidor saw the boy's body get bigger and rise, almost with pride. A smile crossed Senmen's lips.

"Yes," Senmen hissed. "Yes. I see him choking. I see him dying."

"Good, good," Isidor continued.

"I see hate covering him and killing him. Sucking the life out of him the way he did me," Senmen continued in a voice that sounded like a snake crawling across a stone floor. "He will die, he will die."

"Yes, yes," Isidor agreed, "he will die. You and I will make sure he does so in the most unpleasant of ways."

Senmen rose from his chair and raised the wand over his head. Isidor felt a dark shift in the room and a charge of energy swirl around the boy. Senmen laughed—a cold, evil laugh that Isidor had heard only in the presence of Set.

"*Death*," Senmen cried out as a breeze swirled around him, causing his tunic to flutter. Isidor wrapped his arms around himself as he sucked in a startled breath.

He'd never seen anyone channel Set's energy with such ease. It had taken Isidor years of approaching the god of chaos before a connection had been made. The boy was a natural.

"Good, Senmen," he said with pride. "I think you're the student I've been looking for."

Senmen dropped the wand and turned to Isidor, his body now deflated and eyes fluttering to stay open as exhaustion took hold of his body. Isidor helped him to the table and poured him a glass of wine to ground him.

"Keep the wand," Isidor said, "but don't let anyone know you have it. I don't think Metakryon would approve. Practice the hate exercises every day during your private meditation time. It will make you stronger, and when you're a man, you'll find yourself quite capable. In the meantime, do what you must to learn here and keep the pact between your father and the pharaoh. It's important. But know this, your father did not send you here to be used in this way. When I tell him—"

"*No*," Senmen roared like a caged animal.

"Excuse me?"

"No," Senmen said in a calmer voice. He took a deep breath before continuing. "You mustn't tell him. No one can know this. Please, Isidor. I'd never be able to face anyone in Behdet if they knew I'd been . . ." He stopped and drank his wine, unable to continue.

"If you insist, I will keep this secret," Isidor answered. "But if it happens again, you must let me know."

Senmen gazed at the priest over his goblet and nodded. "Yes, my lord, I will."

"Good. Now back to your quarters. It's best you remain together tonight. Your collective hate for the pharaoh can be powerful if you know how to work with it," Isidor said.

"Will you teach me to work with group emotions in such a way?" Senmen asked. There was a devious look in his gaze. "So much anger in one place must be a formidable force."

Isidor looked at the boy and was amazed at how similar they were. Senmen looked like Queen Keket, yet his talent and temperament were nothing like hers. She was manipulative, yes, but had no command for subtle energy magic. Nor was he like his father, who was charming, but dull-witted. Senmen, on the other hand, was a priest rather than a princeling.

"Yes, my prince," he said with reverence for the child's skill. Senmen was remarkable. "When you return to Behdet, I'll teach you the magic of Set, and you'll never be hurt by anyone again."

The next day, Isidor was informed that the pharaoh and his entourage had left for Alexandria. It appeared Ptolemy IV had begun suffering from a lung infection and cough and desired the care of his own healers at his palace. When Isidor left for Behdet, he was certain whom he would employ to help him reinstate the Dark Brotherhood and restore Egypt to her former glory.

5

Children of the Light

The royals of Behdet practiced Anit-Shadya, "the Purest Pleasure of Isis, the great Goddess of Love." Ecstasy opened the path to perfection, not a solitary path, but rather Anit-Shadya required a partner with whom to travel the road to bliss. The Priestesses of Isis practiced this sex magic, with the goal of becoming vessels of divine love and delight for the royal men so that great warriors would be born—warriors who would reclaim their lands from the intruders.

Behdet, Egypt 211 BCE

Natasa threw herself into those first months of training, soaking up as much knowledge as possible from the various leaders of the temples of Behdet. Her favorite teacher was Iu-Amon, the high priest in the Houses of Healing, who showed the girls the ways of physical healing with plants, massage, medical procedures, and sanitation. They also spent time with the scribes learning to read and write. Lessons in music were a complete joy; Natasa had taken to the harp with ease. Playing the instrument felt as natural as breathing. One day, after what seemed like an eternity, Natasa and her classmates were called to train in the temple of Isis with High Priestess Neferu-ankh-maat herself.

Natasa made sure she arrived in the courtyard early, finding a seat next to Alexa, another of her childhood playmates. Natasa had often spent hours with Alexa and Senmen growing up, and she told her girlfriend how he had kissed her in Abdju.

"I still can't figure why Senmen would do such a thing," Natasa said to her friend, making small talk as they waited for the high priestess to arrive.

"He's in love with you, that's why," Alexa replied.

Natasa cocked her head to one side as she considered her friend's words. Did Senmen love her? Moreover, did she love Senmen? Natasa wasn't sure someone her age could be in love. She was about to say so when Alexa tapped her on the shoulder and pointed. Natasa followed Alexa's gaze and found her mother entering the courtyard. She, along with every other girl in the room, rushed from the ground to stand at attention. Her fellow classmates included several daughters of priests, priestesses, the most important southern nobles, and two of the crown princesses—Bithiah and Weret.

"Why are they here?" Alexa said, nodding her head at the princesses.

"Bithiah is promised to my brother, Nefermaat," Natasa explained. "I guess she has to train in the temple. But I'm not sure why Weret is here. She's going to grow up to marry one of her brothers and have children, so she doesn't need to study."

"Nefermaat is going to marry a princess? Shouldn't he marry a priestess instead?" Alexa asked.

"Why, jealous?" Natasa teased.

"Of course not," Alexa said, but the color on her cheeks suggested otherwise. "It's strange for the son of the high priestess to marry outside of the temple.”

“I overheard him arguing with mother before I left for Abdju,” Natasa replied. “Since she wouldn’t let him train in Memphis, he demanded Bithiah’s hand in marriage. The king agreed.”

“But Bithiah is so bossy,” Alexa said, wrinkling her nose in disapproval. “She doesn’t seem like a consolation prize.”

Natasa shrugged. “I think my brother wants to be part of the court, now that Mother won’t let him inherit the temple.”

“I still think your mother is wrong to have denied her own son his rightful place,” Alexa said.

Natasa looked to the high priestess, who was now staring at Natasa and Alexa as she drew nearer.

“Shush,” Natasa whispered, hitting Alexa’s arm. “She can hear us.”

“No, she can’t, she’s too far away.”

“Perhaps she can read our minds?” Natasa suggested.

Alexa stood taller and nodded. “Oh dear, you might be right.”

The high priestess stopped before the group of girls, and they bowed.

“Welcome, my dear children,” Neferu-ankh-maat said, a warm smile crossing her beautiful face. “It is with a joyous heart and immense gratitude that I meet with you today, and we begin your training in the alchemies of Horus and magic of Isis.”

“Good morning, Lady of Isis,” the girls said in unison, as they had been instructed to do.

The high priestess nodded to them and turned away as she spoke. “Line up behind me.”

Without so much as a peep, the group formed a long line across the temple courtyard behind their teacher. Neferu-ankh-maat raised her arms out to her sides and wiggled her fingers. The girls followed. She raised her arms above her head, and lowered them to her sides, each movement elegant and intentional, making a circle formation around herself.

"For the next three years," the high priestess began, "we will study the alchemies of Horus."

She continued to raise her arms, circling behind her and in front of her body. Again, the girls followed without question. She dropped her arms to her sides.

"We will begin with walking," she explained as she took a slow, small step forward. "As you walk, feel the earth below your feet. This is your home, our home. The earth is you. From the earth our Khat is made, and to the earth it will return."

They walked in silence, and Natasa felt every bit of stone and dirt beneath her feet. She'd never paid attention to her feet before, nor the ground upon which she lived. Now she knew what color the dust made as it pooled above her toes. It seemed like a strange way for her mother to begin their priestess training, but it felt right.

The high priestess raised her arms around her, drawing circles in the air around her body in all directions. "Around us and in us runs the power of life," she explained. "This is our Ka, the vital life force that makes our hearts beat and our lungs take a breath. Our Ka is one with the goddess, for she is the life of the world. Through her, we breathe in, and to her, we breathe out. The Ka surrounds us, like an apple, and our Khat, our flesh and blood, is the core. Faithfully the Ka pulses, feeding us, guiding us, creating us. All life has a Ka, and all life lives within the goddess. Every flower, animal, and tree has a Ka, and with time you will see it. For though it is subtle to your eyes, the Ka is life and the root of all true power."

The girls continued to walk back and forth in the courtyard, drawing circles around themselves with their arms.

"The Ka is also a force that surrounds every living thing. Unseen, it can touch and be touched. It can even," she turned and stopped, "push." The line of girls also stopped, matching her step. Every face was rapt upon Neferu-ankh-maat.

"With time, you will learn how to use the Ka's energies to touch, ever so gently, the world around you. First, you must find your own Ka, for this is the most important thing to know—yourself. Your Ka is faithful, steady as your breath. Firm as your beating heart. But it is not everlasting. The Ka's flame weakens as the maiden becomes the mother and the mother becomes the crone. Eventually, the candle sputters out, and the body, with the light, dies."

Several girls gasped, including Natasa. The Ka could grow weak. This was death. Even as a child, Natasa felt the horror of it, and she shivered.

"However," Neferu-ankh-maat continued, "we are not mere passengers on the river of life. We are not powerless to our mortal fate. The alchemies of Horus nourishes the Ka. Through movement, prayer, breathing, plant medicine, massage, music, and song, we enliven our life force and live in strength."

The high priestess began walking again. The girls followed, drawn to her as the dung beetle to the flame.

"At the end of your training, you will know your Ka and how to care for it, as well as you know your body. Some of you will pursue work in music, contemplative life, or the Houses of the Healing, using your knowledge to heal the broken and the sick. Others will continue your training in the temple and become true Priestesses of Isis. The goddess will teach you how to renew your Ka with another person, united in love, through Anit-Shadya. Not all men are granted a spiritual companion, only those chosen by the king. Upon these chosen ones, the Vessels of Isis pour out her divine strength and vital élan. In return, we are rewarded with health beyond measure. For where two are united in love, there is the greatest blessing."

She paused and turned to the girls.

"The only way to access the mystery of the cosmos is with an intact, pure Ka, in tune with the goddess herself. This is enlightenment when Khat and Ka are so perfectly attuned, and the Ba can separate itself from the bond of flesh and unite with the Divine, without death. This is what we seek. It is the promise of life, abundant and lasting. It is around us, in us and through us. We need only have the eyes to see."

It was a lot for Natasa to grasp. But she heard one thing clearly—that through the temple she would find eternal life. This was an activity worthy of her time. As she followed her mother's footsteps across the courtyard, she thought about Senmen, and how it had felt to kiss him. There had been something between them, like the heat of a flame. Perhaps this was part of Anit-Shadya? An energetic connection formed between two people?

"Natasa," her mother called out.

She stopped and discovered she was lagging behind the rest of the group.

"Yes?" she said, wishing she were invisible.

"Keep your head out of the clouds and in your feet," Neferu-ankh-maat reprimanded.

Bithiah let out a snort of laughter, and Natasa swallowed the urge to snap back. Alexa was right; the middle princess was horrible—what in the world did her brother see in her? Natasa took a deep breath to calm herself and focused on her feet, sensing the ground below her. She drew her hands above her head and lowered them. She put one arm in front and one behind, making a circle in that direction. Over and over she sensed the air around her, how it moved, how it danced. The dust rose behind her as she stepped forward. She imagined her feet extended down to the center of the Earth and felt connected to life in a whole new way. And after twenty minutes of this quiet, slow movement exercise, she sensed it, not with her sight, but with a deeper sort of knowing, around her was a living force, a being as real as her physical body. It shimmered like diamonds. She'd seen this shimmering before, around objects and people, connecting things like a web.

Yes, the energy was a web, but it danced as it spun, and she was in the middle—a sacred part in the rhythm of life.

When they were dismissed for an afternoon break, Natasa continued to sense these connections around her. Rather than eat in the kitchens with the rest of the girls, she decided to go back to her apartment and seek her meal with her father. She rarely saw him now that she lived with the others in the temple dormitories. Her path took her past the training facility, and she followed an instinct to go inside and watch the men fight. When she arrived, she found several men sparring in various rings. She could see the energy between them and knew who was going to fall before they did. Natasa found it fascinating as she predicted the winners and losers of each match. The web of life was strong between the warriors.

In the center ring, Ankhmakis fought her older brother, Nefermaat. Strong energy fields surrounded both young men. She imagined that they too had been taught the alchemies of Horus in their own trainings. Natasa sat on a bench to watch the men fight and was startled to discover that she knew Ankhmakis's actions before they happened. Somehow, she sensed him lifting his sword to strike Nefermaat on his right side moments before he did so. She knew when he was about to jump back. Nefermaat, however, also knew these things and blocked and parried each movement with ease. Ankhmakis was tiring, and Natasa didn't want the fight to end. He fell to the ground after one of Nefermaat's aggressive strikes.

Without thinking, she focused on her own Ka and found it pulsing around her in all directions. She expanded the force and sent it toward Ankhmakis. When her energy was mere inches from his, she allowed their Ka's to blend for a brief moment. As they connected, he burst up from the ground and attacked Nefermaat with a renewed strength. Onward he pressed, and within moments, he held Nefermaat on the ground and under his sword. The swordmaster, Ikui, called the match and awarded Ankhmakis with the victory.

Natasa allowed her Ka to grow smaller and withdrew from Ankhmakis. The prince turned to her and gave her an accusing look. She was frozen, trapped in his dark gaze, as the world melted around her. A flash of heat raced across her skin, and she felt the sting of shame within her heart. Rising from her place in the stands, she darted out of the arena as fast as she could, for fear that the young man would follow her. She wasn't sure herself what had happened, but one thing seemed clear—there was a lot more to this than her mother had let on in her lessons.

Natasa made her way to the small home she had shared with her father and Corinna, who was also her nursemaid. As Natasa entered the small garden of her childhood home, someone grabbed her arm from behind.

"Hey," she cried out as she spun around to face her captor.

It was her brother, Nefermaat. Three years her elder and a cubit taller, his hand shook as he dug his fingers into her upper arm. His face was covered with sweat, dirt, and small scrapes—evidence he'd been working hard in the ring.

"What the hell were you thinking?" he yelled as he dragged her into their small yard.

"I have no idea what you're talking about," Natasa replied, tugging her arm from his harsh grip.

"I'm not stupid. I know what you did back there in the ring. You made me lose to Ankhmakis."

"Oh, yes," she said, admitting her guilt. "Honestly, Nefermaat, I had no idea what I was doing."

"Don't give me that. You're the high priestess's daughter, you should know how to control your magic."

"Nefermaat, I'm so sorry. I didn't mean anything. My Ka sort of fell into his."

Her brother stepped back and laughed. "Your Ka fell into his? It's bad enough the king gave my inheritance to his stupid youngest prince. Now you're going to help Ankhmakis in his training?"

"Senmen didn't want to go to Memphis," Natasa cried out.

"What is it with you and the princes? Why do you protect them? They're useless, just like their father."

"He's your father too," Natasa pointed out.

Nefermaat put his hands on his hips. "I'd watch your step, sister. King Hugronaphor can't be trusted. If he'd betray me, his only son with the high priestess, what's he going to do to you, the daughter of Hecataeus, a Greek and traitor?"

"My father is not a traitor." Natasa's blood always boiled anytime someone mentioned her father's Greek heritage.

She shoved Nefermaat as hard as she could, but he remained still as a temple statue. She might have tackled a wall—his military training was turning him into a hardened warrior.

"War will come to these lands," Nefermaat said in a low and threatening tone. "We'll see who is loyal when the time comes."

"Is everything okay, children?" a female voice asked.

Natasa turned from her angry brother to find their nursemaid, Corinna, holding her own baby, Eleni. The infant struggled to be put down.

"We're fine," Nefermaat lied.

Corinna cocked her head. "If that is true, then why did Natasa hit you?"

Nefermaat smiled as if nothing were wrong. "I was teasing her for being in love with two of the three princes."

"Nefermaat, how could you say such things?" Natasa said. She made to hit him again, but he backed away.

"Would you like to come in, Nefermaat?" Corinna said, ignoring his comment. "It's been so long. I've missed you since you left to live in the military dormitories."

Nefermaat looked at Corinna and for a moment his face softened, only to be covered again with a scowl.

"No, thank you, Corinna. I must be going." He looked at Natasa. "I'm due to guard the princes this evening. While Senmen steals my inheritance in the temple, I have the esteemed honor of watching over Silus and Ankhmakis as they get drunk with the whores. Do you understand, Natasa? How in the world do you expect me to honor them, or my father?"

"Nefermaat, I'm sorry," Natasa begged. "I won't help Ankhmakis again."

"You'd better not." He looked to Corinna and nodded, then turned and left, leaving dust in his wake.

"Natasa, don't take his anger personally," Corinna said as she placed baby Eleni on the ground and opened her arms to Natasa for a hug. "He's been angry since I married your father. I think he feels left out."

Natasa walked toward her nursemaid, entering the

woman's welcome embrace.

"You've always been here for us." Natasa sighed as she hugged the woman.

Until her temple training, Natasa had lived in this small mud-brick home at the outskirts of the temple complex, with her brother and Corinna. Neferu-ankh-maat might have given birth to the children, but the moment she could re-enter public life, the high priestess had handed them over to Corinna for care. All of them—Nefermaat, Natasa, and even Hecataeus—had been second to Neferu-ankh-maat's love of Isis and her role as the high priestess of the temple.

Hecataeus hadn't abandoned Natasa. From the beginning, her father had spent his spare time doting on his daughter and visiting her in Corinna's home. It was only a matter of time before he fell in love with and married the nursemaid. Corinna was stunning to behold. A mixed-blood herself, she had golden highlights in her dark hair, deep brown eyes, and skin the color of copper. After many years of loneliness, Hecataeus had pursued Corinna with vigor, and eventually, the couple had their own child, Eleni. Right after Hecataeus had moved in with them, Nefermaat asked to leave. First, he'd begged to be sent to Memphis to train in the temple, but the high priestess and the king had denied him. They insisted he become a warrior instead, and within a season of Corinna's marriage, Nefermaat had left for the military complex.

Natasa had never put the two events together before.

"Do you think Nefermaat hates Papa?" she asked, feeling horrible. It hurt to think that her brother hated her father— she loved them both.

"No, he doesn't hate Hecataeus, just the attention he pays to you," Corinna answered. "Nefermaat's own father pays him little heed. It hurts to be reminded that both of his parents are too busy with their duties to consider his needs."

"But you've always considered his needs, Corinna. So why is he mad at you?"

"He's not mad at me. Nefermaat is mad at life."

"Why didn't Hecataeus marry my mother?" Natasa asked.

Corinna let her go to chase down the baby Eleni, who had begun to eat the ants that lived in the rich, black garden soil.

"Your father did ask her to marry him," Corinna answered honestly as she picked Eleni out of the dirt. The baby laughed and tugged her mother's hair. "Neferu-ankh-maat turned him down. It isn't proper for the high priestess to take a husband. She has to be available to all of the men of the court so that she can bestow the love of the goddess in the kingdom."

"But what if I want to marry someday?" Natasa exclaimed, now horrified at the thought of becoming the high priestess herself.

Corinna shook her head, her expression stern. "My dear, if you inherit your mother's role, you will never marry."

Natasa stumbled backward, stunned by the revelation. She'd never considered it before.

"Corinna, what if I don't want to share the goddess's love with more than one man?"

"Don't let it concern you right now," Corinna advised. "You're only thirteen. There's time. Trust me. Focus on your lessons, and you will know better when you're older. Now come, it's time to wash up. Your father will be home soon to eat his mid-day meal."

As she stood at the stone basin scrubbing her hands, Natasa inhaled the scent of the roasted goat cooking over the fire, and her stomach grumbled. She was too hungry to consider her future. Natasa had until her sixteenth year before she had to decide her path. In the meantime, she had a meal to take, and many lessons yet to master.

6

Rivalries

During the Middle Kingdom, the Egyptian kings built two fortresses along the Nile, one in the north near Buhen, and one in the south near Semna. Used to control and restrict traffic along the Nile, these fortresses were periodically housed with soldiers and police for centuries. Rarely did battle ever take place; however, Semna was the more active of the two—for it had been built to secure the Empire's southern border with Nubia and did so until Egypt's last breath.

Three Years Later, Semna, Egypt 208 BCE

The Egyptian navy sailed without issue up the languid Nile River. Ankhmakis stood at the helm of one of the ships, taking note of everything around him. He and Silus commanded seven boats with twenty rowers each, constructed from cedar wood imported from Byblos. Their red sails, bearing the black Ibis of Behdet, flapped in the breeze. This was a perfect day to storm the fortress.

Per royal decree, the Greeks controlled the ancient fortress at Semna. However, given the relative peace with Nubia, they'd long ago abandoned stationing anyone loyal to the Ptolemaic Dynasty, instead staffing Semna with Egyptians, Nubians, and sometimes slaves from other countries. Semna was considered a poor assignment by many counts within the Greek nobility and military. For seven years, since his victory in Raphia and subsequent gift of an army and navy, Hugronaphor had offered to oversee the maintenance of the fortress, providing the most secure border in the Empire to Ptolemy IV.

There was no strife on the border, and this outpost in the middle of nowhere, between Egypt and Nubia, had become the perfect secret training headquarters for the native rebellion. Ankhmakis and Silus were on a mission that would put their years of training to the test. They were to "take" the fortress from Hugronaphor's men. No one was to die, and injuries had to be kept to a minimum. Straw-filled bags lined the fortress walls as targets for the archers to practice upon. They had to breach the walls to gain entrance, and once inside the fortress, would have to fight hand-to-hand combat until they retreated or captured the fortress's flag hidden deep within the compound.

The exercise was the perfect training experience, and the thrill of adventure filled every bit of Ankhmakis's being.

"Are you ready, brother?" Silus said behind him.

"I've been ready for this for years," he replied.

Silus slapped him on the back and stood beside him. "Let's begin."

His older brother turned and called out to the crew, "Steady now. Dock the four supply boats along the western shoreline one mile north of the target. The other three, sail on to the entrance and breach the river access. Archers, take down the soldiers on the riverfront walls. The rest of us will take the landside entry. The first group to gain access to the fortress must drop their weapons and fight. Remember, our king doesn't want us injured in a manner that would prevent our training. Nothing more than a scratch."

The men nodded in agreement and scattered around the deck, readying the boat for their landing. Ankhmakis turned his gaze back to the river and watched as they approached the Fortress of Semna. He smiled at the brilliance of his forefathers in choosing this site, the Semna cataract, the narrowest passage in the south, where large rocks stood across the Nile, slowing its flow. This was a sound choice for securing their border with Nubia.

The fortress had one small entrance at the river—a square building lacking windows, with a single door. The small building was connected to the larger military outpost by means of a long narrow passage up the shore and onto the land. On the east bank stood a second, insignificant, dilapidated building, used to ensure Nubians didn't shepherd their goats to pasture in Egyptian territory.

The walls of the fortress itself were forty feet high. Ankhmakis would need to scale them to breach the complex. There was also a large door for supplies located on the western wall. While the others worked the river entrance, Ankhmakis, Silus, and their men would cover the land.

"Steady," the captain of the boat called as the rowers slowed their speed and prepared to dock. When the ships drifted up to the shoreline, men jumped from the decks and swam to the shore with long, flax ropes in their hands. They tugged the vessels as close to the bank as possible. As soon as they were given clearance, a dozen men on the boats slid long, wide planks over the sides and toward the land. The men on the land threw ropes with grappling hooks at the planks, and after assuring they had a secure hold, helped to heave them to the shoreline.

Once the planks were secured on both land and ship, Ankhmakis called to his men, "Disembark."

One hundred men clambered down the ramps. The planks were wobbly, as were the men's strides, for many of them had developed sea legs on the journey up the Nile. Silus himself looked shaken and pale, but Ankhmakis decided now was not the time to point it out. They were his father's generals and had to look strong and capable of the mission.

"Sebastos," Ankhmakis called to the horse master. "Deliver the horses."

The journey had been harder for the horses than expected; the animals hadn't enjoyed their time on the water and were unsteady as they were herded down the ramps to the shore. But Sebastos's men did their jobs, and within moments the horses were bridled and ready to ride. Ankhmakis strode up to his horse, a rare white stallion, and a precious gift from the king of Pergamon to his father after the Battle of Raphia. Given the horse's natural speed in a sprint, Ankhmakis had named him Biriq, or lightning, in the native tongue.

"There, there, Biriq," he whispered into the horse's ear. "We've got this, eh?" The horse whinnied, and Ankhmakis mounted with ease. "Ready, men," he cried. "We ride."

Silus approached on his black mare, nodded to his brother, and raised his sword. "To the fortress."

The thundering of horses could be heard from a mile away. Ankhmakis felt his bow and quiver rub on his back as he and Biriq led the charge. His sword clanked at his side. As they approached the fortress, he could see the targets lining the walls. They had to take down every single one before they could raise the ladders and enter the complex. He scanned the scene and made a quick count—there were over four hundred targets, one hundred on each side of the fortress. The boats would take the riverside targets; he and his men would take the rest.

"Ansel, Min," he called, "take the northern wall. Nefermaat and Pontius, lead your troops to the west."

"And what will you do, brother?" Silus asked.

"I'll take whatever you don't want," Ankhmakis answered, regretting his words. Giving Silus an option never worked out in his favor.

"You go around back to the south," Silus suggested. "I'll stay with the men on the north side."

Ankhmakis nodded, realizing his brother had left him with the most work. A chance to show his mettle, but typical of Silus. His plan was obvious—work with Min to secure the front, scale it, and get inside first, capturing the flag before Ankhmakis was even done securing the backside. Ankhmakis sighed, determined to beat his brother to the flag, no matter what.

"Fine," he agreed, "but I get Min and his men."

"No, you don't," Silus argued. "You'll do it on your own."

With that, Silus kicked his horse and raced ahead of Ankhmakis, calling to Ansel and Min to follow him. Ankhmakis looked behind him to the men Silus had left behind. There were twenty-three, and all were novices.

"Follow me," he cried. "We go around. Hurry."

Ankhmakis kicked Biriq, and the horse jutted forward. He galloped ahead, leading his men to the west past Pontius's troops, and south, around to the back wall of the complex. He passed the northern wall, where the men were firing at the targets, but many of them were missing the mark by a cubit's length and would run out of arrows before taking the wall if they continued with their incompetence. He watched as Silus took aim and failed time and again. Ankhmakis rounded the western wall, where the situation wasn't better, but he had no time to help them. He had to get to the backside and take down the one hundred targets before his brother did, or he'd fail in his mission.

"Take your positions," he commanded as he led his line down the southern wall.

He sat tall in his saddle, closed his eyes, and allowed himself to become silent, searching deep within and without. Taking a deep breath, he filled his body with the energy around him. Exhaling, he felt his Ka pulse through his body. When he opened his eyes, he allowed himself to join with his Ka and the space around him, sensing the movements of his soldiers, the horses, and the mud-brick wall that towered before him. He gazed up at the top and created the shimmering connections between himself and each of the straw targets.

With ease, he nocked his bowstring with an arrow and raised it above his head. As he led his men down the line, he made the energetic connection between the tip of his arrow and the target forty feet above him. He drew back and released, allowing the space between the target and the arrow to grow smaller as the arrow made its flight. He'd executed a perfect shot, and even before it hit its target, Ankhmakis had drawn a second arrow and repeated the act. *Thwump, thwump, thwump* sang the arrows as they met their mark. By the time he rode to the end of the wall where he met the men fighting along the river, he'd taken out two dozen of the targets himself. There were men waiting for him at the shore with handfuls of arrows. He reloaded his quiver and rode back down the wall, repeating the feat.

He'd first discovered the lines of energy that connected everything when the temple girl, Natasa, had helped him fight her older brother. She'd joined her energy with his, and at that moment, the path between his sword and Nefermaat's failed defenses had become clear. She'd awakened something within him that day, and even though he'd never spoken to her or anyone else about it, he'd continued the practice until sensing the web of life had become natural. After beginning his training as a warrior, Ikui had officially given him the name of what he was working with: the Ka, both his own and the energetic fields of everything that surrounded him. His instructors, from Sebastos who worked with the horses and hawks, to Kyros, the Greek military officer Hecataeus had employed to run their training, spoke of using space to predict and manipulate one's surroundings both on and off the battlefield.

What he'd discovered wasn't a secret—everyone in his father's court knew of it—but Ankhmakis was able to master the skill with ease. At times, it seemed his Khat and Ka hummed a cohesive tune, especially when fighting. When he emptied his quiver a second time, he looked up, grateful that all the targets had been hit. His men began hoisting the ladders up against the wall, and Ankhmakis jumped from his horse, leaving his weapons behind. He ran to the first ladder secured and scaled it as fast as he could, hoping he wasn't too late.

As he leaped from the ladder to the roof of the complex, he was relieved to see that his brother's wall still had a dozen targets to disable.

"To the keep," he cried as his men flooded the rooftop.

They sprinted toward the stairs, where they were met by the first of their enemy foe. Ankhmakis ran up to the biggest one and allowed himself to connect with the energy around him. He swung and punched the man in the stomach, who returned the favor with a slug of his own that Ankhmakis sensed before the man's arm had even moved. Ankhmakis crouched low and took the man out at the knees.

The fighting continued in this way, and as Silus and Min's men were climbing on to the roof, Ankhmakis had broken through the line and was heading down the stairs toward the inner fortress, where the flag was hidden. A group of five men stood at the base of the stairs, and Ankhmakis beat them off with the help of two of his soldiers. They entered a large hall and searched for the flag. Within minutes, they determined it wasn't there and ran to the exit to continue their explorations farther within the fortress.

As they did so, dozens of men entered and fought them. Ankhmakis took several punches to the gut, back, and face, but he returned more than he received. His men weren't as lucky, and it looked as though they were in trouble when the archers who had stormed the entrance on the river finally entered the fight and took control of the situation. At that moment, Silus made it down the stairs and yelled to Ankhmakis to halt.

Ankhmakis looked over his shoulder at his brother and smiled. "Come and get me," he taunted as he sped around the fighters and into the hall.

The bulk of the fortress soldiers were engaged in skirmishes already, and Ankhmakis ran around and through the mess, reaching out with his Ka and sensing their energy, enabling him to avoid contact with the bodies in motion. He was surrounded by complete chaos, and Ankhmakis thrived in it. He wove his way through the men and in moments found a small door at the end of the hallway. This had to be it.

He heard Silus call his name, but he paid no attention. He tried the door, but of course, it was locked. He beat at it and threw his body onto the hard cedarwood to no avail. He glanced behind, relieved as Silus took a strike to the head and fell to the floor. Searching around, Ankhmakis panicked. How to get the door open?

He silenced himself, and the narrow hallway became clearer; the noises of the men fighting faded away. He turned in a circle and found what he needed—an ax affixed to the wall, placed there for the one who would arrive at the door first. Drawing upon the energy of the fighting around him, Ankhmakis took the ax from its place and slammed it into the door, cracking it slightly. He repeated the act, creating an opening, and the next thing he knew, Min was with him, throwing himself into the hole in the door and falling on the two soldiers who lay in wait, guarding the flag.

Ankhmakis followed Min and took a hit to the groin. He breathed out with a heavy grunt and struck the man with a blow across the jaw. The force caused the man to stumble.

"Now," Min cried. "I'll hold them both."

Ankhmakis nodded and raced across the room to the wall where the flag of the Semna fortress hung. He ripped it down and held it above his head.

"We've got it," he yelled, showing Min and the men he fought. They lowered their hands and nodded.

"We surrender, Your Highness," the man he'd hit said, rubbing his jaw. Blood flowed from his mouth.

"Hey, sorry about that," Ankhmakis offered. He held out his hand and the guard shook it.

Min chuckled. "Always the gentleman, even in battle. You look pretty bad yourself."

Ankhmakis touched his jaw, which throbbed in pain, and spat on the floor, noting a large amount of blood in the liquid.

"Indeed," he admitted. "Time for us to clean up and celebrate."

One of the guards opened the broken door and Ankhmakis stepped out, holding the flag above his head for his men to see. The fighting stopped, and everyone cheered. Everyone, that is, except Silus, who had been knocked unconscious during the fighting.

☥

The healers tended to the wounds of the men and tents were raised around the fortress. Inside, kegs of beer and loaves of bread were shared. Fish, caught on the journey to battle, were smoked and distributed. The soldiers laughed and taunted each other, no longer two opposing sides, but one cohesive group. Silus and Ankhmakis sat at the front with the twins Min and Pontius, their half-brother Nefermaat, and Ansel, a half-Greek soldier with a wicked sense of humor. Silus stewed in silence, arms crossed over his chest and face sullen, as the others joked and recounted the battle.

"Ankhmakis was like Ramesses II," one of the soldiers on Ankhmakis's team proclaimed. "He took out half of our targets before the rest of us were even drawing our first arrow."

"You're exaggerating," Ankhmakis said with a laugh.

"So that's how you guys scaled your wall first, even though you had the longer ride," Min noted.

"Indeed," the soldier continued. "I'd never seen anything like it."

"Yes, yes," Silus said with a dismissive wave of his hand, "my brother is a wonderful archer. Why don't you write a love poem about it?"

The soldier fell silent, and Min stared at the older prince.

"Silus," Ankhmakis warned, "that's no way to treat our men."

"Our men," Silus replied, jabbing the air with his clenched

fist. "Our men? This was my mission, Ankhmakis, and you stole it from me."

Ankhmakis held his tongue. He refused to fight with his brother in front of the others. This was his father's golden rule—present a unified face to the people, regardless of how you feel toward your family. He was going to say so himself when the men in the room rose from their seats—as if on cue, King Hugronaphor had arrived.

Both he and Silus sprung to stand, the argument forgotten for the moment.

"Wonderful job today, soldiers," Hugronaphor announced. "I watched from the eastern bank and was rather impressed."

He strode across the room, speaking with the various groups of soldiers.

"Riverside ships, you captured the water entrance with ease," he continued. "However, you stalled clearing the passageway to the keep. The passageway was built narrow with low ceilings for a reason, to ensure that only two men could enter it at a time. A better use of your skills would have been to send in a small group of your best men to defeat those in the passageway while the rest joined the fighting along the southern wall."

"They didn't need our help, Your Majesty," a soldier cried out. "Prince Ankhmakis took out their targets before we'd even docked the boats."

Hugronaphor smiled and looked at Ankhmakis, who felt a mixture of embarrassment and pride. His father hadn't often looked at him with such admiration, and it made him feel insecure.

"Yes, I saw," Hugronaphor agreed as he made his way to Ankhmakis's side. "Good work, son. Where ever did you learn to shoot? It almost rivals my own skill at the Battle of Raphia."

Ankhmakis had heard the stories of his father's prowess in the infamous battle. Hugronaphor's military accomplishments were what drove him to better himself every day.

"Yes, sir," he answered with a strong voice. "You're my inspiration."

Silus rolled his eyes. Hugronaphor gazed at his elder son but said nothing.

"As you were, men," Hugronaphor said to the room. "Sit, eat, drink, and rest easy. I'm grateful to the gods that I have such fine soldiers serving me."

Hugronaphor took a seat next to his sons and blended in with the group of young men. Ankhmakis noted how his father made the soldiers comfortable while still maintaining the air of commander. Yes, he was above them, but he also knew them as men and kindred spirits. As the evening was winding down, the king turned to his sons.

"Meet me in my tent," he commanded. "I wish to discuss the exercise with you before heading off to sleep."

"Yes, sir," Silus said.

Ankhmakis nodded and followed his brother and father out of the hall. Min, Nefermaat, Pontius, and Ansel followed behind and took their positions outside of the king's tent to guard them. As he entered, Ankhmakis admired his father's tastes—the tent was a mini-palace, with animal skins on the flaps and other luxuries like soft pillows and thick mats upon a wooden bed, the images of the ibis, alligator, and falcon carved upon its face, for Hugronaphor to sleep upon. Ankhmakis and Silus stood at attention before their father's chair as the elder man sat and poured himself a glass of wine.

Hugronaphor cleared his throat. "That was exciting. What did you think?"

Ankhmakis remained silent, allowing Silus the first

word, as was protocol. His elder brother pointed his way, lips screwed up into a sneer.

"Ankhmakis cheated," he accused.

"What?" Ankhmakis cried. "How dare you? You're the one who sent me around to the south, taking the easier route for yourself."

"Nonsense," Silus argued. "You let me choose my own path, and I did."

"How did I cheat?" Ankhmakis challenged him.

"You carried more arrows than the rest of us, and your horse is faster," Silus said.

"*Enough,*" Hugronaphor yelled. "Silence, both of you."

The boys ceased speaking and looked at their father.

"This is no way for my princes to act," Hugronaphor continued. "Silus, what you say is false. While you were missing every shot, Ankhmakis took his horse and focused on the targets. He carried no more arrows than you; rather, he met his mark."

Silus looked at his father, nostrils flared and face flushed with anger. Ankhmakis could feel it pulsing around them. In addition to being able to live within the web of life, he also knew what others were feeling, especially stronger emotions such as anger, jealousy, and lust.

"Yes, Father," Silus said, but Ankhmakis knew he didn't mean it.

"Ankhmakis won fair and square, even against the odds," the king continued.

"That's not true, he had extra men—" Silus argued.

Hugronaphor raised his hand, silencing Silus. He looked to Ankhmakis.

"As a reward, you are granted two regiments of your own to begin training as soon as we return to Behdet."

"That's one thousand men," Silus complained. "I have only one hundred at my command."

"And so that shall remain until I see improvement, Silus," Hugronaphor said. "You need to focus on your lessons with General Tsui. Strategy is as important as your skill with the blade. Today's exercise was to see if you understand your lessons. You're both incredible swordsmen, yet it appears Ankhmakis alone has grasped the concept of military strategy."

Silus glared at his father, jaw clenched so tightly a vein pulsed at his temple.

"Now, if there's nothing else, you're excused to rest," the king finished.

"There is something else," Silus said, cocking his head, a grin twisting his face.

"Yes?" Hugronaphor asked.

"I believe it's time for me to take a spiritual companion," he proclaimed.

Ankhmakis startled in surprise. What in the world would prompt him to make such a request? Hugronaphor, however, laughed.

"If you think a priestess will improve your military skill, fine by me," their father replied with a shrug as he took a sip of wine from his goblet.

"What?" Ankhmakis asked. "I don't understand."

"You're twenty years old now, Silus," Hugronaphor continued, "I imagine it's time. You're also old enough, Ankhmakis, if you feel like it."

"No," Silus demanded. "I get first pick. I'm the eldest."

Hugronaphor raised an eyebrow. "There are several young women to consider."

"Is Natasa available?" Silus asked.

Ankhmakis's skin tightened as a wave of angry heat

flashed over him, which surprised him. Why should he care if Natasa was paired with Silus? He hadn't seen her in years, as his training kept him busy and often away from Behdet. Besides, she was a child. He swallowed down the protest forming upon his lips and instead remained silent.

"No," his father said, "she's not done with her training until the end of next season. If you're willing to wait so be it. Otherwise, you'll need to choose someone else."

"Never mind," Silus answered. "I don't want to wait. She's not worth it. I want a spiritual companion now. Would you consider Tyia's eldest daughter?"

"Kawit? Yes, I believe she's available to bond," Hugronaphor answered. "I will speak with Neferu-ankh-maat and make the arrangements."

Silus nodded. "Thank you, Father."

Ankhmakis's father turned to him with a nod. "And you, son? At nineteen years of age, you too can be bonded in the temple of Isis if you so choose."

He looked at Silus's smug face and considered what was being asked. A spiritual companion would be a benefit, and he risked allowing Silus to grow stronger than he if he refused Anit-Shadya. But his gut told him now was not the time. Besides, he wasn't attracted to any of the priestesses, not even the high priestess herself. They weren't the ones. He'd know her when he met her, he was sure of it. He could wait.

"No thank you, Father," he answered, still looking at Silus, "I don't need a priestess. I have a thousand men to train."

Silus flinched but said nothing.

"Wise choice, my son." Hugronaphor yawned. "Now leave me, I must rest."

As they left the tent, two guards sauntered up the path from the docks, escorting several women. The group approached his father's tent and two of the females entered.

"I'll take one of the extras," Silus said to the guards, tossing his head toward the women and running his tongue over his parched lips.

The guards nodded, and Silus approached his father's whores, inspecting them the way Sebastos did when new horses arrived in the stables. The women looked Ankhmakis's way and smiled, beckoning him. He felt a fire awaken within him and considered taking one himself but shook his head. Even the concubines were no longer interesting. After unlimited access to them for years, he'd tired of the game. Besides, he now found training in the Way of the Warrior a better use of his time.

He turned away and Min followed him. They walked back to his tent, where he'd spend the night alone, basking in the glory of his father's praise, and begin planning how he would build an army that followed him as their true leader—and a man worthy of their loyalty.

7

The Golden Child

There were three seasons in ancient Egypt—Akhet, also known as the Inundation or the flooding of the Nile; Perit, the time of sowing and growth; and Shemu, the time of harvest. Each season was four months long. The appearance of the Star of Isis, called Sopdet, rising in the sky moments before the dawn marked the end of the old year and warned that the floods of Akhet would soon arrive. Egyptians lived, celebrated, and perished by this cycle of life, death, and rebirth.

Behdet, Egypt 208 BCE

The high priestess entered the small inner temple in reverent silence. Four of her faithful priestesses knelt, heads down, before the altar of Isis, upon which stood a golden statue of the goddess, illuminated by the warm fire burning in a brazier at the statue's feet. Tyia, the eldest priestess, looked up from her supplicant, prayerful posture and nodded at the high priestess's arrival. "Welcome, Lady Neferu-ankh-maat. We are ready to serve."

"May Our Lady Isis show us the way of truth," Neferu-ankh-maat responded.

She wore a white ceremonial tunic, handspun by the royal women and woven by the temple priests. Upon her head, the golden circlet of the high priestess glowed in the firelight. At her brow shone a set of golden cow horns with the sun disk between them. She radiated power and peace as she approached the altar and placed the ceremonial Ankh before the goddess.

"We come today to serve you, mighty Isis," the high priestess continued. In her hands she held a copper bowl of burning frankincense from the land of Punt. She walked around the altar, wafting the smoke into the air as she invoked the power of the goddess's sight. "Come to us, Our Lady, and show us the path for our acolytes, who now approach their time of initiation. We have three women who are ready for temple life, and we seek your guidance."

Neferu-ankh-maat stopped before the altar, and her four priestesses sang. She knelt beside them and raised her arms. "Dear Isis, reveal the roles these women shall occupy so they might shower your love upon the kingdom of Egypt."

From a colorful, woven basket she picked up a small olive branch and placed it upon the altar. "Alexa, the olive tree, ripe with nourishment and faith." She placed a small stone frog upon the altar. "Tatianna, the tree frog, as fertile as the abundant Nile and the Goddess Haquet." Lastly, she took a hawk's feather in her hand and held it before her face. "Natasa, high priestess-in-waiting, the little hawk who sees far and wide."

The women sang together with deep voices, thickened by the smoky air, and fell into silence, each one breathing in Ra's love and light, filling their bodies with his power. As she relaxed, Neferu-ankh-maat widened her gaze and activated the eye within her mind.

"Tell us Isis, mother of Egypt, how you wish to call the women into your service."

They remained silent until Tyia cried out, "Alexa, my daughter, shall serve by loving the royal men. Always she will keep them in her heart and advise them in the ways of wisdom."

"Yes," Neferu-ankh-maat agreed, seeing the young girl in her glory. "She shall be initiated into Anit-Shadya and serve the princes."

Again, they returned to silence, and Neferu-ankh-maat felt her Ba drifting from her body. She struggled against it as she heard a second priestess call out.

"Tatianna will serve in the Houses of Healing. She is needed to birth the children and heal the wounded."

Neferu-ankh-maat nodded, unable to speak. She fell into the arms of Tyia as her Ba left her body and journeyed into the astral plane. It appeared the goddess wished to grant her a vision, and she had no choice but to obey.

She found herself in the Tunnel of Illumination, deep below the Great Pyramid in Egypt, in a room carved from the womb of the earth long before the birth of Egypt herself. From its ceiling hung crystals, glowing in the torchlight, and the floor was covered in crushed quartz, as fine as sand. Neferu-ankh-maat crawled on her knees through the tunnel, following a light that glided before her.

"Hurry," a voice commanded. "We long to meet with you."

Neferu-ankh-maat crawled faster until the tunnel disappeared, and she entered a cavern filled with tall beings, radiant and emitting light. They sat in thrones around a purple-blue flame burning in a copper bowl. A web of golden threads surrounded them, connecting each one to the other.

The forms of love and acceptance permeated the space, and she felt as if she could stay with them forever.

"Come," a deep voice said.

She obeyed and walked to the beings. Their faces were nondescript, yet glorious all the same. For as long as she lived, she would never find the words to describe their elegance and power. Fear left her. They never looked at her yet told her many things. She felt them connect to her mind and read her thoughts, sharing with her the wisdom and power of the cosmos. Her consciousness expanded across the universe, and for a moment, life made sense.

Then the screams began. Pain, unlike anything she'd ever felt, consumed her. Fire erupted in her vision. She saw the temple of Isis in Behdet burning to the ground as the Ptolemaic army slaughtered her people. The form of hate surrounded every soldier—its geometry so horrible it made her stomach turn in agony. As she focused on the scene, the hate swept over her, and she felt the rage-filled act of taking another's life. Before she knew it, she shifted inside the victim, running for her life. The form of fear danced around her, its heavy oppression slowing her step. She stumbled away, but the sword of her pursuer cut through her stomach. The form of death permeated the city as the palace burned in the night.

The city was surrounded by hate, greed, fear, death, and malice. These forms were entities, beings that entered her soul. She was in agony. She searched for her body to escape the madness but found herself stuck and surrounded by the evil of humanity. On and on she jumped from form to form, knowing how it felt to kill, maim, harm, and torture. She knew without a doubt she was seeing the future of Behdet, and if the city fell, their entire civilization would also vanish into flame.

When Neferu-ankh-maat thought she couldn't take

anymore, the vision left her, and she stood once again before the great beings in silence. After a time, the purple flame in the center of the room danced, and a new being extracted itself from the fire—a female child. She walked toward Neferu-ankh-maat, glowing and radiant.

"A Child of the Light," Neferu gasped, knowing this was the child she'd been searching for since receiving news of the Oracle of Memphis's prophecy. "You're the Golden Child Stamatia spoke of years ago."

"Yes," she said, jumping up and down as if playing a simple game. "I'm coming, Grandmother. I wanted you to know."

Neferu-ankh-maat gazed at her beauty. Her heart felt like an unseen hand was squeezing it. The experience was both painful and blissful.

"Natasa shall be your mother?" she gasped. Could this be her daughter's calling?

"Yes, my parents left the Halls of Amenti to incarnate into the world of men many years ago," the child continued, nodding to the chairs around the flame. One was empty. "Their Ba split and became two. Natasa must be paired with my father, and through them, I will come to Egypt's aid."

"Your parents are twin flames?"

"Yes. Male and female, yet one song. One Ba in two bodies. This is how it must be."

"And who is your father?"

"Ankhmakis, the true pharaoh of Kemit. His banner will one day fly at Thebes, and I will take my place by his side. You must make sure they are bonded within the temple."

Ankhmakis and Natasa were one? Neferu-ankh-maat considered it and nodded. The child spoke the truth, even if she hadn't noticed the connection between the two young people before.

"And what of my vision of Behdet burning?" she asked the child, unsure she wanted to know the answer.

"We shall not let Egypt die, Grandmother. I must come—

to balance the scales between love and chaos."

"I will do what you request," the high priestess vowed. "I'm at your service."

The child laughed, and Neferu-ankh-maat felt her body tingle. Her vision blurred and darkened. She was no longer in the hall with the beings of light. Instead, she was in Tyia's arms. She shook her head and sat up, trying to get her bearings.

"What did Our Lady show you?" Tyia asked as she helped Neferu-ankh-maat to her feet.

"The Golden Child is on her way," the high priestess answered, brushing the dust from her linen shift and straightening her crown. "Natasa will be the one to bear her unto our lands."

Despite her fear for her country, Neferu-ankh-maat felt like she glowed inside and out. The Golden Child was coming. Isidor and King Hugronaphor had long believed the child would be male, but it appeared they were wrong. It would be through the female form that she would guide Egypt back to her glory, and Natasa would be the vessel of the divine. Could she and Ankhmakis be one Ba in two bodies? Such a pairing was rare—twin flames didn't often incarnate together. Yet the vision had to be true. That Natasa should be bonded to Ankhmakis was so obvious, how could Neferu-ankh-maat not have noticed it before? Yet, until the pair recognized themselves as such, there would be no holy union. Somehow, Neferu-ankh-maat had to provide a situation where they could discover their love for each other and convince them of their destiny.

The two needed to spend time together, and soon, before Ankhmakis chose a different companion.

8

Of Herbs and Bees

Because they had perfected the art of mummification, Egyptian healers had a remarkable knowledge of anatomy and sterilization. If the cause of an affliction was visible or known, practical treatments such as the cleansing and bandaging of wounds, minor surgery, or herbal remedies were used. If the cause was hidden, magic was employed. No disease was considered untouchable and the sick were always treated with dignity. Those in the Houses of Healing made sure of it.

Behdet, Egypt 208 BCE

Natasa stumbled into the healer's garden, tripping over her own feet. She was late again, having lost track of time on her break visiting with her father and little Eleni. She always envied the time her younger sister had with their father, Hecataeus. She missed her childhood days when she'd play in his office as he worked on documents or treaties. As a child, she'd never understood what her father's role entailed, but three years of temple training had made it clear—her father was the one who allowed Hugronaphor to train an army in secret by keeping Ptolemy IV's eye elsewhere. She didn't envy her father's role—politics was not her strong suit.

"You're late," Bastyre said as Natasa approached the low table at the center of the garden.

Situated under a linen overhang to keep the sun off the acolytes's heads, the long wooden table ran the length of the garden, covered in colorful woven baskets filled to the brim with rosemary, thyme, calendula, scotch broom, marigold, poppies, and many other herbs, as well as stone mortars and pestles. On both sides of the table sat her other classmates—Alexa, Molyruse, Tatianna, Weret, and Bithiah. At the head of the table stood Bastyre, the royal midwife and herbalist. She was a dark, round woman with huge breasts. Her long hair was wrapped in four thick plaits that fell to her waist. Around her head, she wore a yellow and blue scarf, and upon her ears hung large gold earrings that sparkled in the sunlight. Her strong upper arms also shone with bands of gold.

Bastyre was neither young nor old, but she did seem to know everything there was to know about the herbs and flowers and their healing powers. Natasa loved her as she loved the high priest of the Houses of Healing, Iu-Amon. The two had been her dearest teachers the past three years, and she felt terrible for being late.

"I'm sorry, Lady Bastyre," she said, lowering her head and speaking with respect. "I lost track of time."

"I'd lose track of time in Hecataeus's office if only he'd invite me for tea. Speaking of tea, sit, girl, and get chopping. We're running low on mint," Bastyre commanded, returning to the basket she was weaving.

Natasa grabbed a pile of dried mint leaves from a red clay bowl and chopped them. As she did so, she imagined the spirit of the plant, and how it infused the green leaves with its healing properties. She recited them in her head—digestion, sore throats, and calming nerves. Per her instruction in the Houses of Healing, she recited prayers of thanksgiving to the Goddess Sekhmet, and praise to the mint, and asked the plant to serve those who needed the herb to heal. The group worked this way, without uttering a single word, for another hour chopping, binding, and grinding the herbs.

"There," Bastyre announced, breaking the silence. "Done. What do you think?"

She held up the basket she'd been weaving, and the girls praised it.

"It's one of my best, isn't it?" Bastyre said. She rose from the table and looked around her. "Get up. The time has come for you to meet the queens."

"Excuse me?" Bithiah asked.

"The queens," Bastyre replied. "They await us in the apiary."

"Oh," the youngest princess, Weret, said with a frown. "You mean the bees?"

"Indeed, child," the older woman agreed. "There are no other queens worth meeting in Behdet."

Natasa wasn't sure what to make of the comment; it felt like a swipe at Queen Keket, and no reasonable person insulted the high queen. But then again, Bastyre wasn't known to be a reasonable woman. She enjoyed stirring up emotions within the court.

As if reading her mind, Bastyre smiled. "The queen of the hive has something to teach us today."

She turned, and the girls followed her through the lush gardens to the far corner where the royal beehives were tended. They passed under an iron arch long ago covered in ivy. Above the entry to the apiary was the figure of a bee carved in stone, surrounded by flowers and the rays of the sun. Natasa shivered as if meeting royalty for the first time.

Bastyre stopped inside the gate and raised her hands. In front of them were rows and rows of deep, circular baskets turned upside down on the ground. Some were covered in mud, others were bare, but all were surrounded by hundreds of thousands of bees, buzzing every which way in the hot sun. Along the walls of the apiary were long, mud-filled tubes the size of large hollow logs stacked upon each other, with bees flying in and out, coming home and going off to work.

"Welcome to the apiary, where the most precious and valuable of our medicines are created by the Queens of the Sun," Bastyre said with loving pride. "We use two types of hives, the baskets that you see and the mud tubes. The baskets are easier to harvest, and that's where we take our honey, pollen, and propolis to meet our needs. The mud tubes are used to house the extra hives that will split and be moved to the baskets."

"Why does a hive split?" Natasa asked.

"Ah, my dear, that's the real magic," Bastyre answered. "Life in the hive is rather straightforward. There are three types of bees—drones, which are male, and workers, which are female—"

"It figures that the women do the work," Bithiah interrupted.

Bastyre smiled. "Now that's the truth, isn't it? However, a king doesn't run these hives. No, my children, in the beehive it's the queen who rules."

"How many queens?" Weret asked.

"Only one," Bastyre answered.

"They only have one queen?" Bithiah asked. "How does that work?"

"When the hive decides it needs a new queen, the workers shape the cells where several larvae have already been laid, to turn them into new queens. The old queen determines who will join her and who will stay behind to help the new queen. When the time comes, she leaves the hive and swarms to a new location with her bees. Nineteen days later, the first queen is born. The instant she breaks free from her honeycomb cell, she must kill the other queens before they hatch. If she doesn't, they fight to the death. When one queen is left standing, she flies out of the hive to the Sun God, Ra, and the males follow her."

Bastyre raised her hand to the bright sun above them and pointed to it with a wistful gaze.

"They chase her to the sky, and there, under the loving gaze of Ra, she mates with the finest of the males—only the fastest and strongest may approach. It is her one moment under the glory of Ra, her one chance to be out of the hive. When she's done mating, she returns with enough fertilized eggs to manage the hive for five years. At that moment, she's like the high priestess, taking all the lovers she wishes."

Bastyre paused and looked at Natasa, who felt prickles of shame run across her skin. She looked to the sky and squinted, avoiding her mentor's gaze. Natasa still wasn't sure she could ever follow in her mother's footsteps. How could she bestow the love of Isis on so many men? One lover seemed scary enough. Part of her wanted to deny her place in the temple of Isis, and spend her days with Bastyre in the apiary, taking care of the bees.

Bastyre continued, "However, once she is done with her maiden flight, she will not frolic among the flowers ever again, until the hive is too full, and she becomes the old queen flying away to a new home and making room for another new queen and her workers."

"Only one queen bee," Weret said in a voice so quiet, Natasa had to strain to hear her. "There can be only one."

Bithiah scowled at her younger sister. "In a hive, but there are thousands of hives in the apiary. That's thousands of queens."

"She speaks the truth," Bastyre said to Weret. "The apiary is a system of hives working together, each one run by their individual queen, and served by their thousands upon thousands of workers. And we humans are the better for it."

"What happens to the drones?" Bithiah asked.

"The males? Many are made when a new queen is born to serve her. But after she has mated, they're allowed to die off, keeping only enough to warm the hive."

Bithiah smiled, opening her mouth to speak, and Natasa readied herself for an anti-male rant.

"What does honey do for us?" Alexa asked, saving them from Bithiah's complaints about her brothers. "Other than taste good on soft, warm bread?"

"Honey is used in our food and in our brewing of ales," Bastyre continued. "Mead is a favorite of King Hugronaphor. The priests offer it to the gods in the temple, and it is placed in the tombs of the dead to enjoy in the afterlife." She walked them closer to the hives and the droning of the busy worker bees filled the air with a lazy, yet purposeful sound. "It's also a wonderful way to administer our harsher medicines," the herbalist continued. "A touch of sweet makes even the bitterest treatment taste good. We also put it on wounds to keep them free from infection and heal scars. And the propolis is fed to the high queen when she's first married, to help her conceive her children."

Natasa looked to Bithiah and imagined the princess on

her wedding day. Would they still feed her propolis since she was marrying Nefermaat instead of a crowned prince? Or did Bithiah's marriage to a priest mean her children weren't important enough to receive such a gift?

"Queen Keket also mixes it with oils and bathes in it," Bastyre continued. "It's one of her beauty secrets." She rubbed her own cheeks and smiled. "How old do you girls think I am?"

Natasa watched the girls shake their heads.

"Older than the queen," Natasa said, though she had no idea how old the women of the court were.

"Yes, by over ten years." Bastyre smiled.

"No," Natasa cried with the girls in unison.

"That can't be true," Weret squeaked. "You look so young."

"I never lie," Bastyre continued, looking over her shoulder as if to guard a great secret from the bees that swarmed behind her. "The priestesses may have Shadya to keep them youthful and vivacious, but I have access to the bees, and use propolis both on my body and as a tonic to keep my youthful looks."

Natasa was impressed. Perhaps the secret to long life was simpler than the path that temple life entailed? She longed to take a place in the Houses of Healing, rather than at her mother's side. But oh, what would Neferu-ankh-maat say if Natasa gave up her inheritance and instead chose to work with Iu-Amon? Her stomach twisted in fear as she considered her mother's reaction when she told her. But Neferu-ankh-maat had always counseled Natasa to follower her heart, and her heart longed to become a healer.

"Now listen," Bastyre instructed, "we're going to stand among the ladies. But first, you must understand something—they choose you. Not the other way around. Bees can see your emotions, so connected are they with the energetic Ka of the world. They know if you're afraid or angry and will mimic you.

An angry person attracts the angry bee. A bee sting won't kill you, but it does hurt. If you're not worthy, don't approach. Only those with a loving heart can stand among them."

She looked at the princesses as she spoke. Bithiah crossed her arms.

"What?" she cried. "I'm loving."

"I suggest you don't think about the princes when you approach the hives," Bastyre advised. "Neutral also works. If you can't be loving, please do us a favor and be neutral."

Bithiah opened her mouth as if to speak, but Bastyre turned and sauntered toward the hives, her back straight and her head proud. Natasa knew Bastyre had connected to her Ka and was surrounding the beehives with her love and patience. Natasa found her own heart beating a heavy rhythm, her pulse quickening as a bee flew by her face. The droning grew louder and louder with each step she took. She closed her eyes and took a deep breath, making sure to close her mouth, to avoid sucking in a bee. She focused on her heart and calmed it.

Steady and sure, she thought. *Only love. Only love.*

The next thing she knew, her fear was gone. She opened her heart and allowed the low hum of the bees to draw her in. She walked between two rows of hives, and her skin tickled as the bees buzzed around her and crawled along her arms and legs. She raised her arms out to her sides and felt them exploring under her palms and her stomach. When one landed on her nose she almost cried out and ran away, but instead, she remained in her heart and slowed everything down. The sound of the bees filled her soul, and for a moment she experienced the world as they did—a dance of golden streams of light. Every human, flower, bee, tree, even the wind, and the sun was a part of a golden dance that beckoned her closer to hear their song. She was nothing, and she was everything.

A scream cut through the apiary, and the moment was gone.

Natasa turned to see Weret running from the garden, screaming and swatting at her head. Natasa turned and backed away, beyond the hives, and out of the bee's range before she panicked and was also stung. Alexa joined her on the sidelines as they watched Tatianna start screaming, too, from the bees stinging her. Bastyre ran after them, telling the others to follow and wait for her in the garden.

Bithiah stood beside Natasa and snorted. "Weret is such a baby. She's always been afraid of bees. I can't believe she even tried."

"Will she be okay?" Alexa asked.

"Of course, she will," Bithiah answered. "It's a bee sting, not an arrow through her head."

"Why are you always so mean to her?" Natasa asked.

Bithiah rounded on her. "I'm not mean."

"Yes, you are."

"No," Bithiah continued. "I'm mean to the princes because they're spoiled. Weret on the other hand, I don't think she's spoiled. Her life is as unfair as mine."

"Why do you mock her?" Natasa continued, unwilling to give it up.

Bithiah paused and picked at her fingernail. "Am I unkind?"

"Yes," Alexa admitted.

Bithiah shrugged. "I guess it's because she's the one who killed our mother."

"What?" Natasa asked.

"Our mother," Bithiah continued. "Ruia, Weret, and I have a different mother than the princes. She died giving birth to Weret."

"The king had a second queen?" Natasa asked.

"Yes," Bithiah said, her voice softer. "Her name was Queen Mafuane, and everyone says she was Father's favorite."

"But why doesn't anyone ever speak of her?"

The middle princess looked at her with a frown, and her bottom lip quivered. "Because there can only be one queen."

Shoulders slumped, Bithiah walked from the garden, as did Alexa. Natasa didn't feel like returning to class. She'd had an epiphany—she was going to pledge herself to the Houses of Healing and spend the rest of her life with the bees and flowers, making medicines and healing the sick. Maybe she'd even become a midwife and train with Bastyre forever.

She ran past the other two girls and straight into the healing wing, where she found the high priest asking a patient how they felt. Natasa stood at the edge of the bed and waited for Iu-Amon to acknowledge her. After he was done asking his patient questions, he turned to Natasa and nodded.

"Lady Natasa," he said. "I understand the Princess Weret had an unfortunate event in the apiary today."

"Yes, my lord," Natasa replied.

"Are you here to report?"

"No, I would like to talk to you in private. I've made my decision."

He nodded and held out his arm. She took it, and he escorted her to his study. The walls were lined with woven linen blankets depicting various healing ceremonies and glyphs. Elsewhere, deep holes were carved into the walls and filled with scrolls. Their entire medical knowledge stored in one place. Wooden tables and plush animal skin chairs filled every corner. In the center stood a copper brazier, lit only at night to keep away the desert evening chill. To Natasa, Iu-Amon's study was the most beautiful place in the whole world.

"I love your chambers."

"Do you?" Iu-Amon asked.

"Oh yes," she continued as she traced her fingers along the handle of a scroll. "This knowledge can help others. Here, the secrets of the gods are written down. It's so wonderful."

"If you think this is wonderful, you should join us on our trip to Alexandria."

"Alexandria?"

"Yes, the Library of Alexandria is considered the greatest place of learning in the known world," he continued. "Your father and I are joining King Hugronaphor and his sons when they visit the pharaoh in a month."

"That does sound fantastic, but I don't think Mother will let me."

"This part of your training ends soon, and after you are required to remain in solitude until you come to a decision as to what role you wish to take within the temple. If you don't take too long to decide, you'll be able to join us for a quick trip before beginning your next phase of temple life, whatever that may be."

"That's what I'm here to tell you, Iu-Amon," Natasa exclaimed. "I have chosen. I wish to pledge myself to you and the Houses of Healing."

Iu-Amon eyed her and took a seat. His gaze unnerved her, but she followed his lead and did the same. He was quiet for so long, she feared he was going to reject her.

"Why?" he asked.

"To serve the people," she explained. "To heal the sick, work with the bees and the flowers, or to sing and play the harp. I'll do whatever you need me to do."

"If you do this, you can never know a man," Iu-Amon replied. "We take a pledge of celibacy, directing our life force toward our patients rather than a lover."

"I understand this," she answered.

"Do you?" Iu-Amon asked. "Tell me, child, are you aware of the prophecy of the Golden Child?"

"No," she admitted.

"If you enter my cult, you can never be a mother."

"So?"

He looked at her again. "You're young and haven't fallen in love yet. You can't comprehend that the pledge of celibacy is a serious one. The punishment for failure is death, both for you and your lover."

"I understand. There is no one I love more than the goddess herself."

"What is it that you seek from the goddess?" he asked.

"I'm not sure what you're asking."

"What do you seek in this lifetime?"

Natasa felt a shiver run down her spine and felt clear and alert. "I desire the secrets of immortality."

"And you think you can find that here, in the Houses of Healing?"

"Can't I?"

"You can't," he said. "Here you will learn of illness and recovery, as well as birth. But you will learn most about death, and merely prolonging life until that inevitable day when the Ka extinguishes and life among the living is over."

His words struck her like a blow to the chest, and she gasped at his honesty. He leaned forward and clasped his hands together. "Natasa, I love you, and I'm honored that you have chosen me. But my heart tells me you will not find the secrets of immortality here."

"If not here, where?"

"Isn't it obvious? You will find them in the arms of your true love."

Natasa jerked away. "You believe I should become a priestess in the temple of Isis?"

"Yes," he agreed. "Follow your mother's footsteps, and I think you will go further down the path of immortality than anyone has before you."

"But what can be greater than healing those who are dying?" she asked, lowering her head to hide her tears.

"Teaching them how to avoid having to die."

She rose from her place and wiped her eyes. She knew Iu-Amon spoke the truth.

"I trust you, Iu-Amon, and will do as you suggest. I will enter the temple and train to be a spiritual companion, though which man I might serve remains a mystery to me. I don't love the men of the court."

"Don't worry, my darling." Iu-Amon patted her shoulder and gave her a comforting smile. "You will know him when you are ready to love him."

"May I go?" she asked, her body now weak from disappointment. A moment ago she had been so sure of her path, and now she was searching for her next step in the dark.

"Yes," he answered, "and tell your father you wish to join us in Alexandria. You'll enjoy the library. There's nothing else like it in the entire world."

9

A Journey with the Men

In 525 BCE, at the Battle of Pelusium, the Persians disarmed and subjugated Egypt when their king, Cambyses II, captured Psamtik III, the last native Egyptian Pharaoh. Two centuries later, the Macedonians took the power of the rich nation. Thus Egypt's kings had been bowing to an occupying power for many generations. When Ptolemy IV Philopater armed the natives to help him win his war against the Syrians at the Battle of Raphia in 217 BCE, he unwittingly gave them the keys to a long and brutal civil war.

The Nile River, Egypt 208 BCE

In the distance, pyramids dotted the horizon. Palm trees lined the banks of the river. After two days of nothing but birds, fish, and the occasional merchant ship, Ankhmakis was relieved to see signs of civilization. They passed a group of dark, naked children fishing from a dock, and the prince waved. The children jumped up and down, flapping their bare arms like cranes and waving back, eager for him to throw them a souvenir. The passage of a royal boat was always a treat to the locals.

He searched the deck and found a small, wooden figurine of the god of the Nile, Hapy, and tossed it to shore. The children scrambled for it upon the banks and a young boy, at most eight years old, raised it above his head. Ankhmakis delighted in the joy on the child's face.

"That was kind of you." A feminine voice laughed behind him, and his heart skipped a beat.

Turning, he bowed his head to Natasa, the only woman on the boat. Behind her stood Hecataeus, her father, who hadn't left her side the entire journey.

"Natasa, Hecataeus," Ankhmakis replied, forcing his voice to steady. "Just doing my job."

"I didn't realize charming the locals was a part of the royal duties," she said with a slight smirk.

Hecataeus chuckled and patted her on the back. "That's my girl."

Ankhmakis didn't know how to respond. Natasa made him speechless more often than he wanted. They'd left Behdet weeks prior, and from the moment she walked onto the boat, he hadn't been able to focus. When his father had told him that the vizier and his daughter were joining them, he hadn't given it much thought. The vizier joined the king on diplomatic trips, and everyone knew Hecataeus enjoyed traveling with Natasa. Yet, Ankhmakis had been expecting a sassy, unkempt girl—not a beautiful, elegant young woman. The men on the boat perked up when she walked by. Many of them would whisper inappropriate comments to one another, which was probably why Hecataeus never left her side.

"Hermopolis ahead," the captain called, saving Ankhmakis from having to respond.

He glimpsed Natasa, noting her perfect dark-bronze skin, high cheekbones, full, red painted lips, long black, plaited hair, and charcoal-lined green eyes. Those eyes unnerved him—a physical sign that she was both Egyptian and Greek. Yet, they were also what made her stunning to behold.

"Duty calls," he said to the pair and ran to help the men prepare to dock at the Castle of Hermopolis, where the upper kingdom crafts were registered and paid their toll to enter the lower kingdom.

The city was the capital of the fifteenth nome in Egypt and stood as a border town between the upper and lower kingdoms. Over time it had become a resort town of great opulence, second only to Thebes in its beauty and glory. The entourage hadn't been off the ship since their stop in Thebes, and everyone, including Ankhmakis, couldn't wait to enter the town and explore it.

"Oh, thank the goddess, civilization," Silus said as slaves threw the heavy ropes out to the Hermopolis attendants. The vizier and the mayor of Hermopolis stood at the end of the docks under a shade tent, held aloft by several dark-skinned servants. They were expecting the royals of Behdet.

"I agree," Ankhmakis replied. "I've had enough of this boat. It's amazing how little there is to do when traveling for pleasure."

"Ha." Silus smiled. "You'd rather be training the troops, eh?"

"Please be quiet," Ankhmakis hissed. "We're not to speak of those things. North of Abdju we are stewards, not princes."

Silus's smile disappeared, and he nodded as the two of them stood back to let Hugronaphor, Hecataeus, and Natasa disembark first. Iu-Amon stood beside them. He rocked unsteadily on his feet, and Ankhmakis was about to offer help when Ennaeus, the vizier's assistant and tutor to the princes, grabbed the healer's arm.

"Here." Ennaeus smiled as he took Iu-Amon's hand. "I've got you."

Iu-Amon nodded and allowed the younger man to escort him off the boat. Ankhmakis and Silus followed behind.

"Hermopolis, home of the great god Thoth, fine wine, and even finer women." Silus laughed as he put his arm around Ankhmakis.

The failure at the Semna fortress had changed Silus. He now spent extra time on his studies and did everything he could to show Hugronaphor his quality. Within months, he had won in an exercise against Ankhmakis and earned a thousand men of his own to train. When Ankhmakis asked him how he'd managed to improve in such a short amount of time, Silus's answer had been copious amounts of Shadya. Ankhmakis wasn't sure he believed the claim, even though he'd heard from others that the art of love made one stronger and clearer of mind. Prior to their journey, his father had pestered him to consider taking a spiritual companion. Given the improvements in Silus, perhaps he should give it thought.

Hermopolis shone under the sun. Glowing white buildings stood seven stories high, the tallest in all of Egypt. The streets were lined with palm trees, lush gardens, and water fountains. Everywhere he turned, there were beautiful people, dressed in fresh linen and covered in jewels and gold. But what was most noticeable was the Greek influence. Dark-skinned servants followed the fairer Greek nobles, fanning them with palm leaves. Thoth was the patron god of this town, but the Greeks knew him as Hermes and had changed the name of the city to Hermopolis. This was by far the Greek elite's favorite southern city to vacation in.

Ankhmakis and Silus stood at attention, backs straight and chins up, behind their father as the local vizier and mayor, both of Greek blood, greeted them. Hecataeus knew of them already, and once Hugronaphor had been acknowledged, Hecataeus led the conversation. Natasa stood at her father's left elbow, smiling at their comments and watching the men as they discussed the tolls to be paid and what arrangements had been made for their stay. She was as natural a diplomat as her father. Hugronaphor's money would be accepted here, but his skin color made him a minority in the noble class.

"This city is not Behdet," Silus said later as they dressed for dinner in their apartment. "I don't think they're used to Egyptians dining in their decadent halls."

"True," Ankhmakis replied as he tied his sword to his waist. He wore a simple white kilt and blue and gold headpiece— not the regal attire of a prince. Their bloodline was not to be flaunted here.

"I wouldn't be surprised if they ask us to fan them," Silus continued, "or serve them their wine."

"The Egyptians of the north have suffered, that is clear," Ankhmakis replied. "Father has often said we're the last in the line of native kings."

Silus stood still for a moment and looked at Ankhmakis as if he'd never quite understood their predicament. "What we work for is important for the whole country," Silus answered, a serious look upon his face.

"Indeed. What we do isn't a game, brother. The purpose of our rebellion is to free our people from slavery."

Ankhmakis turned and left the room. The entourage was staying in a two-story house a brief walk down the boulevard from the mayor's mansion. Min, Pontius, Nefermaat, and the rest of the King's Guard were stationed outside to keep watch. Hermopolis, being a town of Greek influence, was the sort of place Ptolemy IV could have his loyalists execute them.

Ankhmakis nodded to them as he approached. "What are we waiting for? Let's go. I'm hungry."

"We have to wait for the Lady Natasa," Min advised.

Nefermaat nodded his head. "Our father and Hecataeus are already at the mayor's, probably drinking his best wine. We are to escort the two of you, and my younger sister."

Ankhmakis knew Nefermaat was his half-brother, born of his father's union with the high priestess. What he often forgot was that Nefermaat was also Natasa's older brother. Nefermaat should have been a priest, but Hugronaphor had demanded he train as a guard, and as a warrior. The king felt he had too many priests and not enough fighting men. Nefermaat never complained, but then again, Ankhmakis had never even thought to ask him how he felt.

"Right, the Lady Natasa." Ankhmakis sighed. How long would it take the girl to get ready?

The next moment, she arrived, wearing a light blue dress spun from the finest of linens. Her hair was piled up on top of her head, and at her throat she wore a small amulet that shone in the setting sun. They bowed, and she curtsied as she laughed. "Manners, even among family."

Ankhmakis felt his spirits lifted by her smile. The politics of the evening faded from his mind.

"Shall we?" Nefermaat said, not even a hint of humor upon his stoic face. "The king awaits us."

"Of course," Natasa said with an innocent grin. Nefermaat didn't return the smile. They walked for a block in silence before she spoke again. "My, you're a boring bunch. I never would have expected it."

"What's that supposed to mean?" Ankhmakis asked.

"It's quite funny," she continued. "The princesses think you're spoiled and lead wonderful, exciting lives. I can't wait to go home and tell them the truth—that while you might get to go on adventures, you're as boring as lessons with the scribes."

"That's not true," Silus protested. "We have fun."

"Do you now?" she challenged.

"*Yes,*" he said. "Not the kind you're invited to."

"Oh, yes," Natasa replied, "men's business."

"Yes, men's business. Things unbecoming of a lady such as yourself," Silus admonished.

They approached the door to the mayor's mansion, and Min and Nefermaat held the door open. Natasa looked at Silus, and Ankhmakis found himself dying to know what was going on in her mind.

After a moment she said, "I know what men do for fun, and it's unbecoming of everyone, not just women." She held up her chin and strode toward the palace, leaving the men speechless in her wake.

A man stood at the door to greet them. "Welcome, stewards of Behdet." He took Natasa's hand. "Let me show you the way."

She fell into step, and the princes had no choice but to follow. They entered a large hall filled with plants, flowers, and water fountains. Through the open-aired roof, he could see the sky was ablaze with the pinks, golds, and purples of the setting sun. Scattered throughout the hall were secluded seating arrangements with silken pillows, thick, plush mats, and low serving tables. Bare-chested, dark-skinned women sat in each alcove, serving food, playing the harp, and singing. Jugglers roamed from table to table, making the guests laugh. A man wearing a skimpy loincloth blew fire from his mouth in the center of the hall, dancing around the giant gold-plated statue of Hermes—Thoth without his animal presentation.

At the front sat Hugronaphor and Hecataeus alongside the mayor and his other administrative officials. The man led Natasa to the end of the table, and she took a seat. Ankhmakis sat beside her, and Min and Nefermaat stood at attention to the side with the other guards.

Ankhmakis was too far from the older men to participate in the conversation, so instead, he gazed about the room. His court in Behdet was full of beauty and extravagance, yet Hermopolis was opulent. A serving girl filled his cup with wine. Natasa held out her own goblet, and the girl obliged.

"You drink wine?" Ankhmakis asked her.

"Yes," she replied. "What should I drink? The water of the Nile?"

"I guess I don't know," he answered. "I didn't think girls liked wine."

She laughed. "My father's been giving it to me for ages. Often, it's the only drink he has around."

"Your life is so different than my sisters,'" he noted.

She nodded. "Yes, I'm fortunate my father isn't a noble. It's allowed me to get away with . . . things. I didn't realize it when I was younger, but after entering the temple and working with my mother, it's become clear that my time as a child was blessed."

Ankhmakis smiled at her radiant face. "That's quite wise of you."

"Does my wisdom also surprise you?"

"Yes," he answered, surprised at himself for believing she was so simple. "I guess it does."

There was an awkward silence, in which Ankhmakis finished his wine. A moment after he set it down upon the table, a serving girl refilled it. He stared at Natasa and found himself speechless. Why did she silence him this way? He pasted on a smile and noticed that she fingered an amulet at her neck.

"That's an interesting stone," he said, hoping she'd be a normal woman and talk about it forever, and he wouldn't have to initiate conversation anymore.

"It's a bloodstone," she explained. "Senmen gave it to me before he left for Memphis."

"Senmen?" Ankhmakis exclaimed. "Why in the world would he give you a gift?"

She glared and raised an eyebrow. "Because he's my best friend."

"Your best friend?" Ankhmakis asked, surprised again, this time at the flash of anger he felt with the idea of his younger brother romancing this girl. "How can that be?"

"We grew up together and played in the gardens, the river, even in my father's study."

"Oh," Ankhmakis replied, "I never noticed."

"Of course you didn't," she continued, shaking her head as if she'd caught him being naughty. "You never paid attention to us. We aren't important to you."

"What?" he cried, caught off guard by her accusations. "No, that's not it. Senmen's younger than Silus and I. We never spent time together."

She fingered the amulet at her throat, and he marveled at how graceful her hands and arms were.

"Is he actually your best friend?" he asked. For some reason, it mattered.

"He was," she answered, a faraway look upon her enchanting face as she stared at the candles, "but I haven't seen him in years. So much has changed."

Ankhmakis drank down his wine, and Natasa followed his lead, draining her entire goblet in a few gulps. The girl would be drunk if she continued. He encouraged her to eat her food, and she did so while making small talk. He relaxed and let her lead the conversation, nodding and smiling when appropriate to give her the impression that he was listening. In reality, he was wondering why the idea of her caring for Senmen made him so irritable.

"Thank you, Mayor," he heard his father say from across the table, "but it's time we take our leave. We need to rest before we disembark in the morning."

They stood and thanked the mayor as they left. The walk back to their guesthouse was animated—they were sloppy drunk. When they arrived home, Hugronaphor turned to them.

"Come to the study. I've arranged for libations to be delivered. It's too early to sleep," he commanded.

"But I'd like to explore the town, Father," Silus whined.

Hugronaphor shook his head. "Not wise, son," he answered. "No one, not even the whores, can be trusted here. Get your instruments and meet me in the study. Trust me, this is safer."

Ankhmakis did as he was told, and when he entered the small study Hecataeus and Natasa were already there, sitting in front of the fire, tuning their instruments. She'd changed into a simple gray tunic and let her hair down, so it fell around her head in dark, luxurious waves. She had a small drum at her feet and a harp that fit upon her lap. Hecataeus held a lyre, the same instrument Silus played. Ankhmakis sat across from Natasa and smiled as he tuned his pandura, the three-stringed instrument he preferred. Senmen's bloodstone upon her chest felt ominous as if his brother had marked her as his own, and Ankhmakis found he was envious.

"Going to sing us temple songs, dear enchantress?"

Ankhmakis teased.

She frowned.

"No, little hawk," Hecataeus suggested, "I think we should sing my Greek sailor songs."

"Papa," she cried, tossing her hair over her shoulder. Ankhmakis felt his knees go weak.

"Why not?" Hugronaphor asked, handing her a mug. She took a sip and smiled.

"Oh," she cooed, "mead. My favorite."

"Mine too," the king agreed. "Now, play us those sailor songs."

Hecataeus looked to Ankhmakis and Silus, who sat awaiting his instruction. He gave Natasa a hearty grin. "How about *Poor Tanny?*" Natasa nodded, smiling at her father as if plotting a prank. "Follow me—there are only a few chords. Ready, Natasa?"

"Oh, yes."

She put down the harp and picked up the small drum, beating out a rhythm as her father played the melody. What followed was a vulgar tune in which the hero of the song gets drunk, loses his dog, finds a golden ring, and pawns the ring to try to find a whore for the night, only none will take him. Instead, he drinks himself blind and wakes the next morning to find himself left behind by his crewmen. Which would be fine except . . .

"Oh, poor Tanny, you couldn't even get a hen, but it's not your fault because the women here don't like men! The women don't like men? No, the women don't like men! It's not that you're ugly Tanny, to lie would be a sin! It's just that the women here don't like men!"

Natasa and Hecataeus sang the last chords together and everyone, even the king, joined in. Min was guzzling his mead and laughing so hard he spit it up. Ankhmakis had tears in his eyes.

"Oh, my," Hugronaphor cried when they finished, "Greek sailors have such wonderful songs."

"I don't know what's stranger," Ankhmakis laughed, "the idea of an island full of women who prefer the woman's touch or witnessing a priestess of the temple of Isis sing such a vulgar song."

"Neither is strange," Natasa said, giggling. "There is an island in Greece where the women don't like men—no men are allowed."

"No," Silus cried, shaking his head in what Ankhmakis could only assume was denial. "That can't be true."

"It is," she replied, her giggle warming Ankhmakis's heart. Everything she did enchanted him as if he were caught in her web of charm. "Furthermore, contrary to what Prince Ankhmakis thinks, I'm not a fragile temple maiden. Women can be vulgar too."

Hugronaphor's body shook as he chuckled, his laughter booming throughout the room. "Dear Natasa, we mustn't tell your mother about this." He tipped the pitcher to her mug. "Now, here, let me refill your mead and sing me another song."

"If it's the king's orders, I must oblige," she declared, toasting him before taking a sailor-sized gulp.

The night continued as thus until the wee hours of the morning, the men and Natasa singing by the fire. Hecataeus had no lack of bawdy tales, and when they stumbled to bed Ankhmakis couldn't help but notice where Natasa's bedroom was, and that her father had chosen to sleep on the floor outside her door.

10

Alexandria

The Royal Library of Alexandria was the greatest library of the ancient world. Dedicated to the Muses, the nine goddesses of the arts, it flourished under the patronage of the Ptolemaic Dynasty and became a prominent research center for the ancients. The most illustrious thinkers of the age studied there, until that fateful day when she was burned to the ground, and centuries of knowledge were lost to the flames.

Alexandria, Egypt 208 BCE

Their arrival in Alexandria had been quiet and discreet. Ptolemy IV was expecting them, but he didn't bother to have his administrators sent to greet them. Instead, Hugronaphor's boat was docked in a slip reserved for visiting nobility, and they arranged for their own wagons and litters to carry their belongings to their lodgings, which were nowhere near the Royal Palace. They were within walking distance to the Royal Library, and this delighted both Natasa and Iu-Amon. Iu-Amon had reserved an entire alcove for research purposes during their stay. Ankhmakis overheard the two planning their days of reading and scribing together. He wasn't sure what the allure was, but once they were settled he decided to offer to take Natasa for an initial walk to the library before they were expected for dinner that evening.

He knocked at the door to her suite, with as much confidence as he could muster, and of course, Hecataeus answered.

"My Lord Chaonnophris," he said, using Ankhmakis's Greek name, "what a surprise."

"Ah, yes," the prince answered, feeling awkward in the presence of the imposing man. Hecataeus was a force of nature unto himself, and it didn't help that he was Natasa's father. "I was wondering if the Lady Natasa would be interested in a visit to the Royal Library."

At the sound of her name, Natasa appeared behind her father, her eyes twinkling with delight. "Oh, yes," she answered, elbowing her father out of the way.

"Not so fast," Hecataeus said with a grimace. "You need a chaperone, and I'm busy. Ennaeus and I have business with the pharaoh within the hour."

"Min will guard her," Ankhmakis offered.

"I don't need a guard," Natasa protested.

"Yes, you do, young lady," Hecataeus warned. "Fine, Min will have to do."

She shook her head at her father but said nothing. Ankhmakis held out his arm, hoping she'd take it. Natasa hesitated, a hard look on her face, and Ankhmakis feared she would reject his gesture. The next moment, her gaze softened, and she accepted his offer. A jolt of electricity ran through his body when she touched his arm.

"How long do we have?" he asked Hecataeus.

"Both of you are expected for dinner later tonight with

Queen Arsinoe and the pharaoh," the vizier replied. "But the rest of your day is quite unplanned. The pharaoh won't attend to business with the stewards of Behdet until tomorrow."

Natasa gave her father an adoring smile. Ankhmakis almost laughed at how Hecataeus melted at her gaze. "Can I spend the afternoon at the library?" she gushed.

"Yes. Iu-Amon should be there within the hour," Hecataeus gave in with a sigh.

"Tell him to meet us there," Ankhmakis said.

"Natasa could wait here until the high priest is ready himself," her father suggested.

"Stop being such an old man," Natasa teased. "I want to go now. I'm not a child."

Hecataeus shifted his gaze between his daughter and Ankhmakis. "Oh, don't I know it—which is the exact reason why you need a chaperone."

She hit her father on the shoulder and smiled at Ankhmakis. "Now, princeling, how about that promised tour?"

Min stood guard outside the apartments, and the three strode toward the Royal Library, stopping along at various vendors as they walked, admiring the merchandise. There were instruments, blankets, copper bracelets, and pottery. At one stall, Natasa discovered a Greek parasol and tried it out, spinning for Ankhmakis and asking if he liked it. At another, she grabbed an Asian turban and placed it on the prince's head. Min shrugged and said it looked rather nice, but Ankhmakis could tell by the expression on his friend's face that he looked ridiculous. She spent time with an old woman who sold scents—driving Ankhmakis wild as she asked him which one he liked best. The markets in Alexandria had everything for sale, from songbirds and snakes to furnishings and fortunes.

Natasa spent several minutes haggling with a vendor over the price of a small beautiful blue flower made of papyrus. The artwork was delicate and splendid. As she was taking out her purse to find coins to pay for it, Ankhmakis handed the vendor twice the amount she'd negotiated. The dark man smiled and presented the flower to Natasa with a flourish.

"For the beautiful lady," the man said with a lisp, for he was missing both of his front teeth.

"Ankhmakis," she cried. "How could you?" The prince shrugged. "You're being rather kind. I'm beginning to get suspicious."

"If Senmen can give you a gift," he answered, "then so can I."

"Hmm." She tapped her pursed lips and gave him a wink that made his head swoon. "Then if Silus also gives me a gift, I'll have a princely collection. Now, where is our eldest prince? I must find him and convince the fool to buy me something."

"How dare you call the eldest prince a fool?" Ankhmakis feigned offense. He raised a hand to his chest in mock shock.

Natasa tossed her head back and laughed. "Please, don't tell him. I don't want to get in trouble, but he's such a bore. Then again, I've always thought you were boring, and you've turned out to be quite wonderful."

Again, he found himself in an awkward silence, fearing that whatever he said next would sound trite or stupid. How in the world would he command armies, if he couldn't even be witty in front of a girl?

"Come," she said, tucking the flower behind her ear, "we have business to attend to. The Royal Library is around the corner."

Ankhmakis held out his arm, and this time, she took it without hesitation. Yet again, his knees felt weak. He hoped

Min didn't notice his affection toward Natasa. His guard was loyal, but teasing him about women was one of his favorite pastimes, and Ankhmakis was falling for this girl. The trio entered a larger promenade, so filled with people, Ankhmakis grasped Natasa closer to his side for fear of losing her in the crowd. The street vendors no longer captivated their attention, for at the end of the wide road stood the Royal Library of Alexandria in its entire splendor.

The complex was built upon a high rise over the city. A large, wide alabaster staircase led from the street to the agora, perched upon the hill. On either side of the staircase stood two enormous statues.

"Thoth, of course," Natasa pointed out as they passed by. "Our beloved scholar."

"They call him Hermes in the north, remember," Ankhmakis corrected.

"Yes," she agreed. "And who's that?"

She pointed to the second statue of a bearded god, curls framing his face and wearing a Greek tunic—rather unusual dress for an Egyptian deity.

"Serapis," Ankhmakis replied. "Invented by Ptolemy I Soter, the first Greek ruler of our lands."

"How can you invent a god?" she asked.

"When you're the pharaoh," Ankhmakis answered, "you can invent whatever you want. He is Ptah himself, remember?"

"Gods inventing gods," she murmured as they walked up the steps. "That doesn't make sense." They approached the agora and Natasa gasped. "It's so beautiful."

Before them stretched a large rectangular pool, lined with sidewalks and palm trees. In typical Greek fashion, low storied stoa ringed the agora and at the end of the pool stood the library itself.

"Come," Natasa said, pointing to the classic Greek structure. "That's where I'm to meet Iu-Amon."

She let go of his arm and ran forward through the crowd and up the next set of stairs. Ankhmakis and Min had to work to keep up. As they crossed under the lintel and approached the main entrance, the guards informed them that women weren't allowed in the library. Fearing a disastrous end to their morning, Ankhmakis asked the guards where he might guide the lady.

"Females are welcome only on the balconies," one of them answered, and showed them the way.

Natasa hurried down the corridor, her robes flying behind her. Ankhmakis followed, keeping up. Her excitement was catching. She arrived at the balcony moments before him and gazed at the wonder below.

The Library of Alexandria stretched out in all directions. The domed ceilings were tiled with pictures from the great myths, stretching to the heavens. Natasa craned her neck as she peered above her head to gaze at the magnificent scenes. Ankhmakis was in awe. The walls were covered with narrow holes filled with scrolls from all over the world. Engraved columns supported the building, and benches and tables covered the floor. Statues of Isis, Horus, Serapis, and Hermes stood at attention. Fountains bubbled, and the lush indoor gardens scented the room with rosemary, sage, and flowers. Scribes, scholars, and pages milled to and fro.

"It's the most beautiful place in the world," she said in a deep, almost breathless voice.

Ankhmakis turned and looked at her face, which was alive with excitement. Her cheeks were flushed, even with her dark skin, and her painted mouth was set in a smile that stretched wide across her face. She continued to eye the room. She'd placed her hands on the railing right next to his without even noticing their skin was mere centimeters apart. It was a bold thing to do, but in her excitement, she was oblivious to rules and regulations. She was free in her bliss, and he felt his pulse quicken.

"So much wisdom, so much information," she continued. "So many answers in one place."

"They won't let a girl enter. You heard the guards, only qualified scholars may study in the Library of Alexandria."

She turned on him, her green eyes lit with a fire that consumed him. "Iu-Amon will get me in. I'll dress like a boy and pretend I'm his page if I have to."

Ankhmakis laughed at the idea. "Why in the world would you do that? What does a girl want with things like manuscripts?"

She stood taller and placed her hands on her hips. "I am no mere maiden from the House of Hugronaphor. I will not grow old, locked in a room, spinning wool and weaving the king's clothes."

Ankhmakis gasped. He was both shocked and intrigued. He was a prince, an heir to the throne. How dare she talk to him like that? "Tell me, my lady, what sort of woman are you?" he challenged.

She turned away and gazed down again at the vast library below them. A soft smile graced her perfect lips. She was no longer a child throwing rotten berries from the tops of the trees in the royal gardens, but a full-grown woman, mysterious and cunning. Her year's training in the temple had been transformative. Her skin glowed under the light of the sun as it poured through the roof and shone upon her like a halo. She inhaled and turned to face him.

"I am a woman who seeks the answers to the universe,"

Natasa said. "One who weaves words and spells—not blankets and robes."

Passion flooded his soul and his groin ached. His heart beat a rhythm too fast for his mind to follow. He was falling in love, and there was no stopping it.

"I'm sorry I misunderstood you," he said, his voice now thick with desire.

If Natasa noticed his need, it didn't show in her serious face.

"You didn't misunderstand me—you underestimated me."

He nodded.

"Don't ever do that again," she warned, and she turned on her heel and walked toward the exit.

"My," Min said when she was out of earshot, "she has you under her spell."

Ankhmakis turned to his friend, his mind foggy as if waking from a deep sleep. "What?"

"You're in love with her, aren't you?" Min replied.

Ankhmakis's heart was still beating hard beneath his breast. "Is it that obvious?"

Min slapped his shoulder. "To love such a woman is dangerous, my prince."

"No, it isn't," Ankhmakis demanded. "It's clear now. I'll request her as my spiritual companion. She's to be initiated into the temple of Isis after we return to Behdet. I overheard her talking to Iu-Amon."

"Ah, now there's a plan," Min agreed. "You need to make sure you talk to the high priestess before Senmen does."

Ankhmakis's stomach tightened in panic. Min was correct. He couldn't even stand the idea of one of the priests giving her First Rites; he didn't want any other man to touch her. Worse would be sending her into Senmen's arms forever, for if that happened, he would never know her love.

"Right," he said, his heart still racing. "I must have her."

"Yes, but right now we must follow her," Min advised. "She can't walk around Alexandria alone. Hecataeus would kill us."

They ran down the steps and found her waiting for them at the pool.

"Take me back to the apartments," she said, arms folded across her delightful bosom as they approached her. "Iu-Amon and I need to form a plan to get me into that library."

"As you wish, my lady," Ankhmakis replied, offering his arm. She wrapped her arm in his, and this time he didn't care that his knees felt weak.

"Thank you, my lord," she said, her lips softening into a smile.

He wanted nothing more than to serve her for the rest of his life.

11

Disguises

Women in ancient Egypt had the right to divorce, own property, inherit wealth, and work for wages. While only the princesses and priestesses were taught to write, most women knew how to read. They could train in the temples as enchantresses, musicians, midwives, and healers—and in three specific temples within the ancient empire, a select few learned the holy techniques of Anit-Shadya. The Greeks, however, never acknowledged these rights for women, and thus the native Egyptian females of the Ptolemaic Dynasty lived without the freedoms their great-grandmothers had enjoyed.

Alexandria, Egypt 208 BCE

Two hours later, Natasa found herself carrying a pile of scrolls to Iu-Amon's table. He'd agreed to let her dress as a young male page, so she'd purchased the turban she'd earlier forced Ankhmakis to wear and hid her hair under it. She removed her eye makeup and jewelry and bound her breasts close to her body. She donned simple, silken trousers and a linen blouse she tied at her throat. She was dressed like a male Syrian servant, and she felt a thrill when the guards at the door fell for it.

"Here you are, my lord," she said as she dropped a pile of scrolls on the table. "*Herbal Healing Methods* from Athens. *Sound, Tone and the Golden Ratio* from Persia, and a volume describing the domestication of bees in Nubia."

"Thank you, son," Iu-Amon replied. "What is it you carried back for yourself?"

"Oh, nothing," she said, nudging aside the scroll so he couldn't see it. She didn't want him to know she'd found a volume on the history of witches and love potions from Gaul. Of course, she wanted it for academic reasons; she had no need of love potions. Her training in the temple had included learning to cast her Ka as to charm those around her. She felt a rush of heat course through her body when she considered how often she'd used that specific technique on Ankhmakis during the trip. She knew she was to remain neutral toward Ankhmakis and Senmen, or any of the male priests for that matter, for any one of them could be her spiritual companion. Time and time again her mother had warned her to not allow her emotions to come into play with men—otherwise, she might find herself disappointed when she was bonded in the temple, and it wasn't with the one she'd wanted.

But Natasa couldn't help it; she wanted it to be Ankhmakis. She knew it was dangerous to allow herself to feel for him, and even more dangerous to encourage him to care for her, yet he'd stolen her heart. Perhaps he was the one casting spells on her? As she contemplated that possibility, she heard Iu-Amon call out.

"My boy," he said, keeping up with her fake identity, "I need you to find me the second volume of this scroll on bee stings and their alchemical makeup."

"Yes, my lord," she answered with a bow.

As she meandered through the library, she allowed herself to eavesdrop on the various conversations. A group of men near a great window that overlooked the sea were discussing Pythagoras and his methods for discovering the height of the Great Pyramid across the river from Memphis. Natasa followed as best she could, but since she'd never seen the structure, it was beyond her to comprehend how its shadow had helped the philosopher. Her mother had been deep inside the Great Pyramid, and soon, so would she. Once she'd completed her First Rites, it would be her turn to take part in the Tunnel of Illumination. Until then, their greatest temple would continue to be shrouded in mystery.

She walked closer to the window and gazed out at the Mediterranean Sea. The harbor was crowded with ships, their wooden masts towering into the sky. Colorful sails dotted the landscape, men strode along the wooden docks, and she could make out the murmur and hum of their activities. Seagulls cried, and the waves crashed upon the shore. Beyond was the wide-open sea, and Natasa felt afraid. She'd never seen the sea, and it stretched out to the horizon forever. She got the sense that if she stared too long, it would drag her into its depths and drown her. Her father had traveled to Egypt from Athens by boat along the sea. He was so brave. Could there be life on the other side? What sort of people lived there? She quivered with fear and hoped she'd never have to find out. The Nile River was her home, and she didn't want to leave it.

The sound of two men arguing over whether the Romans would ever finally conquer the Carthaginians interrupted her thoughts, and she remembered the errand Iu-Amon had given her. She found the section on beekeeping and was searching for the second volume when a low voice whispered behind her.

"You're the strangest looking man I've ever seen."

She sucked in her breath and turned to see who her accuser was. As she recognized him, her heart filled with joy.

"Senmen," she cried and grabbed him to hug him. He stiffened at her touch.

"Men don't greet each other that way," he whispered. "You don't want to blow your cover."

"Oh, yes," she replied and stepped back, rubbing her palms on her silken pants.

"Pants?" he asked, pointing at her legs. "No one wears pants."

"Syrian servants do," she answered. "Oh, Senmen, it's so good to see you."

He was a foot taller and broader in the shoulders than when she'd last seen him. His bald head accented his strong jawline. He wore a black robe with a large, golden necklace. No longer a sweet boy, he looked handsome yet formidable, and a chill ran down her spine. Gone was the laughter in his gaze, replaced with something else. What was it? Anger? Fear? Hesitancy? She searched him and found she was blocked. He had an energetic wall around him, and she knew he too had mastered the alchemies of Horus.

Yet even with these changes, he was still Senmen, and she was delighted to see him.

"You look different," she said.

"As do you." He smiled. "You make a strange looking man."

"True." She laughed, adjusting her turban on her head. "Is my hair showing?"

"No," he answered. "Your disguise holds true. What in the world are you doing in here?"

"Studying with Iu-Amon."

"Studying what?"

"Anything we can. We joined Hugronaphor's diplomatic entourage for that purpose. While you and your brothers are busy with the pharaoh, I'll be here, soaking up as much information as possible. Isn't it wonderful?"

Senmen looked around at his surroundings and nodded. "Yes, the Royal Library of Alexandria is a wonder. I wish I could spend my days here with you rather than in attendance with the pharaoh."

He paused, and for a moment the busyness of the library faded from Natasa's awareness as she recalled their last moments together—the young boy sitting in the window, begging her to remember him.

"You've always had the better life." He sighed.

"Yes," she agreed. "As I was telling Ankhmakis the other day, training in the temple has shown me how lucky I am to have been born to Hecataeus rather than a royal. The freedom is quite a gift."

"Ankhmakis?" Senmen asked, his mouth narrowed. "Has he been stealing your time? I don't recall he ever paid us a moment's attention when I lived in Behdet."

As he spoke, she felt his animosity toward his older brother. It made her uncomfortable. "Will you be coming home with us when we leave?" she asked, changing the subject.

"No." He shook his head. "I will remain in Memphis for three additional months."

"Why? Aren't you done with your tribute?"

"Yes, I'm done," Senmen answered, measuring his words with care. "However, Isidor has invited me to join the Cult of Set and study under him as a priest."

"You mean you won't join your brothers in military training?"

"No. Isidor thinks that being a part of his priesthood will be—" He paused for a moment. He looked at her with his dark, glittering eyes. "He thinks it will be beneficial for me."

"Oh," she said.

"Joining the Cult of Set requires an additional initiation in Memphis that occurs when Sopdet rises before dawn in the sky, which means I must wait until the new year begins. Once I've passed the test, Isidor will retrieve me."

"I hope it doesn't take you too long to travel back," she said.

"Why?"

"I've missed you," Natasa replied. "It's not the same without you."

"From the way you tell it, my brother has kept you quite entertained in my absence."

Natasa once again felt his disdain but couldn't read anything on his impassive face. Whatever was the source of it? She found a scroll over his shoulder titled, *Bee Stings and Their Alchemical Properties, Vol. II* and grabbed at it, her arm brushing his shoulder as she did so. He flinched again at her touch, but said nothing, instead gazing deeper into her soul. This time it wasn't disdain she detected, but a sexual energy, not unlike the looks the sailors had been giving her the entire trip.

She recalled how he'd kissed her in Abdju and felt confused as a jolt of energy flooded through her. "There it is," she said as she slid the scroll from its place in the wall. "Come, let's get this to Iu-Amon."

Senmen followed her back to Iu-Amon's table, where to her surprise, Ankhmakis also now sat. Before him was an open scroll containing a diagram of a temple. He traced the lines on the paper with his fingers as he discussed it with Iu-

Amon. Natasa approached them, and Iu-Amon called out.

"You're back."

Ankhmakis looked up from the table and smiled as she approached. Another pulse of energy surged through her body, this one even stronger, and her heart pounded in her chest. She felt lightheaded. *Oh, dear,* she thought. *I am not neutral toward him.*

"Is this your new page, Iu-Amon?" Ankhmakis asked, rising from his seat. He smiled with a wicked look in his eye and held out his hand. "Nice to meet you."

She took his hand and shook it, trying her best to appear charming in her male disguise. Beside her, Senmen cleared his throat.

"Brother," Senmen said, "flirting with boys, now are we? Made your way through the women of Alexandria already?"

"Senmen," Ankhmakis exclaimed. "Sweet Isis, I didn't even recognize you. Where is my younger brother? And who are you who claims to be him?"

Ankhmakis took Senmen in his arms, hugging him and patting him on the back. They were now the same height. Natasa poked Senmen's ribs, causing him to flinch.

"I thought you said hugging wasn't a typical male greeting," she noted.

Senmen shrugged Ankhmakis off. "I guess Ankhmakis is getting soft in his old age."

"Ah, sarcasm," Ankhmakis replied. "Yes, you're still Senmen, even if you've grown into a man."

Natasa held out the scroll to Iu-Amon and he thanked her for helping. She took her seat next to her elder and sorted through her pile of scrolls, making sure to hide the one on love potions. If the brothers discovered it, she'd never hear the end of it. Oh, how embarrassing that would be.

Ankhmakis and Senmen took a seat at the table to chat. Senmen shared stories regarding his temple life in Memphis, and Ankhmakis informed him of recent court politics, leaving out any mention of the military and their training regimen. As Senmen spoke, Natasa could tell he too was hiding things. She sighed. She'd also been taught secret things she couldn't reveal, not even to her best friend. Not even with her future spiritual companion. Strange how each of them had been schooled in the alchemies of Horus, yet they had to keep things from each other to maintain their Order's commands. It was frustrating their studies had to be so guarded—it made for misunderstandings.

As the sun began to lower on the horizon, Senmen rose and addressed her. "I must go. Metakryon needs me. Will you be at the banquet tonight?"

"Yes, I will," she answered. "I'm dancing for the pharaoh."

Both Senmen and Ankhmakis looked uncomfortable. She could feel desire radiating from each of them, and the intensity of their mutual male need added to her confusion.

"Wonderful." Senmen found his voice. "I look forward to seeing you later."

Ankhmakis grimaced at his brother's words but said nothing.

Neutral, she thought to herself, taking a deep, meditative breath. *Must remain neutral.*

She glanced at Iu-Amon, who was watching her. She'd loved Senmen as a brother since her earliest days, and now it seemed she was falling in love with Ankhmakis, in a different way. Natasa wanted Ankhmakis with her body, heart, and soul, and that wasn't good. She sighed and looked at the statue of Isis in the center of the room.

Dear goddess, she prayed. *Help me let go of both and trust my mother to do the right thing for me.*

For, in the end, it was Neferu-ankh-maat's call. She would choose the best spiritual companion for her, and there was nothing Natasa, nor the princes, could do. Senmen took his leave, and Ankhmakis sat back down at the table.

"Are you studying?" she asked him, unable to stop herself from speaking.

"Yes," he answered. "Turns out the plans for the temples, administrative buildings, and palaces in Egypt are here in this library."

"Why would you want to study those?" she asked.

"Because such knowledge will come in handy," Ankhmakis answered.

Iu-Amon peered at the prince and nodded. "I imagine it will. I've heard you have quite the memory."

"Yes, I guess I do," Ankhmakis replied, his chest puffing out with pride. "I can look at an architectural scheme and memorize it within minutes. It's why I beat Silus repeatedly in training exercises. He can't recall a thing and has to carry the schemes with him into the mission."

Realization dawned on Natasa, and she grinned with admiration. "You're going to memorize the floor plans of the important places for you to seize."

He nodded and placed a long finger to his full lips to shush her. She found herself imagining what it would be like to kiss him. So much for the goddess helping her remain neutral.

"Now then," he said with a sly smile, as if he could read her shameful thoughts, "I think I'll start with Thebes."

12

The Dance of the Knives

Dancing, singing, and entertainment were important to Egypt. This was how the people bonded, shared stories, and passed on information. Every evening would find someone, somewhere, regardless of their rank, playing music and dancing, with ales and wine flowing. Dancing was a part of being alive—and as natural as breathing.

Alexandria, Egypt 208 BCE

"It is so good to see you again, son," Hugronaphor said with a knowing grin and a gleam in his eye. He threw his arm around his son's shoulder as he sat next to Senmen in the Great Hall of the Royal Palace. While awaiting the arrival of the pharaoh to dinner, they had begun drinking the man's wine and eating his bread, cheese, and olives. Senmen forced himself to do these things, feeling sick with each sip he took. He dreaded having to see Philopater.

"Yes, Father," Senmen agreed. "It's good to see familiar faces again."

"Even mine?" Ankhmakis joked.

Senmen looked at his older brother, wishing he wasn't

seated right next to the fool. The way Ankhmakis's lustful gaze followed Natasa's every move bothered Senmen to no end. Still, Ankhmakis was family, and to be honest, Senmen was ready to join the royal court again.

"Yes, even you are better to look at than the lot I've been dealing with in Memphis," he admitted.

Senmen looked across the hall to the table where the other priests sat with Metakryon. Djed, of course, sat next to the high priest, but two of Senmen's classmates, Antonius and Qeny, had also joined. Like him, they were done with their training and ready to head home but had come to Alexandria at Senmen's request—he needed them to attempt dark magic. He recalled how he'd hated Antonius when they'd first met, but after suffering together, they'd become allies. Nothing like mutual hate toward the pharaoh to bond them forever.

"I thank you for your service to the family," Hugronaphor doted. "I will never forget it and will reward you when you return."

"What sort of reward shall I receive?" Senmen asked.

"What would please you most?" Hugronaphor replied.

Senmen knew what he wanted but didn't want to speak it in front of his brothers.

"All rise," the herald cried. "Our Lord and King, Ptah and God, Ptolemy IV Philopater has arrived."

Ptolemy IV stood in the doorway with Queen Arsinoe. Senmen's heart stopped for a moment as his abuser entered the room. Despite Isidor's threats, the man had indeed continued to force Senmen and his companions to participate in his orgiastic ceremonies. Senmen had taken Isidor's advice though and taught his classmates, all twenty-two of them, the hate meditation. Within six months, the pharaoh found himself impotent, and no longer sought out the boys in

Memphis for his sick pleasure. Whether this was directly due to their magic or not, Senmen wasn't sure, nor did he care. It had been over two years since the monster last abused them, and the boys were now men. No, they were greater than men. They were powerful priests, filled with hate for the pharaoh and ready for revenge.

Senmen looked to Antonius, who nodded in return. This was the perfect chance to experiment with advanced magic, and Ptolemy IV had no idea what was coming. As the pharaoh approached the table, everyone in the room bowed. The man struggled to walk up to the dais due to his drunkenness, and his wife, who looked miserable with her station in life, had to help him settle into his place beside Hugronaphor.

"At ease," Philopater said, his words thick from the opium. "Welcome, stewards of Behdet. Please, let's dine."

"Thank you, Lord Pharaoh, my king," Hugronaphor answered. "We appreciate your hospitality and look forward to our time with you. As a token of our appreciation, I present to you a dance by the heir of the high priestess, Natasa the Graceful."

"Dancing?" the pharaoh exclaimed, clapping his bloated hands with delight like a child just given honeycomb to eat. "Oh, I love dancing."

The room quieted as a group of three drummers entered the hall. Behind them walked Natasa, her back straight and tall. She walked with the grace of a puma, and Senmen's heart quickened. Upon her head, she wore a web of gold with small disks sparkling in the firelight. Her shirt was a see-through golden wrap, and around her waist, she wore a dark blue skirt that flowed as she danced. The drummers took their places beside the head table, and Natasa approached. She bowed to the pharaoh and rose to speak.

"Lord Pharaoh Ptolemy, king and master of my lands," she said, "I present to you the Dance of the Knives."

She turned and posed, ready to start the dance.

The dance began the moment the drums started. Natasa's hips swayed as she turned and twirled before them. The gold bangles on her arms made tinkling sounds when she raised and lowered her arms to the music. She was mesmerizing, and Senmen felt fire whip through his body. His desire for her was growing stronger every moment. He recalled what it had been like to kiss her when they were children, and imagined repeating it now, as young adults. Beads of sweat formed on his bald head, and he wiped at the moisture before taking a long drink from his wine.

The beat of the music changed, and Natasa now held in her hands two long, sharp knives. Their metal blades shone as she spun and began a series of military movements. Senmen was shocked at her skill with the blades. He knew his father must have requested this dance—in Behdet, it was known as both the Dance of the Knives as well as the Remembrance of the warrior goddess. Natasa embodied the Goddess of Destruction, Sekhmet, as she battled invisible enemies, with grace. The drums beat faster and faster as she attacked, danced, spun, rolled, and jumped to the tempo. Her skirt flowed, tracing her movements through the room, making the music visible. Senmen lost track of time and fell into her spell without hesitation.

Natasa, he thought, *you will cleanse me and make me whole again. You will make me feel again. You're the one to heal me.*

During his abuse, Senmen had learned how to separate his Ba from the earthly plane and leave his body behind. Often, he lost consciousness and would awaken after the ordeal was over to pain and discomfort in his young body, but unable to recall anything that had happened. With time though, Senmen had lost the ability to feel in his body. He felt separate, like a visitor. His Ka was torn, with missing pieces and dark shadows, and his body felt dirty, used, and unfit for a future king.

Making love to Natasa would change that. She would purify him. He knew what he would request of his father—Natasa as his spiritual companion.

She danced right up to the table, so close Ptolemy IV could have touched her, and the drums ended with one last crashing beat. Natasa held a pose so fierce, Senmen feared her. She crouched before the pharaoh like a tiger ready to pounce, a knife in each hand raised above her head, as if to attack the greedy man. Her gaze bore into the pharaoh, and Senmen could feel the power radiating from her. She was sending the man a message—we are strong in the south. Senmen, along with the rest of the room, held his breath.

She dropped her gaze and stood upright, tucking the knives back into their sheaths at her waist and taking a bow. Ptolemy IV panted like a hound after a hunt. He rose from his chair, Arsinoe offering a steady hand, and began clapping.

"Splendid," he cried. "Thank you, Natasa the Graceful. What do you call that dance?"

"The Dance of the Knives," she answered, panting from her efforts. Her breasts rose and fell under her see-through blouse with each breath. Senmen nearly swooned at the sight. "It is a traditional dance of my female ancestors."

"You were wonderful. Please, come sit beside me and dine."

"If it would please Your Majesty, I shall," she answered. "May I change out of my costume first?"

"My dear, do whatever you must," the pharaoh oozed.

Natasa now looked to Hugronaphor, who nodded and smiled with approval. She let her gaze wander, first to Senmen, and next to Ankhmakis. Did she linger on his brother? Senmen wasn't sure. Perhaps Ankhmakis might be a problem in his quest for Natasa's heart. She left the room, and Philopater turned to Hugronaphor.

"Move over," he demanded. "Make room for the girl to sit right next to me."

"Be careful," Hugronaphor warned, "she is sworn to the temple."

"And what does that matter?" Ptolemy IV asked.

"She's not yours to abuse," Hugronaphor answered.

"Don't worry," the pharaoh replied, his attention now focused on Senmen. "I have other ways to find my pleasure."

Philopater eyed Senmen, and he could feel the pharaoh's desire rise, causing Senmen to look away in shame. He nodded at Antonius and Qeny, signaling the time had come to act. Senmen rose taller in his seat and turned back to face Philopater, who was still looking at him with sexual greed on his blotched, aging face. Rather than cower at the filthy man's perverted gaze, Senmen returned the look with his own glance of hate, spite, and loathing. He bore these forms down deep within his Ka and saw their shadows surround the pharaoh. Philopater wiped sweat from his brow as he cleared his throat, and Senmen knew his friends were also sending their hate to him, reaching out with their Ka to deliver the spiteful curse without even having to leave their seats. Power surged through Senmen, and Philopater coughed.

"My lord?" Queen Arsinoe asked. "What's wrong?"

Philopater's face turned red as he clutched his neck. "I can't breathe," he squawked.

The queen looked around, calling to the servants to help, and Philopater looked Senmen in the eye, his pupils no longer dilated with desire, but terror. Senmen gave him a dark and evil smile, never breaking eye contact.

Yes, he thought. *I'm hurting you, and someday I will kill you. I promise.*

The pharaoh struggled to stand. Senmen broke his contact, and with a slight hand signal, commanded Antonius and Qeny to do the same. As their Ka retreated from his own, the pharaoh was able to breathe again, and the queen was wiping the sweat from his brow.

"There, there," she clucked.

The pharaoh slumped back on his pillows. Servants carried jugs of wine, and the musicians continued playing their tunes. Hugronaphor and Hecataeus both feigned concern while Ankhmakis and Silus shifted in their seats, trying to look anywhere but at the scene in the front of the room.

Senmen felt exhausted but elated nonetheless. He was able to use his thoughts to affect the physical world around him, and this magic was extra powerful with others to help him. As he nodded to his friends, who glowed from their success, his gaze fell upon Metakryon, who was eyeing him. Senmen knew the high priest understood what had happened, and fear tensed his body. What if Metakryon denied him his entrance to the Cult of Set for hurting the pharaoh? What would he do?

What happened was more of a surprise than anything he could imagine—Metakryon smiled and nodded.

Natasa appeared at Senmen's side, dressed in a narrow, green tunic, which matched her eyeshadow, and still wearing her headdress and jewelry. As she approached, she looked to Ptolemy IV with wide eyes.

"Is he all right?" she asked. "What happened?"

"He was choking, but now seems fine," Ankhmakis answered.

"He must have swallowed a bone," Senmen suggested.

"Maybe your dance frightened him, Natasa," Silus said.

"What?" she asked, a look of concern upon her beautiful face.

Ankhmakis laughed and poured a golden goblet full of wine. He handed it to Natasa, and she thanked him with a smile before taking a sip. The casual rapport between the two made Senmen jealous.

"Don't listen to Silus," Ankhmakis said, smiling with delight. "He often confuses female power with domination."

Silus rolled his eyes and shook his head.

"Your dance was perfect," Senmen said.

"Why, thank you." She smiled.

Ankhmakis opened his mouth to try to get a word in—probably a compliment of his own, Senmen thought—but Philopater interrupted.

"Natasa the Graceful," the pharaoh called. "Come, sit by my side."

Natasa did as requested, and Senmen glared at the pharaoh as she walked to him, but the king of Egypt wouldn't even glance his way. The pig was afraid, and Senmen felt on top of the world.

He couldn't wait to tell Isidor.

☥

For the next week, Iu-Amon and Natasa spent their days in what felt like heaven to her—reading books and manuscripts, and often skipping meals at the palace to discuss philosophy, history, and the Punic Wars with the visiting scholars in the library. Natasa met men from Rome, Greece, Gaul, Carthage, and even the mysterious northern lands. Through her various academic conversations, she learned about Ptolemy IV's habits and relations with the Seleucids and the Egyptian natives of the Delta, who were beginning to show their own signs of rebellion. In addition, after years of marriage, Queen Arsinoe had given birth to a son, Epiphanes. Natasa felt like a spy as she copied down what she heard to share with Ankhmakis, who spent his spare time in the library with Iu-Amon and Natasa, studying maps and taking notes on Abdju, Thebes, Luxor, and Karnak. He also memorized the layout of Alexandria and the weaknesses within the administration.

Whether she liked it or not, Natasa understood the civil war was inevitable.

When their time in Alexandria ended, Natasa said goodbye to Senmen, who headed to Memphis with Metakryon. She boarded Hugronaphor's ship with the rest of the men and sailed home to Behdet.

Before sunrise on the final morning of their journey, Natasa woke to the sound of gentle music. She slipped away from her snoring father, who was, of course, sleeping beside her and made her way up to the deck. There she found Iu-Amon standing in the shadows. He was watching Ankhmakis, who stood at the bow playing his pandura, unaware he had an audience. Natasa smiled at how beautiful and noble the prince looked, singing to the rising Sun God, Ra.

"What's he doing?" she asked Iu-Amon.

"He's played this song every morning since Alexandria," Iu-Amon whispered.

"It's beautiful," she sighed. The sky turned purple, and streaks of pink and gold paled the horizon. "Why does he do it?"

"Well," Iu-Amon said, smiling as bright as Ra himself, "it's been my experience that only one thing compels a young man to sing to the sunrise."

"What?" she asked.

"I think the prince is in love."

13

Blood and Chaos

King Seti I had been a warrior, as was his father before him. Their people had practiced the Meditations of the Warrior and worshipped the God of War, Set, as their deity. It has been rumored that later in his life Seti confessed, "One should not serve an evil being, even if it appears to have a good or useful function."

Three Months Later, First Day of the New Year, Memphis, Egypt 207 BCE

Wind and rain slashed against Senmen's face, tearing his flesh and causing his blood to scatter on the wind. Before him rose an enormous thundercloud, engulfing the entire horizon. Lightning bolts struck the ground and the thunder roared his name.

"Senmen. Senmen."

Two fierce green-yellow eyes appeared within the storm cloud. They grew, and a dark and evil laugh penetrated the air. He ran away but was held by the wind. He'd been here before, and he knew what would happen next.

A pair of arms swooped down upon him and tore him

limb from limb.

"Give me your heart, and I will give you the world," the storm creature cried as he tore Senmen's head from his neck.

Senmen woke with a start, sweating and breathing in short, uncontrolled breaths. The room around him was still. He stood and ran to the window—all was quiet in Memphis. The city was heavy with sleep as crickets and locusts droned. A jackal cried out in the distance. There was no storm, and no evil being.

He'd been having this same nightmare since the first phase of his initiation, one in which he'd stood naked before the altar of Set for two days. The moment he'd shown signs of fatigue, the priests had whipped him with their flails. His back was now covered with scars from the ordeal. Ever since that moment of overcoming sleep deprivation, hunger, thirst, and pain, he'd found himself dreaming of storms, dismemberment, and death.

His work in Memphis was starting to take its toll. Nothing was as it seemed. The Rituals of Set forced him to overcome his body's needs and separate his intelligence from nature. In this way, at the point when Senmen's mind was inhabited by his Ba, and his intelligence freed from nature's forms and boundaries, he could be filled with the energy of chaos, death, and pain. It would be from that place he would achieve immortality and travel the dimensions of the universe.

Despite the torture and the pain, he wanted this power more than anything—the power to be an immortal intelligence, just as the gods. But the nightmares were causing him great distress. He shook his head and walked to his basin, where he poured himself a glass of water. He took a vial from his table and drank the contents, a mild herbal preparation to help with the anxiety. Nothing too impressive, an opiate mixed with scotch broom and lemon balm. The priests had given him this preparation the day the nightmares began. Metakryon claimed the dreams were a sign that Set wanted to form a bond. The drug would help open the connection within the mind and allow Set to work within him. Senmen didn't feel like he'd united with a deity, but the opiate did make his heart stop racing and the fear go away.

He lay down on his bed and fell into a disturbed sleep. Hours later, as Ra prepared to return to the morning skies, his attendants entered his chamber. After ten days of refraining from meat and drinking only water, his training as an acolyte had ended. The hour had arrived to be initiated into the Priesthood of Set.

"My lord," his servant, Andara, addressed him. "The time has come."

Senmen nodded and rose from the bed, allowing the men to dress him and shave his head and face. He wore a red robe, something only Isidor would wear in the temples of Behdet. Its hood was trimmed in gold. When the men were finished, they gave him a glass of water—he wouldn't eat or drink for the next three days.

"Come," Andara said, head bowed in reverence, "the morning star will rise in a moment."

Senmen's final ceremony would begin with the rising of the star called Sopdet before sunrise and end in the dead of night, three days later. The intention was to meet Set and receive his blessing. If Set accepted him, he would live. If Set rejected him, he would die.

He drifted down the hall between his two attendants. They each held a torch in their hands. They ushered him down several flights of stairs and into a tunnel that led from the priests's sleeping quarters to the temple. It was a secret path, known only by those who participated in the cult.

The tunnel emptied out into a large, circular room deep within the earth. A twenty-foot statue of Set the Animal was the main focal point. At its feet, a huge roaring fire burned. Twelve red-robed men, hooded and masked, stood in a circle around a black onyx altar, holding torches and chanting. Beside the altar stood a thirteenth man, whom Senmen knew to be Metakryon. The others would be a mixture of Egyptian and Greek priests. This cult had been a collaboration between the two nations, for both wanted to resurrect the worship of the great lord of war, death, destruction, and chaos.

Senmen approached the altar with trepidation—a small boy had been strapped to the granite table. He didn't struggle; rather, he gazed at the ceiling, his eyes glazed over—they'd drugged him into silence. Senmen knew blood was needed to invoke the god, yet he'd never taken part in human sacrifice. Animals had sometimes been involved in various fertility rites in Behdet, but never a human being. Sacrifice was something the initiates did to themselves, not to another. To take an innocent life was against the law in his lands.

But innocent blood was a requirement for the god of war, and Senmen's participation in the temple of Set was necessary—he had no choice. In exchange for their help getting Hugronaphor an army, the king had to allow the Brotherhood to practice in Behdet, and one of his sons had to participate. From the sexual abuse at Philopater's hand to the brutal training in Memphis, Senmen's sacrifice for his country had been great.

He approached the altar and Metakryon raised his arms above his head. A knife gleamed in the firelight.

"Blood for our lord," the high priest of Memphis cried. "Blood for our future. Blood to usher in the end of all things."

He sliced through the child's throat, and with a slight choking sound, blood gurgled from the boy's mouth as the expression on his face fell blank. "Lord Set, may this sacrifice be pleasant to you. We give you young blood in exchange for power and everlasting life."

Metakryon walked around the altar, gesturing and chanting in honor of Set. His attendants forced Senmen to his knees. As Metakryon approached, he threw back Senmen's hood and struck his face. The skin on his cheek stung from the blow, and Senmen fought the urge to strike back. The chanting ended and the temple was still. The only sound was the roar of the fire and Senmen's racing heart.

"Rise," Metakryon commanded. Senmen did as he was told. "Senmen, youngest son of Hugronaphor, the Steward of Behdet, do you reject the station of your birth in favor of everlasting life?"

"Yes, I do," Senmen exclaimed.

"And do you reject the brotherhood of Horus, instead taking up the mantle of Set, the lord of destruction and war, the true father of Egypt?"

"Yes, I do."

"You are now nameless." Two of the hooded men ripped his robe from his body, and he stood naked before them, shivering in the candlelight. "You will enter the tomb," Metakryon continued. "There you shall be locked for three days. If you are alive when we open the tomb, you will be named as one of us. If you are dead, we will feed you to the jackals, for there is no afterlife for those rejected by the Lord Set."

Senmen trembled. To be left to rot under the sun was a punishment worse than any other. Without a proper burial, his Ba would wander the universe for ages, never finding

Amenti, or his people, again.

"Do you accept this challenge?" Metakryon asked him.

"Yes, my lord."

Metakryon held up a cup. "Drink to renew your body and open your eyes," he commanded.

Senmen drank it and tasted warm blood, water, and the bitterness of a fungus that would help him with his journey into the darkness of his soul, with the promise of freeing his mind. He choked it down, knowing the blood had come from the boy.

"Now go," Metakryon boomed.

The attendants grabbed his arms, bruising him with their enthusiasm, and led him to a dark entrance at the foot of the statue of Set. They forced him inside, and slid the solid granite door across the threshold, shutting him in absolute darkness.

The image of blood pouring from the boy's neck filled his mind. He shook with shock. His body turned cold, and he fell to the floor, trembling into oblivion.

☥

Senmen lay on the stone floor, chilled to the bone and writhing in fear, for what seemed like hours—perhaps even days. His head foggy from the drugs; abandoned in the darkness, more alone than he'd ever felt in his life.

After a long, dark moment, warmth spread across his chest. He sucked in a frantic breath, as if taking in air for the first time, and rolled onto his back. Before him, colors appeared. He was still terrified, but in that terror, he found a place of peace. Like the eye of the storm, here was a place where all was quiet.

He closed his eyes, controlling his breath as he calmed himself. With each inhalation and exhalation, he felt his mind separate from his body.

A shock ran through him as his mind opened and the universe unfolded before him. The geometries of chaos, anger, and fear surrounded him, but this time, he wasn't afraid. His body instead grew stronger, and his mind stretched across the cosmos. History played before him, and the future, and he saw himself triumphant.

He would be the one to free Egypt from the Greeks. He would use his family in heinous ways, but it would lead him to glory and strength. He would advance the black magic further than those before him, and Set would love him for it. His blood boiled with lust for that future, for such power.

He found himself before a black altar surrounded by fire. The familiar green-yellow eyes appeared, but rather than a monster surrounded by thunder and lightning, a beautiful, powerful, yet terrifying man appeared, twenty feet tall with hair the color of the brightest copper, his skin a rich, creamy brown, taut over his muscular body. Terror rose within Senmen, for despite the god's beauty, he was the spirit and soul of all that was horrible and evil in the world.

"Come to me, my son, and be my servant," the god spoke.

His voice was melodic, yet cruel and high-pitched, like the sound of metal scraping upon metal. Senmen hesitated.

The god raised his arms, and the scene shifted to a room filled with gold and servants. He was seated on a throne, in the newly built temple of Behdet. Natasa was at his feet, washing them in supplication. He wore the blue Khepresh, crown of the pharaoh of the upper kingdom.

"You shall wear the crown of the Egyptian pharaohs," Set continued, his voice engulfing Senmen and entering deep into his mind and soul. "You will put the Lady Isis in her proper place and bear my power to the men of the south. All shall remember you as the one who ended the Macedonian reign of Egypt."

The room vanished and Senmen was alone in the darkness. The god reappeared and hovered closer, leaning over him as if a lover in the throes of passion. Senmen felt a surge of power and masculinity fill his body. The god drew back, and Senmen rose from the cold floor to face him.

"Yes," Senmen answered, his voice deep and thick with desire. He wanted the god's promise of glory. "I will be your servant. You are my father, and I pledge myself to you."

Set's cold, evil laugh filled the room, causing Senmen's heart to halt with anticipation.

"You shall go forth to the world as Chanax—my faithful servant."

The god disappeared, and Senmen fell to the floor. The cruelty of the god's voice, the evil laughter, filled his soul with terror and darkness.

Senmen passed out of time and remained in a trance, somewhere between life and death.

☥

In the dead of the night on the third day, the assistants returned to the tomb and hauled back the heavy stone. Metakryon stood in the temple. At his side were several red-robed priests of Set. They were amazed to see Senmen standing tall, his body strong. He strode from the chamber with confidence and command, showing no signs of hunger or thirst. The assistants placed a red robe around his shoulders.

"Hello, Metakryon," the young priest whispered, his voice hoarse from three days of silence.

"Welcome back, my brother," the old priest replied. "Has the nameless been given a name?"

"From this day forward, I shall go by Chanax, beloved of Set," he answered with the confidence of a crowned messiah.

Metakryon and the others bowed at his feet, and Senmen nodded as he raised his arms to the ceiling in victory. His shadow cast an eerie, dark specter upon the chamber's stone walls.

"It is time for me to return home and take my place at High Priest Isidor's side," he cried. "Long live the Brotherhood of Set."

14

First Rites

Female First Rites were traditionally administered by one of the priests trained in Anit-Shadya, the Purest Pleasure of Isis. Princesses and the priestesses who sought initiation into the Anit-Shadya of Isis were given this training on their sixteenth birthday. The high priestess chose the man who would be their instructor in the intimate ceremony. The initiate had no input in the matter, yet the high priestess often sought to pair them in the safest and most comfortable way possible.

Behdet, Egypt 207 BCE

The butterflies in Natasa's stomach wouldn't stop dancing. They were causing her heart to pound beneath her breast and her intestines to gurgle. She could hear the din of conversation around her as her attendants bathed her, but she couldn't make out their words. Natasa followed their instructions as they guided her out of the tub and dried her off. The women sat her down, and two of them wound her hair into thick braids. For her part, Natasa stared off out the window, watching Ra begin to set. At nightfall, she would meet the one who would give her First Rites.

"Who is it, Mother?" she murmured. "Who will be the man to teach me the ways of Anit-Shadya?"

Neferu-ankh-maat turned from one of the attendants, who stood holding the white robe Natasa would wear, if only for a moment, to her first experience of Anit-Shadya.

"You will know when you meet him."

"You're not going to tell me?"

"You know I can't. Why does it matter?"

"What if—" She didn't finish, but everyone in the room knew her concern.

What if the man repulsed her? She'd spent three years deep in study of the mysteries, purified her will and her thoughts, and learned of the various subtle bodies that governed life. She knew how powerful the energy field around every human was, and she was excited to explore this part of her being with her spiritual companion. Could Anit-Shadya lead to everlasting life? It certainly led to health, power, and wellness for those who took part in it. But could it work, if she wasn't attracted to her teacher? There were several priests who could train her; it didn't mean she would make the everlasting bond to this person. First Rites were always administered by a priest, and his job was merely to show her the ankh channel, to help her do what she already knew in her mind, and prepare her for her future spiritual companion, one of the princes. At most, she'd spend one night with the man her mother had chosen to perform the ceremony.

Still—what if he were a horrible man? Like Isidor? Natasa shuddered.

"Don't you trust me, daughter?"

Natasa looked up to see her mother standing near. She drew Natasa into her embrace and gave her a squeeze. This wasn't protocol, but Neferu-ankh-maat wasn't the high priestess at that moment; rather, she was a mother, in love with her daughter.

"Yes, I do." Natasa sighed.

She stood, and the attendants covered her body in oil infused with lavender, cardamom, sage, clove, black pepper, juniper, and pine. Each herb contained gifts from the plant world to help her find her ankh channel and through such bliss, connect to her Ba in a deeper way. This evening was the doorway to the ancient magic. Iu-Amon was correct; if she'd chosen his way she'd know only how to help others live longer. The path of Anit-Shadya would allow her to show others how to avoid death. This was her calling.

Her mother placed the white robe around her shoulders. It didn't fasten in the front, revealing a slight hint of her naked body. Into her hands, Neferu-ankh-maat placed a golden Ankh.

"Your offering to the one who will teach you," the high priestess said.

Natasa nodded, unable to hide her fear as she clutched the precious artifact in her trembling fingers

"Do not worry," her mother warned. "There is no room for negative emotions in the place of Divine love."

Several bald priestesses, dressed in white, entered the room. They formed two lines before Natasa and chanted, calling back and forth to one another. Together, the group walked down the hall toward the chamber where the act of First Rites would take place. The doors to the room stood open, and Natasa could hear music drifting through the air, meeting the voices of her singers. Despite her trepidation, Natasa found herself transported outside of time.

She walked, feeling the space around her swirl and guide

her toward her destiny. The vibration from the music filled her cells, making them hum. Her vision cleared, and she could see light particles dancing together in streams of colors, drawing her ever closer to the room before her.

She arrived at the threshold and entered a room of great opulence. The walls were decorated with gilded hieroglyphs, the floors with mats woven from gold and brightly dyed wool. Braziers burned by the windows where soft curtains blew in the late-night summer's wind. Candles decorated every wooden table and flickered in the moonlight that poured through a great window over the ritual bed, which was covered in furs and silken pillows, and sat upon a frame made of solid gold with lions in each corner.

Before the ceremony bed stood a man, his face turned from hers. He was the one playing the instrument, and the pandura's notes filled the air with his romantic tune. He was tall, thin, and proud. Even from behind, she knew who he was—she recognized the song from the journey to Alexandria. Her body ached with desire as she crossed the threshold with confidence, walked to the altar of Isis, placed the golden Ankh before her statue, and bowed to the goddess, giving thanks for this gift.

"I thank thee, Goddess Isis, for the gift of Divine love. I come to thee, open to learn and see."

She looked at her teacher and waited for him to greet her.

Ankhmakis turned to face her and the music stopped. He lowered the pandura to his side and bowed. "I am willing and ready to teach," he answered in a deep voice that cracked, revealing his need for her approval.

Natasa's skin burned with joy and anticipation. She strained to control herself, wanting to throw herself into Ankhmakis's muscular embrace. The attendants took the pandura from his arms, and removed the white robe from Natasa, leaving her naked before him. They left, the doors shutting behind them with a gentle thud. The two stood together, alone in silence breathing short, nervous breaths, each one feeling the electricity forming in the space between them—like a storm rising from the desert. A gentle breeze blew into the room. Ankhmakis untied the string at his waist and his loincloth fell to the floor.

Natasa took the first step, drawn to his rising passion, which she could now see radiating in all directions. She watched in amazement as his body responded, the physical signs of his arousal impossible to ignore. The fingers of time danced around them, enclosing them in a spiral of destiny. She stood before him, so close she could feel the heat coming from his body. When she looked up and gazed at his sculpted jawline, shoulders, and chest, her breath caught at his beauty.

"I'm so glad it's you," she whispered.

Ankhmakis placed his hands on Natasa's cheeks and drew her lips toward his. The moment they kissed, she felt her heart burst. His was an ancient, yet familiar caress—greeting her after a long journey away. His tongue searched her mouth, and his lips consumed hers. He picked her up and took her to the bed.

As he laid her down, she surrendered to his touch; never had she felt anything so wonderful. He kissed her forehead, cheeks, and neck, taking his time to taste every bit of her as he made his way down to the place of her fire. When he arrived at her breasts, he stopped to kiss and caress them. She moaned as desire crept up her spine.

He continued exploring her body with tenderness, and her moans became wild and untamed as he approached her stomach. His mouth wandered between her legs to the lips of the goddess, and she lost control. Ankhmakis touched and tasted her essence, devouring her passion as her body entered the state of eternal bliss. She would experience her first orgasm in this way, and he would drink it in like fine wine.

She arched her back and felt the power race up her spine. It originated from below and traveled at the speed of light to her heart. She could not hold out, nor deny the powerful energy. She allowed it to flow through her, and as it flooded her mind, she cried out his name.

As her moment passed, he climbed on top of her and thrust himself inside. Natasa's mouth opened wide as she gasped with surprise, and she felt a mixture of pain and pleasure. He kissed her, rough and desperate now, and she responded by wrapping her legs around his waist. The prince continued to drive himself deeper and deeper into her mystery.

Natasa watched as pleasure filled him, allowing her vision to widen, now seeing their sexual energy intertwine as he rode along the top, like a snake, controlling his orgasm as it approached his heart. Taking a deep breath, he sent the energy out the back of his body, through his shoulder blades, and into the channel of the Ankh, that most blessed meridian within the energetic field of his body. The goddess Isis had created the ankh channel for the exclusive purpose of recycling the power of human orgasm back into the body, reinvigorating and renewing the Ka, and all life on the planet.

A golden halo of light surrounded Ankhmakis as the power of his orgasm continued up and around the back of his head, past his third eye, mouth, chin, neck, and back into his body at his heart. It shot down his spine to his groin, and his pleasure exploded with such power that she felt it inside her and rose in ecstasy herself. The two of them were bathed in one another's power as they continued in this way, each one rebounding in pleasure from the other.

When he was finished, Ankhmakis fell upon her chest. Sweat dripped from their bodies. Natasa wrapped her arms around him. The bliss she felt was beyond anything she'd ever imagined.

He rolled off her chest and lay beside her, his hawk-like gaze intense and formidable. Natasa found herself in love, and it scared her. What if this was only for one night, and her mother bonded her to Senmen instead? She had to serve one of the princes, but Natasa was sure no other touch would ever suffice again.

"Thank you." She sighed with satisfaction and snuggled her head closer into his chest. The scent of his sweat mixed with musk made her dizzy with sexual need. "And to think that this morning I'd planned to run away and avoid this entire ceremony."

"I'm glad you didn't run away," he murmured as he kissed her. "This is only the beginning, my dear."

"Yes, you have much to teach me," she replied. "I want to do what you did there with your energy body. You entered the ankh channel. I must know how to do it."

"You followed like a natural. I think you'll make an excellent student," he answered, still kissing her neck. Without warning, he suddenly withdrew from her side. She opened her eyes and saw him staring at her, rubbing his fingertips together. He looked nervous.

"What is it?" she asked.

He swallowed hard, rose up on one elbow, and ran a finger down the side of her face.

"I don't want to be your teacher for one night," he said, his voice wavering. "I want you forever, Natasa. I want you to bond with me and be my spiritual companion."

Her heart fluttered under her hard, aching breasts. She'd always known this time would come—that she'd be given to a member of the royal family for life to build the connection between spirit and body and prepare him to be king. It was too good to be true that Ankhmakis would choose her.

"I am a prince in line for the throne," he continued, knowing her exact thoughts. What was this bond that already existed?

"Yes," she said.

"Yes, I am a prince, or yes, you will be my spiritual companion?" he asked.

"Both." She wanted to make love to him for the rest of her life.

He smiled, relief washing over his face.

"Ankhmakis, my prince," she said, rising up to her knees and leaning in toward him, "it would be an honor to serve you and explore the mysteries of the goddess in this way. I surrender to your will."

She kissed him with all her heart and soul and then manhandled him down on the bed to straddle him, feeling his sex harden between her legs. Her body responded with a wetness of its own.

"I think I'm going to like this role." She slipped him deep inside, growing giddy at the sensation as he grew even harder. "Now, show me how to channel that energy."

☥

The next morning, Natasa awoke to the sound of Ankhmakis playing the pandura. Each note filled the air with the sounds of his heart and his mind. She allowed herself to bask in the music, for she knew this was a type of conversation, one where the musician shares his dreams with the audience, encouraging them to go deeper within themselves, if only they bother to listen.

She scooched to the end of the ceremony bed and watched him. He was wearing his loincloth and nothing else. She longed to kiss his neck and muscular chest, for she already loved his perfect, long, and lean body. His thick, chin-length black hair hung around his dark, clean-shaven face. She admired the line of his jaw and felt desire sweep through her. His fingers wandered the three-stringed instrument, from its oval body down along the long neck and back. Both she and the prince had been introduced to music in the first years of their training. The elders believed that understanding music, from the scales to the harmonic progression, was key to understanding the creation of the cosmos—every form has its geometry, and every geometry has its tone, and every tone is the call of life. This was the foundation of their civilization, and everything from architecture, to medicine, to law extended from it.

Ankhmakis's eyes were closed as his fingers danced across the strings in ways Natasa had never thought possible. She was a singer and harpist, yet he was playing chords she'd never heard before. Why didn't he play in the temple, with a gift like this? She opened her mouth to ask him when a voice in her head said, *Be still and know.*

He was staring at her, his expression intense and serious. Had he sent her a message? Could they already speak heart-to-heart? Again, she felt drawn to watch his fingers—fingers that had explored her body the night before with loving attention. Her breasts ached as each note entered deep into her body. The music lifted her from her place, and without even thinking, she closed her eyes and danced to the rhythm. The music played around her, as the notes left his fingertips and traveled through the air to her hips, shoulders, elbows, and hands. They entered her and danced along her spine. She greeted each one and followed their melody while they moved through her body—as if she were a puppet and Ankhmakis held control of the strings, moving her with the music he played.

From this place once again, Natasa found herself outside of space and time. Not beyond them, but beside them, where nothing but harmony existed. Stars were being born within her soul, her body guiding them into life. To dance without a care was a gift she'd experienced before, yet this took her deeper, to a place no other musician had guided her. Not even her own music generated such a selfless joy. She felt him wind down and knew without a doubt the song had been composed for her. He plucked the last note, and it rode upon the air into her heart, causing her to gasp in the silence that followed.

She opened her eyes and found Ankhmakis standing before her, naked once again. Her lover leaned in and kissed her, his mouth lingering upon hers, breathing with her as if they were one. There was no rush. They were outside of time and therefore, had all the time in the world.

15

Senmen Returns

"But the fact is, I do not believe that the Egyptians came into being at the same period as the Delta; on the contrary, they have existed ever since men appeared on the earth."
~ Herodotus, Greek Father of History, 450 BCE

Behdet, Egypt 207 BCE

Chanax strode between two of his father's guards toward the throne room, his purposeful steps pounding on the marble floor. It had been almost four years since he'd been home, and yet everything felt the same. The fresco-lined hall featured the familiar gods and goddesses. Set, the most powerful deity, did not grace a single frame. He knew Isidor would meet him later in the evening—he would mention the lack of representation of the god of war on the walls, and other things, like assigning him a spiritual companion. Anit-Shadya had been denied to Chanax in Memphis, as had all sex, other than those nights of terror at the pharaoh's hands. He shook his head of the thoughts. He needed to block those horrible memories if he was going to fulfill his purpose.

They passed one of his father's smaller libraries. It

appeared empty, but Chanax heard noises coming from within. He stepped inside the room for a moment and looked around. No one was in there, but the sounds were distinct—laughter, thumping, moaning—the sounds of sex. He looked to the corner and eyed the secret door. As children, he and Natasa had often hidden inside the same space, trying to avoid chores or prayers. Once they'd even fallen asleep and scared their nursemaids into a frenzy when they hadn't shown up for bed on time. How long ago was that? Ten years? Chanax shook his head and smiled. Now someone else was using it for their pleasure.

"Ankhmakis," a woman cried out.

Chanax turned to the guards and shared a sly smile. That dirty dog. His older brother was twenty years old, yet here he was, getting in a quick one with a servant girl. The man needed to be married, and soon. Of course, that meant having sex to produce heirs, which would never be as exciting as stealing a maiden's virtue. But something had to be done to rein Ankhmakis in—a war was on the horizon, and they needed the man to get his head in the game.

"I think we'll leave my brother to his lechery," he said to the guards, who nodded their heads.

They left the room and continued down the corridor. A slight breeze blew through the open windows. The view of the sweeping desert from the palace was majestic. He'd gone only five yards when he heard a commotion behind him. Turning, he found Ankhmakis in a passionate embrace with a young woman. Chanax froze, every inch of his body stiffening when he recognized the object of his brother's passion.

Natasa.

Gaze narrowing, fury rose within him like a flood, and its form surrounded him in the air. Swallowing hard, he pulled his emotions under his control. Chanax signaled the guards to halt and crossed his arms to face the pair.

"Hello, Ankhmakis," Chanax said through clenched teeth.

Ankhmakis extracted himself from Natasa's passionate grip, and she brushed her messy hair from her face as she turned to see who was interrupting them. Her cheeks reddened as realization dawned in her eyes.

"Senmen," she cried as she ran toward him with open arms. "You're back."

She made to embrace him, but he stepped back from her in cold refusal. She halted and dropped her arms. The smile fled from her face, and she paled, surprised with his terse reaction.

"My name is no longer Senmen."

"I'm sorry?" she said.

"Our Lord Set has given me the name Chanax. My initiation is complete. I see yours is as well?"

She turned to Ankhmakis, who put his arms around her. "Yes, in a manner of speaking," Ankhmakis replied, leaning forward to kiss her neck. Her eyes lit up with delight, and she smiled again, despite Chanax's temper.

"I thought you were a woman of the temple?" Chanax challenged.

"Oh, I am, Senmen, I mean, Chanax."

"Rooting like a pig in the closet is not becoming of a Priestess of Isis," he hissed.

Chanax glanced at his brother, noting how powerful he'd become. Ankhmakis's chest and arms were filled out. He bore scars from his training on his arms and neck. He was even more alive than he'd been in Alexandria months prior. A field of electricity surrounded him. He was confident and capable. The same power surrounded Natasa. A silver snake armband adorned her right arm, worn only by initiated Priestesses of Isis. Chanax cringed, knowing that meant only one thing.

"You will not speak that way to my spiritual companion," Ankhmakis replied, flexing his biceps as he crossed his arms.

"You've bonded?" Chanax asked, not wanting to hear the answer spoken.

"Oh, yes," Natasa replied.

"You'll want to do so yourself, brother," Ankhmakis said, drawing Natasa closer to his side. "Don't wait as long as I did. There is nothing else like it in the world."

Chanax nodded, clenching his fists at his sides, trying to keep his face stoic to hide his disappointment. Jealousy was a serpent coiling his insides.

"As for the closet," Natasa said with a mischievous smile, "Shadya doesn't have to be serious all the time, does it? But let it be our secret. I think Mother would disapprove."

"As would Father," Chanax replied. "You should be ashamed of yourself, brother, taking the time to do this when you should be training for war."

Ankhmakis let go of Natasa for a moment, and strutted toward Chanax, stopping almost nose to nose. He placed a firm hand on Chanax's shoulder and drew him even closer; the form of anger embraced them.

"You will soon see, what did you say your name was now? Chanax? Yes, Chanax, you will soon discover that there is nothing better for a warrior than time in the arms of the woman he loves," he said. He squeezed Chanax's shoulder and let go, turning instead to Natasa. Ankhmakis placed his now gentle hands on her cheeks. "Beloved, I'd like to escort my brother to Father's chambers. He's been gone so long. I'm sure you understand we have business to attend to."

She beamed at her lover and nodded. "Yes, my lord. I will

see you at sunset."

He leaned over and kissed her forehead. "I'll send Min to fetch you," Ankhmakis answered. He kissed her mouth, running his hands down her backside, marking his territory.

Natasa drew away with a silly grin on her face and turned to Chanax. "I'm so glad you're home. Now we're all together again."

This time when she hugged him, Chanax didn't stop her. He returned the affectionate gesture, heartbroken when she turned away and walked down the hall. Her steps were sure and graceful; energy danced around her. She was in command of herself in a whole new way. She would never be his playmate again. Natasa was now a Priestess of Isis.

It made Chanax want her even more. He turned to his brother, no longer able or caring to hide his rage. "How dare you take her as your companion?" He snarled. "You knew how I felt regarding my plans for her."

Ankhmakis returned the angry gaze with a disdainful look of his own. "I knew nothing. You were children playing in the mud the last time you were in Behdet. How was I to know you wanted her for a spiritual companion?"

"I told you in Alexandria."

Ankhmakis shook his head. "No, you agreed she had grown to become quite beautiful. But never once did you tell me your true feelings. Not that it would have mattered, I've loved her as long as you have. It took me longer to realize it."

Chanax's blood burned in his veins. Before he knew it, he raised an arm to strike his brother across the face. But Ankhmakis stopped him, holding out his hand to block him as Chanax struck—as if he'd known even before Chanax what his action was going to be.

"What?" Chanax cried, struggling to remove his arm from

his brother's grip.

"I told you, I *have* been preparing for war. Don't underestimate my desire to free Egypt from her situation ever again."

He released Chanax's arm and turned to the guards. "Well, men, what are we waiting for? Let's join our king in welcoming my dear brother home."

☥

The two walked to their father in angry silence. Chanax's mind brewed over the various ways he could hurt his brother. How could Ankhmakis steal her? And what about Natasa? Had she forgotten their kiss? His confession of love? Perhaps his intentions hadn't been clear? His anger was building by the moment, swirling around him like a cyclone. He allowed himself to indulge in multiple murderous thoughts as the doors to his father's throne room opened.

He entered and found Hugronaphor awaiting him at a table near the window overlooking the river. A gentle breeze blew the woven mats strung open to allow in the light. Hecataeus stood beside him, the tutor Ennaeus to his left. In anticipation of the prince's arrival, servings of food and wine covered the table. The men looked up as the guards announced him.

"King Hugronaphor," the guard announced. "Your youngest son, Chanax, has returned home."

"Chanax?" Hugronaphor said as he walked toward his son with open arms. "Is that the name Lord Set gave you in your initiation?"

Chanax allowed his father to embrace him. It seemed important to show an alliance in front of Ankhmakis.

"Yes, Father," he said.

"The god appeared to you?" Hugronaphor asked, clasping

his hands and trembling slightly.

"I'm alive, aren't I?" Chanax answered, head held high. "If I had failed, I'd be dead."

Hugronaphor closed his mouth into a thin smile and nodded. "Yes. I'm relieved you passed the test."

The king turned and beckoned everyone to join him at the table. "Of course," he continued as they took their seats, "deep down I knew you'd be fine. The queen's been fretting for months, but I know my sons, and they are strong."

Chanax wanted to accept his father's praise, but he was too angry about Natasa.

"Is there something wrong, son?" Hugronaphor asked.

"You promised," Chanax hissed.

"Promised what?"

"Natasa," he continued. "You promised her to me for my sacrifice in Memphis."

Ankhmakis nearly choked on his wine, and Hecataeus squirmed. Chanax didn't care.

"Son," Hugronaphor laughed, which made Chanax even angrier, "I made no such promise. I told you there were two things I couldn't guarantee you—your choice of spiritual companion and the throne when I die."

Ankhmakis remained still, eyeing Chanax with his threatening, narrow gaze. The air was heavy with rivalries and unspoken fears. Hugronaphor looked to Ankhmakis and smiled. "Turns out the high priestess chose Ankhmakis long ago for her daughter."

"What?" Ankhmakis exclaimed. "Why was I not informed of this? What if I had said no?"

"Do you think you had a say in the matter?" Hecataeus laughed. "Neffa always gets her way. I should know."

"But she never said a thing to me," Ankhmakis said.

"Why do you think Iu-Amon asked Natasa to join us in Alexandria?" Hecataeus continued. "Trust me, he's in league with the high priestess."

"She was quite overjoyed when you returned from the trip requesting Natasa as your spiritual companion. Therefore, she let you initiate Natasa, even though temple protocol states that honor goes to a priest, not a prince," Hugronaphor added.

Ankhmakis looked down at his clasped hands, his thumbs circling one another. When he glanced back up at his father from under his penciled eyebrows, Chanax saw something he'd never seen in his brother before—humility.

Ankhmakis answered, "I'm grateful that the high priestess is wise. She has blessed me with her daughter's love."

"Yes, you're damn lucky," Hecataeus noted, "because if I had my way, she'd be a virgin for life in the Houses of Healing."

Chanax felt as though he'd disappeared from the room; everyone's attention was now focused on his brother. "Love? Is that what you call taking her in the closet?"

Hugronaphor and Hecataeus now frowned at Ankhmakis, Hecataeus crossing his arms across his chest, the king shaking his head. Chanax smiled, satisfied with the men's reactions.

"It's true," Chanax continued. "I caught them having sex in the secret closet in your library. I get the feeling they do such things on a regular basis."

"I don't think I want to hear this," Hecataeus said, rising from his seat.

"Sit," the king commanded. "Is this true, Ankhmakis? You should know I've also heard from the cooks in the kitchen and the stable masters that the two of you have been taking advantage of their facilities."

Ankhmakis grimaced, embarrassment clear as his face flushed.

"My lord," he began, but Hugronaphor raised his hand.

"She is bonded to you now as a spiritual companion," the king admonished. "She is not a concubine."

"Don't you think I know that?" Ankhmakis argued. "Natasa is precious to me."

"It appears you've forgotten what it means to practice Anit-Shadya," Hugronaphor continued. "You're to take ceremony together in private. In public, she is your advisor, and you are hers. You pray together, meditate together, and explore the mysteries of life together. If you practice it properly, you will find more power than you ever could have imagined in the company of a woman."

Ankhmakis stared at his father in silence. Hecataeus shifted in his seat.

"Do I make myself clear, son?"

Ankhmakis nodded. "Yes, sir."

"I will speak to Neferu-ankh-maat regarding this transgression. She can set the two of you in the right direction," Hugronaphor said. He turned to Chanax. "She has also agreed to give you First Rites as soon as possible." Again, Hecataeus shifted uncomfortably. If Hugronaphor noticed, he didn't acknowledge it. "And Isidor has suggested a wonderful priestess for you if you still wish to take a spiritual companion. Her name is Alexa, the youngest daughter of Tyia. I believe you're close?"

Chanax sat up straighter in his seat. Alexa? He hadn't considered her. Yes, they were close. She was one of his best friends from childhood. He recalled her sweet temperament and laughter, and his heart felt lighter.

"Isidor has initiated her and she's ready to bond with you, if you agree to it," Hugronaphor continued. Chanax appreciated the gesture. It showed both respect and love—two things that were unfamiliar after his long years in Memphis. "I know you're disappointed, but I think Alexa will grant you the happiness you deserve," his father finished.

"Yes, Father," Chanax said. "I accept her. Thank you for your efforts. Alexa is dear to me."

Hugronaphor released a huge breath of relief. He waved to Ankhmakis. "You're dismissed. I have other business with Chanax and would like to spend the day getting to know the young man he's become."

"Yes, sir," Ankhmakis said. He was ashamed, and Chanax relished seeing his brother admonished.

"Expect a visit from the high priestess within days," Hugronaphor warned. "Natasa is one of our best priestesses, and I won't have your undisciplined lust ruin what potential the two of you have together."

"Yes, sir," Ankhmakis replied. He stood, hustling toward the golden doors as if the room were on fire.

Hugronaphor rose and smiled at his youngest son. "Come, Chanax, let's visit the stables. You are long overdue your own horse."

Chanax joined his father, basking in the attention and rejoicing that he'd returned home to Behdet, the true center of Egyptian royalty.

16

Anit-Shadya

Anit-Shadya is as profound as it is practical. Between initiates, it has been known to increase health, vitality, intellectual capacities, and wisdom. Yet between twin flames, those unique pairings of lovers who share the same Ba, Shadya is a miracle. When twin flames experience their love in this way, they can't bear to be separated. They become one. Their love is rare and precious and thus causes great envy among others—everyone wants a piece of it, and they will go to great lengths to control it.

Behdet, Egypt 207 BCE

Natasa swam under the warm, silky water toward her lover. When her hands touched his hips, she placed her feet on the tub floor, rose, and stood before him, water and oils dripping down her hair, face, neck, and breasts. He grabbed her and kissed her as if he'd never had her before, and she wrapped her legs around him, slipping him inside her in one graceful movement. Ankhmakis moaned, almost like a purr, into her ear as he bit it as if he were a wildcat. She thrust down on him harder, and their lovemaking sent waves in all directions. He drove deeper within. She threw back her head, the ends of her long hair floating on the surface of the pool. Ankhmakis held her over the water, and she screamed out his name.

Never in her life had she felt this powerful and free. She was in every particulate in the room, sensing and pulsing with the whole of life. She heard the song of Earth. The stars whispered wisdom into her heart. Being with Ankhmakis in this way was like learning to fly, and the entire cosmos was hers to explore. As her lover climaxed, he drew her up to his face and kissed her again, sweeter this time, as he opened himself to her sexual blessing. She felt his orgasm surround her in a channel of spiraling light, and then it burst, sending waves of energy out into the entire room. There was a humming in her head and heart, and it sang only his name.

"Ankhmakis," she whispered, "I love you."

He kissed her forehead, and she melted. "And I love you. You're more beautiful than the sunrise, Natasa. To me, you're a jewel, magnificent and precious—the greatest treasure in the empire. Kings fight wars for love such as this."

She nudged away from him and floated upon the water.

"We should keep it a secret," she suggested, staring at the tile-covered ceiling. Fish, crocodiles, and other river creatures adorned Ankhmakis's bath—a place so private, only he and his guests were granted access. Even the guards remained outside. Each prince had one built off his chambers. Ankhmakis inherited his father's former rooms when he'd become a man, and now Natasa slept there every night, bathing with him, loving him, and holding him. It was torture to be away from him during the day, but after dinner, Min would call for her, and she'd follow him to this place of supreme bliss and sanctuary. Never would she forget these moments exploring and getting to know Ankhmakis, for in his arms she was also discovering her true self.

"Yes," he agreed as he glided toward her, "we must keep our love to ourselves." He paused and looked at her with a frown. "Though, I'm not sure we've been discreet."

"Oh, that was embarrassing when Chanax found us earlier," she admitted.

"He told Father," Ankhmakis said as he kissed her neck.

"What? How could he?"

"He's an ass, that's why," Ankhmakis replied. "And jealous."

"Jealous? Of what?"

"As smart as you are, Natasa, sometimes you're quite naive," he teased as he grabbed between her legs.

She swatted at his hand and sat upon the steps of the bath, feeling the chill of air on her exposed breasts. "I have no idea what you're talking about," she said as she wrung the water from her hair.

"He's jealous that we've bonded," Ankhmakis explained. "He wanted you for a spiritual companion."

"That's absurd," she exclaimed.

"It doesn't matter," he said, his gaze hungry. She loved it when he looked at her that way. "Father has also heard things from the servants. Remember when Sebastos found us in Biriq's stall?"

She giggled and rose from the tub, grabbing a linen blanket, spun as soft as feathers, to dry herself. She walked through a stone archway to his bedroom. He followed her.

"What did he say?" she asked.

"He was angry," Ankhmakis admitted. "He demanded we behave. Worse, he's going to have your mother give us instruction in proper meditation, prayer, breath work, and other lessons."

Natasa's stomach lurched. "Mother? Give us lessons? Together?"

"I know, it's awkward," he admitted.

"Oh, dear, this isn't good."

"They want us to become disciplined."

She nodded and sat on the bed. It made sense. It was hard to not touch him whenever they were near each other. The instant she was near him, all she wanted to do was kiss every part of him, which she often did, and that always led to Shadya in whatever place they could find.

He sat next to her, and her breasts hardened. "They don't understand how hard it is for me to keep my hands off you," she said, wanting him inside her yet again. "The mere sound of your voice makes me ache."

Natasa crawled to him and sat upon his lap. She loved the way his body responded to her touch, and how the heat rose between them. He kissed her, and turned her down on the bed, sliding across her chest and down toward her legs, inching his way to her sex with his perfect kisses. Her skin was alive, rejoicing in the song of her pleasure.

"No," he admitted with a muffle, continuing his oral exploration of her body as he spoke, "they don't understand. Let's not think about it right now. They can teach us how to behave in the daylight, but the nights will always be ours."

Natasa spread her legs wide and arched her back. "Oh, yes," she moaned.

☥

Neferu-ankh-maat looked at the couple, feeling a mixture of disappointment with them and shame of her own. She remembered her own love affair with Hecataeus and recalled that they'd also had sex in the closets, stables, and larders long before Ankhmakis was even walking. But this was different. Ankhmakis was a prince, and Natasa was the high priestess-in-waiting. They needed to learn how to practice Anit-Shadya with discipline.

They sat before her on their knees, each dressed in proper temple attire. Their hands rested upon their thighs, and they gazed at her from beneath their brows, waiting for her to address them. The sexual energy pulsed between them.

This is what it's like when twin flames mate, she thought to herself. At that moment, it became clear to her that this couple could take Anit-Shadya further than any other if she could only instill within them the discipline they needed for such a task. The fire in his eyes, combined with the passion in Natasa, made the hair on her arms rise. This was not going to be easy.

She crossed her arms and cleared her throat. "It appears my lessons didn't sink in, Ankhmakis," she began. His bronzed cheeks reddened. "Recall that as Natasa's teacher, you're to show her the ways of Anit-Shadya, not merely the ones in which the two of you end up in a stable, unable to control your impulses."

He nodded, his shoulders slumped as he turned his gaze to the ground. It hurt Neferu-ankh-maat to be stern, but it had to be done. She walked to the small altar behind her. In the center was a golden statue of Isis with candles burning around her. Dried flowers, crystals, stones, small papyrus scrolls, food, incense, and other offerings were scattered at the statue's feet.

"It is important, Ankhmakis, not for your pleasure, but for Natasa's development. She's to enter the Tunnel of Illumination to complete her initiation into the Cult of

Isis within the year. You need to help her prepare for this important quest. Many do not return, and I don't wish that to be my daughter's fate."

His eyes widened at the mention of the danger Natasa faced, and she knew she had his attention. "Now, this is the ceremony room in which your First Rites took place," she explained. "It's one of several in the temple of Isis. In this place, the two of you can experience complete privacy."

She lit a candle and bowed to the statue. She placed a small piece of jade as an offering in a copper bowl at the goddess's feet. "It's expected that during this initial bonding period, you perform Anit-Shadya together once a week, and as most of the servants can attest, the two of you are keeping that part of your contract. Only, you're merely having sex, not Shadya, when you fall upon one another wherever you happen to be."

"Merely having sex?" Natasa blurted out. "Is there anything more divine than sex?"

Neferu-ankh-maat shook her head and kneeled before the couple. "Anit-Shadya includes sex, in addition to other, important techniques. It isn't sex—it is the purest pleasure, the greatest gift of the divine. Thus, it is important to give thanks to the goddess first, before indulging in one another's bodies."

Natasa grimaced. She wore the look of a puppy caught chewing on her master's rug.

"You must learn how to honor Isis and often pray to her together as a couple, which will open both of you even deeper to one another's souls. Therefore, we encourage ceremony, in this room. Ankhmakis, I showed you this ceremony. Have you instructed Natasa yet?"

He shook his head, gazing into his lap. "I've been busy, Lady Neferu-ankh-maat."

"Nothing is more important than this," she admonished. Sighing, she continued. "I shall show you again, this time with your lover at your side. Ceremony begins with giving thanks to Isis and her consort, Osiris. There are breath work and meditation together, and sometimes, Anit-Shadya, where each of you climax together, and at the same time become aware of your Ka, enabling it to take part in the rich, magnetic fields created by such bliss."

The high priestess paused, overwhelmed by the love she felt for the couple. She wanted to help the man before her take up the mantle of pharaoh, and he needed Natasa's love to accomplish such an impossible task.

"Ankhmakis, do you want to be king?"

He raised his chin and threw back his shoulders. "Yes, I do."

"Do you wish to be pharaoh of Egypt?" she challenged.

"If it is the goddess's will," he answered, meeting her gaze.

"Then you will need this even more than Natasa. Training in the breathing exercises and using them during your lovemaking will purify each of you, such that Isis will enter her, and Horus will enter you. At that moment, you'll both become the gods themselves. Do this often, and you will inhabit Amon-Re when crowned pharaoh. Forsake this, and you'll be nothing but a footnote in history. Average men make average kings."

As he considered her words, his dark eyes glittered in the firelight, reminding her of the pharaoh eagle owl that haunted their deserts at night. A vision of Ankhmakis wearing the crown of Thebes flashed within her sight.

"I am not an average man, High Priestess," he answered as if he too had seen the vision.

"Good, let's get to work," she replied, shaking off the

image and focusing on the moment at hand. There was no use getting ahead of themselves. Ankhmakis would never be king until he mastered the ways of love.

She led them through several breathing exercises in which she showed them how to fill their abdomens with the golden light of the Almighty Ra, and activate their core energy channel, the djed, that ran through the center of their bodies. They learned the skill with ease. She now needed to teach them how to draw the serpent energy that resided at their root chakra.

"Ecstasy is food and nourishment for the Ka body," she said to them. "One can achieve enlightenment by studying the alchemies of Horus alone. But ecstasy is supercharged and will advance you further in your spiritual development. Between lovers, ecstasy is natural. Therefore we practice Anit-Shadya. To create a strong line of kings and queens. A family line that has survived the occupation of not one, but two foreign nations. It is no coincidence the last line of native Egyptian kings resides here; most other native nobles have perished over the centuries. As Initiates of Isis, we draw upon one of the oldest alchemical streams, ecstasy, to build our Ka and ensure our livelihood."

Natasa nodded, her face open with interest.

"As a Priestess of Isis," she said to her daughter, "you support the line of kings by bonding with this prince and assisting him with the building of his Ka body, that he might continue this native line and serve his people.

"The important thing is that in the moment of ecstasy, you both become aware of the Ka body itself. This causes the ecstasy to spread throughout your physical body, which is absorbed by the Ka, strengthening and revitalizing it. Thus, the Rising of the Two Serpents exercise is something you should practice several times each day. This way when you're together in a moment of ecstasy, you can raise the energy up your djed, around your chakras and into your minds, where you will find greater bliss than orgasm as you know it now."

Her students looked to one another and smiled in a knowing way that led Neferu-ankh-maat to believe the pair could already communicate mind-to-mind. She could only imagine what favorite sexual moments they were sharing in this intimate way.

"It's easy," Neferu-ankh-maat instructed, raising her tone to gain their attention. They turned to look at her as she continued. "Once again, fill your abdomens with the golden light of Ra as you breathe in, and on your exhale, imagine two serpents, one dark and one golden, residing in your pelvis. With each breath in, feed them with the golden light of Ra; with each breath out, see them rise through your chakras, winding between each, dancing with each other as they pass. Eventually, they meet in your head. Can you do this?"

The lovers nodded, and all three of them closed their eyes. Neferu-ankh-maat settled into her abdomen and breathed in the light of Ra. She felt her energy swirl and come to life. She exhaled, and the two serpents appeared inside her. She'd long ago mastered this exercise and allowed them to take form. The dark one rose on the left side of her djed, the golden one on the right. At each chakra, they crisscrossed. She felt the power rise her spine and her head begin to vibrate in a low, loving hum. As the two serpents met within her mind, she opened to the universe, and her Ba shone above her.

The high priestess hadn't been intending to astral travel but trusted the goddess would guide her. Within moments, she discovered Natasa and Ankhmakis had left their bodies as well—yet rather than two distinct Ba, there was only one being of light before her—beautiful and golden, shining like a star. Neferu-ankh-maat beheld them in their splendor; never had she seen such a magnificent union. As one they pulsed, and she followed them. Together, the trio flew above the temple, the gardens, and stables. Behdet stretched out below, and yet they continued. Neferu-ankh-maat feared she might lose her students, for they had no training in astral travel.

"Do not worry," a musical voice called.

The Golden Child had joined them, and as usual, she was laughing. The star that was Natasa and Ankhmakis surrounded the being, radiating in all directions as the parents met their child in this spiritual plane.

"Aren't they beautiful?" the Golden Child asked.

"Indeed," Neferu-ankh-maat answered, "too beautiful for words."

"Soon you will hold me, Grandmother."

The next moment, Neferu-ankh-maat found herself back on her knees in the temple. She opened her eyes, and tears poured down her cheeks. Before her knelt Natasa and Ankhmakis, in two physical bodies, yet surrounded by a golden pulsing light that hummed a distinct melody. This was their tone, and they were one within it. The high priestess's heart sang with joy.

"Who was that?" Natasa asked.

"Your daughter," Neferu-ankh-maat replied.

"Daughter?" Ankhmakis said.

"Yes," Neferu-ankh-maat answered.

"When will she come?" Natasa asked, the glow around her growing with excitement.

"As soon as you're ready," Neferu-ankh-maat answered. "Keep training this way together. Astral travel together often and learn what you must. When the time comes, she will ask you to conceive."

"How will we know it's time?" Ankhmakis asked, his head tilted to one side as if puzzled by the revelation that he would soon be a father.

"Oh, she's quite clear in her instruction." Neferu-ankh-maat smiled. "Trust me, I know. This isn't the first time I've met her on the astral plane. It is, however, the first time I've seen the two of you there. Do you understand what you are?"

Ankhmakis turned to Natasa and took her hand into his own. "I am her, and she is me."

"We are one," Natasa answered, beaming at Ankhmakis with a devotion reserved for the gods. "One being in two bodies."

"The perfect female, the perfect male," Neferu-ankh-maat whispered. "It's an honor to have met you in this way."

The high priestess rose and gestured for her students to do the same. "I think that's good for today," she said, wiping the tears from her cheeks. "I'm sure you can see where this could lead you, should the two of you decide to undertake Anit-Shadya and ceremony with discipline."

Ankhmakis bowed low and stood to meet Neferu-ankh-maat's gaze.

"Thank you, my lady," he said, taking her hand and kissing it. "I will never neglect this duty again."

The man who-could-be-king took her daughter's hand, and the two walked together out the door. Neferu-ankh-maat watched their images fade into the hallway. In the light of the doorway, their two bodies merged closer, and to her wet, tear-filled eyes, appeared to meld into one graceful form.

17

Dark Magic

The talk of war became real. Rebels in the Nile Delta spoke of insurrection. The men of the south formed alliances. Cries for justice filled the air. Anger filled men's hearts. Yet Natasa and Ankhmakis didn't notice it. They cared for nothing but their love and desire. They were on the path to immortality. This is why it is said that lovers are fools—because in their passion they become oblivious to life's darker forces.

One Year Later, Behdet, Egypt 206 BCE

"Welcome, Chanax."

"Thank you, Lord Isidor," the younger priest answered.

"Are you ready for another lesson?" Isidor asked.

"Of course," Chanax replied. "Why wouldn't I be?"

Isidor rose from his place and walked to the door, locking it for good measure. He dared not practice with Chanax in the temple, not yet. Thus, he decided to tutor the young man in his private chambers, deep below the temple of Horus, where no one, not even Neferu-ankh-maat, was allowed. Only one other person joined Isidor in his domain, and the queen was good at keeping its location a secret. Isidor's groin ached when he considered his affair with Keket. It had began years ago, long before Chanax's birth, and Isidor marveled at how he'd kept the secret from Neferu-ankh-maat for decades. His skills at deception were improving with time, which was good, since running the temple of Set required activities the high priestess would find unseemly.

Isidor understood the dangers of keeping Queen Keket as his secret lover, for only the king was permitted to touch the queen's body, but he couldn't resist. Their sex was dark, angry, and painful, often involving various techniques of torture, leaving marks only their servants would see. But the sex was powerful, and Isidor craved it like nothing else in the world. When he was hurting her, he could feel Set in his body, touching her, entering her, and goading her to her limits. The fear in her soul as he abused her always left him stronger. Set had blessed him with an obedient sex slave.

"Isidor?" Chanax asked, his voice interrupting his mentor's lecherous fantasies. Isidor smiled at the boy. He needed to focus on the prince, not Keket.

"Please be seated on the mat in front of the fire," he instructed.

Chanax knelt in front of the brazier, behind which stood an altar to Set.

"Why isn't there an image of Set on this altar?" Chanax asked.

Isidor bowed to the altar and knelt beside him.

"In the ceremony rooms of Isis," Chanax continued, "we give thanks to the goddess's image."

"Indeed," Isidor replied, "and how is that going for you?"

"Anit-Shadya with Alexa?" Chanax asked, blushing.

"Yes. Your father told me you were quite angry you hadn't

been given Natasa," Isidor probed. "I wondered if my selection for you was satisfactory."

"Alexa is good," Chanax said. "I feel stronger with her. I see why the magic is practiced."

"Love is not necessary," Isidor advised, "but honor is. Trust me, Alexa is a better choice for a man such as yourself."

"Why do you say that?" Chanax asked, gaze narrowing.

"Because she's a true Egyptian," Isidor answered. "Not a filthy half-breed like Natasa."

Chanax's teeth ground together, seething with anger, which was what Isidor had expected.

"I know you don't like to hear it, but her Greek blood stains her," Isidor continued. "We've been rather lenient in the temple when it comes to the Greeks, but trust me, when war breaks out, her kind will pay."

"She's also Egyptian," Chanax cried.

"But not pure," Isidor said. "Set does not accept Greek blood. Oh, they think he does. Ptolemy imagines he's a part of the cult, and that it serves him. Nothing could be further from the truth. The power and chaos that Set controls are not something a Greek could ever access. Therefore, you need a pureblood as your spiritual companion. Natasa would have harmed your Ka with her imperfection."

"Does the high priestess know you feel this way?" Chanax challenged.

"I have forgiven Neferu-ankh-maat for tainting her body with the touch of her Greek lover," he admitted. He pointed to the altar that was clear of objects except one—a crystal skull. He opened his leather pouch, grabbed a handful of frankincense and myrrh, and threw it into the fire. The flames grew stronger and crackled in the dimness of his chambers.

"You asked why there are no images of Set on my altar,"

Isidor said, changing the subject.

"The temple in Memphis has one, but I've not seen him anywhere else."

"That's because Set needs no image to remind us of our true nature," Isidor explained. "Set lives within the minds of all men. Anger is his call to action. Even a man who's never thought of Set is under his spell if there's anger or hate in his heart. Since men are angry by nature, Set is always alive and ready to help us find our power and strength.

"Isis represents love. Thoth is wisdom. Anubis reminds us of death. Horus inspires kings. These aspects of glory are not natural in humans. We must work to achieve love and wisdom, not all are born kings, and as for death, we appreciate a reminder that we're not alone when we cross the threshold. Thus, we surround ourselves with their images. We pay homage. We try to connect to them, and often, we fail. But the daily offerings are a reminder that perhaps if we practice the magic, we will find ourselves such things as love and wisdom. Grace and work, this is the method to rise above human nature."

He raised his hands to the sparse altar and drew in a huge breath.

"Set, however, is always with us. Anger is always ours. Common humans misuse their anger. They let it rise within them and throw a tantrum, or attack, without warning or discipline. Like the ecstasy you feel in Alexa's arms, anger can be recycled and channeled, if only it's guided to the mind. This is what a dedication to Lord Set reveals with time—your mind is the key to your freedom. If you can take your anger and hate, and observe it within your mind's eye, you can influence world events and even strike out at others from a distance. Therefore, I display a crystal skull on my altar to Lord Set, as both a reminder and an aspiration. My intellect is my prize possession. Cool, calm reflection of events is always necessary. Otherwise, the gift of anger, which is a blessing bestowed upon us by Set, is wasted in meaningless violence."

"If I need only to practice the dark magic, why did you encourage me to take a spiritual companion?" the young man asked.

Isidor studied Chanax's face. The young man was intelligent, that was obvious. But he was also broken and untamed. Philopater's orgiastic habits had harmed Chanax—both physically and spiritually—and Isidor needed to help him.

"There was a time I thought I no longer needed the Anit-Shadya of Isis," Isidor admitted. "But years later, it became evident that while man's intelligence needs anger to enhance clarity, his Ka still needs bliss. I discovered that my work with dark magic is amplified when my Ka is radiant and alive. Of all the alchemical streams in the planet, ecstasy is the most powerful and the most efficient. Which is why I returned to Neferu-ankh-maat, even after her affair with Hecataeus."

Chanax nodded.

"Now," Isidor said, "let's begin with the breath."

They both closed their eyes and placed their hands on their laps.

"Lord Set, almighty harbinger of chaos, we come to learn and travel, seeking the wisdom needed to use the anger of our people to free our nation and remove the infidels from our lands," Isidor said. "We give thanks for your blessing of this anger and promise as your servants to use it with respect."

Isidor took a deep breath, and as he exhaled, he expanded his Ka body. He noted that Chanax did the same. After moments of silent breathing, their life force filled the room.

The two of them blended, and each one investigated the other's emotional state. As usual, Chanax was blocked. His energetic wall needed to be broken, a task that Isidor feared might prove to be difficult.

"Chanax," Isidor called out, raising his voice for effect, "whom do you hate?"

"The pharaoh," he hissed in a low, animal-like sound.

"We shall not touch him today," Isidor said. "Someone else?

"Ankhmakis," Chanax said, his voice unsteady.

"Yes, your brother," Isidor agreed. "We can work with that today. See him, Chanax, see him in your mind's eye."

The image of Ankhmakis kissing Natasa flooded Isidor's inner vision. This is what Chanax was holding on to. Silly to want such a woman, but perhaps it would be helpful.

"Your Ka is the energy that surrounds you," Isidor said, now using a gentle tone. "It renews your body and makes it grow. And it connects you to the life force of the Earth. Your emotions ride along this streaming power, like smoke on the wind. See your anger in your mind's eye. Visualize what you want to happen to Ankhmakis, and send it out along your Ka to your brother. We are all connected in this web of life."

Isidor sensed Chanax's anger and jealousy building and beamed with pride. How wonderful to have a new source of anger other than the pharaoh within his student. In truth, killing the pharaoh was the ultimate purpose of their work, but practice was needed. Ankhmakis would make a fine object for their training.

Chanax's hate filled the room, and Isidor watched him send it out to the image of his brother. The dark gray swirls crawled toward the kissing couple, inching ever closer like worms seeking to devour.

As the tendrils of Chanax's darkness whisked toward Ankhmakis, a golden light, more intense than anything Isidor had ever experienced, pulsed out toward them. It hit the room with such a force both men were knocked to the ground.

"*You cannot touch them,*" a voice whispered within Isidor's mind. It wasn't Set, nor was it Isis. This was someone else, protecting the couple from their dark magic.

Isidor opened his eyes and looked at Chanax, who was beginning to panic.

"Isidor," the prince cried. "What happened? What was that golden light? That's never happened before."

Isidor stood from the floor and dusted himself off. He grabbed Chanax and dragged him to stand.

"We've never attempted to infiltrate your brother's energy field before," Isidor noted. "It's possible to protect yourself from dark magic. Such techniques shall be shown to you soon, but how would Ankhmakis know of them?" he murmured, more to himself than Chanax.

Chanax wrapped his arms around himself, trembling. "Do you think he knows what we did?"

"It is not likely for a man such as him." Isidor pressed his lips together. "But we cannot be certain."

The high priest of Set walked to his table and poured them each a glass of wine. He handed it to Chanax. "Drink this, it will ground you."

Chanax accepted the offer without question.

"I do believe," Isidor said after a moment, "that your brother is inaccessible to us at this point in time. We can't take him down with our skill."

"What?" Chanax exclaimed.

"It matters not," Isidor chided. "Ankhmakis is not our target right now. The pharaoh is, as well as the anger of the people. We must be able to arrange for his death and stir the hearts of men, including your father, to begin the battle. This is what we're working toward. We'll need a different object of disdain to practice with."

"If not Ankhmakis or Natasa, who?" Chanax asked.

"What do you want above all else in the world? Envy works as well as anger," Isidor suggested. He looked at the young man's face and raised a hand. "Don't say Natasa. She's beneath you."

"I want to be king," Chanax said, rising taller in his seat.

Isidor raised an eyebrow. "As the third son, that is quite ambitious. It remains to be seen which one of you shall succeed your father. However, putting the competition at a disadvantage at this point in the game might help you." He twisted his lips into a smile.

"We've already discovered that I can't touch Ankhmakis," Chanax said, brow wrinkling in frustration.

"But we can attack Silus," Isidor suggested. "I'm not impressed by him. He must have a weakness we can encourage or expose. Death and harm aren't the only things dark magic can be used for. Manipulation is easier."

Chanax shrugged. "I don't hate Silus, but he's a buffoon. He's spoiled, drinks in excess, and is insecure. Did you know he demanded to marry our eldest sister? He's upset with how powerful Ankhmakis has become since taking a spiritual companion, and he demanded that he marry Ruia as soon as Father will allow."

"Yes, I heard," Isidor replied. "The wedding is this month, isn't it?"

"Yes," Chanax said. "He's the eldest, and if he has a son, he'll secure the throne. That's why he's marrying her."

"Thus, securing his place as pharaoh, if your father is

successful in his mission." Isidor paused, contemplating. "That wouldn't be good. I think we have a target, Chanax. Your homework until we meet again is to observe Silus. Watch him and tell me his weaknesses, his habits, and his desires. I want to know everything. We can devise a way to develop our skill while also altering the course of history."

"Yes, sir," Chanax said.

"Wonderful. You're dismissed."

"Thank you, Lord Isidor," Chanax said with a bow. As he made to leave, he turned and asked, "Isidor, may I grow my hair back? I hate being bald."

"Baldness is a sign of mental clarity," Isidor answered. "So, no, you may not."

"Yes, sir," Chanax replied, lowering his gaze to the floor and bowing again before leaving the room.

Isidor reclined on his settee and exhaled, his dark thoughts returning to Ankhmakis and Natasa. "How in the world are you two protected?" he whispered to the empty room. "I must discover a way to breach it before others learn how to do the same. It would do us no good if the people can protect themselves from my work."

18

The Tunnel of Illumination

"The Egyptians were also the first to assign each month and each day to a particular deity, and to foretell by the date of a man's birth his character, his fortunes, and the day of his death. The Egyptians, too, have made more use of omens and prognostics than any other nation; they keep written records of the observed results of any unusual phenomenon so that they come to expect a similar consequence to follow a similar occurrence in the future. The art of divination is not attributed to them by any man, but only to certain gods."
~ Herodotus, Greek Father of History, 450 BCE

Giza, Egypt, 206 BCE

"Are you ready?" High Priestess Neferu-ankh-maat asked.

Natasa trembled under her white ceremonial shift. She'd been given three months to prepare for this next stage of initiation—the last step to full membership in the temple of Isis. Neferu-ankh-maat had done her best to train her in the art of mastering fear, the most important technique for this phase. Many had attempted the initiation under the Great

Pyramid, and many had died. It was all part of the process. Natasa was determined she would survive it and keep her promise to return to Ankhmakis. He needed her, and she could not fail him now. Even with the great distance between Giza and Behdet, she felt his fear for her deep within her heart, so strong was their connection.

"Yes, Mother," she answered.

"We shall begin."

The high priestess raised her arms, and several other priests and priestesses stood at attention. They were in a room without angles, deep within the Great Pyramid, more like a cave than a chamber, and no one, not even the wisest of elders, knew who had built it. For the Room of Initiation was older than the pyramid itself. A stone well stood in the center. As the chantresses sang, Natasa stood taller. She walked toward it, focusing her consciousness on each step. When she arrived, she yanked on a rope until a copper pitcher filled with crisp, cool water appeared. She held the container before her breast and bowed to the high priestess.

"My mother, I come seeking purification and initiation into the alchemies of Horus and the temple of Isis."

"Are you willing to enter the tunnel?" Neferu-ankh-maat asked her.

"In the name of Isis, I ask permission to connect to the womb of the Earth."

Neferu-ankh-maat raised her arms above her head and chanted a blessing in a language from the beginning of time. Natasa felt chills run along the surface of her skin. A breeze stirred in the torch lit room. The tunnel shone brightly as the mid-day sun for a moment before darkness fell once again.

"You have been granted permission. Go and see your true self and hear your true song. Return to us only if you have passed the test."

Natasa bowed to the high priestess and rose to take a drink from the pitcher. The water was cool and cleansing to her senses. Her vision grew clearer, and she could see the energy patterns in the room—both the frequencies that surrounded each person and the light that danced between the torch flames. She placed the pitcher on the stones surrounding the well and continued toward the tunnel. As she approached, two temple acolytes held torches into the narrow tunnel for her to see. She would have to crawl on her belly.

She got down on her hands and knees, and dropping to her stomach, she crawled like a snake away from the room and toward the end of the tunnel, to the zero point of creation. The soft floor was made of ground silica sand. The walls and ceiling were covered with quartz stones that shone like diamonds in the firelight. She trembled in awe at their beauty.

The acolytes blew out their torches, and she was surrounded by darkness. She continued crawling at a snail's pace, onward toward her destination—the end of the tunnel. In their instruction, the elders had told her the tunnel was eighty feet long. Her breath echoed off the dirt walls in the silence. As she progressed, she felt the weight of the Great Pyramid above her. Her heart beat faster, and it felt like she was being buried alive. Yet, she couldn't turn back. There was no way but forward.

Finally, after what seemed like ages, her head collided with an earthen barrier. She'd found the end. This part of the tunnel was roomier, and she was able to sit up and put her back on the wall before her. Her head grazed the ceiling. She folded her legs under her and focused her breath. It didn't calm her. She couldn't concentrate. The weight of the mountainous pyramid above her head suffocated her. What if she died? What if the tunnel caved in? As if in response, bits of earth fell from the ceiling onto her face. She clutched her throat and gasped for air.

She opened her eyes to utter blackness. The darkest place on Earth. She put a hand on her nose and couldn't see it. The walls around her vibrated and hummed. Were they getting smaller? She wanted to scream but couldn't find her voice.

"*My child,*" said a familiar voice in her head, "*it is time to sing the words I taught you.*"

"Mother?" she whispered.

"*You don't need to speak, sing the ancient song. It is the way through.*"

Natasa nodded in the dark. She breathed the life of the Earth into her abdomen. She breathed out through the central energy channel of her body, the center of her Ka.

Breathe. In and out. In and out. Breathe.

The panic subsided, and she sang the "Song of Light," taught to her by her mother months prior. She sang in the ancient language—understanding everything, and yet nothing as well. Over and over she repeated the words, and her voice echoed in the chamber as if there were a choir of singers joining her, all singing in the same key. The air felt heavy. She continued to sing despite its oppression. The sound of enormous wings flapping filled the tunnel as if she were surrounded by a flock of golden eagles taking flight. Her body froze. The sound increased in her ears. She could no longer open her mouth as her consciousness, her Ba, was ripped from her body and tossed into the astral plane of humanity—the place of emotions, desires, action, and destiny.

Time had no meaning. The darkness gripped her. Her Ba flew into the silence. She was in an unknown land, filled with trees and rain—a place unlike her own country; she knew she was no longer anywhere near her body. Her Ba had left Egypt and was now traveling the globe. This land was beautiful, but in the blink of an eye, fire consumed it. The fire continued, across an entire continent. Her body was lost to her. In her terror, she'd forgotten to lay a trail to follow back. Her training had been for nothing.

She was alone in the cosmos. She might never make it back to her body.

Natasa felt a tug and found herself over an unusual sight: a city with buildings hundreds of stories high. The form of death surrounded it, permeated every particle. A metal object, like a bird, flew in the sky overhead. In it, the form of malice rose, and she felt the deep cold of great evil. An object fell from the metal bird and plummeted toward the city. Natasa followed it and sensed danger. The object connected with the ground, and unimaginable fire and heat spread in all directions. It burned the people. She found herself in each of those people as they died. Their fear and surprise at death weighed her down. She couldn't move. A dome-shaped cloud with a long bottom, almost like a tree of life, rose from the ashes. The buildings fell on top of her, reduced to nothing in mere moments.

She floated away from the Earth. As she ascended, evil pulsed around the planet, trying to force its way into each bit of light and life. She drifted like a feather upon the wind and the form of panic took hold of her. It swirled around her, cutting her off from her own Ka, the life force of her physical being. She was going to die if she didn't get back to her body. She couldn't abandon Ankhmakis. The world burned below her, and yet knew she needed to return. What had her mother taught her? How did the initiate return to her body? Apathy took hold in her soul, and she no longer felt like trying.

No. She couldn't die here, separated from her body—

separated from Ankhmakis, her true love, lost in the cosmos and adrift in time. Natasa scanned her mind. Her mother flashed before her.

"The cord," the high priestess advised. *"Remember the cord."*

She searched for the shimmering cord that attached her Ba to her body. After what seemed like an eternity, she found it, a light golden beam that began at her heart space and spiraled out into the distance. She followed the spiral, up and over the dark forms around her. She still felt the pain and hunger of humanity, but now she had hope as she rode the spiral closer and closer to the Earth. Down, down, down, and around she followed. The Great Pyramid shone below her, and with great relief, she sensed her physical self.

The next moment, she could see her body lying prone in the tunnel, now illuminated by flames. Had they set her on fire? Panic rose within her. They were going to burn her to death. She followed the golden spiral right into the head of her body and felt her skin—burning in pain from the fire. She struggled to sit up but couldn't. Her body was paralyzed, held back by a force greater than herself.

She'd made it back, only to burn to death.

"What will be, will be," her mother's voice said again. *"Focus on the light that is you. The eternal flame."*

Natasa took another deep breath, and relaxed. Within the fire glowed her Ka, the energy body that encircled her and connected her immortal Ba to her physical self, stretching fifty feet in diameter. She spun the geometric form with her mind, and the flames turned to golden light. The crystals on the walls and ceilings sparkled, almost blinding her.

"Behold the beauty of humanity," her mother sighed. *"The divine essence of mankind."*

Her Ba sparkled and glowed in the tunnel, and she experienced what she'd been taught—her immortal, true self. The energy of life pulsed through the tunnel, and she knew it as her own. Truly, her body was nothing compared to the vastness of her Ba, her light body, and her spirit. She, Natasa, was a perfect stream of energy, pulsing throughout eternity like the rays of Ra, her eternal father.

"Yes," Natasa said, her heart about to burst with gratitude. The light was her true self, and it was exquisite. "I am pure and perfect energy. The body is a temporary vehicle. A mask we wear to experience matter."

"*Good,*" her mother replied. "*You may continue.*"

The tunnel disappeared and Natasa found herself transported yet again to another place. However, this time the forms of evil were not present. Instead, Natasa was now standing in a chamber with beings that sat in a circle around a copper bowl, chanting in low voices. They weren't human in form, yet they spoke to her mind. She allowed them to penetrate her consciousness, sharing with her their wisdom and power, until a female child appeared in their midst. Natasa felt her heart grow at the sight of such a perfect being.

"*Hello, Mother,*" the child said.

"*Daughter?*" Natasa asked, not sure what to make of the spirit's words.

"*I approach you,*" the child continued, "*and I desire to live among you.*"

Natasa dropped to her knees and placed her hands on her cheeks in wonder. "*My child? You are my child? But you're so glorious, how can I be your mother?*"

"*Why do you say such things, Mother? After everything you have learned, how can you doubt the love of the goddess?*"

Natasa trembled. "*Forgive me, but I'm still young.*"

"*No,*" the child answered. "*You are ready. Tell Father I desire to incarnate.*"

Natasa's heart burst at the idea of creating a child with her beloved. "*Yes, I will. There is nothing I desire more than to carry Ankhmakis's child.*"

"*And there is nothing I desire more than to become your family,*" the girl said in her musical voice. "*Go now and tell my father my time has come. You have passed the test.*"

The child laughed, and Natasa felt her body tingle. Her vision blurred and darkened. She was no longer in the hall with the beings of light. Instead, she was in the tunnel, and she was surrounded by the now familiar pitch black. A wave of profound joy washed over her, and she cried. War might be on their doorstep, but her daughter was on her way. Knowing her initiation was over, she began the long crawl back out toward those who awaited her.

19

The Invitation

"And the flock of the foreign countries will drink at the river of Egypt. They will cool themselves on her banks, lacking anything to make them fearful. This land will go to and fro; the consequence is unknown, and what will happen is hidden."

~ The Words of Neferti, poem from the Twelfth Dynasty, 1991—1802 BCE

Behdet, Egypt 206 BCE

Ankhmakis parried the sword's thrust and spun around the backside of his competitor, nicking the man in the back. Crying out, the soldier shoved Ankhmakis to the ground. As quick as an adder, the prince got to his feet and charged forward, striking the man with a series of lightning-swift moves. The sound of his sword as it clanked against the soldier's shield echoed through the training center. Ankhmakis could feel the interested stares of those observing the exercise from the sidelines.

"Faster," he cried to the soldier. "Lift up your shield and advance toward me. You need to find a way to break through my defenses."

The man was tired, but it didn't matter. He was a soldier, and he needed to be trained.

King Hugronaphor had built an impressive military center with the pharaoh's coin, but since the Battle of Raphia ten years prior, Philopater had reduced the number of men Hugronaphor could accept at the facility. It made sense; Hugronaphor's military outpost was supposed to train enough Egyptian men to keep the southern border safe. But this made arming the rest of the men loyal to Egypt's rebellion, without raising the suspicion of the Greeks, rather difficult and agonizing in its pace, irritating Ankhmakis to no end. He itched to launch the civil war and set out with his men to take back their land.

To create a larger army, Hugronaphor had begun hosting small groups of men from each of the cities in his alliance, no greater than one hundred at a time, in the city of Behdet. Once they completed their training, they returned to their homes along the Nile and trained the other men in their villages with the weapons Hugronaphor smuggled to them via his various ships. These men were listed as his "guests" in the official records Hecataeus sent on to the pharaoh, but they spent their time in Behdet endlessly training with Hugronaphor's experts in weapons, wrestling, fitness, and military strategy.

Ankhmakis was considered one of Hugronaphor's best warriors. After working with hundreds of men from Abdju to Aswan, he'd already become a legend. His intense physical fitness, combined with the accuracy of his bow, were often the talk of the young men during those precious moments of rest that were granted in the evenings at the end of a hard day's work.

"Strike at me," he commanded the soldier before him.

In response, the young man raised his sword but hesitated at the last minute, his eyes flicking away from his opponent. Ankhmakis's brow furrowed. Why didn't he strike? He took a stride closer to take advantage of the man's hesitation when he heard a voice in his head.

"Watch it, my love. Min has joined the fight."

Ankhmakis turned to find his best friend pouncing from behind. He swept a kick at Min's knees, forcing him to the ground, and spun to do the same to his original competitor. Both men were panting with surprise at the strength and speed of the prince's takedown.

Breathing hard from the exercise, Ankhmakis turned to the stands, delighted to find Natasa sitting in a shady spot, her long dark hair blowing in the warm desert breeze. She held a lotus flower in her hand and waved. His entire body melted under her bright gaze, and his shoulders relaxed. He stepped over the men lying in the dust at his feet to approach her.

"That's not fair," Min cried. "She told you I was behind you, didn't she?"

Min rose from the ground and held out his hand to the visiting soldier to help him up.

"How is that possible?" the young man asked as he brushed the dust from his dark, sweaty body. His bare chest heaved with short, exhausted breaths. "She's on the other side of the arena."

"Oh, you think Ankhmakis is talented?" Min laughed. "It's Natasa who gives him the advantage. Aren't I right, my lord?"

Ankhmakis turned back to his friend and grinned. He enjoyed the power his connection with Natasa granted him in a fight. "Did you see her touch my sword? Was she in the ring with me?"

"You know she was," Min accused.

"I don't understand," the other man said.

"Astral travel," Min explained. "Somehow, Ankhmakis and his spiritual companion can communicate to one another without words."

The young man shrugged. "I wouldn't want a woman in my head."

Min smirked and shoved the soldier, his look of irritation replaced with a grin as he nodded up to Natasa in the stands. "You would if it was the Lady Natasa."

The man's eyes grew wider, and Ankhmakis knew what he was thinking.

"She is beautiful, isn't she?" Ankhmakis said as he shook the trainee's hand. "Good work there, by the way. Now, if you two will excuse me, I must see my lady."

"Ankhmakis," Min said, now wrinkling his forehead in concentration, "if there was a way you could get her to help you without being in the arena, it could be pretty helpful in the field."

"I never considered it," Ankhmakis answered. "I'm not sure how far apart our astral communication will work. It's an interesting idea though. I'll take it up with her. In the meantime, both of you need to work on the element of surprise. You never know what advantage your opponent will have. Be prepared for anything."

Ankhmakis smiled at the two, and made his way to Natasa's side, springing up the amphitheater like a gazelle. She'd been away for weeks, traveling to Giza for her final initiation into the temple of Isis. He was grateful she'd returned home—not everyone passed the test of the Tunnel of Illumination. Yet here she was, alive and radiating power in a whole new way. She rose from her place as he kissed her sweet lips. He felt his passion begin to rise before she withdrew from his embrace and held the lotus flower between them.

"What is this?" he asked.

"For you," she said. He took the flower from her hands. A hint of a glow, as if Ra himself shone from within her breast, surrounded her as she stroked his sweaty hair. "You're always dirty."

"This *is* a military training ring."

"No matter, I know how to clean you up," she said.

"I'll be taking my mid-day break soon," he replied, snuggling closer, but she put her hands up to keep him at bay.

"My lord, I come here today to make a request."

"A request? Right now?" Ankhmakis could think of several pleasurable requests he'd love to fulfill, but he could tell something other than Shadya was on her mind.

"Yes," she said. "I have something to share with you regarding my initiation in the Tunnel of Illumination."

She paused, as if unsure of her next words. He glanced at the lotus flower in his hands, and then to her eager face. "Natasa, what is it?"

"I have something to ask of you, and it's important. Can we go somewhere private?"

"Of course," he answered, leading her out of the noisy arena to the arsenal. They passed men cleaning and storing shining swords and heavy, metal shields. In a corner table, several young boys were carving wooden shafts to be used for arrows. The artisans who made the bows worked in a small courtyard, surrounded by various pieces of select wood imported from the Syrian Peninsula. Ankhmakis led Natasa through the larger room to an office in the back. When he entered, Ikui, the weapons trainer, was at a desk, making inventory notes.

"Ikui," Ankhmakis said, "do you mind leaving for a

moment? Natasa and I need privacy."

The older man gave him a knowing look, and Ankhmakis almost blushed. He recalled those first months after bonding with Natasa—more than once his sword master had discovered the pair in various states of sexual bliss in his military compound. Since their training with the high priestess, they'd learned to behave and now refrained from impromptu sexual activities, keeping their passion to his chambers, or the ceremony room in the temple. It hadn't been easy; he still constantly craved her touch. To be near Natasa was to want her.

"Of course, my lord," Ikui said. Natasa was so preoccupied she didn't even notice the wink the old man gave them as he shut the door.

As soon as they were alone, Natasa turned and spoke. "Ankhmakis, will you make a baby with me?"

He froze, stunned by her request. To be honest, he was terrified.

"A baby?" he stuttered, his hesitation plain upon his face. "I must admit I've been wondering why you haven't conceived yet."

"A priestess is taught when she is young how to control her fertility," she admitted. "I conceive only when I want to."

"Oh, I didn't know that," he said, still unable to wrap his head around her desire to have a child. A baby between them made sense; their holy union required it. But now? Was he ready?

"My love," she continued, "I'm here because I want to have a child. Our daughter approaches, and she has asked me to receive her."

Ankhmakis continued to look at her with doubt. The idea of a child seemed sudden and was the last thing on his mind.

"Why do you need my permission?"

"Because your permission gives her power. When both parents want a child, the Ba of the child is freer to incarnate into the physical body. Your desire for her will also make our own energy bodies stronger, giving her greater benefits."

"Why are you sure of a daughter? Why not a son?"

"Because I'm the high priestess-in-waiting. A king needs a male heir, and I need a female successor. It is the way of things."

"You can determine the sex of your children, as well as when you are fertile?" he asked.

"No." She laughed. "I'm not that powerful. I met the spirit of our child in the Tunnel of Illumination. She told me the time had come to give birth. I know without a doubt the child wishes to be female."

"I see," he said as he took in her determined face. She looked more divine than ever. Her bright eyes shone with the wisdom of knowing her path. He envied her. He wished his own path was as certain.

Natasa put her arms around his shoulders, drawing him nearer. She kissed him, and her passion whirled around them. In response, he rubbed his body against hers and returned the kiss.

"Don't think too much," she whispered. "I want to have a child with you. That's all. Are you willing?"

He kissed her neck, and she moaned with delight. His love for her took his breath away.

"When do you become fertile?" he asked as his hands traveled down her back. He untied her shift, and it fell to the floor.

"Weeks from now, when Khons's silver ship is fullest," she answered, shoving him down on the document-covered table.

He swept the papers to the floor in a flutter as he fell onto the table and yanked his lover upon him.

"I guess we'd better get practicing," he said, lifting up his robes as Natasa guided him in between her legs. "I want to do it right."

She moaned as he thrust deep inside her. "Oh, you always do it right, Ankhmakis."

20

Philopater

By the time Ptolemy IV Philopater took the throne, Egypt had been an occupied nation for four centuries. First by the Persians for two centuries, and next by the Macedonians after the death of Alexander the Great. Under his father, Ptolemy III Euergetes, the country prospered, but Philopater's rule would come to be known as the beginning of the end of Egypt.

Alexandria, Egypt 206 BCE

Ptolemy IV Philopater, the pharaoh of upper and lower Egypt, was bored. Worse, he was sweating like a pig. He was grateful he wore almost nothing but a traditional white Greek tunic and his small, informal golden crown. Yet, despite the shade from the fig tree, and the three servant boys fanning him, his skin still beaded with perspiration. Flies buzzed around his head. The weather in Alexandria was quite warm, and he'd sought out the cool peace of the royal gardens. As if in response to the god-king's need, an ocean breeze from the harbor below rose to greet him, and he sighed with desire, glancing at the three boys assigned as his attendants.

The pharaoh had picked them out himself. They stood

around him, wearing nothing but white loinclothes around their waists—their dark, smooth, pre-pubescent chests glistening with sweat. He felt a flush of desire rush through him. He grabbed a cup of wine and sucked it down. Thank Zeus he was under a fig tree. This allowed him both the luxury of shade and delightful glances up the boys's loincloths when he made them climb the tree and get him something to eat.

"Your Majesty," he heard a voice cry behind him. Without hurry, he turned his middle-aged, swollen face toward the noise, and was unimpressed to see his sister, the High Queen Arsinoe, and their three-year-old son, Epiphanes. Behind them walked the royal nursemaid. He turned to the woman who sat to his side, Agathoclea, sister of his advisor Agathocles, and his lover for the past five years.

"What do you think she wants?" Agathoclea asked, her own gaze wandering to the Royal Guards who stood at attention as Queen Arsinoe arrived.

"Nothing important," he purred as he rested his bloated, bejeweled hand on her thigh, brushing up under her skirt to swipe a feel of her moist sex. Her bare breasts rose and fell with each short, excited breath she took.

"Philopater," his sister repeated as she arrived, "what are you doing here?"

"Resting," he answered, turning away from his lover and gesturing to one of the boys to pour him another cup of wine.

"But Sosibuis and Agathocles are waiting for you in the palace," she admonished.

"Why?" he answered.

"They have news from the south," she replied as she let go of Epiphanes hand.

The boy ambled away from his mother's side and chased a butterfly down the well-manicured garden path. The Royal

Garden was situated at the northwestern-most corner of the harbor—a short litter ride from the palace and the city. The gardens were the pharaoh's favorite place to hide away from the endless duties of the court. He sat upon his low, silken couch in a courtyard surrounded by fig, olive, and pomegranate trees with low hibiscus bushes that filled the lush gardens with their scents. Fountains bubbled in the four corners and water poured from the mouths of gilded statues of the gods and goddesses. Bees buzzed among the bright flowers. The sounds of the harbor and seagulls filled the air. How dare his sister destroy his special place with her incessant demands?

"What news?" he asked, eager to get rid of her.

"They have a witness who claims the steward of Apollonopolis Magna is training an army."

"Nonsense," the pharaoh replied. "Vizier Hecataeus has reported that they train only enough men to watch the southern border."

"I don't trust that man," she argued.

"Father trusted him, why shouldn't I?"

"You are not Father," she hissed. "Hecataeus isn't loyal to you."

"I rule the land, thus I also rule Vizier Hecataeus," the pharaoh replied. "He is as loyal to me as he was to Father."

"Haronnophris has sailed to Aswan with a contingency. Why would so many southern nobles meet together at once? I think you should take troops and sail to Apollonopolis Magna yourself," Queen Arsinoe suggested.

"Don't pretend to be pharaoh, my dear. It doesn't suit you," he said, finishing off yet another cup of wine. "You there," he said to the pretty boy standing closest. "Fetch me a handful of figs."

The boy climbed the tree, and Philopater looked up the

boy's skirt as he rose higher. The pharaoh slipped his hand between his own legs as he grew hard with desire. His sister slapped him hard across the face.

"What was that for?" he cried, rising from his place in anger. Agathoclea sat up at attention and glared at the queen.

"You're a pig," Arsinoe screamed.

"Quiet," he answered, holding up a hand. "Our finest philosophers encourage the bonding between men. Aristotle even encouraged Alexander the Great to enjoy men often, but women only for the purposes of breeding heirs. You're jealous."

"Stop," she said again.

"You wish you weren't my only sister, don't you? You wish you'd never been forced to marry me."

"What I wish is that you would stop violating the slave boys and pay attention to your advisors. You need to become a pharaoh worthy of this nation."

"You shall not speak to the lord of Egypt in such a manner," he called out.

"Philopater, you must do something about Haronnophris. Agathocles's source says he's meeting with the nobles of Aswan as we speak. I know it's to plan an uprising," the queen demanded yet again.

Pharaoh Philopater glared at his wife. He looked down at his lover, who wore a bemused look upon her face. "What do you think, Agathoclea? Should I listen to this wretched woman?"

"If my brother Agathocles thinks there is trouble in the south, you should attend to it, my lord," she answered, batting her eyelashes.

Philopater hated Arsinoe, but she was right, which was unfortunate, for he had no desire to visit Apollonopolis

Magna. The place was uncivilized compared to Alexandria. Besides, he didn't want to be anywhere near their High Priest Isidor, nor his assistant, Chanax. Desire pulsed through Philopater's body when he recalled the ways he'd dominated Haronnophris's son when he was younger, but the last time he'd seen Chanax, the young man had tried to kill him with nothing more than an evil gaze. Pharaoh might own the land, but the dark magic of Set scared him. Best to send someone else.

"Tell Agathocles to take six ships and sail to Apollonopolis Magna tomorrow at sunrise. Imagine Haronnophris's surprise to return from Aswan and find my men at his docks waiting for his arrival. I have other things to attend to here in Alexandria."

Queen Arsinoe frowned with disgust. "Like forcing yourself on our serving boys while your whore watches?" She turned to her son, who had captured the butterfly and was tearing it apart, leg by leg. "Epiphanes, come."

The prince threw down the insect, now in several pieces, and ran to his mother. Pharaoh sat back down on his blanket, and Agathoclea snuggled up beside him. He looked up at the slave boy still in the tree, holding on to a handful of figs and staring at his pharaoh with fear. Philopater liked that look. Others' fear excited him—made him feel alive.

"Remain where you are, boy," he said as he lay back in Agathoclea's arms, hand sliding up his own skirt once again, allowing himself a full view of the boy's naked underside. "Don't come down until I'm finished."

He poured himself another cup of wine and relaxed, enjoying the view.

21

A Change of Plans

Ramesses the Great lived to be ninety-six years old and had over two hundred wives and concubines. He was considered the greatest pharaoh of Egypt, and he reigned for so long that when he died, the majority of his subjects had been born knowing only him as their pharaoh. King Hugronaphor studied the monuments and steles in Ramesses the Great's honor and often dreamt he would be the next great pharaoh of his people—the one who would save Kemit from her ultimate demise.

The Nile River, Egypt 206 BCE

King Hugronaphor rapped his knuckles on the wooden desk in agitation as he contemplated the week's events in Aswan. His sons, Silus, Ankhmakis, and Chanax, as well as his general, Tsui, Vizier Hecataeus, and the High Priest Isidor stood before him. Through the portside window, a soft Nile breeze cooled the otherwise stuffy captain's quarters.

"This hasn't been easy," he said.

"No, Your Majesty, it hasn't," General Tsui agreed. "But it appears our hour is now close at hand."

"I think the trip was successful," Silus offered. "We now have several older Egyptian families on the side of the rebellion."

"And their priests," Ankhmakis pointed out. "Temple support is vital."

"I'm grateful Lord Setep accepted your invitation, Isidor," Hugronaphor noted. Setep was the most powerful of the Egyptian-born priests left in Thebes, and his loyalty was a great prize. Isidor's dark eyes glittered at the king's praise. "What did you get the man to promise us?"

"The Khepresh crown of Upper Egypt when you conquer Thebes," Isidor answered with a satisfied grin.

"The blue crown of Thebes?" Ankhmakis gasped. "But no one has worn that crown since Ramesses the Great."

"I know," Isidor agreed. "It has been in the Theban vaults since antiquity. The Ptolemys have never seen it. They prefer their crown of twelve golden spikes. It reminds them of Macedonia in addition to the Sun God, Ra. But a true Egyptian pharaoh shall wear the blue crown."

As the priest spoke, Hugronaphor found it hard to contain his excitement. "This is wonderful news," he said as he jumped from his seat and paced the room. The boat swayed in the downstream current that bore them home toward Behdet. "We have the loyalty of the priesthoods in Aswan, Elephantine, Behdet, Abdju, and now Thebes. That will be enough to launch the war. Thank you, Isidor, for your tireless efforts."

"It has taken a long time," Isidor answered, "and for that, I am sorry, Your Majesty. Priests by their nature are cautious. Yet our temple brothers long for pure Egyptian blood to sit upon the throne in Thebes."

"It's taken too long," Hugronaphor said, his excitement turning into frustration as he slumped back into his chair.

"Eleven years ago, I managed to gain an army and training center from the pharaoh. Yet still, I haven't launched the civil war."

"Soon, my lord," Isidor said, placing a long-fingered hand on Hugronaphor's shoulder to calm him. "We shall be rewarded for our persistence."

"Why has it taken so long, Father?" Silus asked. "The Battle of Raphia was ages ago."

"For that war, I was granted an army of five thousand men, and that was enough to help Pharaoh conquer the Seleucids," Hugronaphor explained. "We were successful, but my squadron wasn't capable of driving the Greeks from our country. I needed to build a larger army behind Philopater's back. You know that's the main mission of the training center in Behdet, and it has been delicate work. It has been difficult recruiting those loyal to our cause without raising suspicion from their Greek rulers. Here in the south, we may be free of the pharaoh's constant attention, but Greek viziers, mayors, and other officials run every city and town. Why, according to the pharaoh, Hecataeus runs Behdet, don't you Vizier?"

"Yes, Your Majesty, that is true," the big, handsome Greek agreed with a slight grin.

"I've had to convince the Egyptian nobles in each of the cities south of us that it's safe to join the rebellion, and then train and arm them, without their viziers reporting us. This has meant precarious negotiations, secret communications, and large sums of money for both weapons and bribes."

"I see," Silus replied.

"After a decade of effort, I have armed the native southern kingdoms, as well as procured the loyalty of the Egyptian houses from Hierakonpolis north of Behdet to Aswan in the south, and the priesthoods of a majority of the southern nomes. Our work has come together, and now we can launch the war. We need only to give the signal."

"And what signal is that, my lord?" Ankhmakis asked.

Ankhmakis was studying him with a hard look. The king looked to his son's hand, noting the golden ring bearing his phoenix signet. The men of Ankhmakis's company had begun painting the symbol on their shields, and it bothered Hugronaphor.

"That is the final task," Hugronaphor answered. "The priests in Thebes suggest we throw a festival in Behdet, one which our allies are invited to attend. We could honor Sopdet with a feast, or perhaps the re-enactment of Osiris's resurrection, like they do in Abdju."

"But wouldn't that raise suspicion in Alexandria?" Chanax asked. "If we've never held the festival before, why would we start? It's rare for a steward to do such a thing. Only the pharaoh can create festivals."

"He is correct," Isidor agreed. "We can't afford to draw that sort of attention."

Hugronaphor eyed Ankhmakis once again. The young man fidgeted under his father's appraising gaze. "I have an idea. I'm still working out the details."

He debated telling his plans to the group. They needed to know, but given Ankhmakis's extreme passion for his spiritual companion, he wasn't sure now was the time to tell the young man his new plan. Ankhmakis's love for Natasa was intense, and Hugronaphor thought it better to spring the news that the young man's wedding to his half-sister, Weret, was the festival Hugronaphor had in mind when there was no chance of turning back.

"I'm sure you do, my lord," Isidor said. "I look forward to serving you in whatever capacity you require. Remember, it must look like a celebration, and not draw Alexandria's eye."

"Yes, Isidor," Hugronaphor began, but he was interrupted as Min and Nefermaat entered the room in haste.

"Father," Nefermaat called. "We're approaching the docks, and it looks like trouble."

"What do you mean?" the king of Behdet asked.

"The harbor is filled with ships from Alexandria," Nefermaat panted, "bearing the pharaoh's flag."

"No." Hugronaphor jumped from his seat. "What are they doing in Behdet?"

"We don't know, my lord," Nefermaat continued. "They sent no runner ahead to greet us, but it appears a dozen of the pharaoh's soldiers stand guard at the dock, waiting for us."

Hugronaphor's heart sank. The pharaoh knew. Someone must have passed information to Alexandria regarding his meeting in Aswan. He'd known it was risky to have the Egyptian nobles gather in one place, yet how did the pharaoh's troops get here before he'd returned? There must be a weak link in his chain of command, and someone had given him up.

"Hurry," he said as the group of men left the captain's quarters. "Let's meet them without fear."

As he walked out to the prow of his ship, he took count and found six royal ships docked in his harbor. The flag of the Ptolemaic Empire flew high upon the tallest mast of each one. At the end of the longest dock stood twelve soldiers, armed and waiting for their return. As his ship sailed nearer, a litter, carried by his own servants, approached the dock from the palace. Had Pharaoh paid a visit himself? If so, it meant only one thing—his plans had been discovered, and his life was forfeit. If this was the case, it was best to get it over with.

"Rowers," he called out. "Make haste and get me to my dock."

Twenty men drew long, golden paddles across the languid Nile's surface, causing them to gain to speed. As his ship approached the docks, several men jumped ashore, holding long ropes. The Macedonian soldiers stood still and did not offer to help while the Egyptian men struggled to position the craft along the dock. Hugronaphor remained standing at the prow, Ankhmakis and Silus at his side. No one spoke. When the men secured the craft, and a ramp was lowered, the litter halted. Out stumbled Agathocles, along with two other men Hugronaphor didn't recognize. He let out a sigh of relief. Pharaoh had sent one of his favorites to see what he was up to. He hadn't come himself. That must mean he didn't feel threatened, and this surprise visit was an act of posturing.

Hugronaphor disembarked from his ship and walked, back straight and chin held high, to Agathocles. He and his sons bowed low to address the visitor. "My Lord Agathocles, favorite of the pharaoh," Hugronaphor said in Greek. "To what do I owe the pleasure of your company? You should have sent word ahead of your arrival—I would have been here to greet you."

Agathocles glared with disdain. "This is not a pleasure visit, Haronnophris."

"Then why have you traveled this far from Alexandria?" Hugronaphor asked. "We don't often see Macedonian nobles in these parts."

Agathocles looked around him, the disgust for Behdet obvious in the tight smile that he forced as he spoke. "Our Pharaoh, Lord Ptolemy IV Philopater, Ptah and God of this land, sent me."

"And why would he do that?" Hugronaphor asked.

"To deliver a message," Agathocles answered with a note of anger in his voice. "We see you, Steward, and we won't tolerate native uprisings."

"Uprisings?" Hugronaphor said, allowing a smile to grace his face. Someone *had* turned him in. "This isn't the Delta, my lord. We have no need for uprisings in the south. Please, feel free to search my armory and training center, as well as the palace. You will see we train only soldiers to watch your southern border, in addition to a small standing army for you to call upon to serve Egypt in military campaigns against the Seleucids."

"I already have investigated your holdings," Agathocles said. "I arrived three days ago, and my men have combed through the city."

"And what did you find?" Hugronaphor asked, staring the man in the eye as a challenge. He hoped Ennaeus and Ikui had kept their secret. He'd ordered them to hide excess weapons and documentation in the family tombs while he was gone.

Agathocles remained silent, but from the sneer twisting his lips, Hugronaphor knew his men had done their jobs.

"Nothing," the Greek spat. "All is in order, but I must know, what were you doing in Aswan, Haronnophris?"

"Visiting family," he answered. "We keep an estate in the south. I was also trading for Nubian wares, such as gold and wool. They have the finest sheep."

"I see," Agathocles said, still stern. "I will report my findings to our lord and pharaoh."

"I'm sure he'll be pleased to know I'm keeping my end of our promise," Hugronaphor said. "And next time His Majesty decides to check in on us, do have him come in person. It's been far too long since I last enjoyed his company."

Agathocles shook his head and wrapped a red silk around his shoulders as if he were cold. He raised his hands and the soldiers lined up behind him. "We will take our leave,

Haronnophris. Remember, we are watching you."

"Yes, my lord," Hugronaphor replied.

He watched in silence as Agathocles boarded one of the pharaoh's ships, and within moments, the Ptolemaic vessels left Behdet's harbor, sailing downriver toward Alexandria. Hugronaphor let out a sigh of relief.

"We were fortunate," Hecataeus said as he watched the fleet fade into the distance.

"We have a rat," Hugronaphor replied.

"Indeed," Hecataeus agreed, "and I think I know who."

"Really?" Hugronaphor asked.

"Yes," Hecataeus sighed, distraught. "I believe it is Kames, the young nephew of Ikui, our sword master."

"Kames?" Hugronaphor asked. "How can that be? Ikui is one of our most loyal men."

"Yes, but his nephew disappeared for several days before we left for Aswan. The roster reports his absence from several training exercises. I found it odd and made a note. It appears I will have to ask the young Kames where he was, and why the town rhapsodist has reported to me that Kames's wife now goes about village adorned with silks and gold."

"I see," Hugronaphor muttered. It pained him to hurt Ikui in this way, but if the young Kames had betrayed them, there was nothing else that could be done. "If this is true, do what you must to see that the informant's mouth is shut for good."

"Of course, my lord," Hecataeus answered.

Hugronaphor turned and looked to his entourage. "All except Isidor are excused."

His sons and the other men bowed before walking away, concern etched upon each of their faces. Ankhmakis, however, jogged toward the palace, eager to see Natasa, who was heavy with child. His love for the girl was something Hugronaphor himself had felt once in his life, for his second queen, Mafuane. He'd never recovered from her death and shuddered to think his son might ever know such a sorrow as his. Hugronaphor's throat tightened as he recalled Mafuane's sweet smile. Goddess, he missed her. Yes, he understood Ankhmakis's love for Natasa, and thus also understood his reluctance to marry Weret. Hugronaphor had never liked his youngest daughter because her birth was the cause of Mafuane's death. Weret was as difficult in life as she was in birth, always demanding more than her share, and more like the foolish Keket than his beautiful Mafuane.

But duty was duty, and Ankhmakis had to take Weret as his wife. As soon as everyone was out of earshot, Hugronaphor turned to Isidor and spoke, "We need to schedule the wedding date sooner than originally planned."

"Ankhmakis and Weret's wedding you mean?" Isidor asked.

"The wedding of my sons," Hugronaphor answered. "That will be our cover. Let us arrange it for six months from now after the season of Akhet and the waters of the Nile have receded. We will launch the war during the festivities. No one in Alexandria will find it odd for the southern nobles to gather for such an event."

"Sons, my lord?" Isidor asked.

"Chanax will also marry. Three sons with royal heirs will ensure the throne is secure. You know how the Egyptian people desire security above all else."

"But whom will my apprentice marry?"

"Bithiah."

Isidor took a step back and shook his head to object. "But you promised the high priestess—"

"I will do as I see fit. I do not fear the high priestess, and my word is final in these lands. Now, plan the double wedding for six months from this time, and I'll plan my attack. Our work must come together in perfect timing."

"And when will we tell your children of your plans, my lord?"

Hugronaphor considered the question. Tell them too soon, and both Ankhmakis and Nefermaat could turn on him. "I think it's best we tell them as close to the date as possible. After official invitations are sent to my allies. The invitation to this wedding is the signal they are waiting for."

"Yes, my lord," Isidor said with a slight bow of his head. "I shall see it done."

"Thank you. You're excused."

The red-robed priest turned and walked toward the temple. A litter arrived, and King Hugronaphor allowed himself to be lifted inside it. Ankhmakis would be petulant, he knew this. But Ankhmakis didn't concern him. With time, the middle prince would come to understand that he didn't have to love Weret; he just had to get her with child. Hugronaphor had survived his miserable marriage with Keket all these years, and his sacrifice had brought him three strong sons. Ankhmakis would do the same. Nefermaat was the son he feared, but he'd deal with the young man. Sacrifice was part of royal life, rebellion required it, and it was expected of his sons, Nefermaat included.

Yet as his litter approached the palace, Hugronaphor couldn't shake the feeling that the wrath of his daughter, Bithiah, might be the worst of all his children.

22

Claiming His Own

"Time abandons me when I'm in her arms, and my heart is always seeking her."

~ *"The Song of the Sunrise," written by Ankhwenefer, the last native Egyptian king*

Three Months Later, Behdet, Egypt 205 BCE

Ankhmakis ran to the apartment Natasa shared with Hecataeus and Corinna. Now that she would have a baby of her own, it made sense she returned to the place she lived as a child. Before her pregnancy, Natasa had preferred Ankhmakis's chambers to her simple dormitory room in the temple, but now that her pregnancy was advanced, she had moved back in with her father. Corinna could help her raise the child. Ankhmakis visited her every night before she fell asleep, playing his pandura and singing lullabies. In this way, he hoped to remain in her soul and dreams while she slept.

This evening was her last before moving into one of the birthing rooms until their daughter was born. Separation from everyone except the midwives allowed the mother to prepare for a successful birth. As he approached her small quarters situated between the Royal Gardens and the temple of Isis, Ankhmakis shivered in fear—this could be the last time he saw Natasa if something horribly wrong occurred during the birth. He remembered his father's second queen, Mafuane, and felt his stomach tighten at the thought of losing Natasa in the same manner. He couldn't lose Natasa, not now, not ever.

"Good evening, my love," Natasa said as he arrived. She was leaning on the doorframe, her hands resting on her belly, which seemed as big as a keg of ale.

"Good evening," he said as he took her face into his hands and kissed her, feeling the butterflies come to life in his stomach.

"You're early tonight," she noted as they walked into the apartment.

"Hello, Ankhmakis," a cheerful voice called out.

Natasa's younger sister, Eleni, skipped into the room and threw herself at Ankhmakis. He picked her up and swung her in a circle, and she giggled.

"When you laugh," he said, "it sounds like the temple bells."

"No," Eleni cried. "Temple bells mean seriousness. I sound like the flowers when the breeze plays around them."

He placed the girl, who was now seven, back on the floor, and rummaged through the bag he wore at his hip.

"I think I have something for you," he said, holding his fist above her head.

"For me?" She giggled, jumping up and down to try and open his clenched hand. "What is it?"

"You're going to spoil her," Corinna chastised as she entered the small, open room, moving aside baskets and herbs that hung from the ceiling.

"Not possible to spoil something that's already perfect,"

Ankhmakis replied with a smile.

"My, you are charming." Corinna shook a slim finger at him.

Ankhmakis opened his hand and held out a carved stone bumblebee. "Father's master stonemason made it. When I saw it, I thought of you," he said as he placed it in the girl's palm.

"Oh, thank you, Ankhmakis," Eleni gushed. She planted a wet kiss on his cheek.

"That's kind of you," Corinna admitted. "I can see why it reminded you of her. She's always buzzing around, aren't you little one?"

Corinna's mother had been Egyptian and her father a Greek soldier, yet for the most part, the middle-aged woman represented the dark southern race. Eleni, however, was paler and had green eyes like her older sister. Her hair was still dark, and her skin bronzed in the sun, but Hecataeus's Greek genes were strong in her—even stronger than they were in Natasa.

"We must go, busy bee, and visit Papa in his study," Corinna continued. "Time to leave the soon-to-be parents alone."

"But why do we have to leave them alone?" Eleni demanded.

"So that Ankhmakis might have time with Natasa before she goes to the birthing rooms tomorrow."

"Will the baby come tomorrow?"

"No. But soon, and Natasa must prepare."

Eleni didn't answer. Instead, she ran out the door with her bee, pretending it could fly.

"Goodnight," Corinna said to them. "I'll take you to Bastyre in the morning."

Natasa nodded. Ankhmakis's chest tightened. He wanted

to be the one to deliver her, but custom didn't allow men to participate. Instead, Corinna, Neferu-ankh-maat, and Bastyre would witness the birth. His heart raced at the injustice. What if she needed him? He felt his throat tighten as panic choked him, and Corinna placed a hand on his shoulder as she left.

"She's going to be fine."

"How can you be sure?" Ankhmakis asked.

"Because this is the child we've been waiting for," Corinna answered before following Eleni.

Natasa waddled to her bedroom where Ankhmakis helped her lie down and get comfortable.

"Does it hurt?" he asked.

"No," she said, shifting around, "but I never feel quite comfortable anymore. The baby is always moving, kicking, and jostling me. Sometimes my insides feel squished like there isn't room inside me."

Ankhmakis ripped off her tunic and reveled in her full, naked body. He kissed her face and massaged her shoulders and arms. She relaxed at his touch. He held her swollen breasts and felt desire sweep through his body. He kissed them and placed his hands on her belly. As if saying hello, a foot extended out on his hand, and he smiled.

"She knows I'm here," he whispered.

Natasa nodded. "She recognizes your voice."

He leaned in closer, and kissed the foot, causing it to withdraw, and then push out again. "Hello, my daughter, I can't wait to hold you."

He looked up at Natasa, beaming with pride, and felt her love surround him like a blessing. He swooned at her beauty. No woman in Egypt compared.

"I also have a gift for you," he said as he rummaged through his pouch. Sitting beside her on the bed, he took her left hand into his and slipped a golden ring with a big, blue stone upon her finger.

"A ring?" she asked as she gazed at the gift. "It's stunning."

"Made from the finest Nubian gold and lapis lazuli from the Caucus Indicus Mountains," he explained.

"What is the symbol?" she asked.

"My signet," he answered, "the Phoenix. My father gave me that symbol when I came of age. It's on my banner and shield, and my men wear it upon their shields. I wanted you to wear it because I love you, and I want everyone to know that you, and your child, are mine."

She started to cry, and he held her in his arms. "I'll never take it off," she sobbed into his chest.

"Good," he answered, also feeling the sting of tears. "Because I'll never stop loving you. Now, lie back and relax."

He propped pillows up behind her on the bed and massaged her. He spent time on each part of her body, feeling her warmth and soft skin. The baby might have changed her figure, but her touch was still familiar. As he massaged her foot and calf, she purred with delight.

"That feels wonderful, thank you."

"You carry the child, and I'll care for you," he answered.

She lounged in the candlelight, one arm resting above her head, her black hair spread out on her pillow. Ankhmakis smiled at the look of satisfaction on her face.

"I love you," he said again, and he lay down in the bed, snuggling up behind her back, his arms resting on her bulging belly.

"Sing me a song," she murmured as she yawned.

He rose from the bed and picked up his pandura, strumming a gentle tune, one he'd written years ago. As he sang, her eyes drooped shut, and before the last note, she was breathing as if asleep. He put down his instrument and arranged a linen blanket over her naked body.

"Ankhmakis," she sighed, "what is the name of that song?"

"'The Song of the Sunrise,'" he answered.

"Is that the song you were singing on the boat from Alexandria years ago?"

"Yes," he replied. "How did you know?"

"I watched you," she admitted.

"You spied on me?"

"I guess. I was young and smitten with you. I thought you were romantic."

"I wrote it for you," he said.

She peeked out from under her drowsy, drooping eyelids, and placed her ringed finger on her belly. Ankhmakis felt his heart burst with pride. She was now marked as his, no matter what happened within the court.

"For me?" she replied, fighting a yawn. "You were already in love with me?"

"I think, my dear," he answered, "I've always been in love with you. I didn't realize it until that trip to Alexandria."

Natasa smiled, and he rose to kiss her goodbye. As he stood, a new sort of terror overwhelmed him.

"Natasa," he said, "are you sure we're ready for this?"

"For what?"

"To be parents?"

She patted her belly. "Too late, we accepted her invitation long ago. You were there, remember?"

"Yes, but what if something goes wrong? Women die in childbirth, and I won't be there to protect you."

"You think you're better with babies than Bastyre?" she teased. "I'll be fine. Trust me."

"But I won't be there," he continued.

"Ankhmakis," Natasa cooed, "you will be there, remember? When I go into labor, I'll connect to you with my Ka. If you're able, you can join me in that plane, in the place where we are always one."

He nodded. They'd learned to excel at astral travel the past two years, connecting to each other via the mind whenever their duties separated them, which was often these days. Min had been correct; they could speak in this way across large distances. It not only gave him an advantage in training but also kept them connected. Natasa smiled, and her eyes fell shut as she succumbed to sleep.

"Good night, my love," he said as he kissed her forehead. "I'll miss you."

"I will see you on the other side, with our daughter in my arms," she murmured.

He left her and made his way back to the palace. His men were drinking and playing games in the kitchens, and he decided to join them, though he didn't have the heart for it. He plucked the strings on his pandura as the men's conversation and laughter buzzed around him, wanting the birth to be over and to have both Natasa and his child alive and in his arms.

23

As Above, So Below

It is written in the Temple at Luxor that, "The birth of divine man depends on the transformation of the universal mother." Midwives, the keepers of the cosmic threshold, know that every human participates in the alchemy of life unfolding, either in an awakened manner through the intentional expressing of one's higher nature, or unawakened, through the tumult and suffering of karmic experience. The freedom to choose one's path in life is what makes one human.

Behdet, Egypt 205 BCE

Two mornings later, Natasa awoke to faint contractions in her private birthing pavilion in the Houses of Healing. She regulated her breathing as her abdomen tightened. After the moment passed, she stretched her arms and legs and lingered in her small bed for a moment longer. In the corner stood a birthing stool next to a simple altar to Hathor and her two assistants, Bes and Taweret. The sight of the statues prompted Natasa to rise, struggling with her engorged belly as she shuffled to the altar. She brushed her fingers over the coarse fibers of the thick mat that served as a wall as she knelt before the statues. Upon each side of the pavilion hung one of these, which could be lowered for privacy. There were six birthing pavilions in total, and one other woman shared the complex with Natasa now—Ruia, the eldest princess, who had married Silus the previous year and was now expecting their first child. After finishing her prayers to Bes and Taweret, Natasa left the privacy of her room and found the princess in the garden, sitting by the fountain in the center, watching small songbirds drink the water as it sprayed from the Goddess Hathor's mouth.

"Good morning," Natasa said as she shuffled to join her. "How are you feeling today?"

"Full," the princess muttered, holding her belly. "Contractions have started."

Natasa sat, feeling as graceful as an elephant stuffed inside a royal litter, and shifted her own abdomen. "I can't get comfortable," Natasa complained.

Ruia laughed. "Don't I know it? I can't wait for this to be over."

"Pregnancy has its moments," Natasa agreed.

A set of three acolytes of Hathor arrived carrying trays with tea to aid the beginnings of labor, fish eggs, broth, and hearty bread covered in butter and honey. Natasa's stomach grumbled.

"Thank you," she said to the girls, each twelve years old, beginning their training as healers.

As they left, Ruia peered after them with a strange look on her face. "What a marvelous thing it must be to dedicate your life to birthing other people's children."

"What do you mean?" Natasa asked.

Ruia continued with a huge bite of bread in her mouth, too hungry to be polite. "You and I didn't get to choose our paths. I'm born of the king; thus, I'm to marry and produce heirs. You're born of the high priestess of Isis; thus, you train in Anit-Shadya and provide love to the royal men. But those who pledge to Hathor remain celibate, meaning they have no heirs. Every single one of them has chosen to take part in this role. They do it out of interest, not duty."

Natasa looked at Ruia and noted sadness in her face. "You give Silus love," she offered.

Soft tears rolled down Ruia's cheeks. "It's not me whom I cry for. I cry for my daughters if I should have one. I do love my family, and yes, it's comforting being Silus's wife. But we don't love each other, not in that way. True, he demanded to marry and requested me, but he's busy, and ever since I became pregnant, he's had nothing to do with me."

"You make it sound sad," Natasa answered. "Every girl wants to be a princess, don't they? You're the future queen of this kingdom, and maybe all of Egypt, if the rebellion is successful. Isn't that good?"

"Would you trade your position for mine?" Ruia asked. She shifted in pain as a contraction started.

"No," Natasa admitted. "I enjoy being a priestess."

"That's because you share Isis's love with the men of this court," Ruia replied. "The royal males have a spiritual companion for their heart and health. They take a wife for land, heirs, and titles. The royal women aren't given a spiritual companion, only a husband, and their duty is to provide heirs. We aren't given love for love's sake. Often, we don't even like each other. Look at Father and Queen Keket—they don't speak to one another. I fear he hasn't taught my brothers how to take care of those of us who will bear their heirs. He's no example of a loving husband. Father has the high priestess, and in her arms, he finds solace. Who loves the queen?"

"You have a point," Natasa admitted. "I'm sorry princesses aren't given spiritual companions. To be loved is one of the most divine things in the world."

"Do you know why we aren't?" Ruia asked, her expression hardening.

Natasa shook her head.

"Proof of ownership. If I made love to both Silus and a spiritual companion, the way he does with me and his spiritual companion, Kawit, and the concubines for that matter, who is the father of my children? If a prince can't prove his son is his, he has no claim to the throne when the king dies. Thus, I'm denied a lover due to ownership of the children."

She patted her belly and winced as she endured another contraction. When it passed, Ruia finished her tea and smiled. "I don't mean to hurt you with this—just to make you understand what you're up against."

"What do you mean?" Natasa asked.

"Do you know why my brother gave you his ring?"

"As a gift for carrying his child?" Natasa said, trying to say the right thing without hurting the princess's feelings. While her younger sisters, Bithiah and Weret, were hard to handle at times, Ruia had always been cheerful, loving, and kind.

"No," Ruia insisted. "He did it as a sign to Father."

"What?"

"Father wants him to marry Weret before the war begins," Ruia admitted, struggling through another contraction.

Natasa's heart jolted with a sudden ache. She'd known this would happen, but not so soon. Ankhmakis had planned to put off the event for as long as possible, hoping the war would keep his father's mind preoccupied. He didn't like Weret, but Bithiah had been promised to Nefermaat long ago, and that left the youngest sister for Ankhmakis. If he wanted to inherit the throne, he needed her and the heirs she would bear him.

"Ruia," Natasa said, wanting to change the subject, "I think we should call a priestess to get Bastyre. Your time has come."

Ruia nodded, but continued talking. "Silus said they had a huge argument. This is the first time Ankhmakis has ever questioned Father. He refused, and Father said he had no choice in the matter and arranged for them to go on a diplomatic tour, hoping Ankhmakis might calm down and see reason."

The princess looked at Natasa's hand and pointed. "He gave you his signet as his way of telling Father that you, and your child, are his. He's a smart one, Ankhmakis. The smartest of them all."

"You mean, by claiming me he doesn't have to marry Weret?" Natasa asked.

"Don't be foolish," Ruia reprimanded. "He can't be king unless he produces an heir with one of his sisters. If you love him, you'll encourage him to listen to Father, and do it. That is his only chance for stability. A civil war on the horizon, plus three brothers fighting for the throne—it's a hard situation for any man. But that ring is his way of saying his soul and his love are with you and lets both Weret and Father know that while he accepts his role, he has already chosen the bride of his heart, and your child together is his favorite."

Natasa's throat tightened. Could that be why Ankhmakis did it? She looked down at the ring, and the image of the Phoenix rising from the flames. Like his personal guard, she was marked as one of his own. However, there was more to it than possession.

"This isn't merely making a statement to the king," she said, jutting out her chin in defiance "This was to make it clear to me that he loves me, regardless of what he must do to maintain his honor with his father. He's sending me a sign, that I might never doubt him, even when he goes to his sister's bed to mate."

Ruia grimaced again. "I imagine you're right, but you should know it's not a regular thing. No other prince, not even Father, has claimed his spiritual companion in this way. It has upset Weret."

Natasa felt fear at the princess's warning. "Why are you telling me this?" she whispered.

"Because I like you. I always have, even if I do envy you. But Weret doesn't feel the same way, and I fear she can make things difficult. It's best for you to know."

"Thank you," Natasa replied. "Now, we need to get you to your room and summon the priestess of Hathor. The first heir desires to be born."

Ruia wore a weary look, and Natasa took her arm to help her stand. The two waddled toward the princess's pavilion, swaying from side-to-side, their huge, pregnant bellies touching one another's. Natasa felt her daughter lean against Ruia's baby, who shoved back in return.

"What a pair we are," Natasa said as she rubbed her belly and laughed. "We look like a double-headed hippopotamus like the Goddess Taweret."

"Oh, dear," Ruia answered in delight. "I do believe you're right."

Natasa escorted the princess to her bed, took a smooth hammer, and struck a large brass gong to draw their attendants. As she worked to make Ruia comfortable, two young girls appeared.

"Yes, my lady?" the taller one asked.

"Attend to the eldest princess," Natasa commanded. "Her

child is ready to be born."

"Yes, my lady," the acolyte replied. One ran to fetch Bastyre while the other made to ready Ruia's room. The girl lowered the mats on all four sides of the room for privacy and left Natasa standing in the garden alone.

Natasa returned to her own pavilion and lowered the mats to be alone. She lit several candles at the altar and knelt upon a silk pillow. In her hand, she held a figure of Bas, the gnome-like god of the household, and protector of women and children.

"Dear Bas," she prayed. "Protect Ruia in delivery. Usher her child into the world without issue or trouble."

The distant cries and moans of labor began in Ruia's room, and Natasa shut her eyes, breathing in and out and recalling the birthing meditation Bastyre had taught her. Breathing in the light of Ra and the blessing of Hathor, breathing out fear. She raised the serpent energy up along her spine and opened herself to the heavens. Within moments, she found herself outside of time, in the place of light, the All-One, where she could see that the unfolding of the universe was a dance of streams of light—each one a life, a pulse, a dream, a story— taking life in the material realm. Like lightning bugs on a humid summer evening, the entire cosmos pulsed with the light of spirit. Here lived the idea behind everything in the material world. The world behind the world. In this place, Natasa was free of the body, obligations, and rules.

In the place of the All-One, the only rule was love.

"*Daughter,*" she said, not with words, but as a burst of light and tone.

"*I am here,*" her child answered.

A spiral of light swirled around Natasa, and the sense of complete joy and acceptance filled her.

"*Are you ready to descend?*" Natasa asked.

"*Yes,*" the light replied. "*Are you ready to birth?*"

"*Indeed,*" Natasa answered. "*I open myself to you. You may use my body to enter into the stream of humanity.*"

"*Thank you,*" the being answered.

Natasa felt a surge of power course through her light body—Ankhmakis had joined them.

"*Beloved,*" he said to her heart.

When both focused their consciousness on their Ba and traveled out of their bodies at the same time, they entered this world—the world behind the world—with the same eyes and felt the music of the spheres with the same spiritual sense. Nothing separated them. Their power grew, and the child spiraled a bright yellow stream around them. Together, their spirits soared, interacting and dancing with the light that surrounded them. As three, they became one in spirit, and they expanded their field of awareness to the edges of the cosmos.

As above, so below.

Natasa held her consciousness in that state of bliss for what seemed like hours. When the moment arrived to enter her body, Natasa searched for Ankhmakis and felt his love. They'd spent hours in astral travel and now they could speak to one another even when their bodies were hundreds of miles apart.

"*It's time for me to prepare my body for birth,*" Natasa said.

"*I miss you,*" Ankhmakis answered.

"*Leave a connection to me in the back of your mind,*" she advised.

"*Soon I shall be a father.*"

"*Yes, and you will be the best father. I know it.*"

At their child's urging, the lovers let go, and Natasa followed the thread of life back to her body. She re-entered, allowing herself to feel her head, arms, legs, and feet. She was lying in bed, the figure of Bas still clutched in her hand. Light, linen covers had been placed over her. An attendant must have checked on her and moved her while she was journeying.

With Herculean effort, she rolled to her other side, and found Bastyre in her room, eyeing her.

"You're quite vulnerable when astral traveling like that, child," the midwife chastised.

"Ruia?" Natasa asked.

"Fine. Baby's fine. It's a boy. His name is Senui."

"Oh," Natasa answered.

"Yes," Bastyre continued. "Good for Silus. Eldest son has a son. That should quiet everyone down."

"Yes," Natasa agreed.

"Eat the food I've left at your side. Drink the tea. The plant will prepare your Ka for birth. Go to sleep. I imagine you'll be in full labor soon, and there's no stopping that when it starts," Bastyre advised as she rose from her place.

"How do you know?" Natasa asked.

"I also connected to the All-One," Bastyre admitted. "I sensed the three of you together. The unborn children speak to me in pictures as they prepare to descend. Yours has contacted me."

"I've heard you're a prophetess," Natasa said. "Can you see the future when you travel?"

Bastyre nodded. "Indeed. But like the Greek prophetess Cassandra, no one listens to me."

"Cassandra?"

"Yes, a princess of Troy. She predicted the city would be destroyed the moment her older brother Paris arrived with

Helen at the city gates."

"Helen was the most beautiful woman in the land. A goddess, I believe. Men are bound to act like fools around her."

"True. But burn a whole city? Of course, her father didn't listen to her warning. For her service, she was locked up. Burned to death in her cell when the Achaeans torched them."

"That's a terrible story, Bastyre," Natasa said, feeling wary.

"Yes, however, it's one worth remembering. Even when you know what's coming, what matters is what the royals decide to do with the information," she answered, a warning in her low voice. "Now, do try to sleep."

Bastyre left the pavilion, securing the mats behind her. Natasa sighed, squeezing her eyes shut as she breathed through her pain, and despite the regular contractions now racing across her abdomen, fell asleep. She dreamt of her child, and ten hours later, she woke to the most excruciating pain she'd ever known. She crawled out of bed, and fumbled toward the gong, striking it as best she could. Soon Bastyre was at her side.

She walked her room and the garden for what seemed like miles and squatted for hours as her mothers, Neferu-ankh-maat and Corinna, held her steady and Bastyre chanted and sang. As her child descended from the quiet warmth of the womb, Natasa's body was on fire and she screamed out a primal wail, bearing down on the birthing stool. A cry like a screeching kitten mewled out from between her bloody legs. Bastyre reached under Natasa's body as her child slid into the midwife's trained hands. Natasa shook as the woman held her baby up to inspect her. The newborn wailed, and Natasa cried with her. She felt the surge of power that was Ankhmakis in her heart and knew he was there.

"She's so red," Natasa exclaimed.

Bastyre handed the baby to Neferu-ankh-maat and took a carved knife from her hip. After pouring hot water and soap over it, she muttered a chant and cut the cord that had connected Natasa to her daughter for ten moons.

"You're not done," the midwife said. "Bear down again, child. We plant the afterbirth in the garden to grant new life to the entire kingdom."

Natasa bore down as her daughter cried. She was weak, and she almost fainted. The next moment, Corinna laid her on the bed, washing her face and legs with great care. Natasa, however, wanted nothing but her daughter.

"Give her to me," she demanded.

Neferu-ankh-maat approached the bed and placed a clean bundle of baby into her exhausted arms. The child stopped crying and looked up at Natasa. As the two of them gazed at each other, Natasa saw the entire universe unfold within her daughter's eyes. No longer a thought, the child was now real— the idea made manifest.

She's beautiful. She heard Ankhmakis speak in her heart. *Like her mother.*

The baby whimpered, and Natasa placed her to her breast, as Bastyre instructed. The baby suckled and relief coursed through Natasa's body.

"She has accepted you," Bastyre said. She bowed low to the baby. "Welcome, daughter of Isis, child of Natasa, and heir to the temple."

Neferu-ankh-maat also bowed. "Welcome, Granddaughter. Blessed Golden Child. Princess of Peace."

Golden Child? Natasa had heard that term before, but where? She gazed down at her baby, the infant's face was a blur through her tears. It was her turn to speak and give the child a name.

"Welcome, daughter," she said, her throat stinging from her screaming and crying. "You shall be known as Helena, for you are the most beautiful child in the kingdom."

Neferu-ankh-maat nodded and smiled, wiping her tears with the back of her hand. "Helena, it's good to finally meet you."

24

The Young Family

In ancient Egypt, women were kept in seclusion for two weeks after delivery because the process of birth opens a woman to the pure energy of the cosmos. The baby itself is a whirlwind of energy and power. The world of men is unclean, and women and newborns are vulnerable until their Ka has thickened and they are ready to be exposed to the drama of others.

Behdet, Egypt 205 BCE

Two weeks later, when Natasa and Helena completed their time in the birthing rooms, Corinna and Eleni escorted them home. Upon entering her apartment, Natasa let out a sigh of relief. No other room in the palace compound, other than Ankhmakis's chambers, granted her such peace. Even better was the sight of Ankhmakis sitting at the table with her father. Both men jumped up upon her arrival.

"This is my granddaughter?" Hecataeus asked with a playful grin on his face. "It seems I'm destined to have only females in my life."

"Isn't she tiny?" Eleni asked as she ran a chubby finger

along Helena's face. "Bigger than a kitten, but smaller than a loaf of Mama's bread."

Ankhmakis drew Natasa into his strong embrace and kissed her. As he did, her heart soared. The mere touch of his skin made her swoon. "This is my baby?" he asked as he drew away, gazing at the bundle in her arms.

"The one and only," she answered, holding Helena out toward him. "Would you like to hold her?"

He cuddled his daughter near his chest. Helena looked small in his strong, muscular arms. Every day Ankhmakis changed, becoming more of a warrior with each training exercise and challenge issued. A part of Natasa loved his fierce look, yet another part feared losing him to the war once it started. A shiver ran down her spine as he kissed Helena's forehead.

"She's quiet," he noted. "Everyone says babies are a great disturbance."

"She eats and sleeps, that's it," Natasa replied.

"Enjoy it while it lasts," Corinna advised.

"What do you mean?" Natasa asked. As if on cue, Helena cried.

Natasa took a seat in a chair near her bed to nurse her. Ankhmakis drew up a stool and sat beside her, fascinated by the action of feeding their child.

"Soon she'll cry, and you won't know what she needs," Corinna answered. "Until she can talk, crying will be her number one way of communication. Wait until she crawls. Not a moment's rest once that happens."

The sounds of the baby's suckling filled the air. Eleni played with her toys in the corner. Natasa gazed at Ankhmakis and smiled.

"It's good to see your handsome face again," she

murmured.

He leaned in close to kiss her, and she felt a flash of desire run through her groin and up her spine. To her immense disappointment, Bastyre had advised waiting another three weeks before making love.

"This is going to be difficult," Natasa said while he continued to kiss her.

"I know," he groaned.

Corinna cleared her throat. "She and the baby are to remain inside the apartment for another three weeks. You can visit as often as you want."

"I'll be here every free moment," Ankhmakis answered. "I can't go even a day without my family."

He smiled and once again, Natasa felt her entire being melt with desire. She couldn't wait to be in his bed again, spending her nights intoxicated with their bliss. In the meantime, there was a baby to get to know.

☥

For the next three weeks, Ankhmakis did come every day to visit, and as he held Helena and played with Eleni, Natasa fell even deeper in love with him. She couldn't help it. He completed her, and it seemed Helena completed them. Hecataeus and Corinna also doted upon the newest member of the family, and others visited, including her mother, Alexa, and Bastyre. The days passed in a blurry haze of nursing, kisses, moonrises, and sunlight. Those quiet moments of nesting were blissful.

The day that Bastyre released her, the first thing Natasa did was wrap Helena around her chest in a sturdy, papyrus blanket and, grabbing a basket filled with bread, figs, wine, and cheese, set out to find Ankhmakis. He was in the stables, brushing down his stunning white horse after the day's ride.

"Hello there, handsome," she said, her body trembling with need and want. It was time to reunite with her lover. "This stall brings back good memories."

He kissed her, careful not to crush the baby strapped to her chest.

"I'm going to have to get used to her being there, aren't I?" he asked as he patted the sleeping baby's head.

"For now," Natasa replied. "Before you know it, she'll be riding a horse of her own. What are you doing?"

"I've been riding Biriq," he explained. "I like to be the one to brush and tack him."

"Oh." Natasa patted Biriq's massive, thick neck. "Were you training?"

"No," he answered. "Sometimes I take him out into the desert as far as I can."

Natasa shook her head at the thought. "You do? But no one goes into the desert, except in banishment."

Ankhmakis laughed, that wicked look in his eye—a strange mixture of passion and resentment—and it stirred her soul. She felt her entire body yearn for him, and this time, she'd be able to act upon it.

"I ride to the west often," he bragged as he continued to brush the horse. "When I need to unwind. The endless desert feels alive and free. I'm insignificant in the vast sandscape, and no one can find me."

"Has someone made you angry?" she asked as she untied Helena from her chest and found a soft spot in the clean hay across from Biriq's stall. She looked up and down the barn, and found it empty of other people. They'd retreated in the heat of the day for their rest. She removed her tunic and let it drop to the ground.

"Planning the war isn't easy, and Father doesn't listen to me," he explained as he bent over to check Biriq's foot and clean it.

Natasa stood behind him, rubbing naked flesh up against his backside. He placed Biriq's foot back on the ground, stood, and turned around to face her.

"Let me take your anger," she murmured as her hot flesh molded against his chest, "I know what to do with it."

"My goddess," he groaned, "I've missed you."

He grabbed her and picked her up. As she wrapped her legs around him, he shoved her up against the stall, plunging himself inside her. She'd gone months without their bliss, and Natasa felt complete within his lustful embrace. The sex was hurried and rough, yet she hadn't felt this good in months. As he climaxed, he called out her name, and at that moment, she was free. Helena mewled like a kitten. Natasa giggled. Ankhmakis thrust himself deeper into her, as if unable to let her go.

"I think I might leave her with Corinna tonight," she said.

Ankhmakis let go of her, and she put on her tunic and rushed to the baby. "No," he replied as he adjusted his loincloth. "She can sleep with us in my chambers. We both need you right now."

Natasa sat and placed Helena to her breast, feeling her own passion simmer down for a moment.

"It looks like you made us lunch," Ankhmakis said, pointing to the basket at her feet. "I'll be finished with Biriq in a moment. Let's take a boat out."

She watched him work, placing the bridle, crop, brushes, and other tools in their proper place. She loved his muscular body, and the perfect dark skin of his bare back and chest, and longed to kiss every part of him. When he'd completed his tasks, he grabbed his sword and strapped it to his lean waist. Natasa gazed at her lover with pure adoration as Helena drew away from her breast and fell asleep. Ankhmakis held out a hand to Natasa to help her up. She readjusted Helena on her chest, and he grabbed the basket. They walked hand-in-hand to the docks in silence, instead enjoying the sexual energy that danced around them. Words were becoming meaningless in their relationship. Instead, she found that his gentle touch, soft smile, or even his wild eyes spoke volumes.

As the boat made its way down the shoreline, Natasa and Ankhmakis drank wine and fed each other figs. She rested in his lap while he played with her hair. They made love again, this time her riding on top of him as the sunlight warmed her chest, face, and back. She rocked her hips to the rhythm of the boat, her breasts inches from his mouth and allowed the bliss to circulate first in her groin, and snake up her spine, weaving its way up to her heart to access the ankh channel, bathing her in ecstasy and bliss. As she climaxed, Ankhmakis did as well, and the two raised the serpent energy and held their state of bliss in perfect union and balance. From this place, they peered into the other's soul.

"*I love you,*" he said without speaking.

"*And I you,*" she replied in silence.

They returned their attention to their sweaty bodies, and Natasa sighed with delight.

"What?" Ankhmakis asked.

"I'm quite relieved," she said.

"About what?"

"That I can still experience bliss with you," she replied.

"What? Why would that concern you?"

"I don't know," she said as she rolled off him and filled their goblets with wine. "A lot of changes occurred with the pregnancy and birth. It's been months since I've experienced bliss, and I was worried I might have forgotten."

Helena whimpered, and Ankhmakis jumped up to get her. He picked her up with great care, as if handling a delicate piece of pottery, and carried her back to their day bed. The baby was more alert these days, and her bluish eyes were wide open and gazing at the water as they sailed down the river.

"You'll never forget bliss in my arms," he said with a crooked grin as he tickled the baby's stomach.

Natasa sipped her wine while Ankhmakis played with his daughter. A smile crossed Helena's face, and Ankhmakis jumped back, almost knocking Natasa's goblet out of her hand.

"What is it?" Natasa asked.

"Helena," he explained. "I think she's smiling."

"Yes, she is smiling," Natasa replied. "Either you've made her happy, or she has gas."

Ankhmakis frowned. "It's not gas."

"I'm sure you're right," Natasa said as she leaned forward to kiss him. "You make both of us happy."

And they were happy—the happiest young family in the entire city. Natasa often pinched herself to make sure she wasn't dreaming as she spent her days caring for her beautiful baby girl, and her nights in Ankhmakis's bed, making love with wild abandon. Waking in his chambers each day and watching Ra's morning rays fall across his and Helena's sleeping faces gave Natasa a rush of delight she'd never known was possible. She vowed to store these blissful moments deep within her memory, for the number of soldiers in Behdet grew each day, and Natasa knew without a doubt that once the civil war began, things would never again be as sweet between her and Ankhmakis.

25

A Poisoned Mind

By the year 3150 BCE, Egypt was already an empire with an established language, art, religion, and culture. No one knows who founded it, nor how it evolved from simple river tribes to a great civilization. Much Pharaonic knowledge is lost. Yet for thousands and thousands of years, the people of Kemit, the Black Land, nourished their culture and kept it alive. Until that day when darkness spoiled it from within.

Two Months Later, Behdet, Egypt 205 BCE

Chanax plodded along the streets through the city of Behdet, his attention focused on Isidor's latest plans. The war was about to begin, and they needed to prepare within the temple. This required blood ceremony, to call in the god Set to their side as his father took to battle. He rounded a corner and found what he was looking for—an old tavern, filled with undignified people. Not the sort a prince would converse with, but the type that might be able to help a priest in need of children to sacrifice.

He recalled the boy on the altar at his initiation ceremony and felt sick. Was murder necessary? Yes, it was. Set demanded blood, and only young, Greek blood would do. Chanax took a deep breath and entered the dark tavern. He was met with the scent of dirty, unclean people, mixed with the aroma of roasted meat, and the sounds of men arguing, an out of tune lyre, and the thick accent of a Greek woman bargaining with a pair of men over the price of their meal. Chanax skirted past them and made his way to the back where an old man sat. He was small, dark, and hunched over the table, and when he gave Chanax a toothless smile, his insides turned.

"Ilias, I presume?" Chanax said as he took a seat.

The man nodded and cracked his knuckles upon the table. "You here for the boys?"

Chanax nodded. "How much?"

"Twenty drachmae each."

"Twenty drachmae?" Chanax feigned insult. The price was a bargain, but part of him wanted Ilias to become angry and storm out of the tavern. Chanax wanted to return empty-handed to Isidor without punishment.

"It's a fair price," the man slurred. His eyes were bloodshot, and Chanax could smell the sickly sweet smell of opium from his side of the table.

"Fine," he said. "I'll take two."

"Two? In my experience, royals like them in bunches."

He knew of what the man was inferring, and he felt his stomach roil. Royals did buy children to add to their concubine collection. Filthy people like Philopater. Chanax's blood surged as he recalled the pharaoh's vile touch. Shaking his head, he glared at Ilias. Chanax didn't need the children for sex—he needed them for sacrifice upon the altar.

"What makes you think I'm royal?" Chanax asked.

"The way you walk. No common man would carry himself that way."

"I need two, for now. We'll place an additional order in six months."

Ilias raised an eyebrow, perhaps assessing whether Chanax was serious. The scoundrel took a sip of ale from his mug and wiped his mouth with stained, unwashed hands. "Fine. I'll have them by the docks. Pick them up at sunrise."

"I'll send my men," Chanax said. He wanted nothing to do with the children. He was there only to make the purchase. Others in the temple would pick up the merchandise. He threw a bag of money at the man and waited while the merchant counted the coins.

Chanax rose from the table and shuffled back to the palace, shoulders slumped. The streets were filled with commoners singing, playing music, and dancing together, Greeks and Egyptians alike. Dark women sat on Greek soldier's laps, and Egyptian men danced with their wives while children of various races chased each other through the narrow alleyways, their laughter filling the air with the melodies of freedom. It was a normal evening for them; the people of Behdet loved to celebrate at the end of a long day of work. How many of them understood their children were a wanted item? That people like Ilias would steal them, and sell them to the highest bidder? In a world where all were fed and housed, why were children taken from their homes and forced to do the bidding of horrible men? Chanax shook his head—he knew the truth— evil was what governed such things. And he, Chanax, was becoming an evil man.

He'd tried to avoid it. He wanted to work within the temple of Set and remain the person he once was. But it was impossible. His only choice was to deny his feelings and build a wall around his heart. Otherwise, he'd go mad. In his nineteen years on Earth, he'd seen too many horrible things to remain open to love and happiness. Better to bury his hope, along with his conscience.

When Chanax arrived at the palace, he took the long way through the royal gardens to his chambers, where he knew Alexa was waiting. As he approached, he heard familiar voices.

"She's the most beautiful thing, isn't she?" a woman cooed.

"Not more beautiful than you," a male replied.

There was a silence and the rustle of bodies moving against one another before a baby cried out. Chanax hid behind a cypress tree and peeked around to see them. Ankhmakis kissed Natasa's neck while their baby, Helena, lay on a blanket chewing on a toy carved from a solid piece of wood. The two were beyond happy, their joy radiating on their faces like sunshine. The form of passion swirled around them, and Chanax allowed himself to feel it before envy took hold and pierced his heart.

This was the real reason he couldn't feel. Not only was his life one of torture and pain, but knowing Natasa had rejected him, for Ankhmakis no less, magnified his hurt, like oxygen to a flame. He hated his brother beyond comprehension. Chanax glanced at the delighted couple and watched Ankhmakis pick up his girl and kiss her on the forehead. The child giggled as she tugged at her father's long hair. He grimaced and Natasa laughed as she unwound her lover's locks with care from the pudgy, tiny hand.

Alexa was pregnant. Chanax would soon have a holy child of his own, but he felt no joy. Instead, there was a hollow feeling, as if his baby was yet another thing happening to him, but not by his own choice. Could he look at a child the way Ankhmakis looked at Helena? Chanax loved Alexa, in his own way, but something held him back. The wall he'd built to survive his duty as an offering in Memphis was too tall.

Perhaps not even Natasa could have saved him from this feeling of separation. Perhaps he was too broken.

"Chanax? I see you over there," Natasa called out.

He glided toward the happy family with a false smile on his face. Chanax was the master of shape-shifting; he knew how to become what people wanted.

"Natasa, Ankhmakis, you must excuse me. I didn't mean to disturb you."

"It's no problem, my friend," Natasa answered with a smile. "Come, sit and join us."

"No, thank you. I must be going."

"Come on, brother, I have extra wine and snacks here," Ankhmakis offered. "Don't tell me they work you harder in the temple than they do in the army. Every man needs time to enjoy life, don't you think?"

Chanax looked at his brother and raised an eyebrow. He thought of the children he'd bought and grinned, forcing his face to relax. He surrounded himself with a feeling of contentment. It was an act he was used to portraying.

"Why, brother, I've spent the day in prayer and meditation. I think my life is more relaxed than yours. Now if you'll excuse me, I have a priestess to attend to."

Natasa rose from the ground and took him into her arms.

"Alexa told me she was with child. A true holy child between priest and priestess. Congratulations, my dear friend."

He hugged her close and breathed in her scent: a mixture of musk, warm skin heated by the summer sun, and rosemary. To be in Natasa's embrace was to be in heaven. It took all his control to hide his desire from her. When she let him go, he breathed a sigh of relief.

"Yes, I hope we have a son. I would like a priest to train."

"I'm happy for you, Chanax." Natasa's face shone with a genuine look of joy.

Chanax's heart beat faster under her adoring gaze, and he glanced at his brother, who was preoccupied with his baby. He looked back to Natasa, grabbed her close, and planted a kiss on her lips. She jerked away, and he grinned at her response.

"All is good, isn't it, my dear?" he whispered and left her standing by her lover with a confused look upon her face.

Chanax knew his life was a series of falsities: acting like he loved Alexa, acting like he enjoyed his duties in the temple of Set, acting like he didn't still want Natasa. The only thing that interested him anymore was the power of emotions, and how he could manipulate others with them. As he turned the corner around a large hibiscus shrub, he looked behind him to see Natasa staring down the path where he stood, bewildered by his bold affection. The form of sadness surrounded her, and he tugged at it to lure her deeper into his Ka, hoping to trap her in his field.

But Natasa sensed his action and blocked him. Her look of confusion turned to one of realization, and he flinched. Someone in the court could see through his act.

And that wasn't a good thing.

26

A Wish Denied

"I shall show you the land in catastrophe, what should not happen, happening: arms of war will be taken up, and the land will live by uproar . . . I shall show you a son as a foe, a brother as an enemy, a man killing his own father."
~ The Words of Neferti, poem from the Twelfth Dynasty, 1991-1802 BCE

Behdet, Egypt 205 BCE

Nefermaat approached his childhood apartment filled with rage, storming into the living area and finding it empty. He'd been a fool to think his mother would be here—she'd never visited the place when he was a child, why would she now? As he turned to leave, he heard her laughter coming from the back garden.

"Oh, aren't you perfect?" she cooed.

He didn't think at this point he could be more furious, but hearing her doting voice added fuel to the fire burning within his gut.

Nefermaat strode through the apartment and out into the small garden where he found High Priestess Neferu-ankh-maat, his mother and namesake, tickling the stomach of the baby Helena. The child nudged her grandmother away with her pudgy hands and rolled onto her stomach. Neferu-ankh-maat lay beside the child in the dirt, looking ridiculous and inappropriate. She was the high priestess of Behdet for goddess's sake.

Sensing her son's arrival, Neferu-ankh-maat looked up from her supplicant position on the ground with a smile. "Nefermaat," she exclaimed, leaning back onto her knees. "What a wonderful surprise. Are you here to see your sister's baby? She's rolling over now and will be crawling as fast as a gecko soon, won't you, my darling?" She swept the baby into her arms and kissed the child's stomach, sending the infant into a fit of giggles.

"I've been looking for you everywhere," Nefermaat said, anger constricting his throat. "I never expected to find you playing in this garden, a place you avoided in my youth if I remember."

Neferu-ankh-maat stood from the ground, allowing the baby to roll around on the ground. "Your sister is taking Shadya with Ankhmakis, and Corinna had errands to run in town, so I offered to watch Helena. Family helps one another, Nefermaat."

"Making sure Ankhmakis finds time to bed your daughter is part of your family duties, is it?"

"Nefermaat," she asked, taking measured, hesitant steps toward him, "what has made you upset?"

He shook as the pain of her deception flooded his entire body. Why did it have to hurt? "When were you going to tell me?"

"Tell you what?" she asked, still oblivious to the cause of his grief.

"About the double wedding?"

"What in heaven's name are you talking about?" she replied.

"You promised me Bithiah," he spat.

"Yes, I did, and your father approved your request six years ago. Has she changed her mind?"

Nefermaat felt the urge to strike his mother and stepped back from her side for fear of hurting her in his moment of wild madness. "Changed her mind? Are you crazy? Ever since Helena and Senui were born, Bithiah has been begging me to marry. She wants to start her own family."

"Then I don't see the problem," Neferu-ankh-maat answered as she turned to Helena, making sure the baby didn't eat anything from the ground that would hurt her as she grabbed at the weeds, flowers, bugs, and dirt that surrounded her blanket.

"I asked Father that we perform the ceremony a month ago," he continued, his hands clenched so tightly, his fingernails were digging into his palms, "and he told me to wait because he was busy with launching the war, and complications had arisen. He said he'd get back to me."

Neferu-ankh-maat picked up Helena and placed her down on a well-manicured part of the garden. "Well?" she asked. The tone in his mother's voice led him to believe she knew nothing of the matter, and it made him even angrier.

"You don't know, do you?" he yelled, kicking a stone from the path.

Natasa and Ankhmakis arrived in the garden, holding hands and beaming up into one another's faces. They had eyes for no one else, and Nefermaat's heart ached with jealousy. Oh, how he longed to walk by Bithiah's side in that way. Why was the prince allowed to live in luxury, granted his every whim, while Nefermaat was denied his wishes again and again? Ankhmakis leaned forward to tuck Natasa's hair behind her ear and kissed her neck. She tipped her face to the sky in delight.

Neferu-ankh-maat smiled at the couple and said, "Welcome back," before turning to Nefermaat again. "Son, I don't know what you're talking about."

"Do you know?" Nefermaat spat at Ankhmakis, who now had his arms around Natasa.

"Know what?" his half-brother asked with a goofy smile as he drew away from his lover's neck. He wore his desire for Natasa without shame for the whole world to see. The man was unaware of what their father had in store.

"Given the blissed-out look on your face, I imagine not," Nefermaat replied with harsh disdain.

"Nefermaat," his mother cried. "Tell me what the issue is, right now."

"Bithiah is to marry Chanax," he yelled, and his voice echoed off the garden walls.

It was still and quiet until Helena whimpered. Natasa left Ankhmakis's arms and lifted her daughter from the ground. She sat to nurse the child; the garden became so silent they could hear the drones of the crickets in the trees, and the cries of the vultures sailing over the desert. For a moment, no one dared to speak.

"Nefermaat," his mother said, "I don't understand."

"Father got back to me today," he explained, again squeezing his hands into tight fists as he recalled the dreadful meeting. "He let me know he could no longer allow Bithiah to marry me. Instead, he needs all three of his princes wedded to his perfect, pure-blooded princesses, to appear strong and healthy for those he wishes to follow him into the war."

Ankhmakis stepped forward, raising his hands out to his sides. "You must have misunderstood him."

Nefermaat glared. "No, I didn't. He said that in times of war, it's possible you or Silus might die on the battlefield; thus, it makes sense for Chanax to also marry a princess and be ready to reign in case the worst happens."

"I see," Ankhmakis answered.

Neferu-ankh-maat stepped forward. "This is outrageous. He promised me. I will go to that fool of a man to make this right, son."

"Too late," Nefermaat hissed. "He's planned a double wedding to be held in two weeks's time." He glanced at Natasa's stricken face as the realization of what that meant hit her, and smiled, even though he felt nothing but malice for his spoiled sister. "Looks like Natasa understands me. Yes, dear sister, soon your sweet Ankhmakis will be married, along with Chanax, to their sisters. Every nobleman in the upper kingdom has been invited. It's both a show of Hugronaphor's power, for his three sons will ensure the throne is protected during the war, even if one or more of them dies, as well as a reason for them to gather and launch the first attack under the cover of a celebration to the eyes of those in the north."

"Two weeks?" Ankhmakis asked. "He hasn't said a thing to me."

"Yes," Nefermaat answered, relishing in his brother's discomfort. "Father told me Bithiah will go to Chanax in a double wedding extravaganza. That means soon you'll be sharing your bed with pretty, demanding Weret. You'll have two women to keep you company. Not the entire harem of concubines you used to plow through in your youth, but better than none."

"Shut your mouth," Ankhmakis snarled as he rushed

toward Nefermaat, raising an arm to strike him.

Nefermaat turned out of the way and laughed. "You're upset? You've always known you'd have to marry Weret, why do you care if you have to do it now?" He pointed to his sister and panted his rage like a gladiator in his final round. "You'll still spend your nights in the arms of the one you love, but not me. I've been waiting six long years to touch Bithiah, following the law and refraining from her, yearning to be the father of her children. Now that dream will never come true."

"Nefermaat, listen to me—" His mother made to embrace him, but he backed away in disgust.

"Don't try to console me, woman," he screamed. "You stole my inheritance from me long ago and gave it to Chanax, and now he will also have the woman of my heart. He will be the only man she will ever touch, and I will grow old babysitting my brothers while they get the glory."

Without another look at his mother, Nefermaat ran from the garden and toward the palace. He needed to see Bithiah. She was the only one who could calm him down, and he feared he'd murder someone in his rage. How dare his family hurt him in this way?

When he entered Bithiah's waiting room, he found her crying in front of the window. She turned as he approached and fell into his arms.

"Why?" she sobbed. "Why do they have to play with our love?"

"They will pay for this," Nefermaat whispered into her hair. "I promise, if it's the last thing I do, my mother and father will both pay."

She nodded as a cruel smile formed upon her beautiful face. "I believe you and will help. Together we will make them suffer in the most painful of ways. They will see in time what a mistake it is to keep us apart. In the meantime, Nefermaat, there's something I need from you."

"What is it, darling?" he asked her as he wiped the tears from her cheeks. "You know I'll do anything for you."

"Make love to me," she pleaded, "for I must know your sweet touch before I live out a life of duty in my younger brother's bed."

"Yes," he answered, trembling with excitement as he kissed her with all his restrained passion and anger.

She demanded the guards leave her room and not allow anyone else to enter. The instant they were alone, she took Nefermaat's hand and led him to her bed, where he threw himself upon her in a moment of love, lust, anger, and hate. Making love to her was against the law and punishable by death—she was the king's property until she became Chanax's—but at that moment, she was Nefermaat's.

As he climaxed, he cried, for the moment was all too brief.

27

Wedding Eve

It has been suggested the Royal lines of Egypt didn't originate in ancient Kemit, and instead migrated to the Nile Valley from a land far away, fleeing from the destruction of their homeland. When they arrived, they found the inhabitants of Kemit to be barbarians and quickly set to task granting them civilization, thus becoming the new kings and queens of the land. Perhaps this is true, for of all the empires of that age, they were one of the few to practice intermarriage, ensuring the line of kings never be changed by the blood of the commoner.

Behdet, Egypt 205 BCE

Ankhmakis slipped his naked body into the bath, feeling the hot water take away the aches of the day's training. His army was growing in strength and size. He commanded them with ease, and they followed him with honor and pride. They were excellent troops, and he was proud to be one of his father's generals. Ankhmakis was the master of strategy—he always knew the next step, and his men acted on his orders without question. The breath work with Natasa had opened entire worlds for him, making him a beloved general and a man worthy of the soldiers' adoration.

In addition, he'd become even more powerful with Helena's conception and birth. The child was a beam of light in his world. If he'd thought his love for Natasa was intense, his love for his daughter was nothing short of miraculous. They were the perfect family.

If only his father didn't require him to marry Weret. Why now? Why was it important? They were on the verge of war, why even think of marriage? Why couldn't he ride off at his father's side, and deal with marriage later? Why not let Chanax's wedding be the event to launch the rebellion, and leave him out of it? Between launching a war, and his new child with Natasa, he had no desire to take a wife—even if it made his father look powerful. Why should the man control him in this way? He felt like one of Sebastos's finest studs. Yet if Ankhmakis wanted to rule after his father died, he'd need an heir to the throne, and only his children with Weret would count.

He wished that Natasa's father had been Hugronaphor or even Isidor. He might have been able to bargain with his father to make her his queen. But her non-royal blood disqualified her for even a second queen position. His love for her and his desire to become pharaoh of Egypt were at odds, and the conflict was tearing him apart.

"Min," he called.

The soldier arrived without haste. "My lord, what do you need?"

"Fetch Natasa. Tell her she is wanted here."

The guard's mouth fell open in shock, and he shook his head for clarification. "Here, in your bath?"

"Yes," Ankhmakis replied.

"On the eve of your wedding?" Min continued, now scratching his head.

"As a lord of this land, I have the right to request a woman's company in my bath," Ankhmakis answered, his words curt.

Min looked like he wanted to argue, but he nodded anyway. "Yes, sir," he answered, and left the room.

When he returned with Natasa, Ankhmakis gazed at them from the tub. He could feel the tug of his lower lip and knew he was pouting but didn't care. He had no desire to hide his feelings—not even from Min.

"My lord," Natasa said with a slight bow.

"Min, you and the others may take your leave. I will dry myself off," Ankhmakis commanded.

The room emptied, and Natasa lowered her gaze. She was troubled, and he felt it. His heart was breaking at the thought of his wedding the next day.

"Come, join me," he said, with a husky, low voice as he fought his tears.

She took off her clothes and entered the tub, pouring water over her head with a pitcher, as if trying to wash away her sadness. He drew her close, held her wet body against his, kissed her, and breathed in her sadness.

"You're hurting," he whispered into her ear.

"Yes, you know my heart," she said as she cried.

"And you can see mine," he answered.

He trembled in her arms.

"You must marry her," Natasa whispered.

He turned away and wiped his eyes, which were filling with tears.

"It is your duty," she continued.

"And you coming to me tonight, did you do this out of duty?" he answered, now angry with her. He wanted her to fight. "You're mine, it's not like you could have refused me. Is our entire relationship also a matter of duty?"

She shook her head. "No, I'm here out of love."

He touched her face. "Natasa, hear me now. I have no need for queens, or harems of concubines. You are more beautiful than a hundred queens and more wonderful than a hundred thousand harems. No king in the world has more than me, right here, right now.

"You speak to me of duty, something you and I excel at, but you and our Helena are not my duty. You are my soul, the fire that lights my heart. There is nothing Weret can do to compare to you."

"My love," Natasa answered, the words sounding dry upon her lips as if she didn't mean them. "You're destined to be king of these lands. We both know it. You must marry and produce heirs. You and I have created a holy child of the temple. Together we will grow in power, and you will become a legend. But you won't take the throne without Weret. Can't you find love and affection for your sister, who looks at you with such adoration? Her work as the mother of your children will be important for Egypt. You need both of us to see this through."

"How can you give me to another woman like this? Do you care so little for me?"

In response, tears trailed down her cheeks. "Don't think I'm not in love with you. I love you like the stars above. I love you beyond this body and life, for eternity. There is nothing worse than to be separated from you in this way. But for Egypt's sake, I must encourage you to respect her and do what must be done."

She hugged herself, her shoulders stooped and quaking. Ankhmakis put his arms around her, tears of his own forming yet again. They held each other as they rocked back and forth, neither one ever wanting to let the other go. He took her hand in his and kissed the ring he had given her at Helena's birth. The lapis Phoenix wrapped itself around her thin ring finger as if to protect her from everything that was wrong with the world.

"No matter what happens," he croaked, "never doubt my love for you. Remember this ring and my promise to you. You are the one who wears my insignia. Of all women, you are my shining star, the light that guides me. There will never be another woman like you. I will never stop loving you or doing our work together. Ours is the highest and most noble magic."

He kissed her, this time sending his passion through their physical connection, and felt her breasts harden with desire. He wanted to make love to her until the sun rose. As he grew hard, she stroked him—holding his power in the palm of her hand. He leaned her up against the side of the heated pool, forcing himself between her legs and entering her. She cried out and shoved down against him. They continued in this way until the ecstasy rose up their spines together in unison, as they'd perfected. Sensing the Ankh, they connected their hearts and entered their Ba.

How long they stayed in that place of bliss, he couldn't recall. To be in the dimension of divine love was to be out of time. They climaxed, and they both cried out in joy.

They panted together, and she held up her hands. Her copper-brown skin was pruned and wrinkled.

"We've been in the tub for too long," she said with a smile. "I'm waterlogged."

He stood, holding her around the waist, still hard inside her, and walked out of the pool, up the steps, and to the settee, where he lay her down and rode her again. She arched her back and cried out his name in delight.

"I'm going to make love to you until Ra rises in the sky," he whispered in her ear.

"It appears that, once again, my dear, you have read my mind," she murmured.

✝

Outside the door, Nefermaat and the others stood guard. He heard the passionate sounds of the lovers and felt both aroused and ashamed.

"The two of them flaunt their relationship," he hissed to Min.

"Watch it," Min warned. "He is our lord. We support his decisions."

Nefermaat turned and stared at the wall before him. He hated Ankhmakis's superiority, but worse, he hated his sister's power in the court. She had no right to be in her lover's arms the night of his betrothal to another woman. If he couldn't be with Bithiah, why should Ankhmakis be granted this luxury? Shadya or not, there needed to be boundaries. Even if he reported it to their mother, nothing would happen. The high priestess would ignore their infraction. She always protected her precious Natasa.

"I'm sorry Chanax is also marrying tomorrow," Min said, and Nefermaat felt a sharp pain in his heart as if his captain had stabbed him.

"What does that matter?" he said, trying to hide his agony.

"Now I see the problem," Min replied.

"And what problem do you think you see?"

"Bithiah is to be his wife," Min noted. "I imagine you must feel betrayed."

Nefermaat stared at Min with a forced grin. He turned

away and tried to gain control of his emotions. The muffled cries of ecstasy could be heard through the walls, and he thought of Bithiah, alone in her room tonight, preparing to give herself to Chanax tomorrow against her will. The pain had begun to fester within his heart, and he felt faint. He couldn't let the men know how he hurt. He couldn't let them see the terrible darkness tearing at his soul. Taking a deep breath, Nefermaat closed his heart and left that part of his body. He need never use it again. When calm, he turned to answer Min in a steady voice.

"Like my sister, it doesn't matter how I feel, does it? The royals will always do as they please."

"Yes, they will. You'd best remember that and keep your opinions to yourself," Min threatened.

Nefermaat remembered Bithiah's promise to help him get back at their father for betraying them. He imagined Hugronaphor in pain, losing the one thing he desired most. It was only a matter of time. Until then, Nefermaat would follow orders, even Min's.

"I'll keep that in mind, sir," he replied, the thunder of his pounding heart in his ears drowning out the muffled sounds of his sister's ecstasy from within Ankhmakis's chambers.

28

Wedding Day

The diplomatic deals that King Hugronaphor of Behdet had worked diligently to secure were nothing short of a military coup. The man spent his entire adult life calculating, organizing, planning, and taking advantage of opportunity for one sole purpose—to start a civil war. Finally, two dozen years after being crowned king of Behdet, his time had come.

Behdet, Egypt 205 BCE

The high priestess paced the room. Once again, her daughter was late. Where was she? How dare she put the wedding ceremony in jeopardy? She turned as Corinna entered the room.

"Eleni has found her. She's down near the water, with Helena," Corinna panted. She must have run from the irrigation channel by the river to deliver this news. "She will be here soon."

"Thank you," Neferu-ankh-maat replied. "Corinna, why do you think she's doing this?"

"Oh, my lady, you know why," her loyal friend replied. "She loves him."

"It's unbecoming of her station," Neferu-ankh-maat said, her lips pursed. "She is a Priestess of Isis. She could take any number of lovers to practice the goddess's path. He is a Prince of Behdet and is doing what's right for the kingdom. It is our duty to support the union and bless it."

"My lady, permission to speak the truth?" Corinna requested. The high priestess nodded. "Your world is one full of assignments. Duty comes first for you. In such a place of business, I'm sure a love like theirs seems quite odd."

"What do you mean? I am the embodiment of love in this kingdom."

Corinna held out her hands. "Yes. You love the goddess. You love Egypt."

"These are the only things to love," Neferu-ankh-maat replied, feeling angry with the woman. "Other than ourselves, as we are the goddess's children."

"But do you love Hugronaphor when you practice Anit-Shadya or take ceremony? Do you care for his soul?"

"Our work is of the soul," Neferu-ankh-maat argued.

"Your work is of the soul, and also mind and body," Corinna pointed out. "But Neffa, Natasa loves Ankhmakis as he is. They're so close they can speak without words. They're one, and you know it. Their relationship is closer to Hecataeus's and mine than it is to yours and Hugronaphor's. My dear friend, Ankhmakis will never be a duty."

Neferu-ankh-maat glared at her friend. Yes, she knew it. When she'd first discovered their connection, she thought it would be the best thing for the kingdom. As far as the birth of their child, it had been right to put them together. When Ankhmakis begged to do Natasa's First Rites in addition to becoming her spiritual companion, she had found his request bold and outrageous, yet sweet.

She now understood the attraction was more than sexual. Bonding twin flames together with the goddess might have been too powerful of a combination for them to do what they needed for Egypt. Natasa was to be the high priestess of Isis and to take her place in the temple, would need to learn to share not only Ankhmakis with Weret but her own body with the other men of the court, as needed. Ankhmakis could never be Natasa's sole lover. He was one of several whom she would eventually serve.

Natasa entered the room. Her eyes were red and swollen, and her hair was in disarray. She held a squirming Helena in her arms.

"You've been crying," Neferu-ankh-maat accused. Natasa shrugged. "Corinna, can you please take Helena and send in the attendants? It's time to get ready for the weddings."

Corinna nodded, but Natasa shook her head. "I will not," she said through gritted teeth. "Do it without me."

"You will not disobey me." Neferu-ankh-maat placed her hands on her hips.

"Why not? What will you do?"

"Throw you out of the temple."

Natasa glared at her mother. "What need do I have for the temple?"

"Oh, that does it. What need do you have for the temple? May I remind you that your access to Ankhmakis is through your station? Or have you forgotten your place?"

Her words were meant to sting, and Natasa gasped.

"Give me the baby," Corinna said. "Please, love, give me Helena, and get ready to bless your prince."

Natasa looked away from Neferu-ankh-maat to the woman who had raised her. She grabbed Corinna close and sobbed into her chest. "Hold me, Corinna. Hold me, please."

Neferu-ankh-maat fought down her anger and envy as Corinna comforted Natasa, as she had when she was small. "My dear one, please don't cry. This is not the end. You're not losing him."

Natasa's grip loosened, and Helena cried out. Corinna took the child from Natasa and the baby quieted.

"Has she been fed?" Corinna asked. Natasa nodded and rubbed her eyes with a cloth. "Good. Now do as your mother says, and I will see you after the ceremony."

Corinna left the two priestesses alone. Neferu-ankh-maat looked at her daughter in frustration.

"Mother, I can't do this. Please don't make me," she sobbed.

Neferu-ankh-maat shook her head. "Where did I go wrong?"

"What? Because I care about who I share my body with, you've somehow failed?" Natasa screamed, her face red and blotched.

"That is childish nonsense. I have been the spiritual companion of our king for twenty years. He has had two wives and takes concubines to his chambers on a regular basis. That does not mean I share my body with those women. I share the goddess with him, and we care for one another. But what he does outside of ceremony is his own business. He is sovereign, as is Ankhmakis."

Natasa glared at her mother. "He and I are one, and who he sleeps with becomes a part of me. I can't stand Weret—"

"Silence," Neferu-ankh-maat yelled. "If you think I don't know what it's like to love a man and see him with another woman, you are mistaken."

"Please, you've slept with the entire royal line, Mother. Your services are known to the men of the court indeed,"

Natasa spat.

Neferu-ankh-maat slapped her across the face, and Natasa reeled backward.

"I love your father," she said, her heart beating faster with rage. "I will always love him. Letting him go was the hardest thing I've ever done. But while the high priestess has the freedom to take as many lovers as the goddess deems proper, she isn't allowed to marry. Marriage is bondage for a woman. Do not envy Weret for her position. She will serve Ankhmakis for the rest of her life, without any choice. She will never know the arms of another man, lest she is put to death. She will always live in your shadow.

"But you, daughter, will inherit the temple. You will raise children of the goddess. You will be free to love whomever you please. Yes, it means you must deny every man your hand in marriage, but you are free to be loved. Can you not see the blessing?"

Natasa held her palm to her cheek, the red outline of Neferu-ankh-maat's hand still apparent. "I don't want any other man. You should have given me to Silus, or Chanax, for I don't love them, and sharing them with the women of the court would be easier. But I can never stop loving Ankhmakis."

"You don't have to stop loving him," Neferu-ankh-maat said, now in a softer voice. "If anything, you must deepen your love for him. Bringing logic and neutrality to the situation is what's called for, not building a wall around your heart. Believe in your beauty and power. Know you are blessed beyond a doubt as a woman and embrace your role. You are to be the high priestess of The temple of Isis in Behdet. There is no higher honor for a woman in this country. Being neutral toward your lover and his actions is key to your success."

Natasa shook her head. "I can't do that. It's impossible."

"It might be best for you to spend time away from Ankhmakis," the high priestess suggested. "To find the core of your power without him. When you come together again, you will see that your love for each other will not wane with his marriage; rather, it will grow in confidence, as the two of you grow more sovereign."

Her daughter considered it and nodded. "That's a good idea, Mother. Perhaps I can take on a seclusion role?"

"Of course, my dear, I can arrange something. The everlasting flame in the temple needs tending. You can take that duty for the next three days."

Natasa let out a long sigh, and Neferu-ankh-maat watched the girl's shoulders sag. Thank the goddess, she was seeing reason. Three days of prayer, devotion, and silence would be good for the girl.

"Please," Neferu-ankh-maat begged, "get ready to sing and bless the royal couples. You must inhabit the goddess and send her love to them. Alexa will be at your side. The two of you can do this."

"And we dance for the king at the feast this evening in their honor, don't we?" Natasa asked, biting her lower lip. Maybe having her dance at Ankhmakis's wedding wasn't a good idea, but it was too late. Neferu-ankh-maat had to trust her daughter would do the right thing.

"Of course, as is custom."

"Where will you be?"

"With the king and his queen." She smiled. "And Lord Isidor."

The attendants arrived and set to work cleaning Natasa's face and braiding her hair. Alexa was with them, already dressed for the event.

"Natasa," Alexa said, approaching her friend. "How are

you?"

"Look at me, I'm a wreck. How are you handling it with grace?" Natasa asked as one of the servants removed her dirty, white tunic, replacing it instead with a silken, translucent ceremony robe. A second approached with a set of golden cuffs for her arms while a third outlined her eyes in dark charcoal and covered her eyelids in blue color made from ground lapis.

"I look good right now, let's see how I feel at the end of the day," Alexa replied.

Neferu-ankh-maat sighed. "Trust me, girls, these feelings will pass. You must remember to not envy the princesses. They may have the perfect royal bloodline, and legal claim to your lovers, but they would rather trade places with you. Never forget that."

The young priestesses nodded, but the high priestess could tell they didn't believe her yet. The attendants placed a golden web on Natasa's head. She was beautiful beyond words. A look of clarity had replaced her grief. Neferu-ankh-maat smiled.

"Daughter, you are the representation of the goddess in this world. Shine her light on the royal family, and on our great country, Egypt."

Neferu-ankh-maat kissed her daughter, noting the red mark on her face had lessened. She felt remorse for slapping her, but sometimes a slap is the only way to shock a person out of their grief. Resigned, the high priestess let out a long exhale and left to get ready herself for the day's events.

☥

When she was ready, Natasa removed Ankhmakis's ring and placed it on the table. It felt wrong wearing it tonight. She rose from her seat and took Alexa's hand. The two walked in forlorn silence as if going to a funeral rather than a wedding, through the palace corridors to the Great Hall. People poured out of the doors, trying to see inside. A double royal wedding was a rarity. Everyone in the kingdom of Behdet had been invited. Natasa and Alexa stepped into a side chamber and closed the door behind them. They knelt before a small altar, upon which stood the statues of Isis and Thoth, Maat and Horus. They each placed a lotus flower on the altar, and Alexa lit a candle.

They remained silent, still holding hands, as each one called the goddess into her heart. Natasa felt a surge of energy and cried again, this time in awe rather than grief. The goddess appeared to her in her mind's eye and spoke with a clear voice.

"My daughter, I love you. You are a Child of the Light. Trust you will be shown the way to everlasting life."

Natasa took in a deep breath and shook. Never had the Lady Isis been this straightforward with her message.

"I trust in you, my lady," Natasa replied.

"As do I," Alexa replied.

They turned to one another and hugged.

"My dearest friend, how we've changed," Alexa said. "And yet, I think the biggest changes have yet to come."

The stone doors opened, and the sounds of the crowd echoed in the nave. The lead musician beckoned. "Come. It's time."

They rose and took their place among the musicians. Natasa inhaled and started the chant. The group marched into the Great Hall, now thronged with Greeks and Egyptians of every station—nobles, mayors, generals, commanders, and their women. Priests and priestesses from neighboring nomes bowed to the chorus as they walked by. King Hugronaphor's banners flew in the breeze that snuck in through the large open windows on either side of the hall. Hugronaphor and

Queen Keket stood at the front, and below them on the dais were the two couples to be married, dressed in full royal attire.

Natasa felt her heart stop and time stand still. The room seemed silent as she looked at her lover's beautiful face. She could feel his pain and anger rise in her own soul and struggled to find a way to love him while letting him go. She heard the music and allowed the goddess to come through her to sing the song of blessing. Each note was perfect, joined by Alexa's lower voice. The two held hands, still needing the support of the other. They stopped before the couples, and the musicians took their places. The priestesses raised their arms and called forth the goddess of love. Their voices filled the hall with a sweet, yet mournful tune. Singing their lovers's wedding song was the hardest thing they had ever done.

"May Our Lady Isis keep you in her heart.

May Osiris bless your marriage with strength and power.

May Hathor bless you with many children.

May Egypt grow with your union."

Over and over they sang the blessing, and Isidor soon joined them. He tossed thyme and garlic around the couples to ward off evil spirits. He took a stick of frankincense, lit it, and walked around the couples. Natasa and Alexa followed behind him as they continued their song. The scent comforted Natasa and guided her deeper into her soul. Once the high priest finished circling the couples, the priestesses fell silent and left the dais to join the musicians at the side.

Natasa found herself standing across the aisle from Ankhmakis and Weret. The princess looked radiant in her long white dress, golden collar, and crown. Natasa fought her own jealousy as the princess took Ankhmakis's arm and tugged him closer. He looked handsome in his wedding attire—a tall blue hat sat proud upon his head and his long, dark hair had been braided down his back. His white and golden robes were tailored to his strong body. His sword hung from his waist, and on his finger he wore his signet, the same ring he'd given Natasa. She met his gaze for a moment, before turning her face to the floor. She couldn't bear it.

"The time has come," Isidor proclaimed, "to unite the kingdoms of the south. The house of Hugronaphor is now complete, his sons are mated, and they are ready to lead us to glory."

The priest turned to Ankhmakis, the older of the two grooms, and held out a hand wrapped in a golden chain.

"With Osiris and all of Egypt as your witness, do you, Ankhmakis, take Weret to be your wife?" Isidor asked.

Natasa's heart stopped as he said, "I do."

Isidor continued to Weret, her large smile eager and hopeful as she agreed to the union. Next, Chanax and Bithiah were wed.

"By the power vested in me, I present the Princes Ankhmakis and Chanax, and their queens, Weret and Bithiah."

The crowd cheered, and the musicians started to play. Natasa stared at the ceiling, trying to control her emotions. She smiled as the couples made their way to greet their guests, but as soon as Ankhmakis and Weret were swallowed by the crowd, Natasa took her leave, hoping her mother wouldn't notice. She had to prepare for the wedding feast later that day and knew contact with the royal siblings would destroy her. Best for her to hide in her apartment until sunset when duty required her to bless them one last time before the couples took to their marital beds.

29

The Dance

"Who can I talk to today? For the wrongdoer is an intimate friend, and the brother with whom one dealt has become an enemy. Who can I talk to today? There is no one who is content, and him with whom one walked is no more. Who can I talk to today? I am weighted down with misery for want of an intimate friend. Who can I talk to today? For wrong roams the earth; there is no end to it."

~ The Dialogue of a Man and His Soul

Manuscript from the late Twelfth Dynasty, approximately 1815 BCE

Behdet, Egypt 205 BCE

The day dragged on. Ankhmakis found it intolerable, but not useless. He gained information from the visiting nobles and learned of Ptolemy's latest actions. The Greek pharaoh was walking a fine line with his own people, and from the sound of it, his health was failing. A rebellion, also planned by the priests in Memphis, had broken out in the Delta and drawn Ptolemy IV's eye from the south. Hugronaphor would act. This plan was Ankhmakis's only joy.

He spent most of his day locked in meetings with the dignitaries of the land, planning and plotting with the men, which meant he didn't have time to think of Weret or Natasa. The sun set as the last meeting wound down, and he was given a moment to get ready for the evening's feast. Again, he entered his bath and called to Min.

"Fetch me Natasa," he commanded, knowing he was out of order.

Min sat on the bench near the tub. He avoided Ankhmakis and stared at the walls. He spoke in a soft, gentle voice, "The frescoes glitter in places under the candlelight. Are they made of gold?"

"I said fetch me Natasa."

"No, my lord, I won't," Min replied. His high-pitched voice and the beads of sweat above his lip gave away his fear of denying Ankhmakis, but he remained firm nonetheless.

Ankhmakis loved Min and trusted his council. He exhaled with frustration as he held his head in his hands. "My dear Min, how can I do this?"

Min looked to his general, his eyes wide and his eyebrow cocked. "My Lord Ankhmakis, I've known you since I was born, and I watched you make your way through the temple priestesses and your father's concubines. You certainly didn't need love to have sex."

"That was before," Ankhmakis replied.

"Before what?"

"Before I knew Natasa," he admitted. "You don't understand how much I need her. Our Shadya is amazing and powerful. You must have noticed how it's changed me."

"I've seen that you and your spiritual companion have a gift, this is true," Min admitted. "I never believed in Anit-Shadya until you bonded with Natasa. Some have said you have an advantage in strength, health, and knowledge over other men, even those who practice Shadya. There are things I've seen you do that should not be possible."

"That's what I'm talking about," Ankhmakis agreed. "And we've been together only two years. Imagine where this will lead me, given the right amount of time and devotion. I don't want to waste it on anyone else."

Min looked at his leader and shook his head. "More important, sir, she makes you happy. That's what I've seen. The man you've become is noble, honorable, and at times, even funny. Though, you'll never be as clever as me." He struck the prince on the shoulder, and continued in a serious tone, "Three years ago, you were a spoiled prince. Now, you're our leader, and we will follow you to the ends of the Earth. I will fight by your side unto my death, and the other men feel the same."

Ankhmakis stepped out of the water and dried himself off. He put on his evening attire—the blue headpiece with a simple golden tunic. No need for his collar this evening. A servant entered to color his eyelids, lips, and cheeks and to braid his hair. He didn't speak, and neither did Min.

When he was ready, he strapped his sword to his waist and looked to the ring on his finger. It made him think of Natasa, and his heart ached. He smiled at his friend. "Thank you, Min, for keeping me in line. I trust you more than I trust anyone on Earth. Other than Natasa, of course."

Min nodded and bowed to the prince. "You're my prince, and I believe you can do anything you set your mind to."

Ankhmakis returned the bow to his faithful commander, and with a deep breath, left the room.

"Oh, and drink in excess tonight, sir," Min advised as they walked down the hall. "Remember how that makes even the ugliest women look good?"

Ankhmakis laughed. "Excellent proposal. You'll keep my cup filled with wine, won't you?"

The two men put their arms around one another as they entered the banquet hall. Like the Great Hall, this room had also been decorated with great care and thought—Hugronaphor's banner hung everywhere he turned. It seemed showy, but Ankhmakis knew his father enjoyed the attention. He made his way through the crowd, shaking hands and stopping to chat. When he arrived at the head table, he found his father, flanked by the queen on one side and the High Priestess Neferu-ankh-maat, resplendent in a green gown and leaning in to whisper in Isidor's ear, on the other. Queen Keket looked uncomfortable. She was staring at Isidor and Neferu-ankh-maat, frowning as if their love was an affront. King Hugronaphor was already drinking wine and telling jokes, oblivious as usual to his wife. Silus and Ruia sat next to the queen. It was here, between Ruia and Weret, that Ankhmakis found his place. Turning to Min, he nodded to his seat.

"Fetch me a pitcher of wine," he commanded. "Better yet, make it two."

"As you wish, my lord," his friend replied.

Ankhmakis took his place between the two women and grabbed his goblet, grateful it was already full. He drank it down like water and grabbed the pitcher in front of Weret to refill it.

"Hello, husband," she said with a kind, yet careful tone. She was nervous, and Ankhmakis knew it was his own fault, yet found it impossible to play the part of the good husband.

He nodded at his wife. "Weret, you look pretty." It was the best he could do, and it wasn't a lie. She did look nice in her golden gown and circlet upon her head. She was a lady of the royal house and dressed for the part. They made a handsome pair, even if he didn't like her.

The musicians played and food was served. True to his word, Min continued to have pitchers of wine sent to the high table, where Ankhmakis drank them down, speaking to Weret as little as possible. The feast was splendid—roasted goat, smoked fish caught that day, bits of cheese, figs, roasted nuts, vegetables from the Royal Gardens, wine, beer, and thick, hot breads. Hugronaphor laughed with Neferu-ankh-maat; Silus caressed Ruia's hand; even Chanax was enjoying his time with Bithiah. For his part, Ankhmakis sat next to his own bride, drinking himself into oblivion.

☥

Farther down the table, Chanax watched his brother with a keen eye.

"What is he doing?" Bithiah asked, also noticing Ankhmakis's behavior.

"Being dramatic," Chanax replied. "Broken-hearted because he had to marry Weret instead of Natasa."

"He's an ass," Bithiah noted, the bitterness apparent in her voice. "Everyone knows you don't marry your spiritual companion. You men have it made; you get as many lovers as you want, plus as many wives as you can handle. It's the way of men to have many women, and the way of women to mate with whom they're told."

"Ankhmakis likes to think himself above the ways of men," Chanax said.

Bithiah laughed. "Oh, too true. Too true. It's a shame I can't be above the ways of women." She emptied her wine and stared at Chanax as she placed the golden goblet down for a server to refill. He felt strange considering her his wife now, and yet it didn't repulse him. He was more practical and thick-skinned than Ankhmakis.

"I don't want to marry you any more than he wants to marry Weret," she said.

"I know," Chanax replied, aware of the promise his father had broken with Nefermaat. The same thing had happened to him when his father denied him Natasa as his spiritual companion. Funny how his siblings suffered the same broken heart. "I'm sorry."

"But I'm glad I was forced to marry you and not Ankhmakis."

"Why?"

"Because," she explained, her fingers dancing upon the table with excitement as she spoke, "I've always wanted to be a priestess. Of course, I was denied my wish, as well as the husband of my choice. The men of the court think their power is in their fighting. They're wrong. Magic is power, not the sword. You're a priest, Chanax, and a powerful one. Anyone can see this. You can teach me, and together we will be the ones who shape the events of the future."

Chanax looked at his sister with new eyes. This was the wife he needed. She understood the path he and Isidor were laying, and wouldn't try to stop him the way Alexa, Weret, or Ruia would have. He grabbed his goblet of wine and held it to Bithiah.

"I suggest a toast," he said, heart now filled with hope. "To our union, my dear wife."

Bithiah toasted him. "If you share your magic with me, I promise to make the best of this situation. Unlike Ankhmakis, I will embrace our marriage, despite my disappointment, but only if you teach me the secrets of the temple. Trust me, Chanax, I'm not pleasant when denied what I want."

Chanax shivered with both fear and delight. He would teach her, and in turn have the perfect partner in the ways of dark magic.

"I promise," he said and turned to look back at Ankhmakis, taking notes. Everyone thought Silus would become king when Hugronaphor died, but Chanax had always known Ankhmakis was the real threat. He had the talent, the charm, and the loyalty of the army. Yet, he was conceited, and his connection to Natasa made him weak. Thanks to the selfish act of Ankhmakis, Chanax had never made love to Natasa, the true woman of his dreams. Therefore, fulfilling his duty with Bithiah wasn't a hardship. If anything, it made him better suited for the throne. Perhaps Ankhmakis's greed was turning out to be a blessing in disguise. Chanax and Bithiah were, after all, the most gifted and scheming of the family, and both had been denied the lover of their choice; thus, they knew the forms of hate and anger. He could show her how to use them to their advantage in the court. They had potential indeed.

The feast was cleared, and barrels of ale and wine were rolled out. The musicians changed their tune to a slow, melodic, serious song. Chanax rose in his seat in excitement— the priestesses were going to dance.

On cue, several women, dressed in long, see-through skirts and golden breastplates, danced into the room. The Priestesses of Isis had arrived to give their blessing to the new couples, and at the lead stood Natasa and Alexa. Their bodies danced to the rhythm. Chanax eyed them with desire and felt himself become aroused, which was the purpose. Their dance was supposed to prime the new husbands for their first evening with their wives.

Natasa danced as gracefully as always, showing no signs of holding back. Her hips swayed to the erotic music as she twirled her arms around her body, turning in time with the seductive beat of the drums. She was like a snake, winding herself around the notes, making them visible to the audience. The men were held captivated, and the women felt threatened. They were foolish of course, for their men's desire would be turned on them later, of that they could be sure. Chanax was impressed. Natasa was doing her job with enthusiasm.

She danced among the members of the audience. The other priestesses did the same. The music picked up speed, and in response, the women made a formation in the middle of the room. They shimmied, lifted their legs, and twirled around one another. As the music played, Natasa spun faster, her long, flowing skirt following her legs and her hips slinking along the top of the song. The freedom of the dance consumed her, and the audience, including Chanax, fell under the spell she'd woven with her body, like a weaver at the loom of desire.

Chanax turned and looked down the table at the rest of the royal family. Hugronaphor and Silus were of course aroused, Bithiah wore a look of envy, Neferu-ankh-maat looked relieved, and Weret had her eyes closed, but it was Ankhmakis whose expression was the most vivid—Chanax could feel the heat rising from him in waves. His brother had connected to Natasa, and the whole room could feel their passion.

The pain on Ankhmakis's face was heartbreaking, even to Chanax, who had long ago closed himself to matters of the heart.

☥

The music rose to a crescendo, and the other women picked Natasa up into the air and in the last moments settled into a final pose, holding her in an arched position above their heads. The music ended, and the crowd cheered, some standing.

Hugronaphor rose and the priestesses lowered Natasa to the floor. She panted, and her dark skin glowed with sweat under the torchlights.

"Come, Natasa the Graceful," Hugronaphor called out. "Come and receive my gift."

She strode to the head table, not allowing herself to look at her lover. To do so would mean to break the thread of neutrality she'd worked hard to weave. She wasn't strong enough yet to face him.

"My King Hugronaphor," she said as she bowed low before him. "It is my honor to dance for you on this special night."

She was aware of the others in the room, and of the political importance of the evening. The energy coursed through her. She stood to face her king. He was handsome and reminded her of Ankhmakis.

"Natasa, daughter of Neferu-ankh-maat, you are beautiful and honored in this court. May you live long and grant us glory." He took a golden wand from his servant and placed it in her hands. It was a mighty gift, and her arms shook as she hugged it to her breast. "You have served my family with your love. Please know your hard work and sacrifice don't go unnoticed."

She looked up at the king's compassionate face. She knew he understood that the marriage between Ankhmakis and Weret affected her. A sense of peace settled over her. "Thank you, King Hugronaphor. I will learn to use this tool in the service of the kingdom. Your patronage is most gracious."

She bowed again and turned to take her leave, allowing herself to chance a glance at Ankhmakis. She sent him a wave of love. He swayed in drunkenness and put his hands on his head, unable to return the gesture. She turned to flee from the hall, but her father waved to her from a table to the right. He hadn't sat in the king's corner, even though he was the vizier. She gave him a questioning look, and he raised a glass.

"Good job," he mouthed.

The music started again and the crowd mingled. She needed to leave before Ankhmakis approached her. But why was her father seated to the side like this?

"Father," she said as she took an empty seat next to his left, "can we talk?"

"Of course, little hawk, what is it?"

Ennaeus and other Greek clerics and priests, as well as the stonemasons of the temple of Horus, were also sitting at this table. "What is the meaning of this?" she asked, gesturing to the fact he was seated away from the royal family.

"Trying to distance myself, darling." He smiled, taking a chug of ale from his mug. "I'm sure you can sense why."

She shook her head. She'd been so consumed with potentially losing Ankhmakis to Weret, she hadn't been paying attention to the political implications.

"You do know why we're here today, child? Certainly not for the love of the precious royal couples."

Natasa understood. She felt a mixture of anger and fear. "He means to declare war soon?"

"Hush," her father advised. "Not too loud. But yes, that's why I'm here, with my fellow Greeks. Only time will tell what part we each play in the game."

Natasa sensed Ankhmakis making his way across the room toward her and turned to face him. His dark, penetrating eyes were dead set upon her, and she felt his helplessness. "I need to go," she said, grabbing a pitcher of wine from her father's table. "I have a date with Alexa."

She fled the room, leaving Ankhmakis standing alone in the Great Hall, while the crowd buzzed with merriment around him, unaware of his pain.

☥

Later, Ankhmakis dutifully took his new wife to his chambers and commanded she remove her clothes. She trembled, knowing he was drunk and not at all himself. He elbowed her to the bed, had his way with her as fast as his body would allow, and rolled off her in a hurry.

"Ankhmakis, what are you doing?" she asked, tears rolling down her painted cheeks as she drew a blanket to her chest to cover her nudity. A low-level cleric, who'd been there to witness the consummation of marriage, left without a word.

"I'm done here. Our marriage is consummated. Your witness may record it. You're my wife now," he said, yanking on his clothes. "Please make sure you leave my chambers before sunrise."

He left her, not even taking the time to say goodbye. The door slammed behind him, and she started to cry. Ankhmakis fled to the stables and made his horse ready. He jumped on Biriq's back and galloped into the lonely, starry night.

☥

Alexa and Natasa sat, perched high above the city, on the top of the temple of Horus. The Greek builders were still at the celebration, getting high on the king's generosity; thus, no one would discover them watching the Khons's silver boat rise and drinking themselves to sleep. They had a pitcher of wine and took turns drowning away their sorrows.

"My mother hates this building," Natasa said, staring out at the empty desert before them. "She says it ruins the view."

Alexa rapped her fist on the roof of the temple upon which they sat, commissioned by an earlier Ptolemy and perpetually under construction. "This temple? Why?"

Natasa turned her head to look at the far end of the building; its marbled façade glowed in the moonlight, and she could make out the carved forms of Horus upon its towering walls. Candles flickered in the small guard windows. The Greeks had been building the monstrosity for forty years, each Ptolemy pharaoh picking up where the previous one left off.

"She thinks they built that to spy on us," Natasa continued. "To try to learn our mysteries. We won't allow them to enter our priesthood in Behdet, so they built their own temple to try to force us to cooperate."

"Do you think that's what Isidor is doing?" Alexa asked.

"I don't know," Natasa admitted. "I know he and his priests hold ceremony in there by the command of Memphis. My mother doesn't like it."

"Nor do I. Chanax participates, and our Shadya has grown darker as of late. I'm not sure he cares for the child who now forms within my womb. Sometimes Chanax scares me, Natasa. His anger is growing, and I don't know what to do."

Alexa quieted and chewed her fingernails. Natasa took her friend's hand into her own. "Isidor is not a good man, Alexa, and what he does in the temple is evil, I know it. I don't see why my mother loves him."

"Isn't she supposed to mate with him?" Alexa asked.

"No, I don't think she has to. Only the king is her responsibility. He is her spiritual companion, yet she can take other lovers. Isidor was her first spiritual companion, perhaps she never broke it off with him when Hugronaphor became king?"

"I imagine that is the case," Alexa replied. She grabbed the pitcher of wine from Natasa's hands. "When did she fall in love with Hecataeus?"

Natasa felt grief pulse around her. It had always made her sad that her parents weren't together—yet Corinna made a wonderful wife and mother, and her father appeared happy with the life they'd built. Natasa blamed Isidor. She didn't trust the man.

"Father told me he and Mother were lovers when Isidor trained in Memphis. Isidor was the king's first tribute to the pharaoh and during his tour of duty, my mother took Hecataeus as her lover, and I was the result. Father says he asked her to marry him, and she refused. Mother says the high priestess can have all men but marry none."

Alexa shuddered, wide-eyed. "Will you keep Ankhmakis as your spiritual companion when you become the high priestess?"

The thought made her heart begin to beat an irregular rhythm. What if her mother died before Ankhmakis became king? Would she be forced to share her body with King Hugronaphor? Or worse, Silus, should he take the throne? Including Weret in their lives was complicated enough.

"I hope my mother never dies, and I can be Ankhmakis's lover for the rest of my life. I never want to feel any other man inside me."

Alexa looked to her friend, tears shining in her darkened gaze. Natasa trembled and felt her own begin to water.

"Why does it hurt to share him in this way?" Natasa continued as she felt for Ankhmakis in the night, to no avail. His heart was closed. "Shouldn't love be free and flowing? That's what they teach us in the temple. Yet I can't seem to go with the flow and trust it."

"In the temple, they teach us divine love," Alexa replied. "The freest of love, and something we can feel for everyone and everything, including the sky, Earth, animals, stars, and even ourselves. Divine love is the web of life that connects us, the energy that shapes the cosmos and everything in it." She took a swig of wine and handed the pitcher back to Natasa. "And they teach us of passion and the discipline needed to share ourselves in the name of the goddess. But they have no idea what they're talking about when it comes to the love between two people. They ignore it because romantic love is inconvenient. It gets in the way of their plans to control us. But the love of soulmates is as powerful as divine love—people will die for such love. It's quite dangerous. Perhaps this is why they pretend it doesn't exist."

Natasa took a huge drink of wine, allowing it to flow through her and numb her heart. She felt safer, even if the world did swoon. "You're wise, Alexa. You should be the high priestess someday, not me."

A rider sped down the main road, past the temple and out into the desert. Under the moonlight, Natasa could make out the glow of the white horse's coat. Dust kicked up from behind the animal as it galloped past below them. Ankhmakis's face flashed in her mind.

"Where is he going?" Alexa asked. "You haven't planned to meet him, have you?"

"No." Natasa shook her head. "He likes to ride out to the west when he's angry."

Alexa put her face in her hands as if Ankhmakis's actions shamed her, and Natasa put her arms around her friend, watching her lover ride away in the distance. Even though abandoning Weret on their wedding night was a foolish thing for him to do, Natasa found herself hopeful as she gulped down the last of her drink and leaned into Alexa's warm embrace under the stars.

They had to share their lovers with the princesses, and war would erupt at any moment, but thank the goddess the priestesses had each other.

30

Passions

"After death, a man remains, and his deeds are placed beside him in a heap. Now, being There is eternity: the man who does what angers Them is a fool; the man who reaches Them without doing wrong, he is There like a God, free-striding like the Lords of Eternity."

~ Teaching for King Merikare, Middle Kingdom manuscript, approximately 1780 BCE

Behdet, Egypt 205 BCE

Natasa emerged from her three days of fasting and prayer a renewed woman. Her love for Ankhmak had grown, as well as for Helena and her own self. Deep in meditation, she found herself cocooned in their Ba, the place of power, far beyond the emotions of the astral. She understood without a doubt that they were one field of light, sharing their male and female experience on Earth. She vowed to live her life to its fullest, learning from her lover how to support the life of the warrior.

Three priests greeted her as she left the Tomb of the Eternal Flame. In her hands, she held the golden rod that

Hugronaphor had given her. The wand was beautiful, ancient, and powerful. But nothing else had been revealed. She would need to consult her mother in this matter.

As she left the darkness of the temple, another priestess entered the tomb, taking her place to tend the flame of Behdet, and keep it alive and filled with Spirit. The sun was shocking, and she squinted. The hot sand burned the soles of her feet, and sweat formed on her skin.

How interesting, she thought, *the body is quite responsive to its surroundings.*

In the quiet, cool tomb, she'd shut down, using only the minimum effort to keep her physical systems going. Out under the gaze of Ra, the body kicked into full gear. It made her smile.

"Where do you wish us to escort you?" one of the priests asked her.

"Home, to see my daughter."

Helena was asleep in her cradle when she arrived. The sight of her made her breasts ache. She took the child in her arms and hugged her, smelling her sweet, warm flesh as the infant took to her breast. Natasa felt the release of more than her body as she reclined on a hay bale and nursed her child. The connection was warm, safe, and ancient.

"Natasa," Eleni called as she skipped into the room. Her brown hair was beginning to lighten from her days in the sun. Corinna followed close behind the eager child, closing the door as she entered the room.

"Hello there, Starlight." Natasa smiled, using the nickname Hecataeus had given her.

"You're back," her younger sister continued. "I missed you. As did Helena. We gave her tea and biscuits when she was hungry, but she wants only you."

Corinna held out a slice of bread, and Natasa ripped it from her hand. She was famished.

"Of course. Warm milk is better than bitter tea." Natasa laughed.

"Oh, she eats like a horse now," Eleni added. "She even steals figs from my plate if I'm not looking. But still, Helena needs her mommy, as all children do."

Eleni looked up at Corinna, and Natasa felt an ache in her heart. "Yes, Eleni, we do need our mommies. You and I have one of the best."

Corinna wasn't her birth mother, but she'd loved Natasa as her own and continued to be the mother she needed now as she showed Natasa how to care for Helena and raise her.

"What did the goddess teach you, my dear one?" Corinna asked, folding the linens. Flies buzzed between the bundles of lavender, rosemary, and sage that hung drying from the ceiling. Natasa breathed in the smells, enjoying the scent of her true home. Eleni handed her a cup of tea filled with herbs to ground her after her days of fasting and solitude, and she drank it, relishing every drop as if it were her first.

"I heard the song of my spirit. I know who I am, and now I can begin to serve."

Corinna smiled. "I can see that. You're confident in a new way," she answered.

"How come our spirit is a song?" Eleni asked.

"Because that's how matter is born," Natasa explained. "First there is a void, a place without sound. Then, the call of love begins to sing, beckoning life to come forth. Out of that void comes a song, or a tone, in response to the call. This frequency is light and energy. It begins to grow in complexity, dancing with the song of life and taking on a life of its own. This is who you are, light and energy seeking to live in a body on Earth. When you want to become human, part of your Ba slows down and becomes matter. A body is formed within your mother's womb. After birth, you live in the world, where the song is hard to hear. But if you follow the way of your heart, you'll remember your song, and see your true essence. The layers upon layers of energy that make up the matrix of life are too beautiful for words. This is why we invented instruments, when we play them we can remember our divine nature. My mother says that once you have heard your tone that is unique in all the cosmos, you can begin to connect to other tones and create together. This is how Ankhmakis and I created Helena; we asked her to come to us."

Corinna smiled and hugged her. Eleni looked puzzled.

"Oh," Eleni answered. "I can hear the songs of the plants and animals."

"Can you?" Natasa asked.

"Yes, but I haven't heard my song yet." The little girl sighed.

"Yes, you have. Children never forget who they are. You won't lose your song until you're an adult, at which point you will have to follow the way back to your heart. This is the purpose of initiation, why we practice the mysteries in the temple and offer them to those who seek the truth."

Eleni shrugged. "Adults are complicated."

A knock sounded on the door, and Natasa feared Ankhmakis had already come to find her. She wasn't ready to see him yet. Being away from him made her stronger and more powerful. She had no desire to feel the pain and vulnerability she'd felt at the wedding. Eleni ran to answer it, finding Chanax standing against the doorframe, looking handsome, yet hurried from his day's work.

"Natasa," he said, entering without being invited. "I've

been sent to fetch you. You're needed by the king."

"I finished my temple duties only moments ago, Chanax," she replied, pointing to the child at her breast. "Can I please finish feeding my child and change?"

Chanax looked down at her and shook his head. "Can you get her to hurry? Father is at his wit's end."

Natasa sighed and stood, handing Helena to Corinna. "Fine, wait for me outside." She left the room to change.

When she had washed her face and wrapped her hair up in a scarf, she felt better. She returned Ankhmakis's ring to her finger where it belonged. She would never remove it again. She took her baby from Corinna, wrapped her to her chest, and made her way outside to find Chanax leaning against the small house. He looked distracted.

"What is it, Chanax? Why does the king call for me?" she asked.

"Philopater is ill," he said with a slight grin on his face. "Alexandria is in a state of chaos. Memphis has given us the signal to launch our plan. We begin the war in a matter of days."

"What interesting timing," Natasa answered, "considering all the nobles south of us are still here because of your wedding."

"I see you understand politics, my lady," Chanax said, studying her with a hawkish gaze. "It's true the entire wedding was planned as a ruse to throw the pharaoh off and allow us to implement the first part of our strategy. The nobles from the south of us have joined our side and proclaimed Hugronaphor their new pharaoh. When we ride north to war, the other houses will arrest the Greeks in their cities and send their troops to support us."

"I see," she answered. "Congratulations, I guess."

"Ankhmakis and I had to marry, you know this, don't you?" Chanax said, acting defensive. "It's the way of things. Now the heirs are secured, perhaps the princesses are pregnant, and Hugronaphor's house is stable. These things are important."

"Yes, I agree with you, but you still haven't told me why I've been summoned. I don't see how this relates to me. I'm not a princess, remember?" She was getting impatient.

"It's Ankhmakis," Chanax admitted. "He's been a madman since the wedding. He hasn't spoken to poor Weret, other than to try to plant his seed in her before we head north. Worse, he's livid you abandoned him. He thinks your retreat to the Tomb of the Everlasting Flame was a way to punish him. He almost broke down the temple door to drag you out of there. Hugronaphor tried to get your mother to end your seclusion, but she refused and set the temple guards at the entrance. The entire event was a disaster."

"Where is he now?" she asked, concerned for her lover. If only he could allow himself to see the bigger picture, none of this would hurt as it did.

"In the training ring, fighting three men. Father tired of his whining and forced him into several matches. We need you to focus him and settle him down so we can—"

"Ride out to war. Yes, I see." She saw too much. A great battle flashed within her mind—the taste of blood filled her mouth. She was not looking forward to this part of their insurrection.

They approached the arena, and she walked with Chanax to stand beside Hugronaphor, who nodded to her in acknowledgment and turned back to the match. Ankhmakis was fighting three men with his sword and spear. They wouldn't fight to the death, just to the pain. The king couldn't afford to lose soldiers on what was the eve of battle.

One sight of Ankhmakis and Natasa melted like honey on a warm day. Her lover fought like the languid Nile, flowing between his opponents with ease. He was sweating, and his bare chest was covered in dirt and scars. He bent down to avoid a hit to the head, and as he did so, one of the men behind him made to strike.

"*Behind you,*" Natasa said, not with her voice, but with her heart, sending the message into their energy field. Ankhmakis turned and struck the man with a blow so hard, his opponent flew across the arena and landed with a thud. Ankhmakis looked up and she waved. He stood taller as he turned on his other opponents.

Natasa could feel the energy between them grow, like the heat shield of a galaxy. Ankhmakis upped his game and took out the next opponent in one fell swoop. Hugronaphor turned to Natasa. "Do you see why I called you? This connection you have, it's unique. I'm still not sure what to make of it, but right now, it works to my advantage. You aren't thinking of letting him go as a priestess, are you?"

"I have no more say in the choice of my spiritual companion than Ankhmakis had in his choice of wife," she replied in a voice harsher than was proper before the king. Hugronaphor glanced at her before turning back to the fight.

Ankhmakis took down the last opponent, and the spectators in the amphitheater rose and cheered.

"My son has won," Hugronaphor called out, ending the match. He turned back to Natasa and smiled at Helena, who was also clapping her tiny, chubby hands. He patted the baby on the head. "You left him for three days. What on Earth made you do that?"

"I needed time alone for my own good, Your Majesty. His wedding day took a toll on me," she answered.

He gawked at her as if she'd spoken in a different language. Chanax grinned and glanced away.

"If you wish to understand our power," Natasa continued, "you must understand that it is nothing but love, and it is pure and true. To be forced to share that love with others hurts us. We are loyal and dutiful. He will produce heirs, and I will not leave his side. You'll have to pry me from him."

Hugronaphor sighed with a nod. "I don't understand it, but all I want is him fit and focused. Get him ready for war."

"With pleasure," she teased, and the king's cheeks turned red.

Ankmakis made his way through the crowd of soldiers to his father's platform. He ignored protocol and grabbed Natasa, kissing her with raw passion. Helena, still strapped to her mother's chest, grabbed his hair, making him tug back and smile. He touched the girl's small, sweet face, and their child grabbed one of his fingers in her fist and tugged at it. Ankhmakis looked at Natasa and his gaze scared her—there was a madness in him that she had never seen before, as if he could come unhinged at any moment. He was anything but a confident general.

"You left me," he croaked.

"No, I didn't. I'm always with you," she replied, pointing to his heart.

"Then why did you lock yourself away?"

"To go deeper."

Hugronaphor and Chanax shuffled their feet, and the king cleared his throat.

"Now that everything's back to normal, why don't you two spend time together? You're both dismissed for today. Ankhmakis is to report at sunrise to work with the troops. We ride out in four days. Until then, expect to spend the daylight in my company, and your evenings are yours as you see fit. I suggest taking Anit-Shadya as soon as possible."

Hugronaphor looked at Natasa and met her gaze. She smiled without shame.

"Come," Natasa said to Ankhmakis, holding out her hand, "you need a bath."

☥

Hours later, in the prince's chambers, the two lay naked in each other's arms. The breeze of the setting sun stirred the bed curtains and the scents of sage and rosemary filled the room. Ankhmakis sat up and looked at his sleeping lover. Every time she was near, he felt a warmth radiate throughout his whole body. To be with Natasa was to be complete. He took oil and massaged her back, making his way to her buttocks. She stirred, purring like a kitten.

"That's nice," she murmured

"Hush," he answered, kneading his hands into her flesh. She moaned when he slipped his fingers between her legs.

"Ankhmakis," she groaned.

"Let me pleasure you," he whispered.

His oily fingers continued to dance inside her. Her groans got louder. She rolled over, and he leaned down to kiss her breasts, never stopping his sensual massage. She arched her back and lifted her pelvis. Over and over he stroked and explored her sex. He could feel her ecstasy rise and allowed himself to penetrate it with his own energy. Her bliss rose and fell in waves, and he basked in it, storing it within his own body as a reserve of power. When she finished, she opened her eyes and grinned. He leaned in to kiss her.

"What was that for?" she asked in a dreamy voice.

"A reminder," he replied.

"Of what?"

"Of why you should never leave me again," he replied. "I have to give you reasons to keep coming back."

Natasa examined her beloved. "Do you feel guilty because you've had sex with Weret?" she asked. He nodded, shoulders slumped. "My love, you do what you have to do."

"Yes, I know. Duty. I despise that word. When I was younger, I experienced sex without love, but I can't even stand to touch her. I've forced myself to sleep with her every night since the wedding, to see if I could find it in me to play this game. I hate myself afterward."

"Ankhmakis, there is nothing to be ashamed of. Even though you grew up in the same household, you barely know her. Give it time."

"Aren't you jealous?" he asked, hurt by her honesty.

"No, I'm not."

"I don't understand. The thought of you in any other man's arms drives me mad. I would kill him."

"Ankhmakis, you only need to mate with her until she produces a male heir. It's best you do that sooner than later, and that means making love to her as often as you can. Yes, I'm hurt by it, but what can we do? Nothing. Unless you and I run away and pretend to be common Egyptian merchants, this is our fate."

He sighed. He knew she spoke the truth, but his throat was tight and his heart beat irregular. He didn't want to share their lives with anyone else.

"I learned something in my isolation," she continued. "It's a waste to try to change the things that can't be changed. You and I have built something with our love—an energy field that we can step into and wield at our will. This is the highest of magic, and duty can't destroy it. Not even death can destroy it.

We could fight to make things ideal in the physical, but in the spiritual realm, we are forever one. If we but think of the other with love, we are together. It is best to let the laws of men be and focus instead on growing deeper in love with each other. Do you understand?"

They were sitting and facing each other on the bed. He took her hands into his.

"I will have to share you someday, won't I?" he asked. His stomach sank at the idea of her in any other man's arms.

"Yes, the high priestess must bond with the king," Natasa admitted. "And initiate the royal males, as my mother did for you and your brothers."

He frowned even deeper and fought the form of jealousy, jagged and icy, as it wrapped around him. His heart continued to sputter, and he fought back his envy. It was no use; she saw through to his pain.

"Ankhmakis," Natasa said in a tender voice, "do you believe in our love?"

"Of course."

"Then why must you possess it?"

"Possess? I don't understand."

She sighed and placed her hand on his cheek, and at her touch, the flames of passion ran through him.

"I am you, not yours," she continued. "You are me, not mine. You cannot own that which you already are. Our love is. Jealousy is for those who are separate, not for those of us who are one."

The prince trembled. "You speak the truth," he admitted. "Yet it feels unnatural to me. Why can't I surrender?"

"Because you've been raised as a prince," she explained. "You were taught that what you own is your power. Land, gold, armies, women, even love—they're a collection for the royal line, and when you're the steward of the kingdom, it's yours."

"And what does love mean to you?" he asked.

"I've been raised by the goddess, and she doesn't make claims of ownership. Her will is to connect, not to control. Thus, I open myself to our love to become a container for it and become your shelter from the storms of life. However, I can't possess you or claim you as mine, for my blessing would be your cage. The goddess provides nourishment, health, and abundance for everyone. Not ownership, but the freedom to be truly alive."

Ankhmakis didn't reply. Instead, he kissed her. She responded by laying him down on the bed and crawling onto his chest.

"Enough philosophy. Time for pleasure." She smiled. "And after we must get to work."

"Work?" he asked, his body shivering with delight as she gently kissed his flesh.

"Astral travel," she replied, climbing between his legs. "To work together miles apart when you're in battle will be our most difficult task yet, but we must try, to ensure your success as general, of course."

Natasa took him in her warm mouth, and Ankhmakis fell backward onto his pillows, groaning with pleasure.

31

Intrusion

Egyptian initiates possessed a deep understanding of the unseen and understood that what was invisible to the eye was often more important than what was visible. The physical body was the agent of action, but action itself originated in the subtle realms of human existence. This was their power, and innovation appeared first as an idea above and was made manifest below.

Behdet, Egypt 205 BCE

When Chanax entered Isidor's private chambers, he found his master already kneeling in front of the altar. The room was dark, illuminated by three black pillar candles on the altar surrounding the crystal skull, which glowed in the candlelight.

"Come," Isidor said without turning. "We have important work to do."

"Yes, my lord," Chanax replied as he crossed the room and took a place on his knees beside the high priest of Set.

"It's time for you to learn how to cast an energetic cord that will drain another's life force," Isidor continued, his attention fixated upon the crystal skull. He was already in a trance-like state. "You have learned how to connect to other people's inferior emotions, such as Silus and his addiction."

"Yes, my lord. I've maintained a constant connection for a couple of years now."

"And how is it that you do this?"

Chanax knew his teacher was testing him and rose up taller on his knees. "I scanned Silus's Ka and found several emotions I could play with, but his inferiority complex combined with a self-aggrandizement creates a wonderful combination that has resulted in anxiety and the fear of never living up to his promise. I cast a cord around his anxiety and work the emotion in various ways. The only way Silus knows how to cope with this is to drink himself blind. Thus, burdening him with the affliction of alcoholism."

"Excellent work," Isidor whispered. "Your father rides out to battle tomorrow, and I must connect with him before he goes so that I can manipulate him from afar and make him too ill to rule once his army takes Memphis. Since we need him strong until the moment of victory, I will work this connection over time, draining him bit by bit. But of course, his illness will be the result of my primary objective—to use the emotion that makes him weakest for our gain. There, at the darkest part of his soul, I will cast the energetic cord and control him from afar, like a puppet master."

"I understand, my lord," Chanax replied.

"I have attempted this before, but your father is more resilient than Silus. He has protected himself. The only way to connect is to attempt to attach to him during his most vulnerable moment."

"And when is that?"

"During Shadya with the high priestess when he enters

the throes of his bliss."

Chanax gasped. Anit-Shadya with Neferu-ankh-maat? "But, my lord, that is quite an intrusion of his privacy—"

Isidor turned, and his dark eyes glittered with malice. "It is the only way. Come, join with me, and you will learn how to navigate the realm of a man's bliss when his guard is down."

Chanax nodded despite the foreboding feelings now surrounding him.

"Don't be such a child," Isidor sneered, sensing his trepidation. "If I can stand to see him in my lover's arms, you can watch your father have sex."

Chanax gulped, knowing he had to obey, and looked into the candlelight, allowing his gaze to relax. He expanded his Ka and attached to Isidor. He took a deep breath and allowed the man to transport him to the astral plane. His Ba followed Isidor's from their room and out under the night sky. The next instant they were in the temple of Isis, surrounded by the emotions of lust, passion, and desire. The king's lovemaking was obvious and permeated the entire building.

"They're on the edge of orgasm," Isidor told him.

Chanax watched as they entered the ceremony room. The couple's ecstasy swirled around them as beautiful dancing ribbons of purple, pink, and red. To be inside their erotic moment was exhilarating, and Chanax had to fight to stay focused on the mission. Beside him, Isidor surrounded the king with a dark energy, like a storm cloud on the horizon. The next moment, his father climaxed, and Chanax found himself in a whirlwind of the man's emotions—anger, worry, anxiety, fear, inferiority, lust—these forms poured out of the king as he expanded into the realm of bliss. His soul was exposed.

Isidor made his move and sent in his darkness to probe further. As his father's soul opened to Isidor's magic, Chanax saw it, the emotion that would be most useful to their cause—jealousy. It rose above Hugronaphor like a dragon, curling and dancing with envy, and within this jagged and horrible form, Chanax found the object of Hugronaphor's bitterness—Ankhmakis.

Chanax turned to his master and discovered Isidor's own jealousy at the sight of Neferu-ankh-maat in Hugronaphor's arms. He found it terrifying to behold the men's emotions, and he feared Isidor would ruin the plan.

"Master, the cord," Chanax said. "Focus on the cord, or she'll discover us."

Isidor corrected himself and tempered his own envy, sending a black cord out from the tips of his fingers and toward his king. It surrounded Hugronaphor's jealousy of Ankhmakis and hovered for a moment before swooping down upon the king and attaching itself to his liver. As the connection was made, Chanax felt a wave of pleasure radiate from Isidor and knew he was drinking in the couple's bliss.

"It is done," Isidor said, sighing.

"Isidor?" a voice cried out. "How dare you invade this sacred space?"

Chanax saw what Isidor had not. Neferu-ankh-maat's eyes were open, and she was searching for them. Wrenching himself from the scene, Chanax returned to his body in Isidor's study. His master was still in a trance, unable to extricate himself from his lover's magical hold. Chanax threw himself on top of Isidor, and the two rolled across the room. Isidor's head slammed upon the ground, breaking the spell.

"What happened?" Isidor asked, his voice shaking as he struggled under Chanax's weight.

"Neferu-ankh-maat," Chanax replied. "She discovered us. You didn't withdraw when I warned you."

"So, you mauled me instead?" Isidor growled as he shoved Chanax off his chest.

"You've often said physical pain can be a powerful distraction. Did she cut the cord?"

Isidor closed his eyes, searching his Ka for the magical connection. A smile graced his face. "No, I was successful. I now have Hugronaphor under my control."

Isidor rose from the floor, took one of the candles from his altar, and threw it into the brazier. As a fire sprung up to illuminate the room, he poured two mugs of wine.

"Here." He handed one to Chanax.

"What are you going to do now?" Chanax asked, taking a huge sip. The wine calmed his nerves.

"Isn't it obvious? I'm going to use your father's jealousy toward Ankhmakis to ruin them both."

"I meant what are you going to do about Neferu-ankh-maat? She knows we were there."

"Oh, that. Don't worry. I think I can manage to convince her it was her imagination."

Chanax doubted this would be the case—the high priestess was no amateur—but he remained quiet and drank his wine. After a silent moment he asked, "I understand how you used his jealousy toward Ankhmakis's military talent as the emotion to draw upon, but why put the cord on the liver?"

"This way I can drain him of his health for months, perhaps even years. Using the heart might have caused it to stop. Attaching to the brain can addle the mind, rendering him useless as a commander, and the kidneys are too delicate. The liver is strong, steady, and puts up with a lot of abuse. We need him to die at the right time."

"Why must he die?"

"To crown you pharaoh, my dear boy."

Chanax's heart fluttered, but he couldn't tell if he felt more fear or pleasure at the idea. Isidor raised his cup and toasted him. "To Egypt. Long may she be ruled by those loyal to our Lord Set."

"Yes," Chanax agreed, his hands trembling with excitement as their cups met, clinking in celebration. "And by those worthy of his grace."

32

The Taking of Thebes

"In fact, a king from the south will come, called Ameny. He is the son of a woman of Bowland; he is a child of southern Egypt. He will take the White Crown; he will uplift the Red Crown. He will unite the Two Powers; he will appease the Two Lords with what they wish, with the Field-encircler grasped, and the Oar in motion."

~ The Words of Neferti, poem from the Twelfth Dynasty, 1991-1802 BCE

Thebes, Egypt 205 BCE

If their campaign was successful, his father would be crowned pharaoh of the upper kingdom by sunset. Ankhmakis looked over his shoulder and noted the position of the Sun God, Ra, rising from his slumber in the east and casting a pink glow over the sleepy city. He turned and glanced at Hugronaphor, who stood by his side, the king's gaze alert while their crew navigated the three ships into the docks of Thebes. As their craft glided into the slips, a group of Theban men, mostly Egyptian, hurried to greet them as they tied their ships and made ready to disembark.

"Hugronaphor, steward of Behdet," one of them cried out. "We received no news of your arrival. Why are you here without forewarning?"

Hugronaphor waited until the plank was dropped and walked toward the men, who stood at attention, wringing their hands. Ankhmakis looked to the crowd now forming on the docks, calculating the number of Theban soldiers mobilizing in the street. He noted the small, mud-brick buildings that lined the docks and looked to their roofs. Silus and his men weren't in position.

"Natasa," he said within his mind. *"Where is he?"*

"Silus and the others have entered the city via the desert gates. He can't let them raise the alarm, and their advance is slowed by secrecy. There's a skirmish, and many of your men have fallen," she answered. They had mastered the art of astral travel, and her Ba was able to ride with his, even at this distance. She was even able to leave his side and see what he could not. *"But the guards of Thebes have suffered worse. Silus will be at your side soon. You must continue as planned."*

It was a shame to kill his countrymen like this, but what had to be done, had to be done. A group of Greek soldiers, one hundred strong, raced down the street toward the harbor. When the Theban greeters were ten yards from his father, Hugronaphor bowed his head to them.

"For Kemit," the king said in a calm voice. He unsheathed his curved *khopesh* sword and raised it above his head.

This was the sign Ankhmakis had been waiting for, and within seconds, he nocked an arrow and shot the man closest to his father—his first kill. He felt a sense of thrill as his arrow sliced through the target, yet also loss as the man fell to the dusty ground. Gone were the days of training, and

Ankhmakis now killed men. As the man bled out, Ankhmakis felt Nastasa's discomfort, yet he didn't have time to consider her needs. He had no choice but to continue the mission. He nocked the next arrow, and a minute later, the four greeters lay dead at Hugronaphor's feet. The rebel army ran from the boats with spears and swords at the ready and charged the oncoming Greek infantry, who were falling under the archers still aboard the ships. Ankhmakis saw the form of fury dance around the battle and exalted in the thrill. He expanded his Ka into the space around him, relishing in the surprise and anger of the Thebans, drinking it like fine wine into his being. He raised his own sword as he fell upon them, cutting them down as they cried out, "Traitors!"

"No," Ankhmakis yelled at the top of his lungs, falling into the fury and letting it guide him. "Liberators!"

Fighting in the city was trickier than Ankhmakis had expected. He and his men drove the Greeks back from the docks and into the city streets. Buildings flanked the road, dirt filled the air, and women and children screamed as they ran to find shelter. Greek soldiers flooded toward them. Ankhmakis looked to the rooftops, grinning as Silus and archers bearing his father's signet strode across the building tops and took aim at the soldiers below. The Greeks fell before him, and he walked across their bodies toward his goal—the mayoral palace.

"Silus is here," he said with relief as he caught up with his father. "Come, follow me. There's no time to lose."

In addition to the three ships, cavalry troops, led by Silus, had made their way across the desert from Hierakonpolis to the south and as Ankhmakis fought his way down the streets toward the palace, they were infiltrating the city from the desert side, sacking it and killing the Greeks as they shot at them from the rooftops.

The Greeks in charge of the city realized too late what was happening, yet they fought back with the intensity only a dying people could muster. The advance was slow, messy, and bloody. Ankhmakis broke through the line, screaming and wreaking havoc on the Greek fighters gathering before the steps of the palace. The young prince raised his sword and slashed mercilessly at his targets. His guard followed, mowing down the men left in Ankhmakis's wake. He fell deeper into the frenzy, and he lost track of time and place as he spun, ducked, sliced, jumped, and thrust men from the palace steps. As he approached the huge bronze doors, surrounded with palace guards, Ankhmakis threw a dagger at one man's throat, and as his foe fell, he picked the dead man up and threw him at a group of Greeks behind him, causing them to stumble down the steps. Hugronaphor raised his sword and took the head from one of them as they rolled past him in a heap right into the Egyptian offense, where every single one met their death.

"*Ankhmakis,*" Natasa said, interrupting his battle fury. "*Please, listen to me.*"

He felt the draw of his body as he grabbed Theban soldiers and tore at them. He found he couldn't stop the momentum of the moment and shook his head to block Natasa's plea, as he thrust his deadly blade into a man's chest, watching the light go out from behind heavily lidded eyes. The man was Egyptian, fighting against the rebellion, and Ankhmakis let him fall to the ground, feeling a mixture of confusion and anger. Why would an Egyptian fight for the Greeks?

"*Ankhmakis,*" she said again. He took in a deep breath and focused on her, finding he could do both—fight and speak with his lover.

"*Yes?*" he asked as he watched Hugronaphor run up the

steps, taking two at a time, arriving on the front pedestal as Min and Nefermaat broke open the doors while Ankhmakis threw the last of the palace guards over the side. The king's eyes were wide behind his furrowed brow as he watched Ankhmakis finish off the last of those guarding the exterior.

"What is the source of your strength?" he asked his son as they stepped aside, allowing archers to shoot down the interior guards before entering.

"Years of practice," Ankhmakis replied with a grin.

"But this is your first battle," Hugronaphor said, dragging them behind a stone pillar as his soldiers stormed into the open door.

"*Ankhmakis, this is important,*" Natasa said again. "*The mayor has fled to a safe room within the palace. If you don't find him, he will escape, and you will lose him.*"

"Clear," the advanced guard called, and the king and prince of Behdet made their way inside.

"Min and Nefermaat, take your men and secure the throne room," Ankhmakis commanded his men as Natasa simultaneously gave him directions to the location of his enemy's hiding place. Ankhmakis turned to Hugronaphor and nodded, brushing his bloodied hair from his brow. "My king, you'll want to come with me."

"Where are we going?" Hugronaphor asked.

"To their sanctuary," he replied. "Deep within the palace is a room with a secret passage. This is where the mayor and his officials have hidden, hoping to survive the attack. We must take them before they can escape."

"Yes, and force them to crown me pharaoh," Hugronaphor agreed. "If it's secret, how do you know where the door is?"

"I have my contacts," he answered. Hugronaphor's antagonistic question led Ankhmakis to doubt he could trust his father with his secret.

Twenty men followed them deeper into the palace. It was a risk leaving the throne room to Silus, but the entire war would be filled with risks. Waging battles on the streets, killing civilians, sacking and destroying cities, farmlands, and granaries. This was the type of war the rebellion was waging. As they turned down yet another passage, Ankhmakis realized that for all their military training, much of what was about to happen was a first—there were no rules of engagement when taking the cities one by one as they advanced northward along the Nile. They were like the barbarians of the northern lands, far beyond the Mediterranean Sea. It was both terrifying and liberating.

Ankhmakis stopped them in a hallway with walls covered in detailed, intricately woven rugs. He raised his hand to quiet everyone. "Be still. Don't speak. Listen."

The men tried their best. Ankhmakis could hear their heavy breathing and the sounds of footsteps in the distance.

"Arno," he said to the lead archer, "take seven men and secure the far end of the hall."

The soldier nodded, and they got to their places in time to shoot down a group of palace guards as they turned the corner. Hugronaphor tapped Ankhmakis on the shoulder with the hilt of his sword.

"Boy," he said in a low growl, "if we stay here, we'll be dead. This is a perfect place to trap us."

"We've secured the palace, Father," Ankhmakis replied. "Trust me, Silus will clean up."

As his heartbeat slowed, Ankhmakis heard hushed voices—a woman's low cry, men shushing, and the light clatter of weapons. He looked to his right and found it: a large rug hanging on the wall in the center of the stone hallway, swaying as if a breeze was coming from behind it.

A child wailed.

"This is it." Ankhmakis drew his sword and cut the rug from the wall in one elegant swipe, revealing a sturdy brick door. In the center was one stone cut differently than the rest.

"*You need to hit it with three long taps, followed by two short ones, and then alternating short and long four times,*" Natasa instructed him. His men formed a barrier before him, and Ankhmakis tapped at the stone. He pounded, not to destroy it, but to follow Natasa's sequence of repetitive beats. The stone fell inward and, the door slid ajar.

"You got someone to give you the sequence?" Hugronaphor asked, his voice rising as his head jerked back. "Why didn't you tell me?"

"Step aside," Ankhmakis commanded as his men thrust the door open with a hiss. Arrows and spears flew past, missing Hugronaphor, but taking three of his men in the chest.

"Forward," Ankhmakis called out and they stormed into the room.

They found two dozen soldiers in the room protecting the mayor of Thebes, a Greek named Lycus, several of his administrators, and his wife and children. Ankhmakis set three of his men at the door to keep Lycus from escaping and focused on eliminating the rest of the threat. Within moments a pile of bloodied bodies assured that the frenzied attack was over, and the mayor stood defenseless in the center of the room with his wife and children clinging to his body in fear. The woman held a baby in her arms whose wails echoed off the stone walls. Blood dripped from his sword as Ankhmakis and his men held them out, encircling the survivors, who trembled behind the weapons like caged animals.

Hugronaphor strode up to Lycus, who bowed. "Lord

Haronnophris, what a surprise. You weren't scheduled for a visit."

"I've come to take what's mine," Hugronaphor said, holding his sword at the ready as if to strike the mayor.

"Surely you don't mean my city?" Lycus asked, his wife still clutching at his shoulder, shielding her wailing infant with her body. "The pharaoh won't be happy when he hears about this."

"Take them to the throne room," Hugronaphor commanded.

Ankhmakis and his guards surrounded the family and forced them out of the safety of their hiding spot and into the halls. The rest of Hugronaphor's men followed, but the king grabbed Ankhmakis to hold him back. When they were out of earshot, he turned on him.

"Why didn't you tell me of this secret room on the boat?" Hugronaphor demanded.

"Because I first learned of it when we were on the front steps taking the palace," Ankhmakis answered, watching the rest of the men walk away. He needed to be with them, not arguing with his father in the hall.

"And how did you get this information?" Hugronaphor demanded. "I didn't see you speaking to anyone when you were decapitating the palace guards."

"Not now," Ankhmakis replied as he made to follow the men. "We must get to the throne room and demand the mayor give you the city in front of the citizens in the town square."

Hugronaphor raised his sword to block his way. "No. You will tell me now. That's an order."

Ankhmakis wanted to strangle the man for his petty inquiry, but one look at his father's furious expression and Ankhmakis knew he had no choice but to follow orders.

"Natasa," Ankhmakis sighed. "We can, well, it's hard to

explain."

"Please try," the king said through his clenched teeth.

"Her Ba is here, with mine, and she watched the family go into hiding as the fighting broke out. We're connected, you see, and can speak mind-to-mind. She gave me the location of their hideout as well as the instructions to get in."

His father took a sharp breath, his upper lip curled and trembling. "That's impossible, son."

"No, it's not. The kings and priests of old traveled this way. It is written on our temple walls. Natasa and I have perfected our astral travel to the point where she can go ahead of me with her consciousness and show me what to expect. It's as if I have a second set of eyes."

"She spies for you? Is this good for her?" Hugronaphor asked.

"Would it matter if it wasn't?" Ankhmakis replied, losing his patience. "She gave us critical information about the security of this palace that enabled us to capture the most important man in the city. Please, Father, trust she can do this and be grateful."

"And you can visit her the same way?"

"Yes, and I do every night, to keep the connection strong. Often, I watch her sleep. I need to focus during the day on what's happening here. Being with her in Behdet must wait until the army rests."

Hugronaphor grimaced, shaking his head. "Such a spy is unheard of."

"But useful, don't you think?" Ankhmakis said, hoping to quell his father's fear of the intimate connection.

"She could also be dangerous in the wrong hands," Hugronaphor warned.

"She is in my hands," Ankhmakis said, setting his jaw.

His father's reaction made Ankhmakis uneasy. Natasa was a gift to the mission, not a weapon against the crown. Why couldn't Hugronaphor see that?

"You will report to me every day," Hugronaphor commanded, "and tell me everything she sees. Is this clear?"

Ankhmakis ground his teeth together in frustration. "Our connection is personal. Why should I share it with you?"

"Whatever you two see on the battlefield is mine to know. I will have you arrested if you disobey."

Ankhmakis felt a cold stab of fear run through his mind. Never had his father treated him this way. What was wrong with the man? He wanted to argue, but Hugronaphor raised his hand.

"Come," the older man commanded. "It's time for me to be crowned king and pharaoh of the upper kingdom."

☥

Four hours later, with the city secured and Hugronaphor's banner flying over the palace and the temples, Ankhmakis stood behind his father, the day's blood washed from his body and dressed in his prince's collar, a white ceremony kilt, and small golden crown with the single lapis jewel upon his head. Beside him, Silus stood in his own ceremony dress. They were in a small room off the main temple square. Through the stone temple walls, Ankhmakis heard the murmur of hundreds of people who'd gathered for his father's crowning. Priests, acolytes, singers, and musicians thronged the hall. The rebellion's generals, including Tsui, Kyros, and Sebastos, waited in the chamber with them. Egyptian soldiers guarded every entrance—not a single light-eyed Greek had been allowed in the entourage.

Hugronaphor wore his bejeweled collar of Behdet and

a crisp, cotton loincloth, yet his bald head was bare, for he would receive the coveted Khepresh crown of Thebes from the Theban priests when they made him their pharaoh. At his waist was his sword, polished after the day's fighting. He was scared and battle-worn, but Hugronaphor stood tall. Finally, after centuries, a native Egyptian would once again be the high king. Ankhmakis trembled with joy. This was what he'd been working for his entire life—to help take the throne unto Egyptian hands.

A dark priest entered the room and bowed low to the entourage, his attention focused on Hugronaphor as he spoke. "Haronnophris, bearer of liberty, your court awaits you."

They followed the priest through the doors, and Ankhmakis and Silus took their places behind their father. As the priest led them into the temple courtyard, Ankhmakis noted how beautiful the structure was. Luxor was an ancient city, built for Amun over centuries, invested in by the kings of old. Those men had built tombs of grandeur along the west bank of the Nile, stretching long into the valley, as testaments to their royal line. Unfortunately, grave robbers long ago raided the tombs, and there was nothing left for the Royals of Behdet to take.

But the temples in Luxor, and especially this one, the temple of Amun, were stunning beyond words. The procession took them past alabaster columns ninety feet tall, covered in painted hieroglyphs depicting the rise of kings, gods, and Egypt herself. The temple walls rose before them. Ankhmakis made his way through the rows of columns, his father's flag flying in the wind atop four long, red turrets that graced the temple roof. For a moment, Ankhmakis imagined his own flags bearing the phoenix flying, and he felt a shiver run through his body as he crossed the threshold into the darker interior of the temple, which was even more stunning than the outer courtyard. Gold shone on the walls, fire and incense burned in braziers casting shimmering light upon the animal-faced gods and goddesses carved into the structure, and everywhere, the people bowed to Hugronaphor and his men with honor.

Behdet's own temples paled in comparison—in particular, the monstrous temple of Horus built by the Ptolemys. This temple was the place of pharaohs. It felt right putting it back into the hands of those who'd made it—the Egyptians themselves. Every noble from the south had ridden with Hugronaphor into this battle, and they now flanked the sides of a long, woven mat, bowing low as he passed by. At the end of the mat stood the high priest of Thebes, a tall Greek man, and to his side, his Egyptian counterpart, a man Ankhmakis knew as Setep. The Greek priest wrung his hands as Hugronaphor approached, but Setep's expression was serene. Behind the men, the statues of Osiris and Hathor glowed, rising over one hundred feet. The priests looked insignificant before the colossi.

"Lord Hugronaphor," the Greek priest said with hesitation. "I have been commanded by Lycus, the mayor of this great city, to crown you pharaoh of upper Egypt." Lycus stood to the side of the dais with a sword held to his back. The man had no choice but to do Hugronaphor's bidding.

"I accept Lycus's generous offer," Hugronaphor said with a smile. Lycus glared. His face, distorted with malice, looked like a demon's in the light of the temple fires.

The priest raised his arms above his head and glanced with trepidation at Setep standing next to his side. He was scared for his life—as well he should be. "By the power vested in me by Ra himself, I call now upon the gods to bless you. May Amon-Re inhabit you, that you might protect the Black

Land, Our Lady Egypt, for all your days."

Hugronaphor bowed low and rose. The priest Setep strode forward and placed the blue Khepresh crown of Thebes upon his head. The thick crown covered Hugronaphor's entire head with its heavy, lapis-colored, papyrus form. Upon the forehead was a golden Ureaus, the upright form of the cobra signifying his divinity and right to rule the land. The Greek high priest's eyes widened at the sight. No Ptolemy pharaoh had yet worn this crown. The Khepresh was the crown of the kings of old, and the priests of Thebes had been saving it for the return of a true Egyptian pharaoh. Smiling with satisfaction, Setep handed Hugronaphor a hook and flail, also artifacts. Hugronaphor placed them over his chest and stood taller.

"I now declare you pharaoh of upper Egypt," the Greek high priest continued, his pale face and trembling hands betraying his fear. Sweat poured down his brow, sparkling in the firelight. "What name shall you take?"

Hugronaphor turned and looked to the crowd. He raised the crook and flail over his head and spoke with divine authority, "I, who was born Hugronaphor, steward of Behdet, shall become Pharaoh Horwenefer, loved by Isis, Osiris, and Amon-Re, king of the gods. Look upon the last house in the line of native Egyptian kings."

The Egyptians in the crowd cheered, including the priests of Thebes. Isidor had done an excellent job procuring their loyalty.

"I stand before you as your servant," Horwenefer continued, "the agent of Amon-Re, set upon taking our lands from the occupiers and sending them back to Macedonia. Kemit, our dear land, will be ours."

The crowd continued to cheer, and the high priest looked

as though he would faint.

"This will not be easy," Horwenefer continued. "It will mean sacrifice and death. Many whom you love will perish. Fields will be burned, and towns sacked. These things must be done to drive the Greeks out of our lands and cut off their food supply. There are many ways to win this war, but none are kind. These times call for pain and suffering, with the promise of a new day when our work is done."

Setep, who had remained silent for the ceremony, stepped forward. "Lord Horwenefer, the good being, and pharaoh of the south, Thebes welcomes you and our temple is yours."

As Setep finished speaking, a soldier wearing Hugronaphor's ibis signet stepped up and took the Greek high priest into his arms, slitting his neck. Ankhmakis's hand instinctively snapped to his sword. What was happening?

As the man fell limp, Lycus cried out, "Traitor! How dare you shed human blood during ceremony?"

Hugronaphor, now Pharaoh Horwenefer, turned and an eerie smile crossed his dark face. Ankhmakis had never seen his father look vengeful or fierce. "When Greek blood is spilled, the gods rejoice." In a flash, a sword cut through the mayor, and the anger in his gaze was extinguished. Horwenefer turned back to the crowd. "Round up the Greeks who haven't fled and deliver them to the square. Let justice be served."

Ankhmakis stood still at his father's side, in shock over what had happened. Why would his father begin his reign with such evil? Ankhmakis swallowed down his disgust as the new pharaoh handed his hook and flail to Setep and held out his right hand to his sons, a huge golden ring bearing the Theban royal crest shining upon his ring finger.

Ankhmakis turned to Silus and found his brother's face stricken, mouth open as if also in shock.

"Is there a problem, my sons?" Pharaoh Horwenefer asked, still wearing the look of a leopard waiting to attack.

"Human sacrifice isn't allowed in ceremony," Ankhmakis said in a low voice, so only his father and Silus could hear him. The entire room was now silent.

"Greek blood is the price I must pay to wear this crown," Pharaoh Horwenefer answered loudly for everyone to hear.

The pharaoh shook his bejeweled hand, and Ankhmakis knew what he must do, but found himself struggling. He glanced around the room—the men who had joined their cause were waiting for the princes's reactions. They wouldn't fight for the pharaoh if their favorite general refused him. The priests might have given Horwenefer the crown, but the king needed the army to win the war.

Silus fell to one knee and took his father's hand, kissing the golden ring. "I will follow you, in this life and the next, Pharaoh Horwenefer, Amon-Re, lord of the upper kingdom."

Pharaoh Horwenefer glared at Ankhmakis over Silus's back. Ankhmakis needed to give his blessing, yet he found it impossible to speak.

"*Make your oath,*" Natasa commanded. "*You must.*"

"*He killed those men without warning,*" Ankhmakis answered her as he struggled to control his anger, now coloring the world around him red with fury. He could strike down his father and take the crown. The murderous man was unworthy to wear it. The army loved Ankhmakis; they would follow him.

"*Do not create a war within a war,*" his lover pleaded. "*He needs you, Ankhmakis. Make your oath now, before you ruin everything.*"

"*I will not be like him,*" he answered her, his heart pounding in his ears as he bowed to his father, now pharaoh of half of Egypt. *"There will be no bloodshed when I take the throne."*

A scene of his men clearing the dead from the steps of the mayoral palace, each killed by his own sword, flashed in his mind, and he felt Natasa's disgust. Blood for their freedom. Blood for the crown.

He'd already shed much blood for the throne.

Ankhmakis took his father's hand and kissed the ring, the metal cool against his lips. He tasted bile as he rose to speak. "I will follow you, in this life and the next, Pharaoh Horwenefer, Amon-Re, lord of the upper kingdom."

High Priest Setep handed the pharaoh the hook and flail. Crossing his arms like the statue of Horus that stood over the golden altar, the pharaoh turned to follow the rest of the priests out of the temple, through the glorious courtyard and toward the flotillas at the docks that would ferry them across the river to the palace, which would soon become the rebellion's headquarters as their troops continued north, taking back Egypt one city at a time. Ankhmakis followed, surrounded by throngs of people cheering his father's name. Drums beat ancient rhythms, trumpets rang out, and the temple maidens sang the songs of the king. Children ran in the courtyard, women wept with joy, and men joined arms and danced. The natives were overjoyed—after centuries of occupation, they were free. As his flotilla glided across the placid river to where the glittering palace awaited its new king, Natasa broke their connection, abandoning him to the clamor, as Ra set beyond the great Egyptian city of Thebes.

33

The Power of Connection

The Ptolemaic war against the Egyptians is one of the first historically documented guerilla wars, yet at the same time, it is a forgotten war. This is because the Greek historians considered it unfit for history; they needed clear-cut military and political turning points, and this war would give them neither.

Abdju/Behdet, Egypt 205 BCE

Blood sprayed across the temple steps. Farmers burned in the fields where she'd once watched the Pigs of Perit celebrate the plantings of spring. Women and children ran from men on horseback who were slaughtering them and cutting them down as if they were weeds in the rich, dark Nile silt. Everywhere Natasa turned there were chaos and disorder. This was the view from her lover's eyes—death at his hands.

She left him, unable to stay with the fighting. He didn't need her; his command of his own Ka was unlike anyone else's on the battlefield. No foe could take him, for Ankhmakis spread out his awareness into every aspect of the fight. He was unstoppable in his battle fury. She was more helpful farther away, where his awareness ended and hers began. There she could see what the Greeks were doing, where they were advancing, hiding, or perhaps even retreating. They'd been at war for two full months, and she followed him northward, participating in battle as she could. Together, they could see what alone he could not.

She opened herself and allowed her consciousness to spread out past the temple, farther to the north of the city of Abdju. Horwenefer, as the pharaoh was now called, had taken the city of Abdju immediately after his crowning in Thebes. Yet their attempts to breach Panopolis, the next city north, had failed time and again. The Nile River split into two north of Abdju, and they'd found themselves cut off by the Greek navy—every single one of Ankhmakis's men on that mission had died, and the rest were forced to retreat and stay put in the ancient city of Abdju. The Greeks, now fully understanding what was happening in the south, had filled the city of Panopolis with soldiers, food, and weapons to create their own outpost, and launched their first organized attack at Horwenefer in Abdju. The recent surprise attack was a last attempt to gain control before the season of Akhet began, and the rains of the Inundation made the movement along the Nile difficult for four months.

Natasa followed the stream of thousands of Greek soldiers who poured into the city from the north, like the river itself. Abdju would be overrun. Yet Ankhmakis couldn't let it fall and be forced to retreat. They had to hold the line.

"Let the enemy into the city," she told him. *"Station troops to the south to keep them in Abdju and send as many soldiers as you can around the city to the north to clear the desert between you and Panopolis and trap the Greeks within the city walls from behind. They're making camp, and you must*

stop it."

For a moment she felt Ankhmakis's anger. He replied, "*I see. Thank you.*"

"*I have to leave you. I'm needed here in Behdet.*"

"*I love you—*"

The next moment, he was gone. Natasa gasped for air at the pain of disconnection and returned to her body—feeling her toes, legs, chest, arms, and mind. She opened her eyes and found herself lying prone on the stone altar, as she'd been before her trance. Incense burned on the altar before Isis, and in the shadows her mother, Neferu-ankh-maat, sat on the floor, her own eyes shut.

"Mother," Natasa said, her voice parched. Neferu-ankh-maat rose and handed a mug of water to Natasa, who drank it gratefully. "Why are you here?"

"To watch over you," the high priestess replied.

"Why?"

"You're vulnerable when you travel this way," her mother answered. "Anyone could hurt you."

"Who would do such a thing?" Natasa asked as she slid from the table. She shivered when her feet touched the cold stone floors.

"The temple is filled with dark ones," Neferu-ankh-maat said.

"Mother, I don't like it when you talk that way."

"It's the truth," she answered, jaw hard. "And you must be protected. I don't like the fact that you go to war with your Ba like this. It drains you."

"No, it doesn't." Natasa shook her head, even though her mother was right. She did feel drained and woozy, but couldn't admit it, for fear her mother would deny her this work. "I feel fine. I'm careful not to use my own energy, and instead rely on our connection to the All-One."

Neferu-ankh-maat scrutinized her as she rose to stand. "I know what you see when you do this, daughter. War is of men, not of the All-One, and to take part in it is to be corrupted."

"I'm not killing those people." She clenched her hands into fists even as she trembled, knowing her mother spoke the truth.

"Yes, you are," Neferu-ankh-maat said, her tone softening. "When he kills, you kill."

"Would you rather I let him go?"

"Unfortunately, for Egypt's sake, you can't. It is this skill to travel inside his body that gives his army an advantage."

"What, Mother, would you have me do?"

"Two things," the high priestess said. "First, allow me to set a guard when you work with him. Please, you must do as I direct." Natasa didn't like it but nodded. Her mother embraced her, stern face softening with a smile. "Second, you must spend time doing things of love. For when you love others, so does Ankhmakis. He needs love, to balance the actions he must take at this time."

Natasa fell into her mother's arms.

"You're right, Mother," she sobbed. "What he does is horrible. I can't bear to be near him in battle. I can't stand the killing. I don't want to see it anymore." Tears poured from her body as her mother held her. The small alcove was quiet, and her sobs echoed off the stone walls.

"There, there." Neferu-ankh-maat brushed her fingers through Natasa's hair. "I have an assignment for you that I think will help."

"What?" Natasa asked, wiping her eyes and smearing her dark eyeliner down her cheeks.

Neferu-ankh-maat took a cloth from a pouch at her waist

and dabbed the smudges from her daughter's face. "It's time you begin to train the acolytes. When the war began, Pharaoh Horwenefer removed the Greeks from the clergy, and we now have openings to fill. Egyptian children from the town have been selected to join our ranks. They begin tomorrow. I need you to be the one to introduce them to the space around them, and teach them how to move with their bodies, not their feet."

Natasa withdrew from her mother's embrace and turned to the small altar. The smoke from the incense wafted around the goddess's head as the Ka did around her own body. "Yes, Mother. I'm ready to teach."

"While Ankhmakis lives the path of the warrior," Neferu-ankh-maat continued, "you must live the way of the goddess more than ever before. It's the only way he'll survive this, and I don't mean surviving battle. War cuts a man from his highest self and turns his heart stone cold in order to survive what must be done to win. A wall is built around the Ba. If this happens, he will forget his path, and Egypt will be lost."

Natasa continued to look at the mesmerizing smoke still moving around the goddess. She felt a surge of power and knew Ankhmakis was trying to contact her. She sent him her unconditional love. A flash of exhaustion followed by elation passed through her mind's eye, and the next instant, he was gone.

"Yes, Mother," she replied. "I will do the goddess's bidding. If it's your will I teach the acolytes, I shall." She bowed to the statue, and she turned to her mother and did the same.

"Thank you, daughter," Neferu-ankh-maat answered with a look of love and concern on her worried face. Natasa knew her mother's troubles extended beyond her own to issues much greater. The war, as well as the Cult of Set, hurt Neferu-ankh-maat. She was the high priestess of Behdet, and one of the last masters of Anit-Shadya in Egypt; thus, she felt the pain of the whole land.

☥

The next morning, Natasa stood beyond the courtyard of the temple of Isis, out of view of the new students. Several girls between twelve and thirteen years of age made their way past her, none taking notice. They were chatty, excited, faces flushed from nervousness. Natasa's throat tightened when she remembered herself at their age, climbing the steps with Alexa, sharing her first kiss with Chanax, who had been Senmen before he left her for Memphis. A sense of sadness washed over her for a moment as she recalled those days before they began their training. They'd been in heaven, but the moment they turned thirteen, it had abruptly ended. The elders had sent Senmen to Memphis, and he had returned a changed man, serious and dark, with a mission to use the god of chaos, Set, to aid them in their civil war. And they'd set Natasa on the opposite path, to share the goddess of love with the men in hopes of balancing them during these dark times. Natasa had lost not only her carefree youth but also her best friend.

Perhaps initiating these girls wasn't fair? What if by teaching them, she would take from them all that had been taken from her? Innocence. Freedom. Playfulness. Could she show them the adult world, and the mysteries themselves, while allowing the girls to remain open to life? Was that even possible? What had adulthood given her? What had it gained her dear friend? In his case, the new name, and a lead role in a cult her mother despised. In her case . . .

Ankhmakis and Helena flashed before her vision—and she found herself once again outside of time, in the place of light, next to her beloved. Peace filled her body and soul, and her breathing slowed. This was the legacy of her adulthood, the ability to see that life was more than the physical and that all things began first as thought, and then as rhythm, and finally became form. The temple had taught her that beneath the surface of life runs a river of creation and light, seen by those who have mastered the alchemies of Horus and opened their inner sight. This was what she didn't know as a child. This was the wisdom of her training and the gift of her adulthood.

She returned to her body and felt the sunlight on her face as she stepped out of her hiding place. The space around her was alive with intent and power. She expanded her Ka to fill the temple before she entered. Her energy accelerated, and she felt alive in her body. Head high, shoulders back, she walked up the steps. As she entered the room, the girls's chatter died out and they rose from their places, bowing low. She smiled at the pale, yellow form of love now surrounding the acolytes. This form was sweetness, perfect harmony, and balance. It flowed from her solar plexus and swirled and danced among them. She had secrets to share. She had mysteries to reveal. Many wouldn't understand, but some would, and those who did would inherit the Earth.

"My dear daughters of Isis," she began, "it's an honor to meet you. Today begins your great journey with the goddess, who will show you the mysteries of the cosmos. Some of her wisdom will be easier to grasp than others. Other lessons will break your heart. These are times of war we now live in. However, don't make the fatal mistake of thinking Isis is no longer needed. Now more than ever, our warriors need to know her touch. Our men need to hear her call and feel her caress. Her love is what will lead them home and keep them alive. There's no power greater than the love of the goddess, and as her priestesses, you will be the ones to bear her love upon Earth.

"A select group of you will follow the path of spiritual companion and be paired with nobles, generals, soldiers, and our priests. Others will become chantresses and musicians or choose to heal our wounded. We fill different roles as priestesses and yet have one purpose—to incarnate love upon this land. For without love, there is no life. The actions of man must be balanced with love. This is what we work for—to love the warrior and protect his heart—that it will remain intact and full of grace, for all time."

She walked past the girls and bowed before the large golden images of Isis and Osiris. Natasa turned to the girls and raised her arms above her head.

"Let us begin our great work together."

To be continued in...

Song of The King's Heart

Book Two

BLOOD AND CHAOS

About the Author

Nicole Sallak Anderson is a Computer Science graduate from Purdue University, and former CTO for a small Silicon Valley startup, turned novelist and blogger, focusing on the intersection of technology and consciousness. She currently lives in the beautiful Santa Cruz Mountains in California with her husband, where she raises goats and bees. She enjoys spinning, knitting, playing the bass, and dancing, particularly the tango. You can keep up with all her latest writing by following @NSallakAnderson on Facebook, Twitter, and Medium or her blog, nicolesallakanderson.com. Feel free to contact her; she almost always answers any query or comment!